FAMILY IS FOREVER

CONVERSION BOOK SIX

S.C. STEPHENS

This is a work of fiction. Names, characters, places, brands, media, and incidents are either the product of the author's imagination or are used fictitiously. The author acknowledges the trademarked status and trademark owners of various products referenced in this work of fiction, which have been used without permission. The publication/use of these trademarks is not authorized, associated with, or sponsored by the trademark owners.

Copyright © 2017 by S.C. Stephens
Cover design by Okay Creations
Editing by Madison Seidler Editing Services
Formatting by JT Formatting

All rights reserved.
Without limiting the rights under copyright reserved above, no part of this publication may be reproduced, stored in or introduced into a retrieval system, or transmitted, in any form, or by any means (electronic, mechanical, photocopying, recording, or otherwise) without the prior written permission of the above copyright owner of this book.

First Edition: 2017
Library of Congress Cataloging-in-Publication Data
Family is Forever (Conversion Series) – 1st ed
ISBN-13: 978-1974478309 | ISBN-10: 1974478300

*For the Adams clan.
My, my, how you've grown!*

CHAPTER ONE

Julian

THERE WERE CERTAIN things about my life that I couldn't ignore, even if I wanted to. My family was full of vampires, including myself. I had to lie about who I really was, had to hide my abilities as much as I possibly could. A couple of months ago, my sister, Nika, had died. Well, I guess she wasn't completely dead. She had undergone a conversion and become a pureblood vampire with all their benefits and setbacks. The empathic bond I'd had with her was gone now, a fact that both saddened and relieved me. I was the last vampire in the family with a pulse. And, I was the last vampire who could continue the line. If I didn't have kids, the vampiric family tree would die with me. No pressure or anything.

It was the last day of my junior year, and what a hell of a school year it had turned out to be. I was glad it was almost over. Then, after a too-brief summer vacation, I'd be starting my senior year of school. Good or bad, it would be my last year in Salt Lake City—my last year with my friends. After I graduated, my family would be moving to another location and everyone who knew us here would be wiped clean. We'd be ghosts and rumors, with no specifics about us remaining in their memories. It would be as if we were never here at all. And that was the point. Protect the nest, no matter the cost. That was our family motto. Lately, the cost had been high.

Nika had temporarily lost her boyfriend, Hunter Evans. Turned into a vampire against his will, Hunter had experienced some serious adjustment issues. He seemed to be doing better now, but Nika had suffered in the interim. Hunter was one who'd turned her into a fully-fledged member of the undead, something my family was still struggling with. He'd done it to save her life though, so no one truly blamed him for her transformation. Even still, I should be starting my senior year this fall with Nika, but instead I would be starting it alone. Completely alone.

The other price that had been paid recently was my girlfriend, Arianna. I'd had to give her up to protect the nest. I was still ticked about that. Grandma Halina had acted too fast, wiped her mind prematurely. I could have turned Arianna around if Halina had just given me more time. But she hadn't and Arianna was practically a stranger to me now.

I'd spent the last several weeks trying to rebuild our relationship, but it was slow-going. Arianna and I talked during school, but it was just friendly, casual chitchat like we were merely acquaintances. It physically hurt me to have to hold back, to not be able to kiss her cheek and tell her how beautiful she looked, how amazing she was. Pretending I wasn't in love with her was hard, and it was getting harder every day. I wanted what we'd had so badly, I was growing impatient. But I didn't want to risk everything by moving too fast, by being too aggressive. We had to come together organically, or else I would come across as a creepy stalker and she'd tell me to get lost. But on the flip side, if we moved too slowly, I'd become ... her friend. And nothing more. Ever. Walking that fine line between friends and more-than-friends sucked, and every day I was terrified she'd never see me the way she once had.

I wished Nika was in the picture again. Arianna's friendship with Nika had helped spark her interest in me—she'd grown to love me from afar while I hadn't been paying attention. With Nika working behind the scenes to sell me to her best friend, we could have crossed the friend-zone barrier more easily. But Nika was a creature of the night now ... and erased from Arianna's memory just as permanently as I had been. It really bothered me that Nika had lost her friendship with Arianna because of me, and I constantly found myself wishing she could have it back, that somehow, Nika could work on rebuilding her bond to Arianna too. That was impossible though. Nika was different in ways that Arianna would notice if she spent a lot of time with her. And Nika was nocturnal now, so human friendships were much harder to maintain. Nika missed a lot by being up all night and hiding away all day. I was still having trouble adjusting to her new schedule, and I didn't get to see her as often as I liked. I missed her.

Although, my human friends had been keeping me company in Nika's absence. Trey, my always-there, almost-always-high best friend, and Raquel, my ex-crush turned friend. It still shocked me that Raquel and I were buds now. I'd spent most of my time in high school pining over her while she'd been dating a raging asshole. But even though she and Russell were no longer together and I was currently single, we hadn't crossed the friendship line. Whatever I'd been feeling for Raquel before I'd started dating Arianna just wasn't there anymore. Arianna still had my heart, even if she didn't know it.

No matter how long it took, I was going to win her back.

"Julian, you're going to be late." Looking over at my bedroom doorway, I saw my mom leaning against the doorframe, giving me a lopsided grin. "It's the last day of school. You don't want to end the year on a sour note, do you?"

Pulling on my last boot, I quickly laced it up. "I don't think being late today is going to be what sours the year for me," I muttered before I could stop myself.

Mom glanced over at my wide-open bathroom door after my sullen comment. Through the bathroom, she could easily see into the next bedroom. Nika's room. Well, her old room, since she couldn't sleep there anymore. She needed a space impervious to sunlight to sleep away the day now. She stayed below the house, in the rooms Dad had added for Halina. Nika wasn't happy about sleeping down there. She wanted to stay at the family ranch, so she could be with Hunter, her sire. Mom and Dad weren't okay with that idea though; she was still too young in their eyes to be living with her boyfriend.

Mom's expression darkened as she stared at Nika's old room. Standing, I walked over to my bathroom door and softly shut it. Mom's face shifted back to me and she smiled, but I knew she was faking it; there was no warmth in her grin. What had happened to Nika still bothered her—it bothered us all. But as I constantly reminded myself, it was better than Nika dying.

"She's fine, Mom. She's happy." While I used to know that through our bond, now I only knew it because Nika told me. And by the way her eyes sparkled whenever she said it, I believed her. She really was truly happy. It was the rest of us who were reeling.

Mom gave me a stiff nod. Her deep brown eyes shimmered with moisture, and I instantly felt bad for closing the bathroom door. And for my unnecessary comment. Maybe the moment would have passed with only an unspoken elephant in the room if I hadn't stupidly brought attention to it.

"Hurry, so you can grab something to eat before school. I don't want you to go to class hungry." Like all of the undead members of my family, Mom looked young for her age, but with the sag in her shoulders and the lifelessness in her eyes when she turned away from me, I thought she looked closer to her true age for once.

"I'm sorry, Mom," I whispered, "I didn't mean to bring it up."

She heard me, as I knew she would. "It's fine, Julian. Nothing for you to worry about. I'll set out some breakfast for you."

I stifled a sigh. I knew when I walked downstairs there would be a meal fit for a king waiting for me. It used to be I'd just grab a bowl of cereal and a glass of blood in the morning, but ever since Nika had turned, Mom had started making elaborate meals for me every chance she got. It was like she was overcompensating for the fact that I was the only one left who still ate regular food. It was nice, but unnecessary. I never ate as much as she made, and all the excess did was remind me that I was different, that I was alone, and that my twin—my best friend—had been taken away from me.

Looking around my messy room, I searched the floor until I spotted the strap of my backpack buried under a mound of clothes and comic books. When I was with Arianna, I'd tried to be less of a pig, but now ... I just didn't see the point in keeping my room tidy anymore. Both Mom and Nika were disappointed by that fact.

Tossing aside the outfit that I wore yesterday, I unburied my backpack and slung it over my shoulder. Today was a double-edged sword for me. It was the last day that I had to deal with the tedium of schoolwork, but it was also the last time I'd have any sort of a real excuse to see Arianna. Unless we somehow bumped into each other over the summer, I'd have to wait until September to see her again. It was only three months from now, but it felt like three hundred.

Shaking away that disheartening thought, I headed downstairs to where I could feel Mom and Dad in the kitchen. I could feel Nika, too, in the basement. While Mom and Dad were moving around, Nika's position was stationary. She was most likely sleeping.

The smell of breakfast hit me long before I saw it. Pancakes, bacon, eggs, fresh fruit, cinnamon rolls, *and* steaming blood. I swear Mom was trying to kill me with comfort food. I looked at the meal piled on my plate with my jaw dropped. "Mom, this looks amazing ... but I can't eat all this. Toast and blood for breakfast really is fine."

Mom was spooning steaming blueberry filling from a saucepan into a thin crepe dusted with powdered sugar. As she plopped the finished crepe onto a plate already overflowing with food, she frowned. "Hmm, you might be right. This is a lot of food." She sighed as she put the pot of leftover blueberry filling on the stove next to the bubbling pot of blood. "Just do your best. I don't want to see it go to waste."

I gave her a raised eyebrow in response. My stomach hadn't woken up yet, and there was no way I'd get through a quarter of this meal. Seeing my expression, Mom grimaced. "I'll try and tone it down, honey. I guess I got carried away ..."

That was putting it mildly. Mom had made a whole turkey for dinner last night. Just for me. I was going to be having turkey for dinner for the next three months. Unless she made something else tonight ... maybe an entire pan of lasagna or something.

With a smirk on his face, Dad started pouring the hot blood into tall glasses. "I told you that was too much, Em. Yes, he's a growing boy, but he's not Bigfoot."

I laughed as I popped a piece of bacon into my mouth. No, I was an entirely different mythical creature. Mom scowled at Dad for his comment, then at me for sniggering at it. Dad was laughing as he approached her with a glass of blood in each hand. "I'm just impressed that you made all of that without burning anything," he said, humor in his voice. "You're getting better."

Mom tried to frown, but smiled instead. Grabbing her glass, she moved over so that her entire body pressed against his. A seductive grin spread over Dad's face as he glanced at where they were connected; I immediately shifted my eyes to my plate. "Guess I picked up a thing or two after watching you in the kitchen for all these years," she said, her voice low.

"You're a very astute student," Dad replied, his voice equally low.

Even though I wasn't hungry, I cringed and dug into my food. My parents sometimes forgot I was in the room when they started flirting with each other. It was mortifying, and I groaned when I heard Mom giggle like a pre-teen. Then the sounds of light kissing filled the air. Kissing reminded me of Arianna, and everything I'd lost with her. Irritated, I grumbled, "Guys … seriously? I'm eating." I shoveled a spoonful of eggs into my mouth for emphasis.

"Sorry."

I risked a glance at parents to see them pulling away from one another with huge smiles on their faces. I was glad to see them genuinely happy, I really was, but it was difficult too. I missed my girlfriend. A lot.

No longer feeling the need to force myself to eat, I stepped away from my plate. I was just about to tell my parents I was heading to school, when Dad held a glass of blood in front of me. Wisps of steam swirled around the cylindrical opening in an inviting way. The smell overpowered everything else in the room. It was sweet, tangy, and heady. Like a marshmallow-laden cup of hot chocolate on a chilly evening, it was an irresistible draw. I didn't need the blood like my family did, but I sure enjoyed it. And with how tumultuous this day might be for me, I knew I could use the pick-me-up.

I removed the glass from my father's frozen fingers and brought it to my lips. My fangs crashed down the second the liquid hit my tongue. Heaven. The warmth cascaded down my throat, invigorating every part of me. I felt stronger with just a few swallows, rejuvenated, almost invincible. I felt alive. Setting the cup on the counter, I felt like I could take on the world. Blood. Such a great way to start the day.

"Thanks," I told my dad. "I should probably get going. I don't want to be late on my last day." I gave my mom a one-sided grin.

She smiled, and then sighed as she looked over the amount of food I was leaving behind. Guilt filled me, but I tried not to feel bad about it as I headed toward the front door. I hadn't asked her to make a banquet, and I'd told her more than once not to make so much food. It was just her way of coping.

FAMILY IS FOREVER

I fished my keys out of my backpack as I approached the station wagon I shared with my sister. One good thing about Nika's conversion, we didn't fight over the car as much since she was now a night owl. And really, she had the blazing speed and endurance of a pureblood vampire—she could run her ass wherever she wanted to go.

Even though it was early in the morning, it was already comfortably warm—no jacket required. The sky was clear and blue, the same shade as my eyes. Arianna had loved my eyes. If we'd never parted ways, I'd be excited for school. And even more excited that it was the last day, and we'd soon have almost endless time together coming up. We would have talked for hours, kissed, cuddled, and grown even closer than we'd already been. But all that was gone, and I had nothing to look forward to now.

Feeling melancholy, I started the car and made my way to school. Traffic was with me, and I arrived early. Trey was there, hands in his pockets while he lazily skated down the sidewalk beside the parking lot. I honked my horn, and he almost fell off his board. I was laughing as he turned around to glare at me. Parking the car, I felt just a tiny bit better about today. At least I still had my friends.

"Not cool, dude. You ruined a perfectly awesome daydream," he told me. Despite the warm weather, Trey was wearing his signature stocking cap. He tucked some loose blonde strands under his hat while he frowned at me.

I clapped his shoulder as I joined him. "Sorry, couldn't resist. What was your daydream about?"

His scowl instantly shifted to a smile. "Annabeth Phillips doing cheers without her briefs on."

I shook my head as he lifted his eyebrows suggestively. Annabeth Phillips was the captain of the cheerleading squad. Trey had had a thing for her ever since she'd done a pep rally braless. The faculty hadn't seemed to notice the jiggling, but the students sure had. I think half the male population here had a thing for Annabeth. Unfortunately for Trey, she was graduating this year.

While Trey and I walked along the path, laughing at his suggestive imagery, a voice behind us shouted, "Hey guys, wait up!"

Trey and I both turned to see Raquel sprinting in our direction. The sight of her hurrying to me, reminded me yet again how drastically my life had changed since the beginning of the year. Raquel was dressed in a thin, long-sleeved shirt, and shorts as legally short as the school allowed. Her skin was an appealing bronze color that was smooth and soft to the touch. Her hair was a deep, dark shade almost as black as my own. It shimmered in the sunlight as it streamed behind her while she jogged our way. With dark almond eyes and plump lips, Raquel was definitely a beautiful girl. Trey often told me to wake up and ask her out. But I couldn't. I only felt friendship for her now.

When she got to us, she leaned over her knees, catching her breath. Trey took the opportunity to glance down the front of her shirt. I immediately stepped in front of him, blocking his view. He peeked around me, but Raquel had straightened by then. Glaring at him, like she'd noticed him peeking, she flipped her hair around her shoulders. "Last day. You guys excited for summer?"

Trey immediately said that he was. I gave her an inconclusive grunting sound for an answer. There were parts of school I was really going to miss, and I wasn't ready to let go yet. Knowing where my heart was, Raquel rubbed my arm in sympathy. I discretely glanced at her long sleeves. Long, jagged scars were hidden underneath them, the result of a vampire-related attack, but everyone in the school, Raquel included, believed they were self-inflicted. Raquel was a much stronger person now after dealing with the harshness of the rumors that had swirled around her after the incident. Little wonder she was ready for a break from here.

Without discussing it, the three of us headed to the cafeteria to wait for school to start. Trey immediately went to the vending machine and hemmed and hawed until he found some sort of granola bar that looked edible. Our school was a "healthy" school, so all the snacks available were nutritious. And not a soda can in sight. That wasn't really a big deal to me, but some of the kids constantly griped about it. Last year's class president even won the election by making the wild claim that he could replace the bottled water dispenser with a pop machine. As Raquel plopped in her quarters and retrieved her mountain spring H_2O, it was clear that the ex-president hadn't been able to live up to that promise. Oh well. According to my American Government teacher, the entire debacle was a great example of how most electoral promises never came to fruition. Seemed like a jaded way to look at things, but I guess I didn't have as much experience with that as my teacher.

I was full and content after my glass of blood, so I didn't get anything. After Trey and Raquel had what they wanted, we found an empty table. The student body started filtering in, and I made note of all the familiar faces. Becky, the girl who sat behind me in Spanish. Charlie, the guy who always dozed off in science class. Mollie, the girl with lightning-fast fingers in typing. Watching her flying digits, I would have laid money that she was a mixed vampire like me. She smelled completely human though, so I seriously doubted it.

Russell Morrison also strolled into the cafeteria at one point. The blockhead senior looked like a king surveying his underlings. He cast Raquel a particularly nasty look, one that made the hairs rise on the back of my neck and a tickle of a growl start to form in the back of my throat. Gripping the edge of the table, I partially stood from my chair. I hated what he'd done to Raquel while they'd been dating—walking all over her, treating her like garbage. But I loathed the way he treated her now. His hard eyes looked down on her like she was dirt beneath his shoe, or maybe even lower than that. And he spread lies about her that would make hookers blush. Most of the cruelest rumors that circulated the school were because of him. Asshole.

Raquel noticed both his look and my reaction. "Still protecting me," she quipped. "I can handle him, Julian. You don't have to guard me." She lifted her chin. "I'm a big girl."

Letting my tension dissolve, I smiled at her newfound confidence. "I know. I just seriously hate him … I'd kick his ass even if you weren't around."

Trey held his hand up to me. "Yeah, you would!"

We bumped fists while Raquel rolled her eyes. "Well, thankfully he managed to graduate, so he'll be gone soon."

I nodded, equally grateful of that. Mid-nod, I noticed the woman who stole my breath entering the cafeteria. "Arianna," I whispered, unintentionally.

Like she heard me, her golden-caramel colored head swung my way. Hazel eyes locked onto mine, and she gave me a small smile of acknowledgment. Just that tiny grin had my heart soaring, and the need to be near her drove me to action. Grabbing my bag, I stood from the table.

Oddly, Trey stood with me. "What are you doing?" I asked him.

He glanced over at Arianna and her friends. "I'm assuming you're going over there to talk to Arianna, since you seem to have a thing for her." I pursed my lips at his choice of words—I had a lot more than a "thing" for her, but Trey didn't know that. Ignoring my look, Trey nodded at one of the girls with Arianna. "Her friend Sophie is hot, so I'm coming with you. Try and introduce us, okay?"

"Fine," I muttered.

Raquel rolled her eyes at Trey, and then slowly started shaking her head. "Good luck, boys," she said, her tone full of amusement.

Trey in tow, I walked over to Arianna and her friends. "Hey, Arianna," I said, trying to sound casual.

"Hey, Julian." Her voice was polite and friendly, but distant too. It lacked the depth of feeling behind it, and I missed that depth. So much. Looking between Trey and I, she added, "Glad it's the last day of school?"

One of the girls Arianna was with snickered and said, "*I* sure am. I want to meet your new hot neighbor, Arianna."

All of them started laughing, while my chest constricted so tight, I was sure I was having a heart attack. Hot neighbor? She couldn't have a hot neighbor. Not now, before I'd convinced her to see me as something other than a friend. Another guy stepping into the picture too soon ... it was the worst possible thing that could happen. I couldn't lose her to someone else ... I just couldn't. "What ... neighbor?" I asked, feeling stupid, confused, and inexplicably ... hurt.

Arianna's cheeks filled with color as she smacked her friend on the shoulder. "Nobody ... it's nothing ..."

All I could do was stand there and stare at her. Was this how we ended? Arianna looked really embarrassed in the sudden silence, and I wished I could have played it cool, laughed ... something ... but my mind was spinning with worry. Trey was flashing glances between Arianna and me. Just as I thought to break the awkwardness of the moment by introducing Trey to the girl who'd caught his interest, he stepped forward.

"So," he said to the group. "You guys going to Julian's birthday party in a couple weeks? It's going to be the party of the year."

I instantly snapped my gaze to him. Birthday party? What birthday party? Trey winked at me, and I knew right then and there, I was going to regret letting him tag along.

The girls all looked at Trey dumbfounded, like they had no idea what he was talking about. That made sense, since this was the first time a party for me had ever been mentioned. To anyone. Including me.

All of the girls were looking at me now, and Arianna had an expression on her face that was close to interest. Could this be what shifted things for us? Make her see me as more than a friend? But crap ... I couldn't have a party. My parents would *never* agree to that.

"You're having a party, Julian?" Arianna asked. Her eyes sparkled as she gazed at me. Goddamn it, how could I say no to that face?

Smiling bright, I tried to look completely at ease even though my insides were quivering with nerves. "Yep! Party ... huge party ... It's going to be epic." I felt like slapping myself on the forehead. What the hell was I doing? I never threw parties. I rarely even *went* to parties. In fact, the last one I'd gone to at Halloween had been a disaster.

The redheaded girl on Arianna's left—Sophie, Trey's newest love interest—narrowed her eyes at me. "Really? *You're* having a party?"

I wanted to take it all back, but before I could, Trey interjected. "He sure is ... and it's open to everyone. Tell the whole school. I'm Trey, by the way. I'll be there too ..."

While the girls giggled, I felt like I'd just been slapped. *Oh my God ... he just invited the whole school to my house.* Damn it ... this was quickly getting out of hand. Needing to get away, I grabbed Trey's arm and started pulling him back to the table. As we moved toward where Raquel was waiting for us, Trey told Arianna's friends my home address, then said, "Two weeks from Saturday. See you guys there!" I'd never wanted to gag someone more in my life. Crap, crap, crap. My parents were going to kill me.

I was pale when we eventually found our way back to Raquel. Trey was grinning ear-to-ear when we joined her, and Raquel's face scrunched in concern. "You look sick, Julian. What happened?" Her gaze shifted to Trey, like she already knew this was his fault.

Dazed, I fell onto a hard, circular stool attached to the table. "Trey just invited ... *everyone* ... to a party ... at my house." He sat beside me and I instantly socked him in the arm. "What the hell were you thinking?"

Trey looked offended. "I was helping you, dude. You clearly wanted to see her again, and you clearly didn't want her hanging out with her hot neighbor all summer. I was giving you an in."

"By offering up a party at my house? A party my mom will never agree to?" I sank my head into my hands. "My mom's gonna kill me." And my dad, but my friends didn't know about him. The story being sold to the public was that my dad was dead.

Trey cringed, looking apologetic, like he'd just realized he'd overstepped. "Sorry, dude. I wasn't thinking about that. I just wanted you to have your happily ever after. But, hey, maybe it's not a big deal. Maybe they won't say anything, and no one will show up."

All three of us glanced around the cafeteria, and I easily picked out Arianna and her friends. The three of them were filtered among the students, spread out in clumps. All of the clumps were hunched over, talking with one another, and sporadically, someone in each group would raise their head and look over at me. This wasn't good. Wasn't good at all. My family hid who we were by keeping a low profile, not by throwing the party of the year.

Just as I was wondering if I was going to have to enlist both Hunter *and* Nika's help to fix this, Arianna met eyes with me. She again had a thoughtful expression on her face, like she was seeing something different in me. I wasn't sure why, or what I should do about it, but I suddenly knew this party needed to happen. I needed to see Arianna outside of school. I needed her to come over and spend time with me one-on-one. And soon, before this "hot neighbor" became more than a hot neighbor.

Yes, this might be just what we needed. Maybe in a party atmosphere, she'd see what a cool, charming guy I was. Maybe I could be funny and witty and sweep her off her feet. Maybe she'd fall for me all over again. Maybe we could finally start over.

Hope blossomed inside me as I considered what this party could do for us. My mind made up, I decided this was happening. Now I just needed to convince my parents to let it happen. And I had a feeling that having Hunter and Nika wipe the minds of the entire school would be a much easier task.

CHAPTER TWO

Julian

BY THE END of the school day, rumors of a start-of-summer party had spread like wildfire over the school. The tiny detail of it being my birthday was all but lost as the news made the rounds. The various reasons being given for the party were both amusing and alarming. They ranged from rich parents out of town, to an about-to-go-to-jail party, to a dying kid's last request to have a good time. The only thing that people were consistently getting right was my address; that was one detail nobody was messing up. The guest list was already massive, and there was still plenty of time before the party for extra guests to be invited. Shit. If the police were called because a mob showed up for my birthday, it might be my last birthday. Nika was going to piss herself laughing over this one.

On the bright side, the party gave me something to look forward to—one last chance to spend time with Arianna. I was on cloud nine when school ended, and I hadn't expected to feel that way today. Both Trey and Raquel noticed my unusually perky mood.

Trey gave me an odd look as we sat on the steps leading into the gym. He was using his foot to push his skateboard back and forth on the cement; the wheels made a grinding sound like the mortar and pestle my grandmother used to mash herbs. "You high, man? 'Cause I didn't think you smoked."

I pushed him away from me, into Raquel. "Just having a good day. Is that a crime?"

Raquel laughed as she dodged Trey's body. "No, not a crime, but definitely weird coming from you. Especially lately. Your mood seemed to be getting darker and darker with summer approaching, but now you're all rainbows and sunshine."

She gave me a mocking smile that made me want to push her away too. I would have, if she was within reach. "The day turned out better than I thought, and I have good things on the horizon. That makes me cheery."

I spotted Arianna walking toward her house on the other side of the graveyard and immediately leapt to my feet. "I'm gonna walk Arianna home. Catch you guys later." I ran off to the sound of Trey wishing me good luck.

When I caught up to Arianna, she was already passed the first few rows of headstones. It irritated me that she was walking home after school now. I used to drive her when we were together. Nika had thought that was ridiculous since she lived so close to the school, but I'd wanted whatever excuse I could use to spend more time with her. And besides, she shouldn't have to walk through a cemetery alone. Even to me that was a little creepy.

"Arianna, wait up!"

She turned when she heard my voice and I nearly choked on my breath. She was so beautiful. Her hair was more golden in color than it had been when we were together; there were streaks of blonde mixed with the creamy brown. She was growing it longer too. Last fall it had been in a cute, shoulder-length bob, but now it was approaching her mid-back. It was thick and luxurious, and I just wanted to tangle it around my fingers. I stuffed my hands into my coat pockets instead.

A strange expression crossed her face as she stared at me. The look was both intrigued and amused. "You don't have to keep walking me home, Julian. I can walk a hundred yards by myself, you know."

I grinned at her often repeated remark. "I know. You can do anything you set your mind to."

As I gazed at her, my heart seeped into my eyes. I knew I shouldn't let it, since we weren't at that level yet, but I couldn't stop the reaction; she meant the world to me. Arianna shifted her gaze to the ground, like seeing the adoration on my face made her uncomfortable. Knowing I needed to keep the mood casual, I closed my eyes and inhaled a cleansing breath, mentally clearing the love from my demeanor. *Look normal, act normal.* "So ... new neighbor, huh?" I asked, opening my eyes.

Arianna coughed into her hand, and then looked up at me; there was a slight cringe to her face, like she was embarrassed to talk about another boy with me. "Yeah ... His dad homeschools him, so he doesn't get to hang around kids his age much. Mom thought it would be a good idea if I made him feel welcome ..." Her voice trailed off and she kicked at a pebble on the ground as her gaze once again returned to her feet.

Hating the awkwardness I felt building between us, I tried to be mature and understanding. It was difficult. "That's ... really nice of you. I'm sure he ... enjoys your company." I know I did.

Arianna locked eyes with me, and that was when I realized just how much longing I'd imbued in that sentence. So much for causal. "Julian, do you ... ?" My heart sped up as I considered just what she might be about to ask me. *Do I like you? Yes. Do I want to be with you? Yes. Would I do anything for you? Yes.*

Her mouth snapped shut and her lips compressed into a tight smile. Clearly, she wasn't ready to open that door yet, and a huge part of me was relieved that she wasn't. Just her asking the question would forever alter what we were, and while I wanted out of this limbo, I wasn't positive she'd be happy to hear that I had feelings for her—or that she'd reciprocate them. We weren't there yet.

"Will you be at my party?" I asked, hoping I could successfully change the subject.

Relief lightened her face. "Ummm yeah, I was thinking about going. It should be fun."

"Great," I told her, keeping my smile contained to a small grin. Great? More like *freaking amazing*, but I didn't want to scare her off by saying that.

As silence fell between us, we continued walking through the cemetery to her house. When we were in her back yard, I finally said, "I really hope you come to the party. Maybe we'll get a chance to talk ... so we can, you know, get to know each other better, since we ... haven't known each other long." Sadness crept over me as I traipsed across her lawn. *We've known each other for years, you just don't remember.*

A strange, contemplative look crossed her face. "Yeah ... although sometimes, it seems like I've known you longer than I actually have."

Shock made me stand still. Arianna stopped with me, and she again looked embarrassed. "What do you mean?" I asked. Did she remember me?

Arianna frowned, and her brows furrowed in an adorable way. "Nothing, it's just ... a feeling, I guess." She looked around her yard before continuing. "I know this is going to make me sound crazy, but I have these ... blanks in my memory, these holes, and no matter how hard I try, I can't remember what happened to me in those gaps. And when I try to fill the hole with something plausible, nothing feels right—like I'm trying to jam a square through a circle. But when I'm around you ... it feels like, somehow you fit in those gaps ... like ... *you're* the circle." Her cheeks filling with color, she quickly stammered, "I don't know why I feel that way, and I don't know what it means, and like I said, it's just a gut feeling I get sometimes, and it really freaks me out, and I can't believe I told you about it ... and now you think I'm nuts, don't you?"

The fact that she was worried about my opinion of her made me feel like I could fly. But what she'd just said ... If Halina hadn't replaced every single one of her memories with something else, and she hadn't been inside with her long enough to do that, then the "holes" Arianna was talking about made complete sense. The gaps would fade with the natural aging process, but right now, she must be really confused. And miraculously, somehow, her body, her emotions, her heart ... a part of her knew that she should know me. It made it incredibly hard for me to not kiss her, to not tell her I loved her—to not tell her *everything*.

I couldn't though, so all I said was, "I don't think you're crazy. I think there's a lot in this world that can't be explained. And who knows, in another life, maybe we did know each other." In another life, that was just a few months ago.

Arianna smiled, and looked genuinely relieved that I hadn't rejected her. How could I, when she'd finally opened up to me? "Have a good summer, Julian. I'll see you ... at your party, I guess."

My beaming smile couldn't be held back this time. "Yeah ... see you then."

I jogged back to my car with a bounce to my step. This was the best day ever. Okay, maybe not *ever*, but it was definitely the best since "The

Wiping", which was how I referred to that awful moment when my grandmother had obliterated my girlfriend. That day had cast a shadow over my young life, but slim beams of light were shining through the cracks now, and I was going to grasp at that frail hope as strongly as I could. I was going to get her back.

I drove home faster than I should have, but luckily I didn't run into any cops. I wanted as much time as possible to make a good impression on my parents. I would need them pliable if they were going to agree to this party. Parking the car in my typical spot, I started in on operation *Good Son*. After tossing my stuff in the house, I opened all four car doors and started pulling out the garbage that had accumulated over the school year. It was disgusting, and I made a mental note to clean out my car more often. There were French fries ground into the carpet, takeout bags everywhere, and about a tree's worth of old assignments that I'd tossed out of my bag while digging around for other stuff. There were even a couple of half full bottles of juice that, judging by the amount of white fuzz growing in them, I knew I'd better not accidentally open. No wonder Mom always asked me to clean the car out, and Nika cringed whenever she got inside.

After my car was in order, I headed into the house and started in on my bedroom. It was almost as bad as my car—not quite, since I'd been keeping it clean for a good chunk of the year, but pretty close. At least my room didn't have any science experiments growing in it, just one glass of milk on my nightstand that was starting to curdle. My room smelled a thousand times better once I tossed it out. Mom must have been leaving it there to prove a point. Or she was overcompensating in other areas besides overfeeding me. She'd been cutting me a lot of slack lately.

I was vacuuming the living room when I felt my parents coming home. Hurrying to finish before they arrived, I moved lightning-fast over the carpet. I probably wasn't cleaning it very thoroughly, but the track marks of the machine would at least make it seem like they were clean. And at the moment, the illusion was good enough.

When I shoved the vacuum cleaner into a closet, my sister yawned and asked, "What are you doing, Julie? You don't clean. Ever." The suspicion in her voice was clear as day.

"What? Can't a guy help out?" I asked, frowning at the floor.

Nika laughed. "A guy, yes. You, no. What's going on?"

I fluffed a pillow on the couch instead of answering her. The old leather couch that had been my father's for an eternity, or so it seemed to me, had recently been stained beyond repair by massive amounts of blood. The new couch was black leather. Mom said it was much easier to keep clean than white. I had to agree, since a couple of swipes with a damp cloth had wiped away all the slight blemishes on the surface. I hoped it was okay to use water on leather. I really had no idea.

As I was rearranging the couch pillows for the umpteenth time, Nika grunted in frustration and said, "Stop ignoring me, and tell me what's going on."

Happy with the pillows, I turned my attention to the kitchen. I had just enough time to do the dishes and wipe off the counters. "I need Mom and Dad to agree to something, so I'm buttering them up."

"Agree to what?" Nika said cautiously.

I pursed my lips at the floor. "Shouldn't you be sleeping?"

I could almost hear Nika folding her arms across her chest. "Dead or not, I don't need eighteen hours of sleep a night. I'm just waiting out the sun." Her voice faltered at the end and I stopped my sour face. Summer meant longer days, and that meant Nika had to be holed up in her bedroom for even greater stretches of time. Yet another argument she'd tried to use on our parents, so they'd let her stay at the ranch. She'd at least have more room to walk around if she was living there.

Looking around the kitchen, I considered what to do. My sister was obviously lonely ... the clean dishes in the dishwasher and the small specks of food on the counter could wait. And besides, I could explain about the party better face to face anyway. "Hold on, I'm coming down."

"Okay," she whispered.

The entrance to Nika's hidey-hole was buried in a huge hall closet that wrapped under the stairs. I stepped inside, then closed the door behind me. Even though it was bright outside, the seal around the door was tight, and the closet was dark. Up until recently, we'd stored all of our winter coats in here. Shoving them aside every day to get to the back had quickly annoyed Nika, so Mom had moved the coats to the garage. I flipped the light switch, and then blinked in the sudden brightness. The bare bulb illuminated the empty clothing rod and the shelves behind it holding games, various odds and ends, and all the supplies that we kept in here. There were bags of dog food under the shelves, and the closet smelled like kibble because of it, a fact that Nika constantly complained about. Our old pup was upstairs right now, snoring away at the foot of my parents' bed with a wheeze that made me wonder if this would be his last summer.

At the back of the closet, where the stairs above made the roof slant, there was a break in the carpet that was seamless to human eyes, but clear to a vampire. Carefully, I pulled up on a long, shaggy strand of carpet. It came up easily, along with the particle board it was glued to. I held the carpeted cover in one hand as I stared into the dark hole where my sister lived. Aligning the board in my hand with the entrance, I jumped into the hole. The cover hit the rim of the opening, sealing the hole, while I continued on with a soft thud to the ground several feet below it. I smiled as I looked up at the now-closed entrance. I was getting better at closing it like that. The first few times I'd tried, the wood hadn't been lined up right, and I'd had to grab the chair nearby so I could reach the cover and manually put it in the correct position. The opening always needed to be shut in case someone opened the closet door. It was just one of the many protections against light that was down here.

With the entrance sealed, the small room was pitch-black. While I waited for my eyes to adjust, Nika said, "Door closed?"

Even though she couldn't see me, I nodded. "Yep. You're clear."

A wooden door to my left squeaked open and phosphorescent light brightened the darkness. Seeing my sister with glowing eyes was still startling to me, but I was getting used to it. I was getting used to her pale skin too. And the chill that emanated from her. With wavy brown hair and deep brown eyes buried beneath that unnatural glow, Nika reminded me of Mom. She didn't have Mom's current melancholy though. Nika had adapted well to her new life, mainly because of her sire, Hunter.

Nika's lips turned into an amused smile as she glanced at the cover. "You lined it up right on the first try this time. You're getting better at that."

I smirked at her, then pointed to the door that led out of this small, 6x9 room. "Let's go before someone opens the closet door." I knew we'd both hear and feel someone approaching before they could get anywhere near the door, and they'd feel and hear us too and wouldn't approach until it was safe, but now that I was down here with Nika, I couldn't wait to tell her about my day.

Nika seemed to understand and left the room without comment. Even though our emotional bond was gone, we'd been connected for so long that sometimes we could still tell what the other was feeling with just a glance. It helped me still feel close to her.

Outside the room Nika playfully called the "foyer" was a cement tunnel that led to the only other room down here, Nika's bedroom. It was technically part of the crawlspace under the house; the home had been designed with an unusually deep one. From what Dad said, that was the real reason he'd wanted to buy the place from the owners. He'd known he could easily convert the crawlspace into a vampire-safe hideout. He'd never planned on anyone staying down there full-time, but it had all worked out in the end.

Dad had dug out the crawlspace to make it even deeper, so no one had to stoop while visiting. Then he'd used a ton of cement to create the enclosed "foyer," hallway, and Nika's bedroom. The room within a room was completely impervious to sunlight.

The air down here was stale, musty. The only time it was refreshed was when the series of doors into the crawlspace were opened. That made it uncomfortable to be down here if you still needed to breathe, but Nika didn't, so it didn't matter. She hated the smell though.

Nika's room here was bigger than her room upstairs, but all of the concrete made it seem smaller. Plus she was stuck in here a lot, so that made it feel even tinier. Her bed took up most of one wall, with a nightstand beside it. A bookcase, table, and six-drawer dresser occupied the rest of the space. A laptop was open on Nika's bed. Luckily, she could get a bit of Wi-Fi signal down here. It wasn't very strong though, and constantly crapped out on her.

Exposed pipes and air ducts were running here and there beneath the house, sometimes straight through the cement wall of Nika's room. The openings were slathered with sealant, blocking off any light potential, but the pipes detracted from the homey feel of the space. They were noisy too. Whenever someone took a shower, flushed the toilet or did laundry, it sounded like a hurricane in here. Yet another reason Nika wanted to move out.

Looking a little stir-crazy and eager for news, Nika sat on her bed and scooted toward the middle. I smiled at the look on her face, and sat on the edge of her mattress. Dad had run power and cable down here for Nika, and she had a couple of lamps turned on, bathing the room in a soft glow. There was a flat-screen TV bolted into the thick cement opposite her bed, and a mini-fridge full of blood. On top of the fridge was a small microwave for warming it up. Warm blood was infinitely better than cold.

Closing her computer and tossing it on top of her pillows, Nika crooked me a smile and said, "Okay, before they get home, spill it. Why are you doing things that go against your very nature? And did I seriously hear you cleaning out the car earlier?"

I gave her an annoyed expression that clearly portrayed my appreciation of her assessment of my "nature." Smoothing my face, I leaned forward, eager to tell her. "Okay, I need your help. I need to convince Mom and Dad to let us have a birthday party."

She blinked at me. "We always have a party for our birthday."

Shaking my head, I told her, "No, a party party. With friends."

She twisted her lips. "I'm sure they'll be fine with a couple people. They usually are."

I sighed. Yeah, I knew that. Trey and Arianna had gone to every party we'd had since we'd started high school. What I wanted was a lot more than a couple of friends though. "No ... I'm thinking more along the lines of ... the entire school."

Nika stared at me a second, then she started laughing. I smacked her shoulder when she wouldn't stop. Wiping her eyes, she told me, "Oh, sorry. I just ..." she laughed again, "... Mom and Dad will never agree to a party that big."

Gauging our parents' distance, I mumbled, "Well, I sort of already invited everyone ..."

Nika stopped laughing. "You ... what? Without asking Mom and Dad? They're going to flip. They're going to make you cancel. They're going to ground you for a month."

I rolled my eyes, but she had a point. "I need this to happen, so ... how do I get them to say yes?"

Leaning forward, elbows on her knees, Nika narrowed her eyes at me. "Why do you need ... ?" Tilting her head, she said, "Is this about Arianna? Did she agree to go to your party? Is she ... interested in you?" I could hear the hope in her voice. It matched mine. Nika wanted Arianna back, almost as much as I did.

Praying this was just the thing Arianna and I needed to get back on track, I told Nika, "I don't know if she's interested in me in that way ... but she agreed to come, and that seems like a good sign. I need this to happen, Nick. It might be my only chance this summer to get her to see me as more than a friend."

Nika let out a long breath of chilly air. "Okay. Then we need to think of a way to get Mom and Dad on board."

Just then, the squeak of Dad's tires rolled up the driveway. The engine stopped and car doors opened and shut. Nika and I both swiveled our heads to look up at where our parents were. "Well, put your thinking cap on," I whispered. "They're here."

I hopped up off the bed and started jumping up and down as nerves washed over me. This wasn't good. I needed to calm down before I faced my parents. They'd hear and smell my distress before I got anywhere near them, and I wanted to seem calm and confident—like an adult asking for a simple favor, not a teen asking for a party.

Nika stood and grabbed my hand. I relaxed with her icy touch. Her presence was so soothing that for a minute, it was almost like we were still connected. "Wait until I come up to ask," she whispered.

Our parents were close now, opening the front door. I could hear them laughing, but couldn't hear what they were talking about. Not quite enhanced enough for that. I nodded at Nika, gave her a quick, one-shoulder hug, then left her so I could head back upstairs. I hoped I could hold out long enough for Nika to join me. I had a feeling she could phrase it in a way that might sway our parents. I'd probably just blurt it out, then start begging when they shut me down.

When I got to the room under the closet, I closed the door to the hallway, instantly darkening the transitional space. Unfolding the chair against the wall, I carefully stood on the cushy foam seat and popped open the lid covering the entrance. Hazy light filtered into the dark room, making it easier for me to see. I easily jumped up into the closet, then replaced the cover over the hole in the floor. I sighed as I looked back at it. Such a dark, dank, musty place. Being tucked under the house was no way for a person to live, vampire or not. Nika belonged at the ranch now, and hopefully Mom and Dad would realize that soon.

As I was still contemplating my sister's life, Dad's voice carried over to me through the closet door. "Julian? Mind coming here?"

Inhaling a deep breath, I replied, "Yeah, be there in a sec."

Rolling my shoulders to loosen up my tight muscles, I opened the closet door and stepped out to see both parents standing in front of me. Dad was giving me a curious expression while Mom was frowning. Wondering why they looked suspicious already, I shrugged and asked, "What?"

With a straight face, Dad said, "It smells like pine in here. Did you clean?"

"Uh ..." I wanted to drop my eyes, kick a non-existent stone on the floor, but I couldn't do either of those things or my parents would be on me in a flash. Just keeping my heart rate even was a challenge. Guess I overdid it on the cleaning. I should have drawn the line at mopping the entryway ...

Trying for casualness, I threw on as charming a smile as I could manage. "I spilled something, so I cleaned it up. That's what you're always asking us to do, right?"

Now Dad frowned as well as Mom. "Yeah, but you never actually do it." He nodded his head toward the living room. "You spill something in there too?"

With a raised eyebrow, Mom added, "And in your car?"

I looked over both of my protective, suspicious parents while I contemplated what to say. I was a spitting image of Dad—light blue eyes, dark black hair, and a smile to stop traffic, or so Mom said, and Nika was a carbon copy of Mom—same mahogany hair, same warm brown eyes, same fierce devotion to her loved ones. We definitely shared the same DNA.

Not wanting to rush my request, I spread my hands and slapped on an insulted expression. "What? A kid can't be nice and clean a little for his family without getting the third degree? I do like helping out every once in a while, you know?"

My parents glanced at each other, then back to me. Dad smiled, and I began to think that maybe I'd taken that argument just a touch too far. "Good to know," he told me. "I've been meaning to clean out the garage again. You can give me a hand."

A groan inadvertently escaped me. Yeah, I'd massively overplayed the I'm-just-being-helpful card. Dad was on to me, but I wasn't cracking. Not yet. Not until Nika was upstairs to work her magic on our parents.

Dad's smile grew at seeing the irritation on my face. He clapped his hands together. "No time like the present."

Mom rubbed his arm. "I'll get started on dinner while you get started on sorting that mess."

I accidentally groaned again. "Mom, no more food ... please. There are enough leftovers in there to feed about twenty vampires."

Mom pursed her lips, but nodded. "All right, fine. I'll give Tracey a call instead ... see how she's doing today."

Tracey was Mom's best friend from back in San Francisco. She was married to our symbolic Uncle, and Dad's best friend, Ben. To save his crumbling marriage, Ben had told Tracey everything about vampires, and everything he did for them. And he helped with a lot of dangerous stuff for us. He'd been beaten on, thrown against walls, nearly bitten, and not too long ago, shot in the head. Tracey was more than a little stressed over all of the new truths she'd discovered lately. She still shook whenever anyone in my family talked to her, Mom included.

Mom took Dad's briefcase and started heading upstairs to make her phone call. Along the way, Nika chirped, "Good morning, Mom, Dad." It was a far cry from morning, but in Nika's world, it wasn't even dawn yet.

Mom smiled down at where her daughter was hiding. "Good morning, Nika." She laughed after she said it, which I thought was a good sign. She'd shaken off a bit of her melancholy since this morning.

The family dog was waddling down the stairs as Mom walked up them. She reached down and stroked his grey muzzle as he inched his way past her. Spike gave her a quick lick, then continued on his journey to Dad. His nails clicked on the hardwood floors, and his long tail made a slow swish back and forth. It was about as excited as the ancient collie got nowadays.

Dad sank to his knees as Spike trudged over to him. Wrapping his arms around his neck, he rustled his fur. "Hey, boy, you didn't need to come all this way to greet me. I know those stairs are tough for you." Dad placed both of his palms on Spike's right hip; he often limped on that leg. Maybe it was my imagination, but I swear Spike smiled as Dad's chilled skin soothed his aches. Sometimes being really cold came in handy.

As I watched the labored way Spike breathed, the way his back dipped, and the way his body lightly shook with fatigue, a sad thought hit me. I unknowingly said it out loud. "He's not going to be around much longer."

Dad looked up at me with a forlorn expression. "I know. I figure two or three more months is all he's got left in him." Dad shifted his eyes back to Spike. "I can smell it. But it's a miracle he's lasted this long. I swear he's set a record." Dad smirked and rubbed Spike's back.

Spike had been a part of the family longer than I had. The thought of him not being in the house anymore was hard to imagine. "Maybe Nika can turn him?" I suggested, only half-joking.

Dad raised an eyebrow in classic Dad-fashion. "We're not making the dog a vampire."

I heard Nika snort downstairs as I shrugged at Dad. "Has anyone ever turned a pet? Maybe we should ask Gabriel what would happen."

Standing, Dad clapped my shoulder. "We'd have a rabid dog biting the neighbors, and that's way too much cleanup work for Nika and Great-Gran."

"And Hunter," Nika added. He was a pureblood vampire too.

Dad sighed as he looked at where Nika was below him. "And Hunter." Raising his eyes to Spike, who was now lying on the floor with his head on his paws, Dad murmured, "Spike will live and die a natural life ... as he was meant to." From the way he said it, I got the feeling he was talking about more than just the dog. None of us were going to live and die naturally. Well, I supposed I still had that option, if I took Gabriel's shot that would keep me alive. I really hadn't decided yet though, and I had plenty of time to do that. My future was still wide open to me. Unlike my sister. Dad and I glanced at each other, then back at the floor, and I knew we were both thinking the same thing: she'd died too young.

At hearing Dad say his name, Spike thumped his tail twice, but didn't get up. I didn't blame him. He was about a bazillion years old in human years. Hoping Dad had forgotten about the garage, I started inching my way toward the living room. Dad cleared his throat and smiled. "It's this way."

I started to groan in protest, but then I stopped myself. I wanted to appear like an adult so Dad would take me seriously. Whining wasn't very adult-like. Although, I'd seen more than my fair share of adult temper tantrums. I slapped on a smile as I rubbed my hands together. "Okay, let's do this!"

Dad narrowed his eyes at me. "Whatever you're up to, I hope it's worth it."

I rolled my eyes at Dad like he was ridiculous, but on the inside my emotions were doing jumping jacks. *Yes, she's worth it, Dad. She's worth all of this and so much more.*

CHAPTER THREE

Nika

TRYING TO IGNORE the internal sensor in my body that told me the sun was still up, I sat on the end of my bed in my musty room and listened to my family. Dad and Julian were in the garage. Organizing the Christmas decorations from what I could tell. Dad was asking Julian to unpack all the lights and check them, then reroll the strands so they weren't such a knotted mess when he pulled them out again in six months.

With clearly forced patience, Julian said, "Really? We need to do this now?" But then I heard him get to work on his project.

Julian wanted this party so badly that he would agree to do just about anything at the moment. I almost wanted to take advantage of the fact and give him something to do, but I'd never actually do that to him. And besides, I was partly responsible for what had happened between him and Arianna. If she hadn't seen me dead … well, I was positive she wouldn't have flipped out and broken it off with him, then Halina wouldn't have wiped her memory and Julian wouldn't be desperately trying to start over. Yeah, I was the one who should be in the garage helping Dad clean up. But I couldn't. I was stuck down here for a few more hours. It was so boring here, I almost wanted to cry. It was how I imagined prison, expect for the amenities, of course. I mean, I did have a TV, fridge and computer at my disposal. I think it was the lack of a view that made it seem so cramped. And the smell. That didn't help either.

I just wanted space. I wanted to be able to walk around. I wanted to see people, carry on conversations with them, and not just through the walls. But mostly, I wanted Hunter. I wanted to be near him more than I wanted anything else, even blood. It was a nagging sensation in the back of my head that I couldn't turn off no matter how hard I tried. Everything about being at my parents' house felt wrong. I was too far away from Hunter, from my sire. I needed him so much closer. I needed his arms around me, his lips on mine. But even then I would still feel too far from him.

My parents were being ridiculous about not allowing me to move to the ranch. They figured if they said yes and I started staying with Hunter, then I'd start sleeping with him too. They were actually right about that concern, but I wasn't about to tell them that. My body ached for him so much it was painful at times, and I'd gone to sleep restless on more occasions than I cared to count. And it was only getting worse as time went by. I'd had him once, and I wanted him again. Especially now that we were bonded. But Hunter was being Hunter, and refusing to sleep with me under my father's roof. He said it was disrespectful. I said it was annoying. My dad kept a sharp vigilance on the two of us, never closing his soundproof door anymore, but he couldn't stay up as long as we could, and we had plenty of time every evening to fool around. But Dad had told Hunter no, and Hunter was honoring him by telling me no.

And because Dad had told us not to leave the house after everyone went to bed, and Hunter was obeying that request as well, we couldn't even be together under somebody *else's* roof. I'd even take the open air at this point. I wanted my boyfriend. Desperately. But now that he was fully fed, he had this superhuman-like resolve. Our bond drove us both to the brink of passionate madness, but he always pulled back in time. I was dying, again, and Hunter was killing me, again, just in a completely different way this time. But I *would* have him. Eventually this impasse would end, and I was going to get my way, and we were going to make love. He couldn't hold out forever.

I tuned out Dad and Julian and shifted to Mom. She was in her bedroom, shuffling around and talking on the phone. She was probably changing out of her work clothes into something more comfortable. She was talking to Tracey while she moved around. From what I could hear, Tracey was having a mini panic attack.

"He wants me to go to the next group meeting, Em. Me!"

Mom sighed and there was a thump like she'd thrown her shoe across the room. "You should go. It will be good for you to see what he does."

"But ... there are going to be vampires there. And vampire hunters. And who knows what else! Probably a werewolf or two."

Mom laughed and her bed squeaked as she sat down. "Werewolves aren't real, Trace."

"Oh? Just like vampires aren't real, Em? Because I seem to remember hearing that before too!"

Tracey's voice was on the shrill side. Mom answered her in a calm, soothing tone. "Okay, that's a valid point. Well, I have yet to see or hear anything about werewolves, and none are scheduled to be at the meeting. It will only be humans and vampires."

"Only," Tracey scoffed.

Mom continued, unfazed. "All of the vampires there are friendly, and all of the hunters there are in on the cause. We're trying to forge peace between the two species, create justice, end unnecessary killing, on both sides. This is a big deal, and you should see it, so you can understand it, and not be so afraid of it."

Tracey took a moment before she answered Mom. "I never said I was afraid."

I smiled at the stubbornness in her voice, and I imagined Mom was doing the same. "Of course you're not. You should still go though. It will help you understand, and you'll be perfectly safe. No one at the meeting will hurt you. We're all just trying to make the world safe for our children—human *and* vampire, Trace. For Olivia, Julian ... Nika." Mom sighed, sadness in the sound. She was still really affected by what had happened to me. We all were. Continuing, she told Tracey, "That's all everyone in the group wants. Just keep that thought in your mind and you'll do fine."

Tracey sighed, and even I could hear the concession in the sigh. "Are you going? This would be a lot less ... strange for me, if you and Teren were going to be there too."

Mom let out a small laugh, her mood lifting with the sound. "We can be there if you want, if that would make things easier for you."

"Um, well, yeah … it would." Tracey laughed a little now too. "You two don't scare me as much as … some of the others."

I knew she meant my boyfriend and the other purebloods. Probably me too, since I was now in that category. Mom and Tracey went on to talk about other things, and I let my mind drift to other things. Namely Hunter and the cursed sun keeping us apart. I couldn't help but wonder what he was doing right at this very moment. I knew he was at the ranch, I could feel him, but he was too far away for me to gauge whether he was moving around or not. He had to be awake, or maybe just waking up. He was probably with Halina, since the two of them were so close. I tried not to let that bother me, they were bonded after all, just like he was with me. Jealousy wasn't always something that could be controlled though, and sometimes, like now, their closeness to each other was grating. I understood though. And besides, Hunter could be with Gabriel in his lab. Or with Imogen, Alanna, or anyone at the ranch who might be visiting the spacious underground levels. He wasn't necessarily with his sire.

There were still a few repairs that needed to be done on the ranch, especially in the living room and the lower levels. The attack a couple months ago had been bad, really bad. I was a little glad I'd missed it. Julian had told me stories though—running away, trying to keep everyone safe, having to leave people that he was sure he'd never see again. He'd been terrified … that I'd known. Up until I'd died, I'd been able to feel his fear. I'd shared it with him while I'd faced my own scary situation.

But that was then and this was now, and we were all steadily picking up the pieces of our somewhat altered lives.

My cell phone rang while images of Hunter swam before my eyes. I shook my head to clear the image of his deep, piercing gaze, his stubbled jaw. I needed to get control over this bond, not let it have such a hold on me. I wanted him, yes, but I wanted to be my own person too. And if Mom had maintained her identity with her bond to Dad, then surely I could maintain mine too. Taylor women were strong that way.

Seeing the screen of my cell phone once I picked it up off my dresser, I couldn't help but grin. Speaking of strong Taylor women. Pressing the answer button, I brought the phone to my ear, "Hi, Aunt Ashley."

Ashley was my mom's completely human sister. She still lived in California with her husband, but she called whenever she could. She'd flown up for a couple of weeks once she'd heard the news about me. I think it had really helped Mom to have her close again, but Ash had missed her home, her husband, and her job, so she'd reluctantly returned to San Francisco after her too-short visit. She called me at least three times a week though.

"Is this too early? I'm still not sure when I should call?" she asked, her voice warm and familiar.

"This is fine. I get up pretty early," I answered, happy to have someone to help pass the time with, and a distraction from thinking of Hunter. Although he was always in my thoughts.

"It's still strange to hear you say that," Ashley murmured.

I laughed. "Yeah, sometimes it's still strange to say it. It feels natural though." That was certainly true. My body had acclimated to my new routine almost instantly. The vampire in me craved the night, and while I missed the sun, I wasn't overcome with grief by its absence.

"Well, that's good. It makes me happy that you're happy." I assured her that I was great and she let out a soft sigh. "I miss you guys. I want to come visit again. I think Christian and I are going to head up for your birthday. Stay a few days, if not longer."

Even though she was still having a conversation with Tracey, Mom overheard Ashley and exclaimed, "Tell her that's great! And I can't wait to see her. And she should stay here instead of the ranch this time."

I frowned up at my mom. That was one annoying thing about living with vampires; everybody eavesdropped on everyone else's conversations. With our hearing, it was unavoidable, but it was still irritating at times. "Mom says she can't wait, and she wants you to stay at the house with us."

Ashley chuckled. "Wow, vampire ears are amazing."

I laughed with her. "Tell me about it. Mom's got better reception than my phone." I glanced at the screen indicating I was getting one bar, and I'd only keep that one bar if I didn't move from this specific section of the room. An unfortunate side effect of being surrounded by so much cement.

Ashley and I stayed on the phone for a while. She kept me occupied by telling me all about her work at the hospital. Ash had been horribly burned as a kid, and most of her body was scarred. She worked in the burn unit at a hospital in San Francisco with her husband. He was a doctor there who specialized in skin regeneration, specifically skin that grew hair.

Thanks to his work, Ashley had a full head of hair again. Mom said she was a hundred times spunkier now that she could pull all of it into a ponytail. It was still pretty thin hair, and patchy in places, but Ashley was happy as a clam to have it.

When we hung up the phone, I only had to wait an hour or so for the sun to go down. It still seemed to take forever, as it did every night, but I managed to make it through with only a mild case of restlessness. As soon as I felt the sun was safely below the horizon, and all of its poisonous rays were doused for the day, I zipped from my hallway, into the "safety" room, and jumped into the closet. I bound from the enclosed space like I was erupting for air. Closing the door behind me, I leaned against the wood and inhaled the flowery scent of the main floor of the house—so much better than my dank, dark hole in the ground.

Mom stepped out of the kitchen to give me a swift hug. She was usually the first one to hug me when I emerged. Julian was on the couch in the living room, looking dirty and exhausted. He raised his head to glance at me when I entered the room, then dropped it back to the cushions. Dad must have worked him hard with his belated spring-cleaning project. Sweeping my eyes around the immaculate living room, I could see why my parents had been suspicious. Our house was never really dirty, but there was usually some form of clutter here and there. Julian had straightened everything. He'd even vacuumed.

Dad walked around the corner from the kitchen, giving me a hug. "Good morning, Nika," he told me, squeezing my shoulder.

When he released me, his pale eyes searched mine, like he was analyzing me. I knew what he was looking for, some sign that my bond with Hunter had kicked into overdrive. It hadn't yet, Hunter was still at the ranch, probably being detained by Halina or Gabriel. The minute he started surging toward me though, it would activate.

Feeling uncomfortable, I broke eye contact. "Please stop that," I muttered.

His face was both apologetic and unapologetic. Without a word, I could tell he was thinking, *I don't want to be this protective, but I'm your father and it's my job.* "Just ... checking," he finally said.

I could feel his eyes on me still, but I ignored it. Mom indicated the kitchen. "Dinner's ready. Let's eat."

The heavenly smell of fresh blood wafted over and a small growl of delight escaped me. The bloody scent was laced with other things that didn't smell nearly as good—leftover turkey, crepes, bacon, tuna casserole, potato salad and ice tea from what I could make out. Once upon a time, that would have delighted me more than the plasma, but not anymore. Not since my conversion.

Ignoring the revulsion of the human food I was smelling, I walked into the kitchen and took my traditional spot at the table. Julian looked starving when he plopped down beside me. I felt bad that he'd had to wait so long to eat, just for me. That was an unnecessary nicety. I could eat by myself once the sun went down. I was a big girl.

As Mom filled up a huge plate for Julian, I told her, "You guys shouldn't wait to eat until I'm up, especially during the summer." Mom set the heavy plate in front of Julian, where it landed with a hearty thud. Smirking, I added, "Julie's likely to starve to death."

Julian edged me in the ribs. "Fat chance of that," he sighed, looking at the amount of food on his plate.

As Dad poured steaming blood into tall glasses, he told me, "As long as we're able, we'll eat as a family."

I didn't object any further as Dad began setting the glasses on the table. While he set the stainless-steel carafe in the center of the table, Julian nudged my side and gave me a questioning glance. Even without the bond between us, I knew he wanted me to bring up the topic of our birthday, so he could ask his huge favor. I wanted to help him out, I really did—I missed my friend just as much as he missed his girlfriend—but I had no idea how to frame our request in such a way that our parents would have no choice but to say yes. I just couldn't fathom them saying anything other than no. Well, except maybe hell no.

Picking up my blood, the glass pleasurably warm under my fingertips, I started the conversation. "So ... Aunt Ashley wants to be here for our birthday ..."

Mom jumped right in, both feet first. "I know! Even though she was just here a few weeks ago, I'm so excited to have her back." Her eyes shifted to Dad as he sat at the table. "I've really missed having her around."

Dad grabbed Mom's fingertips at the same time as he reached for his glass. "I know."

He brought the glass to his mouth; his fangs crashed down before the rim even touched his lips. My stomach felt like it was eating itself I was so hungry. Watching Dad drink only made the ache deepen. I raised the glass to right in front of my face, but spoke before I drank. "Maybe we should celebrate a little more than we usually do since she's coming up?"

Julian's eyes darted to his plate as he immediately began shoveling food into his mouth. I could tell he was purposely ignoring looking at Mom and Dad in case he gave himself away. I instantly started drinking my cup of blood as I let them absorb my comment for a minute or two; it was best to let the idea sink in before I expanded on it. My fangs dropped the instant the blood hit my tongue. It was like sweet, healing, molten lava down my throat. For a second, it burned away every thought, every care, and every desire. Drinking was all that existed.

Somewhere in my din of euphoria, I heard Dad ask, "What did you have in mind?"

Just as I was wondering how to subtly ask for something I was sure they'd never agree to, I felt something else that made everything in the room seem insignificant ... even the blood. I slammed the glass back to the table so hard, I put a fine crack along the bottom of it. Warm blood started oozing onto the wooden surface of the table, but I didn't care. Clutching the edge of my seat, I fought against the aching desire rising in me. Hunter was coming closer, and everything in me wanted to run to him. Mom cleaned up my bloody mess while Dad told me to try and breathe and relax. I wanted to snap at him that this was too intense, that it was impossible to just calmly breathe through it, but Dad had been through this before and he knew what he was talking about, so I tried to take his advice instead.

Digging my fingers into the hard chair below me, I forced myself to inhale a deep, cleansing breath. It helped, but just a little. I wanted to run, but I made myself sit there. I had to squirm though. He was close, so close...yet still so far away. I needed him. I needed him so much. I needed his hands on me, his mouth on me, his body on mine. A small groan escaped me as I crossed and uncrossed my legs.

"And that's my cue to go," Julian muttered as he rose from the table.

One of my eyes shot open as I glared at him. "You have no idea what this feels like, Julian. No idea." I closed my eyes and clutched the chair harder as the throbbing vibrations rippling through my body intensified. I needed him. Now.

"You're right, I don't know, and I don't want to know. And I don't want to watch ... again." I could hear the horror in his voice. Under normal circumstances, I would have felt it too, but I was too electrified to care about anything Julian was saying.

While Dad told him to go wait in the living room, I shot to my feet and sprang toward the door. I couldn't sit here and wait any longer. Dad anticipated my move and snatched me up. Quite a feat, since I was stronger than him. Struggling against him, I growled, "Let me go. I need to go to him."

Calmer than I would have been, Dad responded, "This will pass, Nika. Just breathe in, breathe out. I don't want you running through the city like this. He'll be here soon. I promise."

Breaking away from him, I again concentrated on my breathing. Anything I could focus on besides the surging rush of desire coursing through me was a good thing. I marched back and forth in frustration. Hunter was approaching fast, but not nearly fast enough for me. I felt like I was going to burst before he got here. You'd think I'd be used to the sensation by now, but I wasn't. It was aching, wondrous, torture. I loved it, I hated it.

"Dad ..." My voice was almost a groan, which was horribly embarrassing. "I can't take this anymore. We need to stay together, so this ..." I sucked in a breath, held it, then released it, "... doesn't keep happening."

Mom rubbed my back. "I know it's hard, honey, but you can do this. It's only temporary. It eases up after—"

I cut her off with a sharp glare. "After a year or more. I can't ..." I ran my hands through my hair, down my body, as fire swept through me. "I can't do this for a year ..."

Hunter was just a few minutes away now, and I felt on edge, prickly with desire. Any second I was going to erupt. My somewhat-calm breaths, shifted to short pants. My eyes locked onto the front door, willing Hunter to burst through them. I heard Julian groan again, and Dad sighed. Mom rubbed my back in sympathy, but her tenderness was grating in my current condition, and I stepped away from her. The small movement toward Hunter was more than I could bear. I shot toward the door like a bullet exploding from a gun.

Dad wasn't quick enough to stop me this time. "Nika!" was all he got out before I was gone.

I accidently ripped the front door off the hinges as I fled the house. I could feel Mom and Dad behind me, but their presence in my head was nothing compared to Hunter's. We crashed into each other's arms at the end of the street, and melded together into one body—arms, legs, lips. Bliss flooded me as our bond finally got what it wanted: the two of us together. Nothing in this world felt as wonderful as this.

Our greeting intensified as we sank to our knees near a stop sign on the corner. Groaning between fiery kisses, Hunter laid me onto the concrete, then pressed himself on top of me. I wrapped my legs around him, pulling him closer. I could tell how much he wanted me. The feeling was definitely mutual. I ground my hips against his, begging him to do the same with a low, throaty moan of pleasure. It didn't even occur to me to be bothered by the fact that we were rolling around on a dirty sidewalk. Nothing was bothering me at the moment. Nothing but the fact that Hunter and I were both wearing way too many clothes.

Just as I thought to rectify that problem, my fingers skimming up Hunter's back, taking his t-shirt with them, Hunter was yanked away from me. I leapt to my feet to return to his embrace, but arms wrapped around me, restraining me. A familiar voice chuckled from behind me, but all I could focus on was Hunter's dark eyes boring into me, drinking me in from a distance. I burned with need, and struggled against the person holding me captive. Hunter wrestled with his restrainer as well, even dropping his fangs and growling as he twisted and pulled.

An amused voice broke through my frustrated fog of desire. "Watching them meet up never gets old. I think I'll miss it when their bond settles down."

I recognized the voice and the sense of humor. Shaking my head to clear away the tidal wave of passion pounding me, I looked over my shoulder. Halina was standing just behind my mother, who was pinning my arms behind my back. Reason flooded into me as my eyes darted between the two women. Mom was holding me back from ripping the clothes off my boyfriend ... in the middle of a public street. We'd been moaning, groaning, and grinding when they'd pried us apart. My grandmother was laughing her ass off at our sexual display. It was mortifying to put it mildly, and the buzz from the bond faded in my embarrassment.

As my breathing started returning to normal, I looked over at Hunter. Dad was holding him tight, and neither man looked happy about it. Dad was annoyed; Hunter was still ... frustrated.

Ignoring Halina, who was enjoying this way too much, I told Mom, "I'm fine now."

I relaxed in her arms so she'd let me go. Once she saw that I was more or less myself, she released me, and I headed over to Hunter. His eyes were wild as I approached. It stirred something primal inside me, but I pushed it back. Not now. Not here. Gently, I placed my hand on his rough cheek and stroked his skin in a soothing pattern. He calmed as he stared at me. When he blinked a few times in rapid succession, I could tell the crazed lust we'd both felt was fading from him too. A part of me was grateful, a part of me was sad. We'd never been able to act on the wild, animalistic intensity. I had a feeling it would be incredible if we ever caved to the rush the bond gave us. But Dad was always around to pry us apart and calm us down. He was just as tired of it as we were.

A smile lifted the edge of Hunter's lip. "Hi," he muttered. If his face could have flushed with color, I was sure it would have. Words often escaped us when we greeted each other lately. At least at first anyway.

"Hi," I laughed back. "I missed you. Obviously."

Hunter made a sound that was both a laugh and a sigh. "I did too ..." He tried to give me a hug, but Dad still had a hold of him. Frowning, Hunter said over his shoulder, "I'm okay, you can let go."

Instead of doing what he'd asked, Dad tightened his grip. "Just to be on the safe side," he answered, smirking.

Giving my father an admonishing glare, I peeled his fingers off of Hunter. "Stop it, Dad." When Hunter was free, he chastely wrapped his arms around me. Sliding my hands under his arms, I put my palms on his shoulder blades and squeezed. He felt wonderful. Firm and hard, yet soft and comfortable too. And now that we were both undead, we were equally warm, or should I say, equally cold. I just wanted to crawl into his lap and burrow myself in the shelter of his embrace. But that couldn't happen right now, so I pulled apart from him after a politely brief hug.

Halina was still laughing at us when we stepped away from each other. Dark-haired and pale-eyed like the majority of our family, Halina seemed the youngest even though she was the matriarch. Of course, her being dressed like she was on her way to a nightclub might have had something to do with that.

Hunter frowned at her. "You didn't have to follow me tonight. The meeting's not 'til later."

Halina shrugged as she shook her head in amusement. "I know, but watching the two of you paw at each other like dogs in heat is too much fun to miss."

I frowned at her analogy. *Dogs? In heat?* Eww. Not a sexy image.

Now that the intensity of the bond igniting was over, my hunger came back to life. Clutching my stomach, I looked up at Hunter. "I need to eat."

His dark eyes were concerned as they washed over me. Being newborn, I needed to eat frequently to be at my best. Hunter hadn't properly fed himself when he'd first converted, so he was very sympathetic to hunger pains. "Okay, let's get you something."

I grabbed his hand and started leading him toward home. Mom, Dad and Halina fell into step behind us. "You probably need to eat too," I told him.

Hunter grinned and leaned into me. His eyes drifted to my neck as he murmured, "I could use a bite."

I giggled at his innuendo. I wish he'd bite me again. We'd only done it once, back when I was alive, but it had been incredible for both of us. I was ready for round two, and so was Hunter. Dad cleared his throat, and I flicked my gaze behind us to see him scowling. He'd understood Hunter's innuendo, and he wasn't thrilled.

Halina lightly shoved Dad's shoulder as she took in the exchange. "Lighten up, Grandson." She pointed at Mom. "You nibbled on your girlfriend often enough, and it's not like Hunter can truly hurt Nika now."

Dad's expression grew insolent. "Yeah, but I wasn't sixteen. Or a girl."

I stopped in my tracks and put my hands on my hips. Mom and Halina took the same posture as me and we all stared Dad down. He looked between the three strong, independent women he'd just insulted. This time, Hunter chuckled.

Dad held his hands up. "I didn't mean anything by it, I just meant—"

Mom crossed her arms over her chest. "That as women we're weaker and somehow inferior to men."

Dad shook his head. "No, absolutely not. You're taking it out of context. I just meant ... you're women, and need to be protect—"

Halina leaned in and cut him off. "I would shut up now, if I were you."

Dad sighed and closed his mouth. After another second of us staring him down, he added, "I apologize if I offended you. I'm an idiot."

Hunter laughed again, while the three of us relaxed. Grabbing Hunter's hand, I allowed myself to giggle too. Maybe chagrining Dad would help Julian and me convince him to let us have a party. It couldn't hurt. Perfectly content, I swung Hunter's hand. My day was going well already, and it had only just begun.

CHAPTER FOUR

Hunter

NIKA WAS HAPPY. Our bond wasn't an empathic link, like the bond with her brother had been before her conversion had broken it, but some things I didn't need to feel to know. Her smile told me everything. She was satisfied—with me, and with her life.

I was finally feeling content myself. I'd accepted what I was, and accepted my new family. I'd fought for them, protected them, and was continuing to protect them. The meeting tonight was just one more step in the road to keeping my family safe. And I'd do anything to keep my family safe. Anything.

Holding Nika's hand, I walked at a human pace with her back to her father's home. I hated that she was living in a hovel under the two-story dwelling, but I also understood and respected Teren's desire to keep his teenage daughter under his roof for as long as possible. I'd probably feel the same way if I was her father. But I wasn't. I was her boyfriend and her sire, and being separated from her was frustrating. Especially with how explosive our reunions were.

If we were just allowed to be together all the time, moments like tonight wouldn't happen. The bond-driven desire wasn't *all* bad, the intensity of it was really, really nice, but it wasn't appropriate. And it certainly wasn't private. Someone was always around whenever we came together, ready to bust us apart. It made me shudder to think what might happen if someone wasn't nearby to separate us. Nika and I could easily end up in a compromising position in a very public place if we weren't careful. Just another reason for us to live together.

Studying the cracks in the sidewalk as they passed underneath my feet, I considered just how public that little moment had been. Stifling a sigh, I glanced over my shoulder at Teren walking behind us. He still looked embarrassed over his earlier comment about women needing protection, but that didn't stop him from watching me like a hawk. I should talk to him again about Nika staying with me at the ranch. I would even promise not to touch her until her eighteenth birthday, if that would make him feel better. Refocusing on the path in front of me, I vowed to do just that. I'd promise him abstinence in exchange for a chance to improve Nika's life. And Nika wouldn't like it, but I'd stick to that promise. It would be difficult, but we were already abstaining, so it wouldn't be that much harder than it was now. And right now, turning Nika down had its moments.

We'd only caved and made love once when she was still alive, but that one time frequently ran through my mind, haunted my dreams. The softness of her skin, the taste of her lips, her moans in my ear, her blood in my throat ... the memory of it all was almost too much to handle. It made me instantly want to be with her again. But she was adjusting to so much; I knew from experience how difficult the transition to a pureblood vampire was. I wanted to give her time before we took the relationship to that level again. Because once we did, I knew we'd never go back.

But I'd happily put sex on the back burner if it meant living with her. I'd tolerate almost anything to never be separated from her again. As for drinking from her again ... well, that might be infinitely harder to resist. I'd wanted to bite her three times already, just this evening.

I sensed Halina sliding to my side before I saw her. Cool and sleek, her long hair dark as night, she had a Cheshire grin on her face as she walked beside me. "What?" I asked, already knowing the answer. She was amused by my relationship with Nika, and she was happy that I was finally a committed member of the nest. Much like Nika, Halina was content.

"Just noticing all the dirt on Nika's back, is all." Her smile changed to a lopsided grin. Frowning, I examined Nika's shirt. Halina was right. There was even a stray piece of litter in Nika's hair. Great.

I brushed off the debris and plucked out the bit of garbage while Halina laughed. "So," she said. "Since you're the commander of the Vampire Justice League, can we talk about your bodyguards? They're driving me absolutely crazy."

I rolled my eyes at her. "Can you please stop calling it the Vampire Justice League? It's starting to catch on. People won't take us seriously if they think that's really the name." Halina had jokingly called the group that from nearly the beginning, but I'd heard others say it too. People were even shortening it to VJL.

While Halina chuckled at my response, Nika laid her head on my shoulder. It instantly distracted me from Halina. "You're amazing, you know that?"

I shook my head, slightly bewildered. "I'm many things, but amazing is hardly one of them."

I heard Teren clear his throat behind me, and I wasn't sure if he was agreeing with my statement, voicing his displeasure that Nika was touching me in such an intimate way, or clearing his throat simply because he needed to clear his throat. Vampires got tickles, same as humans.

Nika lifted her head and gazed at me with clear adoration on her face. "I'm asleep for one day and you decide to change the world."

I smirked at her assessment of what I'd done. "I wouldn't say I've changed the world, just leveled the playing field, maybe. And it's not amazing. I'm just doing what I can to right a wrong, protect the innocent. It's all I've ever done."

Halina leaned around me to look at Nika. "See. Vampire Justice League." Nika laughed at her grandmother, and I smiled at both of the women in my life. When Halina brought her eyes back to mine, she asked, "So? Thing 1 and Thing 2? What can we do about them?" Her eyes narrowed to catlike slits. "Do I really need to get board approval to eat them now?"

I gave my creator a reproachful glance as we reached the Adams' family home here in the city. "No, you may not eat Rory and Cleo." I sighed as I stepped onto the porch. "They're just trying to help."

FAMILY IS FOREVER

Halina snorted, her good mood twisting into annoyance. I understood the reaction. Rory and Cleo were two vampire hunters who had been in the first batch that I'd compelled to join us. Maybe I'd gone a little overboard with that original group, because they were both diehard fighters for the cause. And they took the job of protecting vampires, mainly me, a little too seriously. In fact, they would stay at the ranch with us if they could. They would probably stay in my bedroom with me if they could. I wouldn't be surprised if they were moments away from showing up for guard duty—actually, I was a little surprised they weren't already here.

Passing me to open the front door, Teren said, "They were here an hour ago. They wanted to wait on the steps, but I made them go to the meeting place to wait for you." He held the door open along with an eyebrow; he was just as annoyed with the pair as Halina.

Nika walked through the door, pulling me through it after her. Just her stretching away from me caused a brief flutter of anxiety to flash through my body. That feeling amplified to near-painful levels the farther apart we were. When I met up with her in the entryway, I subconsciously melded into her side. "I'll talk to both of them. Have them ease up on the security detail."

Halina walked into the home, immediately striding to the living room. "Just compel them to leave you alone."

I glanced at Nika, then we followed Halina. Nika's brother was in the living room with Halina, giving her a warm hug. Julian Adams wasn't my biggest fan, so he merely flicked his eyes in my direction in acknowledgment of my arrival. Fair enough. I couldn't really blame him for his dislike. His sister was dead because of me. His home had been attacked, his family threatened. And from what Nika had told me, his girlfriend's memory had been erased. All because of me. I wouldn't like me either.

"We might need their help at some point. I'm not going to get rid of them, simply because they're slightly annoying."

Halina frowned at my comment. "Slightly?"

Ignoring her, I looked down at Nika. "Let's get you fed."

She grabbed her stomach in response, and I knew she was starving. I probably should have given her time to eat before rushing over here, but I couldn't stop myself. Finding it funny to watch me squirm, Halina had amused herself by keeping me occupied after the sun went down. I'd blurred away as quick as I'd been able to though. Nika was an irresistible pull.

I escorted her into the kitchen where I could see that the meal had been interrupted. Several glasses of blood were steaming, mostly untouched, and Julian's plate of food was still heaping. The rest of the family followed us into the room, Halina included. I pulled out Nika's chair for her, which made Teren's lips twitch into a ghost of a smile. His face immediately returned to impassiveness as he sat down across from us. While he watched every move I made, his wife poured a glass of blood for me and then a glass of blood for Nika; by the slight bloody smears I could see on the table, it was clear Nika's original glass hadn't survived our reunion.

"Thank you," I told Emma, as she set our glasses down. She gave me a polite nod in return.

Nika immediately began chugging back her blood, her face a picture of contentment. I brought my glass to my lips and took a sip. The taste of the blood as it washed over my tongue and down my eager throat was indescribable. I'd never get over how the sweet, tang of fresh blood eased the aching that radiated from my stomach, up to my mouth. I'd never felt such discomfort as a human, even at my hungriest. And I'd never felt such joy when I soothed my parched mouth. Just the fact that I could willingly drink was a testament to how far I'd come. It wasn't so long ago that just the thought would have had me feeling sick to my stomach. Now all I felt was ... satisfied.

Halina watched me just as intently as Teren did, but for different reasons. She was making sure I was okay. She was watching for any lingering signs of depression. I smiled at her, lifting my glass. "Sit. Drink with us."

Her serious expression lightened. I was fine, and she knew it. Smirking, she pointed to my glass. "No, thanks. I feel like fresh food tonight."

I stiffened a bit in my chair as I lowered the glass from my mouth. I knew what she meant by that. "Halina, we've made it clear that murder is no longer considered acceptable, on either side. The panel will try you if you take a human life, and if they find you guilty of an unjustified murder ... your life will be forfeit."

I set the glass down harder than I'd planned; the blood in the cup rippled with vibrations, but the glass thankfully remained intact. Halina knew the rules, she'd helped me set them in place. The only way to make it fair for everyone was to make it strict. No vigilante killings. No vengeance deaths. Anyone who had issue with anyone else could bring it before the panel to discuss, but handling it themselves was discouraged. It would just lead to more potential justice murders and never-ending fighting between the species if we let either side continue to kill the other with no consequences. For peace to happen, order needed to happen too.

Halina frowned at my statement while the rest of the family grew silent. "I know that, Hunter. I have no plans to kill anyone. Just a nibble will do." She shrugged, then pursed her lips. "Am I still allowed that tiny luxury?"

I relaxed back into my chair and reached underneath the table to squeeze Nika's hand. "Of course. So long as it's a small amount and they have no memory of the incident, it's fine."

Halina rolled her eyes. "Well, I'm glad I have the Vampire Justice League's permission to eat."

Having heard this before, I sighed. "Halina, you know it's for our protection—"

She cut me off with a swish of her hand. "I know, I know. This is all just very different for me. I'm not used to ... rules and regulations. Aside from my own, of course."

She gave me a wink and I could only shake my head at her. My sire was a complex person—playful and passionate, aloof and fiercely protective. She always kept me on my toes. But her trepidation, resistance, and rebellion to the rules was what we were going to face with the other pureblood vampires. No creature that powerful liked to be told what to do. And unlike with the hunters, we couldn't compel vampires. They had to be convinced it was in their best interest to play along.

Halina walked around the room, placing a kiss on Teren's head, then Julian's, then Nika's. When she got to me, she kissed my cheek. "Stay safe. I'll see you at the meeting."

I nodded at her. "You too."

When she left the room, my gaze drifted back to Nika. Her large brown eyes were locked onto mine. I knew it had to be weird for her to see how close I was to another woman. I felt bad about it, but she swore to me that she understood, and she wasn't jealous. I hoped that was the case. Both women were important to me, but Nika was my life.

Without further incident, we dug into our meals. Julian fidgeted the entire time he ate. He wasn't eating very fast either. He was mainly pushing the food around his plate with a scowl on his lips. I had no idea what his problem was, but every gulp of blood I swallowed, I wished he'd get over it and finish his meal already. The smell of his turkey was stomach-churning.

When Julian started tapping his fork against his plate, his eyes locked on Nika, I couldn't help but think I was missing something. Looking around Nika, I asked him, "Something on your mind, Julian?"

Nika's hand was still holding mine. She suddenly squeezed me so hard, I knew she was silently conveying some sort of message to me. I wasn't sure what she was trying to say, but *Shut up* seemed to be the most likely sentence.

I sat back in my chair and didn't ask any more questions. Julian mumbled, "No," and went back to his meal. Teren and Emma looked between their children with suspicious eyes. Nika gave them a disarming smile, and even I knew something was definitely up.

Emma set her glass of blood down. "Nika, before we were …" her dark eyes glanced at me, "… interrupted, you said something about Ashley and your birthday?"

Nika worried her lip. For a second, how plump and inviting it was distracted me from the awkward look of uncertainty on her face. "Oh, yeah … I was just wondering—"

Interrupting her, Julian suddenly asked, "How come I never get to go to the meetings with you guys?"

Teren and Emma looked over at Julian. My eyes stayed on Nika, and I caught the brief moment of surprise on her face, followed by confusion, followed by blankness. It was pretty obvious to me that she was shocked Julian had changed the subject. So whatever was going on, it must revolve around Julian. She was trying to help him with something, and I had a pretty good idea of what—or who—he might want that Nika would do anything to help him with.

Teren scratched his jaw while he thought of how to answer his son. "Well, I guess because it's potentially dangerous, and you're still young."

"Nika gets to go, so I don't see why I can't," he muttered, jerking his thumb over at his sister.

Nika pursed her lips. "It's not like it's super exciting or anything. Just a group of people arguing about rules and regulations and the evils of compulsion."

She rolled her eyes in annoyance and I had to agree with her. Bickering ran rampant at meetings. Every human there argued against the purebloods being allowed to compel people, but it was the only way to keep vampires hidden from society. Giving up the ability to trance people wasn't an option. And besides, we'd never have persuaded the hunters to our side in the first place if we hadn't "forced" them into cooperating with us, and the group recognized the importance of that step. Whether they liked it or not, they were already under the influence of our "evil" mind games.

Julian frowned at Nika while Teren told him, "She's a pureblood now. She can take care of herself." The expression on his face when he said it made me wonder if he was trying to make up for his earlier misstep about the female gender. I squeezed Nika's fingers, torn by his comment. Sure, she was quite capable of taking care of herself, but I'd prefer it if she never had to.

A look of rebellious insolence crossed Julian's young face. It reminded me of when Dad used to tell *me* something I didn't want to hear. I smiled at the memory; we'd had some good showdowns over the years. The slight grin left me the minute I remembered that Dad was gone, and he was never coming back. He no longer knew me.

"I defended the ranch against a horde of hunters intent on killing every vampire they came across. I think I can handle a roomful of reformed hunters who have been compelled not to hurt me." He crossed his arms over his chest and lifted his chin.

Teren sighed as he leaned back in his chair. Lifting a hand, he told him, "I really don't have a good reason to keep you away. If it's something you feel that strongly about, then yes, you can come. You can go tonight."

A weird look passed over Julian's face. It was a mixture of relief and reluctance, like he'd just won a battle he hadn't actually wanted to fight. Very strange.

Later in the evening, the human warrior of the group, Ben, showed up with his wife, Tracey. Now that he was living in Salt Lake City, Ben usually attended the meetings. His wife had never been to one before, but she was going to check it out tonight. Tracey reminded me of a Chihuahua, but not because of her looks. The slender, blonde woman had bright blue eyes, a soft-looking smile, high cheekbones, and a perky nose that you wanted to press like a button. She still had a youthful attractiveness to her that made her seem younger than the age I knew her to be. The only similarity to the tiny dog was because of the way she slightly trembled whenever she was around me, the way the whites of her eyes doubled in size when she took me in. All I would have to do was drop my fangs with a mild look of interest on my face and she'd either pee her pants or bolt for the door. Maybe both.

She wasn't comfortable with the idea of vampires. She trusted her friends, who were, in truth, only partial vampires, and she felt a little more comfortable around Nika, since she'd known her since birth. But me, a stranger to her, freaked her out. I made sure to move very slowly whenever she was around, so I wouldn't spook her with any sudden movements.

With clocklike precision, I turned my head to face the middle-aged man who was Teren's best friend. "As per usual, the meeting is at midnight." Ben nodded, this wasn't news to him. Midnight was decided as the official meet time, since that wasn't too early for vampires or too late for humans. "The ex-hunters will go in first, and gather all the new hunters into the living room. Nika, Halina and I will enter the house next, and quickly subdue them. The rest of you can come in once it's clear, then I'll begin the process of converting them." Ben nodded again. He really didn't need me to tell him all of this, but I wasn't really telling him for his benefit. I was speaking to Tracey, preparing her for what was to come, and speaking directly to her didn't seem like the best idea.

Tracey whispered to Emma, "Subdue? Convert?"

I paused a moment to let Emma answer her friend. "Every time we convert a new hunter to our cause, we tell them to get as many of their friends here as they can, so they can be … persuaded. There used to be new hunters every night, but now it's only a few times a week."

Out of the corner of my eye, I could see the horror on Tracey's face. "You're obliterating their free will."

Clearly only wanting Emma to hear her, she spoke as softly as a gasp of breath. I heard her though, and couldn't stop myself from replying. "We're trying to stop murders, both human and vampire. We don't have time to … convince...the age-old prejudice out of people."

Tracey backed up a step when my eyes locked on hers. She bumped into Teren, startled, then took a sidestep to where no one was standing. Shaking like a leaf, her eyes swept the room. "So you've stopped the humans from killing ... but what about the vampires? Have you compelled them?"

Her teeth rattled together and fear oozed from her like a heady perfume. I ignored her reaction to me, and spoke as softly and as gently as I could. "Vampires can't be compelled. Actually, no one with vampire blood in their veins can be compelled." I indicated Ben. "Your husband, for instance. And your daughter."

Nika had told me about Ben's distant vampire lineage. Ben had apparently never passed along the information though. Tracey's jaw fell open as she stared at her husband. "You? You're ... ? Olivia is ... ?"

Ben sighed and extended a hand to her. She didn't take it. "I didn't know. None of us knew. It's something I just recently found out." When Tracey still looked startled senseless, Ben added, "I don't have any of the attributes. No fangs, no blood cravings. Nothing. I simply ... can't be tranced." He shrugged, looking a little disappointed that he didn't have any other special powers.

Teren smirked at him. "I still think your fighting skills are related to your blood. You're not superhuman, but you're better than most."

Ben grinned at him. Tracey groaned. To complete my point, I told her, "Vampires aren't inherently evil, and most don't kill humans, same as most humans don't kill humans. Hunters, on the other hand, kill. It's in the job description." A flash of melancholy went through me. I had innocent blood on my hands. A *lot* of innocent blood. It was just something I had to deal with. Like Nika could read my dark thoughts, she put her hand on my back, massaging away my emotional ache.

Tracey blinked then snapped her head to Emma, the one vampire she felt the most comfortable with. "I can't do this, Em."

Smiling, Emma calmly walked over and put an arm around her. "Yes, you can. You're under my protection, no one will harm you."

Tracey seemed minutely cheered by that fact. Ben frowned and twisted to Teren. "What am I? Chopped liver?" Teren laughed at his friend and clapped him on the back.

Still seeing that Tracey was bothered by me, I told Ben and Teren, "We'll wait outside until it's time to go."

Teren glanced at me, then Nika beside me. His smile faded, but he nodded. "Don't go far."

I told him I wouldn't, then clutched Nika's hand and pulled her outside with me. Not surprisingly, Julian followed us. When we got to the porch, he sat on the step and twisted his hands in an obsessive-compulsive way. Curious, and feeling the need to chide him, I asked, "You, ah, don't seem overly thrilled that you won the right to go to the meeting tonight. You *do* want to go, don't you?"

Julian looked back at the window of his home, glowing with warmth. "Uh, sure, yeah, I want to go." When he returned his eyes to mine, it was clear his answer was all for his parents' ears, since they could hear everything we were saying.

Nika, not looking satisfied with his answer, grabbed his hand and yanked him to his feet. Since she was so much stronger now, she ended up hurtling him down the steps. He stumbled on the sidewalk, but remained upright. He glared up at her. "What the hell, Nick?"

Nika put her finger against her lip, indicating silence, and then pointed down the street. Julian understood. Looking up at the front door, he informed his parents, "We're going for a walk," then blurred away before they could protest. Nika started to follow him, but stopped and held out her hand, waiting for me; our bond made going our separate ways difficult. Together, we sped off after Julian. I faintly heard Teren say, "Wait," but we were gone before I heard the rest.

A couple of miles away, Nika shifted to a normal walk and I slowed down with her. I didn't see Julian anywhere, but figured he was waiting nearby. I could picture him tapping his foot in irritation while he waited for us, but he'd have to wait. Nika seemed to want some alone time with me, and I wanted the same. The day had been too long. Wrapping my arm around her side, I inhaled her sweetness, then placed my lips upon her head. She sighed in contentment. We walked along for a few minutes in blessed silence, then the evening started replaying itself in my mind. Remembering Julian's oddness, I murmured to Nika, "Your brother seems antsier than usual. He wants something. What is it?"

She looked up at me, surprised, but then her expression relaxed. Between his actions then and now, it was pretty obvious that Julian was up to something. She shrugged. "He wants what he always wants. Arianna back."

I nodded, suspecting as much. Nika swung my hand as she looked at the beauty of the night all around us. Crickets chirped, faint heartbeats thudded in the distance, and the moon white-washed everything. It was spectacular ... and yet it didn't hold a candle to her.

Glancing up at me, she continued. "He's thought up some elaborate plan to finally win her over, but it involves a massive high school party that my parents are never going to agree to."

I thought about that for a second, and then suggested, "Maybe I could get your parents out of the house for a few hours? Help him out a bit."

Nika paused in her steps. "You'd do that for him?"

I held her gaze, fighting back the guilt that was creeping up. "It's kind of my fault they're apart. I owe him one." Nika gave me a light kiss on the lips in answer, and my momentary gloom vanished. She loved me. I could do anything with her by my side. Even get her mopey twin back together with the girlfriend who had no recollection of ever being his girlfriend.

Julian was waiting for us on a covered bus bench; his eyes were locked in our direction and his expression was annoyed. He appeared even more irritated when I sat down simultaneously with Nika. He obviously wanted to talk to her alone. A part of me wanted to let him have his privacy with his sister, but I just couldn't leave her side yet. "Took you long enough," he mused, glaring at me like it was my fault we'd taken so long to get to him. "I was sure Mom and Dad would come collect me before you two even got close."

Blocking Julian's view of me with her body, Nika ignored his sullen comment and asked, "What was that about, Julian? Why the heck were you fighting to go to a meeting? You've never cared about them before. And why did you change the subject? I was just about to ask them about the party. I thought that was what you wanted?"

Julian slumped back onto the bench, defeated. "I know, and I do. I just ... I panicked. There's no way they're going to say yes, Nick. I wasn't ready to hear them say no. This is my last shot with Arianna before the summer. She'll forget all about me. She'll move on. She'll meet someone new. She might have already ..."

Seeing the despair on his face, and knowing I had to do something to help lift it, I leaned forward and said, "I normally wouldn't suggest this to a couple of underage teenagers, but what if you don't ask them? What if you just have the party without their permission?"

Julian gave me a wry expression. "At the house? I think they'd notice that."

I hid my smile. He had a point. An idea started forming, a way that I could kill two birds with one stone, and I stopped hiding my grin. "I'll keep them occupied somewhere else. You'll have the house all to yourself."

"And how are you going to do that?" Julian asked. He seemed skeptical. So did Nika. They both knew their parents a lot better than I did, and they probably knew that the hope I was offering Julian was just as unlikely as the two of them getting their parents to say yes to a school-wide party. I was fairly certain I could do this though.

My smile widened. "I'll think of something, don't you worry."

Nika and Julian were concerned about their parents getting antsy and coming to get them, so we leisurely headed back to the house. Halina caught up with us along the way. She was being flanked by Rory and Cleo, and seemed none too happy about it.

The pair of industrious hunters were keeping an eye on our surroundings as they walked behind her. They acted as if we were all about to be attacked at any moment. I didn't sense any danger around us—no odd, out-of-place heartbeats, no foreign smell on the breeze. It was a calm, quiet, beautiful night.

Rory nodded his head at me when our two groups met up. Any day now, I expected him to start saluting. Thankfully, he wasn't quite there yet. Rory was a brick wall of a man—6'5" and solid muscle. He was surprisingly quick for his size though, and agile too, with a liquidity to his movement that made him a formidable opponent. Even though I had an edge with my enhanced powers, I was grateful he was on our side, and I didn't have to fight him.

Cleo was very much Rory's opposite physically—slender, with long, lean muscles, and a dancer's lithe, graceful body—but she was just as eager to serve me as her massive counterpart. The dark-skinned girl moved to stand in front of me. With her arms behind her back, she looked like a solider awaiting orders.

"Two new recruits are waiting at the house. Avery is with them. The others are waiting nearby and will enter the meeting place once you've had your say." She smiled, showing a row of perfect, white teeth. "So as to not create suspicion with the newbies."

I nodded, pleased that at least a couple of hunters would be converted tonight. Every new person we touched now was one less person we had to worry about later, and they were also a pipeline to more hunters. And getting new hunters to come to the meeting place to be compelled was of critical importance. Having the numbers was the key. If we had more people *on* our side than against us, then we stood an even better chance of truly making a difference.

Our slightly larger group finished walking back to Nika's house to pick up the others, then we all started out together. Tracey had a death grip on Ben's hand as he pulled her along. I made sure to walk as far from her as possible, but my sharp ears still heard her say, "Can't we drive there? Just the two of us?"

Ben answered her with, "It really is faster to walk. And then the hunters won't hear us coming."

She swallowed, and her heartbeat quickened. "Why does it matter if they hear us coming? I thought this wasn't dangerous."

Turning my head, I answered her question. "The unconverted hunters are still dangerous. But they don't expect to see a vampire tonight, let alone several, so we'll be able to disarm them very quickly. You won't be in harm's way. One word from me will freeze them in their tracks."

She only stared at me in response, so I turned away and let her dwell on that in silence. I supposed it was a lot to take in.

As always, Nika held my hand as she walked beside me. Julian kept pace alongside her. He seemed deep in thought. Whether that was about what we were doing or Arianna, I couldn't say. My old home came upon us faster than my wandering mind expected it to. It was still a girly shade of pink, and was still mostly empty inside, although I *had* recovered my father's and my stuff from storage. Soon after the very first meeting with hunters, I'd found the landlord and had him re-rent the house to me; I'd had to compel him to do it, since Dad and I had sort of trashed the place, then left in a hurry. Since I didn't have a paying job, Halina and the others paid for it. I felt a little guilty about that, but I needed a neutral meeting place for this ... and I just wasn't ready to part with the last house where my father and I had lived as a family. A place that had started to feel like home to me, especially when I'd opened up and let Nika into it. I thought my life would change for the better when I'd moved here and met her. It hadn't happened in quite the way I'd expected, but I'd been right—my life *had* changed for the better.

Being a pair of nonthreatening humans, Rory and Cleo entered first. They left the front door cracked open, and I could hear the sound of curt greetings from the living room. I paused on the doorstep with Nika. "Halina, Nika and I will go in next. The rest of you wait out here until I give the word."

Like he always did whenever he came with, Teren stepped forward. "I'm going with you."

Like I always did, I let him. Halina entered first, then me, with Nika and Teren a few steps behind us. We used to spread out and enter the house at different locations, but now that the compelled hunters were on hand to "herd" the new ones into one place, we didn't worry so much about surrounding the enemy.

I wasn't sure what vibe I gave off to humans that immediately alerted them to my otherness, but I wasn't in the living room five seconds before the two new hunters were pulling guns on me. Maybe it was just due to the fact that they didn't know me yet. Maybe Rory and Cleo had been greeted with a barrel in their face too, and it just hadn't fazed them enough to say anything.

It took me one word to make them harmless. "Stop." Neither man in the room so much as twitched. Voice gentle but firm, I commanded, "Lower your weapons." Both guns slowly drifted to their sides. "Put the guns away. You will not harm anyone here tonight." Both men complied, and tucked their guns back into their jackets. The sudden tension in the room began to dissolve as the threat was neutralized. Over my shoulder, I called out, "It's safe, come on in."

Ben came through the door first, followed by Tracey, Emma, and Julian. Tracey looked ill, Emma calm, and Julian curious. He'd never witnessed me compelling a group. I sort of wished there were more than two new hunters here now. It was much more impressive with six or seven.

While Ben rubbed Tracey's back, he turned on her loud, rock music so she was immune to my compulsion. That had been Ben's request; he wanted his wife to come to accept vampires naturally. Seeing they were ready for me to begin, I returned my attention to the hunters. They were still rigidly standing in place, eyes wide open, hearts pounding with adrenaline. I realized I'd disarmed them, told them they couldn't hurt anyone, but had never assured them that they wouldn't be harmed as well. I frowned. This wasn't my first time, and I knew better than to leave them lingering in a fearful state. I wanted peace between the species, and to have that, I needed their innate sense of mistrust gone.

Holding a hand up, I told them both, "Please, sit, relax. No one here is going to harm you. We just want to talk. We want peace."

One of the heartbeats started slowing as the man attached to it sat down. The other man didn't move. His pale eyes flicked to his friend, and his heart started thudding in his chest. My frown deepened. This hadn't ever happened before. If I told them to relax, they did. If I told them to sit, they did, without hesitation.

Stepping toward him, I again repeated, "Relax. Sit."

The man's jaw dropped as his breathing picked up. I could see beads of sweat forming on his brow, could feel the fear and tension emanating from him. Seeing that I wasn't having any luck, Halina tried. "Sit, human."

The hunter's face slowly swiveled her way, and then he finally started sitting. I relaxed a bit, seeing that he was finally complying. Kind of odd that he hadn't right away. He wasn't wearing any protection from trancing. I should have had him from the first word.

Knowing she was probably a second away from bolting, I threw on a bright smile and twisted to Tracey standing next to Ben. "See, there's no danger here."

No sooner had I said that, then the man Halina had commanded to sit shot to his feet. I jerked my head around just in time to see his arm shoot out in my direction. From within the folds of his loose jacket, a sharp stake exploded into the air. Shock kept me frozen, staring at the projectile in disbelief. I compelled him to sit, not to harm anyone. He shouldn't be able to do this.

Tracey screamed as the entire room burst into action. Nika shoved me back at the same time Halina blurred in front of me. I felt completely useless in my stunned state, but I snapped out of it the second Halina grabbed the wooden weapon out of the air; it was centimeters from burying itself into my chest.

Dropping my fangs, I growled at the man who'd just tried to kill me. Reason went out the window as I momentarily imagined ripping him limb from limb. I lunged at him, but he reached into his jacket pocket and blew something at me. A small cloud of grey dust drifted over Halina, Nika and me. Silver. It burned as I inhaled, and, crying out, I clawed at my face and throat. It was like someone had just sprayed me with acid. I hear Halina and Nika cry out in similar pain, saw both of them falling to their knees. I struggled to remain standing, to fight against the torture and defend the women I loved, but the burning sensation was too powerful. All I could do was drop to the floor and curl into a ball.

Amid the sounds of screaming, mine as well as others, I noticed that the compelled hunter was idly watching the deadly showdown; he wasn't taking part in murdering us, but he wasn't stopping it either. From the corner of my eye, I watched the free-minded hunter grab a stake from a strap at his waist. He raised it high, preparing himself for the death blow. The silver had made its way into my lungs at this point, and my stomach was clenching as I resisted the urge to upchuck blood. As my insides sizzled, I almost welcomed death.

With all the strength he possessed, the hunter brought his arms down toward my chest, since I was closest. I thanked whatever gods were listening that he was aiming for me and not Nika. Surely, one of the others would stop him before he could kill her.

Just as his momentum was past the point of no return, a body rammed into his stomach and knocked him to the ground. I tried to struggle through the pain to see what was happening, to maybe help in some way, but I lost control on my stomach and started heaving blood. After that, I didn't care anymore.

CHAPTER FIVE

Julian

EVERYTHING HAD HAPPENED so fast, I almost couldn't comprehend it, and, as a vampire, I was used to things happening fast. One minute, Hunter was telling the strangers to lower their weapons, and the very next second it seemed, people were screaming and Hunter, Halina, and my sister were sprawled on the ground coughing up blood.

When the stranger attacked, lunging toward Hunter with a sharpened stake, all I could think about was stopping him from hurting my family. Using the strength my heritage blessed me with, I tackled him the way I'd watched the footballers at school tackle each other. It was surprisingly painful to knock someone over. The jolt of it ran across my shoulder, down my side. It made the healing wound in my leg throb, but I didn't care. I was stopping this madman.

I grunted in pain when I landed with him on the ground. My first thought was *Yes, I did it*! My second thought was *Crap, he's still armed*. Ignoring the tremors of discomfort running through my body, I attempted to hold him down *and* keep him from staking me. I was stronger than he was, but he was squirmy. Just when I almost had a hold of him, he twisted out of my grasp. I managed to wrestle the stake out of his hands, but before

I could clamp onto his wrists and bind him, he reached into his other pocket and grabbed something shiny. I swear the man was a walking armory.

He held a metallic cross against my face, and I blinked at him in surprise. A cross? Wow, that was old school. But the cross was definitely silver, so I guessed it was an effective weapon. For a pureblood. I wasn't a pureblood though. The silver pressed against my skin was no more an irritant than the wood against my palm had been. The hunter's eyes widened in shock. He'd been so sure I was a vampire, but now he was doubting himself. I took his momentary distraction to firmly subdue him. Grabbing his arms, I shoved his hands to the floor, on either side of his head. I sat on his chest, hoping he couldn't kick me off. Then, because I was irritated at him and concerned for my family, I lowered my teeth and hissed in his face.

"You *are* one of them!" he snapped, his tone condescending. He glanced at the cross still in his hand. "That should have sent you flying across the room in pain. How are you immune?" His demanding eyes returned to mine; he clearly expected an answer.

My father stepped to my side, his shadow partially blocking the hunter's face. I could sense my mother at Nika's side, helping her through the pain, and I could hear Ben assisting Hunter; Tracey was whimpering near the front door, her rock music still blaring. I was a little surprised she was still here.

Dad squatted down and the man pinned beneath me grudgingly looked his way. "You avoided following a direct order. How did you do that?"

The man smirked. "Like I'd tell a monster like you."

Dad looked up at the compelled man, still sitting where he was told. "Do you know this man? Do you know how he ignored being compelled?"

I looked over at the man Dad was questioning. He frowned, his lips compressing into a thin line, but he didn't say a word. Hunter had compelled him to sit and relax, but he hadn't ordered him to cooperate with vampires and answer all their questions. And from all he'd seen, he must assume Dad was a vampire like the rest of us. Well, like most of us.

Sighing, Dad looked back at the man below me. "Well, we'll find out how you did this, one way or another." Dad looked up at me, then over to where Nika was still struggling with losing the contents of her stomach. "We need to know what happened here, and make sure it never happens again."

Standing back up, Dad motioned for me to get off the man. I was hesitant to let him go, but Rory and Cleo were already moving in to take my place. Rory looked steamed that someone had gotten so close to killing Hunter, and he hadn't been quick enough to do anything about it. Cleo looked like she was ready to tear the man's head off. They pounced on him the second I stepped away.

The pair of ex-hunters yanked him to his feet by his jacket, then Rory not-so-discretely socked him in the stomach. The man doubled over in pain, wheezing for breath. It was sort of how my grandmother sounded at the moment, so I wasn't too upset that the creep couldn't breathe. Dad interceded before there could be any further abuse though.

"That's enough. We have rules in place for this very thing. No vengeance, on either side. The panel will convene and we'll decide what's to be done with him." The rest of the members awaiting the meeting had filtered into the house by this point. They took in the chaos around them with calculating eyes. As far as I knew, this was the first attempt made on another species since the league had been formed. This was going to be the first panel trial then too. And Nika said tonight would be boring.

My thoughts on my sister, I turned to head her way. Mom had Nika sitting up now, and was rubbing her back. Mom had somehow urged Tracey to help her, and the shaking blonde was wiping blood away from Nika's chin. Nika had blood-red tears running down her cheeks from where she'd been crying. It broke my heart to see her in such pain, but a microscopic portion of my soul was grateful that I hadn't had to share it with her.

Blurring to Nika's side, I knelt beside her and tossed my arms around her. "God, I'm so sorry, Nick. That looked like it sucked."

Nika weakly put her arms around me, and nodded into my shoulder. "You have no idea."

She lifted her head to look for Hunter. He was a foot or two away, being cleaned up by Ben. He was looking past Nika, to Halina on the other side of her. Halina was still lying down, coughing and clutching her stomach. She had bloodstains all down the front of her, but the worst of it seemed to be over.

Feeling Nika's eyes on him, Hunter redirected his gaze to her. "Babe, are you ... ?" He immediately choked on his words and started coughing. As the adrenaline wore off, my stomach started getting a little squeamish at all the vomiting going on around me. I seriously hoped Hunter didn't lose it.

Thankfully, he pulled it together. Nika stretched a hand out to him. "I'm fine," she whispered, her throat hoarse, like she'd just escaped from a burning building. Hunter nodded as he swallowed over and over, trying to control his spasming throat.

Now that I was able to help with Nika, Mom moved to help Halina. I rubbed Nika's back while Hunter scooted as close to her as he could. Wrapping a protective arm around Nika's shoulders, I watched Rory and Cleo remove the man who'd hurt her. His chin was lifted in defiance, like he didn't have a care in the world what they did to him.

"What do you think happened?" I asked.

Still not able to talk, Hunter only shrugged. Nika massaged her throat as she looked up at Ben. He'd left Hunter's side to go help Dad. The crowd here for the meeting was talking all at once, asking what to do about this unmitigated attack on Hunter, the man the group looked at as their leader. Swift and harsh punishments were being thrown around like Grandma Linda and Grandma Alanna tossed around recipe ideas. These suggestions weren't nearly as pleasant as apple pie though.

"I'm not sure, but I think he was protected, like Uncle Ben." Nika's dark eyes swung back to mine. "He must be a little bit vampire, but so far down he doesn't have any of the traits. I doubt he has any idea what he really is."

She pursed her lips as she glared at the man being led to a back bedroom on one side of the house. "Maybe," I admitted. "Could be something else though, something we haven't seen before." Just saying that scared me, but it needed to be said; all options needed to be considered.

Hunter cleared his throat a few times. His face was splattered in blood, his chin smeared where Ben had tried wiping it away. His shirt had dark patches of blood on it, like he'd been stabbed a few times. He looked like he'd been filming a horror movie. Or living through one. "We'll have Gabriel test his blood. He should be able to compare it to Ben's, and at least answer some of our questions." He squeaked his way through that sentence, then held his hand to his throat when he was done.

Halina was coming out of her misery enough that she heard and understood Hunter's comment. In Russian, she murmured, *"Gabriel can get his sample from my fingers after I grind that man's body into a bloody pulp."* She started coughing the moment she finished speaking.

Hunter looked her way, then over to me. "Do I even want to know what she said?"

I raised an edge of my lip, and saw Nika do the same. "No, probably not."

The meeting never really came together after that. I wasn't sure what happened at a typical one, but this one was focused on what to do with the vampire hunter in the back room. While I sat with the three purebloods who were still nowhere near normal, I halfheartedly watched the bickering going on around me.

After about an hour, Dad squatted down in front of Hunter. He jerked his thumb back at the man Hunter had successfully compelled. He was still sitting like Hunter had told him. "We can't leave him half-compelled like that. Are you up to finishing the job?"

With a long exhale, Hunter nodded and then slowly stood. Every movement he made seemed forced and unnatural. I almost expected him to cringe when he walked, but he made it over to the man with a smooth face and confident eyes; he wasn't showing any of the pain he must be feeling. The man swallowed, looking nervous, yet he seemed relaxed at the same time. All of his muscles were loose and his posture was at ease, but his eyes were wider than they should have been, and they followed Hunter like Hunter was a cobra who was going to strike him down at any moment. He'd been listening, watching, and he knew exactly what was going to happen.

When Hunter stood before him, he licked his lips, then said, "I have no wish to be in your army. Leave my mind, let me go, and I'll leave you and yours in peace."

A sad smile crept onto Hunter's lips. "I'm sorry, but that's not how this works. I need you to listen to what I'm going to tell you, and believe in it with all of your heart." Hunter then proceeded to give the man a new outlook on life.

Hunter told him how vampires were no longer to be hunted and killed simply because they were vampires. They were to be treated as fairly as human beings were treated—innocent until proven guilty. Vampires would be given a chance to live in peace, if they followed the rules. And if they didn't, and they murdered humans for nothing more than the joy of killing and drinking, then it wouldn't be up to individual hunters to dole out their justice. No, a panel of both vampires and humans would decide their fate, much like they were going to decide the fate of the man waiting in the back room.

By the time Hunter was done explaining the new rules to the hunter who was listening to him with rapt attention, it was clear that the man was a diehard fighter for the cause now. His immediate reply once Hunter was done, was to tell him that he was appalled someone had hurt Hunter, Nika and Halina, and that he'd like to be a part of the panel that decided the man's fate. Wearily, Hunter directed the man to Dad, who'd been given the task of forming the Panel of Justice, as Halina was calling it.

I could only shake my head as I locked eyes with my sister. A few years ago, our biggest problem was deciding whether to go to a public high school. And now, here we were, smack dab in the middle of a game-changing political alliance between vampires and their sworn enemies. Life sure was weird sometimes.

When it appeared that nothing else overly exciting was going to happen tonight, Nika leaned against my shoulder and murmured, "That sucked. I'm so tired now. I just want to go home and lie down."

I nodded and helped her stand. She immediately sought out Hunter. He wasn't far from us, but even the few feet he'd wandered away was too much for her. Nika wrapped herself around his arm, and looked up at him with adoration. So much love was pouring from her eyes, I didn't need to feel it to know it was there. "Let's go find a bed," she told him.

Hunter smiled at her, but his gaze flicked around the home swarming with humans. I could tell he wanted to leave with her, but he felt obligated to stay until the "troops" dispersed. He was probably wondering how to tell her that without hurting her feelings. Or he was debating if he could even separate from her right now. The bond made distance uncomfortable, or so Nika said.

Dad intentionally or unintentionally provided Hunter with a way out. "I've asked some of the panel members to finish the meeting for us. We should get your attacker to Gabriel … and away from here." His eyes flicked over some humans who were scowling at the hallway where the man had been taken. With compulsion, Hunter had discouraged the idea of vengeance killings, but they'd still beat the crap out of the man if they could. Looking tired himself, Dad told Hunter, "You and Great-Gran look beat. I'll have Emma go get the car, and we'll drive you home, so you don't have to run in your condition."

Halina snorted at his comment. "I'm right as rain. I could run circles around the lot of you."

Ignoring her, Dad focused his gaze on me. "Julian, we're pretty much done here. Why don't you take your sister home?"

That got Nika's attention. Squeezing Hunter's arm tight, she argued, "I'd like to go to the ranch with you, Dad."

Dad smirked. "I'm not staying. I'm getting everyone settled, then I'm coming right back home. You've been through a lot tonight, and you need your rest. I want you to go home with Julian."

Hope gleamed in Nika's eyes. "Well, then Hunter can come home and rest with me. You said it yourself, he looks beat. You shouldn't make him endure the ride if he doesn't have to."

Dad's jaw twitched. "Nika, I'm really not comfortable with—"

Nika huffed in frustration. "Come on, Dad. I feel like I've been hit with a wrecking ball, and I'm sure Hunter feels the same. We're not going to do anything but rest, and there's no reason we can't do that together."

Dad crossed his arms over his chest. Not a good sign. "I know you don't understand, or you think I'm being unreasonable, but it's my home and while you're living there you'll respect my rules. No sleepovers."

Nika tossed her hands in the air. "I'm only living there because you won't let me move to the ranch!"

She looked about ready to spit fire at Dad, but a fit of coughs grabbed her and she leaned over, hacking. Concern washed over Hunter and Dad's faces. The pained look was so similar, I almost wanted to point it out to them. They both equally loved her, and wasn't that more important than being stubborn?

When Nika was mostly recovered from her coughing fit, Hunter stroked her arm. "It's all right. Go home with your brother. Rest. I'll go with Halina to the ranch. Besides, I want to see what Gabriel can find out about this guy ... and I'd really prefer it if you were nowhere near him."

Nika sighed and stepped away from him. "Fine. But I hate this already," she said.

Hunter nodded. "Me too."

Grabbing Nika's hand, I pulled her away with me. I had to yank her a couple of times to keep her moving. Mom gave Dad a swift hug, and then followed us. Before I could leave the room, Hunter sped over to Nika and gave her one last kiss. I resisted rolling my eyes. Once their lips stopped touching, Hunter turned to me, his hand extended. "Thank you. You saved my life. I guess that's one more thing I owe you for."

I thought about refusing to take his hand, but then I'd be just as stubborn as Dad. I really didn't have a good reason to not like Hunter. Well, okay, I had plenty of reasons, but they were all in the past. Everything had changed since Hunter had truly become one of us, and I was going to have to accept that fact eventually. I grabbed his hand and gave him a firm shake. "Don't worry about it ... I mean that." I raised an eyebrow to punctuate my point. I didn't need him getting all weird, trying to make things right between us. I'd rather just wipe the slate clean and forget about it.

Once we were all out of the house, and Nika was a good distance away from Hunter, she clutched her chest like she was having a heart attack. Mom rubbed her back in sympathy, while I just stared at her dumbstruck. She was cringing like she was physically in pain. "Is it really that bad?" I asked her.

Her eyes brimming with red tears, she nodded. "You have no idea, Julian. It's like someone cracked my chest open, and they're sucking my heart out through a straw."

Grateful that I didn't feel that way, I shook my head. "I'm glad I'm not bonded to anybody." I frowned as I reconsidered. Didn't it cause me physical pain to leave Arianna? Yeah. Sometimes.

When we got home, Mom looked anxious about leaving us. "We're fine here, Mom. It's really late at night, Nika's feeling sick, and our neighborhood is surrounded by reformed vampire hunters who would die to protect us. Not to mention Starla and Jacen are just down the street. We're about as safe as safe can get."

Mom was still reluctant, but Dad was counting on her, so she had no choice. After making sure Nika was as comfortable as she could be on the couch, she kissed each of our heads and grabbed the keys to the Prius. After she left and the light buzz of the car was gone to my ears, I let out an amused grunt. "Well, Hunter did what he said he'd do ... he got Mom and Dad out of the house for a few hours." I turned to give Nika a smile. "It's too bad he did it on the wrong night though. Unless you think we can rustle up a party real quick?"

Nika laughed, like I was hoping she would. Then she started coughing. When the spasm settled, she inhaled a deep breath and closed her eyes. There were dark circles under her skin, like she hadn't slept in days. Silver had never affected her before. I hated the fact that it did now. There were benefits to being a pureblood, but there were serious setbacks too.

"I don't think I'm up to dancing yet," she murmured, sounding sleepy. "Another time."

This time I laughed. "Yeah, next time you guys are almost killed we'll have a party."

Nika cracked an eye open. "Are you okay, Julie? You hit that guy pretty hard."

A smidge of pride went through me. I'd tackled that guy like a pro. A part of me wished Arianna had been there to see it. Thinking of that smack brought to mind the throbbing in my leg, the kink in my neck. They were minor concerns compared to Nika's though, nothing to be complaining about. "I'm fine, Nick. No problems at all."

Her eyes drifted closed as she nodded. Not wanting her to fall asleep here, where she could be exposed to the sun if she didn't move before it came up, I told her, "Let's get you downstairs, so you can rest without having to worry about the sun or anything."

She started telling me okay, but then she inhaled a sharp breath, and her face contorted into what almost looked like pain. I couldn't tell for sure. I hated that I didn't know what she was feeling. "Are you okay? What's wrong?"

Her expression, while still showing signs of discomfort, turned embarrassed. "Hunter ... he's leaving the city. It just ... it aches ... but I'll be fine."

Not knowing what else to do for her, I lamely told her, "Sorry," then scooped her up.

A soft laugh escaping her, she told me, "I can walk on my own," but she didn't make any attempt to get down. She even put her head on my shoulder.

Smiling at her stubbornness, I answered, "I know. You're all powerful now."

Her hand went to her throat. "I don't feel all powerful."

Shrugging, I started walking her to her hidey-hole in the closet. "You'll be fine in the morning. Or ... the evening, I guess."

When I finally got my sister set up in her room, all she wanted to do was sleep. I zipped upstairs and got her some fresh blood to drink first. Blood was a natural painkiller for vampires. It would help her feel better until the tiny silver particles were out of her system. She drank it down, thanked me for making it for her, then curled up into a ball on her bed. She was out cold a minute later. Considering how early in the morning it was for her, I figured she would be up early tomorrow night, which meant she would be bored in her room for that much longer. Mom and Dad had to let her go one day. Locking her up like a caged animal really wasn't fair.

Once Nika was settled, I went upstairs to get myself settled. It was hard to do. My mind was spinning with what had happened, with what could have happened. Hunter had been a moment away from death. If he'd been in a different position, and Nika had been closer to the attacker, *she* would have been targeted. I could have lost her tonight.

Rounding up and converting hunters had somehow turned routine recently. We'd forgotten just how dangerous the other side could be. Reaching through my stretchy sleep pants, I massaged the wound where a bullet had sliced through my flesh. I would never allow myself to forget just how dangerous they could be.

An idea began to form while I waited for my parents to return. They were still at the ranch, getting Halina and Hunter home safely, and making sure Gabriel saw the compulsion-proof man, so he could determine just how the hunter had come to be that way. I wondered if they'd find out anything tonight, or if Gabriel would need a few days to study his blood. I wondered what they'd do with him. Was he innocent? Was he guilty? It was a gray area, and it was hard to say what was right and what was wrong. Yes, he'd almost killed members of my family, but in his mind, he was being attacked and he was just defending himself. Would any of us act differently?

The tiny pinpricks of an idea were a resolute decision by the time I felt my parents heading my way. I stayed quiet and still, waiting for the creak of the front door that heralded their arrival. It was late, mere hours left in the day, and I could tell they were trying to be quiet as they tiptoed through the door. It only took one word to get them upstairs with me. "Dad?"

They were both in my doorway an instant later. "You're still up," my mom commented, walking in and crossing to my bed. She rumpled my hair; her expression was sad. She too realized how close tonight had been. We'd had way too many close calls lately. And just when we were starting to think all of that was over and done with.

I nodded. "I was thinking about tonight. Couldn't sleep."

Dad stepped up to us. "You shouldn't let that trouble you too much, Julian. It was a fluke. It won't happen again." From his tone of voice and the wrinkle in his brow, I didn't think he was entirely sure of that.

Sitting up, I looked at my parents. "Did Gabriel see him? Was he able to determine how he resisted direct compulsion?"

Dad ran a hand through his hair. "He took samples of his blood, but he was still analyzing them when we left. We'll go back tomorrow night and see if he found anything."

I put on my sternest, 'I'm serious' face. "I want to go with you. I want to know what Gabriel found."

Mom smiled and Dad nodded. "We'll all go together ... once Nika's up." Dad frowned. We'd be getting out there pretty late if we had to wait for Nika.

I couldn't resist mentioning the cold fact Dad was avoiding. "You know, if Nika was living out there with the others, we wouldn't have to wait until the sun went down to visit."

Dad gave me a look that clearly told me he wasn't pleased that I was on Nika's side when it came to her living at the ranch with Hunter. Honestly, I wasn't sure if I was or not, I just knew how miserable Nika was cooped up downstairs. I'd want a mansion too if I were in her shoes.

Not wanting to become sidetracked with a situation that was Nika's fight, not mine, I immediately changed the subject. "The man who attacked Hunter ... I want to be a part of the panel that decides what happens to him."

Dad started shaking his head before I was even finished. "You're too young, Julian."

I held his gaze. "I might only be sixteen, almost seventeen now, but I've seen things that men twice my age haven't seen. And I've been through experiences that most grown men haven't been in. That man tried to kill my sister, her sire, and my grandmother. I want a say in what happens to him." I looked down, my mood contemplative. "This is my family, and I want to do my part." I returned my eyes to my father. "Let me help."

A strange look crossed Dad's face. It was a mixture of pride and resignation. "Okay," he whispered. "A group of us are going to be meeting in a few days. I'll let you join in."

"And let me have a voice?" I asked, a little disbelieving that he was actually going to let me be a part of this.

Dad sighed and looked at Mom. She nodded, and his eyes returned to mine. "Yes. You'll have a voice that's equal to everyone else there. But remember," he warned, "just because you have a say, doesn't mean you'll get your way. And ... you might not like what happens to him."

I swallowed. Dad meant he might die, and I might have to condemn him to it. Could I do that? I nodded. "I understand what it means. I accept the responsibility."

Dad beamed at me, then leaned over and kissed my head. "I'm very proud of the man you're becoming, Julian. You're more of a man than I was at your age." Remembering the secret party I was planning on having behind his back made my cheeks fill with color. Luckily, Dad mistook it for humbleness. Still smiling, his gaze swept around my bedroom. "Now that you're a bone fide panel member, maybe you can start keeping your room this clean from now on? Girlfriend or no girlfriend."

Mom sniggered and I pursed my lips at the both of them. Suddenly I didn't feel so guilty about the party. "Sure, Dad," I murmured.

Dad laughed and clapped my shoulder, then he and Mom left for their bedroom. I laid back on my pillows and tried to fall asleep, but all I could think about was that man blowing silver dust into Nika's face. What was I going to do with him? What was fair, what was just, what was moral? What could I live with for the rest of my life? And what in the world possessed me to want to be a part of deciding his fate?

I instantly knew the answer to that though. I was an Adams. The last living member of the line. And there were certain responsibilities that came along with being an Adams. It was time for me to start living up to the name my father had given me. I could do this. I knew I could.

CHAPTER SIX

Hunter

IT WAS LATE afternoon when I woke up. I vaguely remembered the drive home; Teren and Emma talked, while Halina and I rested in the back seat. Rory, Cleo, Ben, and the captive had followed behind us in Cleo's car. Halina hadn't been thrilled that Rory and Cleo were coming to the ranch with us. She trusted them as much as she could trust compelled ex-hunters, but she didn't like the thought of them knowing the main location of our nest. As I'd reminded her though, they already knew it. They were a part of the horde of hunters who'd attacked the ranch at my father's request a couple months ago.

But they wouldn't hurt us anymore. It was no longer in their programming. And besides, we'd needed them to keep an eye on our attacker last night. Halina and I just weren't a match for him then. Other than being a little sore, I felt fine now though. I could take him out by myself if necessary. I was sure of it.

Looking around the room, I could see that it wasn't my bedroom. I immediately recognized it as Halina's. Nearly every piece of art, from the pair of curving metal sconces, to the numerous richly detailed paintings, were odes to the sun. Since Halina couldn't stand in its glory anymore, she surrounded herself in various interpretations of it.

A heavy, down-filled comforter rested over my chest. Beneath me, an electric blanket fitted over the mattress radiated heat; I could feel each thin coil against my back as it twisted and turned inside the fabric. The warmth it generated was contained by the thick blankets on top of me, and my entire body felt warm for a change. It was undeniably pleasant, and I made a mental note to get a heater like this for my bed.

Turning my head, I saw that my raven-haired creator was sharing the space and the heat with me. Both of us were fully clothed under the covers, and from my hazy recollection of last night, I knew we'd remained that way all morning long. The thought of being undressed with her was unnerving for me to think about. I just didn't see Halina in any sort of sexual way. She was like a sister to me, or maybe a mother. I loved her, but she was family, and my heart firmly belonged to Nika. I would never do anything to betray her.

Thinking of Nika brought an ache of loneliness to the surface. She was so far away from me. Too far. But as it was still daylight outside, there was nothing I could do about our separation, except endure it. Like I did every day until the sun sank below the earth, I'd push that pain down and try to think about something else. Usually that was a challenge, but not today. No, today I had plenty to think about.

Halina was still asleep when I sat up and rubbed my eyes with the heels of my hands. Inhaling silver had done a number on my system. I could recall using that same tactic while fighting vampires, but I'd never fully comprehended just how much it hurt. I might have used it more often if I'd known. But it was messy, cumbersome, and didn't completely stop vampires, just slowed them down, so I hadn't relied on it too much back then. Now I kind of felt like the entire substance should be banned. My throat felt like it had fifteen-thousand tiny paper cuts along it. I wasn't looking forward to swallowing. Or talking.

When I pulled back the covers to get up, I let out some of the heat. Halina grabbed the blanket and pulled it tighter around her shoulders. "The sun is still up, child. Why are you?" she mumbled, her voice gravely.

"I'm not tired." Cringing, I swallowed. Yep, talking sucked just as much as I'd feared it would. I couldn't stop now though. I had too much I needed to do today. Looking toward the door, I told her as much. "And there are things I want to do." *Like talk to Gabriel, and see what he found out about the man I couldn't compel.*

Like she could read my thoughts, Halina twisted to face me. "You leave that man alone. I don't want you anywhere near him."

Frowning, I looked down at her concerned, motherly face. "My dad taught me how to hunt vampires before he taught me how to drive a car. I went on my first solo mission when I was eighteen. I think I can handle a human being, especially now, since I'm not one of them anymore."

She sat up, her worried expression not lessoning. "Your father also got you killed."

I bristled at the memory, but made myself relax. I was fine with my fate. I'd made peace with my history. "You keep calling me a child, but I'm not. I'm healthy now, and strong ... thanks to you. You've done your job, so you need to let me go. Trust me a little."

I gave her an encouraging smile. She smirked at seeing it. "Trust me, says the boy who not too long ago, conspired with my boyfriend to run away from me."

Even though humor showed on her face, pain at my recent betrayal flashed through her eyes. The residual guilt from hurting her was one of the reasons why I still let her baby me. It was why I hadn't fought too hard against her last night when she'd insisted that I stay with her because her rooms were closer, safer, and warmer. Besides the warmer part, none of what she'd said was really true, but she'd protested that she wanted me near her for my benefit. I knew the truth of it though. She'd almost lost me to that hunter, and she was scared. Like a child frightened from a storm, she'd needed me near her last night for *her* benefit. Just like she needed me away from that man now ... so *she* wouldn't worry, so *she* wouldn't be scared.

Sliding out of bed, I reiterated, "Agree with it or not, I'm an adult, and I'm capable of making my own decisions, no how matter how foolish they may seem. I'm not going to get hurt, and I don't wish for my own death anymore, so you have nothing to worry about." I pointed at the door I was about to be heading through. "That man shouldn't have been able to do what he did. I have questions, and I need them answered as quickly as possible, so yes, I'm going to go talk to him. You can come with me if you want, or you can stay here and rest, but one way or another, I'm leaving."

Halina rolled her eyes at me. "I really hate it when kids start thinking for themselves." She blurred to her feet an instant later. "Fine. Let's go talk to the creaton."

I smiled, grateful that she wasn't trying to stop me anymore. "The hunter? Or Gabriel?" I asked. Gabriel and Halina's relationship was still a bit rocky since he'd given me the drug that had temporarily broken our bond and allowed me to escape from her. Halina had accepted him back after he'd valiantly defended the family, but it wasn't exactly flowers and sunshine at the moment.

Her lips compressed into a thin line. "Both," she murmured.

I wanted to laugh, but I knew it wouldn't feel good with my raw throat, so I contained it. Walking over to her dresser, Halina quickly combed the sleeping snarls out of her hair. I couldn't help but shake my head at her outfit.

Halina typically dressed like she was heading out to a club. I'd been trying to get her to tone it down a bit. Maybe try wearing pants for a change, instead of thigh-baring, micro-mini dresses. Her compromise to my suggestion was a pair of skintight, bright-red leather pants. All I could say about them was that it was a good thing she no longer needed to breathe. They seemed uncomfortable to me, but she swore they were as cozy as flannel pajamas. I wasn't about to wear leather pants, so I'd have to take her word on that.

"I still can't believe you slept in those all morning."

She glanced at my jeans. "I can almost guarantee that I was more comfortable than you. And anyway, these were your suggestion, and a mighty fine one at that." She examined herself in the mirror, twisting so she could inspect her ass. "These were practically made for me."

I smiled, but didn't argue. Growing up with my sister had taught me that trying to convince a woman not to wear something she really wanted to wear was futile at best, hazardous at most. Evangeline had once pierced me with an eyebrow pencil when I told her that her favorite jacket made her look like she was wearing a dead squirrel on her shoulders. She hadn't even apologized for drawing blood. Man, I missed her.

Halina pointed at me as she set down her brush. "I'm going to change and freshen up. You, stay put." As an afterthought, she added, "Please." Somehow, she made that word sound like a command, same as the others.

I was eager to go, but willing to compromise. "Be quick about it?"

With an amused grin, she blurred away. She was back before I could count to twenty. Wearing a new shirt, but the same pants, and looking as fresh-faced as if she'd taken a shower, she mockingly asked, "Quick enough?" Shaking my head, I turned toward the door. My sire was such a smart ass.

We headed down the hallway in silence, resting our aching throats. A nice, steaming cup of blood sounded fabulous right now, but I wanted to try and get some answers first if I could. The man who'd attacked us was being held in a room right next to my bedroom, which might have also been one of the reasons why Halina hadn't wanted me to sleep there last night. A chain lock had been installed on the outside of his door. Those were typically used on the insides of doors, but it was the best the family could do on such short notice. One of my tasks today was to fortify the captive's cell. At least until he could be properly dealt with. In the meantime, he was being guarded twenty-four-seven. Cleo was standing outside the door now. Rory was presumably somewhere nearby, resting so the pair could alternate shifts. I wondered if they'd let anyone else guard the man, or if he'd somehow become their sole responsibility.

Cleo snapped to attention when she saw me. "How are you?" she asked.

Massaging my throat, I nodded. "Better, thank you." I pointed toward the door. "How is he?"

She puckered her full lips in displeasure. "I haven't gone in there, but I'm sure he's fine."

The fact that she hadn't tried to interrogate him surprised me. "You haven't been in there to check on him since we put him in there? Really?"

Cleo looked across the hall, to the doors that lead to Gabriel's laboratory. "He forbade it. He seems to think the man won't survive an encounter with me." Her sour expression softened into a knowing smile, like she thought the same thing.

My gaze followed hers. "Is Gabriel in there? I'd like to speak with him."

Cleo nodded. "He hasn't left since we brought the hunter in."

I nodded at her answer, and then twisted toward Gabriel's lab. Questioning the hunter *might* give me answers, eventually, but questioning Gabriel would most definitely get me some sort of an answer. He had to know something about the man by now.

Halina let out a long sigh, but followed me toward the lab. She and Gabriel were still working out their differences. Well, she was working hers out. Gabriel didn't have any issues with Halina; he treated her like a queen.

The edge of my lip curled up as I held my hand on the door handle. "You know, it was just as much my fault for what happened as it was Gabriel's, and you seem to have completely forgiven me."

Halina's annoyed expression turned derisive. "You were out of your mind with hunger." Her finger traced a line down the heavy wood in front of us. "Not a centuries old vampire who knew better. Your decision was foolish. His was ... cruel. And it is easier for me to forgive stupidity than cruelty."

I reflected on that for a second before telling her, "But you did take him back, so if the two of you are going to work, you'll eventually need to let it go."

She let out an amused snort. "Since when did you become so interested in my love life?"

Twisting the handle on the knob, I laughed back, "I just don't want to see my parents get divorced, is all."

Gabriel looked up as the pair of us entered the room. He smiled at hearing Halina laughing. She didn't often do that around him anymore. In fact, she stopped the minute she noticed him watching her. Gabriel took it all in stride, inclining his head with a polite, "My love." His jade-green eyes shifted to me. "Hunter. To what do I owe the honor of your visit? Our esteemed guest in the next room perhaps?"

I shut the door behind us. Most of the rooms down here were soundproof, so the volume in the room didn't change much, but closing the door did block out the faint beating of Cleo's heart. That was probably a good thing too, since the thumping reminded me how hungry I was. Halina began examining some of Gabriel's nearby experiments. She watched a glass beaker bubbling with some sort of reddish-pink liquid inside, like it was the most fascinating object in the world. But I could tell it was all for show. She wanted Gabriel to know, without a doubt, that she was angry with him.

Ignoring her immature pouting, I strode over to where Gabriel was holding a vial of deep red blood in the air. "Please tell me you know how he was able to block being tranced."

Gabriel's eyes flicked to Halina before settling on me. Like most of the mixed vampires I'd encountered, Gabriel looked young. He could probably even pass for my age. His youthful face void of emotion, he said, "I believe I do know, although, I do not yet understand."

I frowned at his answer. There wasn't much Gabriel didn't understand. "What do you mean? How did he do it?"

Gabriel shrugged. "He *did* nothing. What is inside him saved him."

More intrigued than irritated now, Halina stepped up to Gabriel's work table. "He is a vampire then?"

Gabriel frowned. "Yes ... and no."

He held the blood out to me. I grabbed it, but didn't see anything overly remarkable with the vial, other than the overwhelming urge I had to drink it, of course. While I stared at the thing in confusion, Gabriel told me, "He has vampire blood inside him, and that is what is protecting him from compulsion. Upon first glance, I believed he had a long-distant mixed vampire relative, like Ben, but upon closer examination, I saw that my initial assumption was incorrect. He is similar to Ben, but different, and it is that difference that I find interesting. And disconcerting."

"Disconcerting how?" I slowly asked, not liking Gabriel saying something as ominous as that word.

He tilted his golden head of blonde hair as he answered me. "Things I do not properly understand are disconcerting to me. I like to know what I'm dealing with." His eyes shifted over to Halina, and for a split second, I felt like he was talking about her, and not about the mysterious man next door.

Halina narrowed her eyes. I was pretty sure she'd picked up on that too. "How is he different? And does it really matter?" She tossed her hands out to her sides. "Either way, he's a mixed vampire. He'll be thrilled with that." A wry smile touched her lips.

Gabriel gave her a soft smile, but directed his answer to me. "Ben has a minute amount of vampire blood cells running in harmony with his human blood cells. He was born this way, so his body accepts the foreignness as his own. This man though, his blood is ... attached ... to the human blood cells, almost forced together ... unnaturally." He shrugged, clearly unhappy with his lack of knowledge. "But like I said, I don't know what I'm dealing with yet, other than he somehow has our blood in his system and it is providing him protection."

Setting the blood on the table, I wondered just what to do with that information. "Born with it or not, the blood is part of his system now, so it's not going to wear off." I locked eyes with Halina. "And that means we have a compulsion proof vampire hunter to deal with."

Halina shook her head, her long, dark hair slid over her shoulders, catching and refracting the harsh lab lights. "Wasn't too long ago that having a dangerous vampire hunter in your midst was a problem easily solved."

Looking over her shoulder, I glanced at the exit. "Yeah, well, times change. I'm going to go speak to him. See what he'll tell us."

Halina crossed her arms over her chest. "I'm going to go out on a limb and say nothing. He's a hunter being held captive in a vampire nest. He won't tell us anything of use."

Dropping my fangs, I gave her a one-sided smile. "We'll see."

I made to leave and Halina moved like she was going to follow me. Gabriel stopped her with a question she didn't want to hear. "Halina, will you stay a while?"

I watched a sulk form on her face that a five-year-old would have been proud of. "Why?"

Gabriel stepped toward her, not in the least insulted by her expression. "I have missed you, and I would like to talk to you."

"We're talking now," she muttered.

Placing a hand on her arm, he calmly told her, "I wish to speak to you alone."

Her face still as stone, she airily told him, "Well, you know what they say about wishing, don't you?" I wanted to roll my eyes. She even sounded like a five-year-old.

Grabbing her shoulders, I pulled her forward, and then pushed her toward Gabriel. This was getting ridiculous. She needed to stop being so damn stubborn and start talking to her boyfriend. My suddenness surprised her, and Halina crashed into Gabriel with a squeak. Then she turned and hissed at me. I found the reaction ridiculously funny, a far cry from when I was human. "Knock it off and talk to him," I informed her, then stalked off before she could threaten to whittle a hole through my heart with a dull butter knife or something.

I hurried into the hallway, closing the door behind me. Before it sealed shut, I heard Halina mutter, "Men."

Cleo's normal ears didn't catch that, otherwise I was sure she'd be smiling too. Her dark eyes watched me as I walked across the hall toward her. Pointing at the door, I said, "I want to talk to him. Open the door."

She frowned, but she twisted around and unchained the door. She trusted me to do the right thing, make the right decision. Plus, she was probably going to come inside with me, and make absolutely certain nothing happened to me. As with most of the women in my life now, she was a bit overprotective.

The man was sitting on the bed when I entered. The bed was pristinely made. Aside from the section he was sitting on, there wasn't a rumple anywhere. He either hadn't slept at all, or he'd made the bed to military perfection. I was guessing the former. Other than look up at me, he didn't move when I entered the room.

Cleo tried to follow me, but I held my hand up to stop her. "Wait outside, please."

Her eyes narrowed as they shifted to the man on the bed. I knew what she was saying without her even having to say it. Smiling, despite the irritation crawling up my spine, I said, "He's been cleaned of his weapons and there is nothing in the room he can hurt me with." That was fairly true. There was a chair but it was a cushiony recliner, a dresser, but it was too heavy to break apart into stake-like pieces, and all of the decorations were round in nature. No sharp edges anywhere. I affectionately called this room the Dr. Suess room. Cleo still didn't seem convinced, so I added, "And, I know you haven't had a real chance to see it yet, but I'm pretty strong. I think I can take him if he tries anything."

I smirked at her, hoping she'd get the message and leave me in peace with the man. Her expression wasn't pleased about it, but she eventually closed the door. The man broke the silence before I could. "She's human. Why didn't you just compel her to leave?"

Not sure if he'd buy my answer, I told him, "I'd rather not compel anyone, if I don't have to."

He snorted. Definitely didn't believe me. "A vampire who doesn't love controlling those around him? Yeah, that's new."

I ignored his taunt as best I could. What else did he have on his side right now but hateful words? I couldn't fault him for that. "What's your name?"

He raised his eyebrows in question. "You asking or compelling? Because you know that crap doesn't work on me."

I raised my palms in an expression of peace. "Just asking. I'd like to call you something other than 'hunter' which happens to be my name."

The man regarded me for a minute, and then said, "Name's Jake."

I thought of extending my hand to him to formalize the introductions, then thought better of it. Jake didn't appear to want much to do with me, and probably didn't want to touch me. Having been in his shoes at one point in my life, I understood. Jake was on the small side for a man, not much bigger than Nika. It gave him the illusion of being harmless, but I knew otherwise, and even though my posture was relaxed as I crossed over to the recliner, I was on full alert. My ears absorbed the rapid beating of his heart, my eyes pinpointed the beads of sweat near his temple, the way his dark eyes flicked from me to the door. I could practically smell the emotion bubbling to the surface within him. He was very nervous to be alone with me.

With a mellow, unintimidating voice, I began my futile attempt at finding out some information. "Jake, I'm curious about something."

His response was instant, his thin smile mocking. "Everyone is curious about something."

I almost laughed. He reminded me a little of my father. And Halina. Jake probably wouldn't like the comparison to my pureblood creator or the comparison to my biological creator. "True. Well, what I'm curious about is you."

His small smile not budging, he replied, "You'll be disappointed then. There's not much to tell about me."

I did laugh then. "From all I've seen so far, I doubt that's true." Like every hunter I'd ever met, I was sure Jake had quite the interesting story to tell.

While I was seemingly distracted, I saw Jake's eyes dart to the door, like he was debating making a run for it. "I'm faster than you, you won't make it." His eyes returned to mine and his smile faded. With a shrug, I added, "And Cleo out there ... well, I have no desire to hurt you, but not everyone here feels the same. I'd just sit tight for now, if I were you."

Even though I was giving him sage advice, he looked like he wanted to finish the job he'd started earlier. "Hunter. Hunter Evans, right?" Surprise washed through me that he knew me. Or knew *of* me. I slowly nodded and so did he. "I knew your father, ages ago. He'd be horrified to see what you've become."

Pain erupted in my chest like he'd finally staked me. My father's face floated through my mind, the disappointment in his eyes, the condemnation. Closing my eyes to banish the vision, I whispered, "He's the one who made me this way." Not wanting to give Jake too long to make a move on me, I quickly reopened my eyes and said, "And yes ... he was horrified."

Jake made a face like he was about to spit on the ground. "I suppose you killed him then? Did you drain him of his blood? Did you feed on him?"

I found that remark really offensive for some reason. Probably because I now found blood drinking to be such an intimate act, one I only wanted to share with Nika. The thought of biting anyone else was disturbing. "Yes, I took care of him ... but ... I didn't drink a drop of his blood. Nor will I ever drink from a human." I made my voice sound as firm as possible, so he would understand I was being completely serious.

It didn't matter though. "Sure," he scoffed, clearly disbelieving me.

It made my gut twist that he doubted me, but that was to be expected. Prior to my conversion, I would have doubted anything a vampire said too. "Believe me or don't, it doesn't change the truth of the matter."

"If you say so, demon."

His disgusted face grew almost comical, and I smiled. Was that what I had looked like? "You sound just like I used to."

His expression eased at seeing my humor. I doubted very much he wanted to amuse me. "Back when you were on the right side."

I sighed. This was exactly why talking to someone with a set-in-stone prejudice was impossible. "There doesn't *have* to be a side. That's exactly the sort of mentality I'm trying to change."

He made a noise that was somewhere between a harrumph and a cough. "Right. By forcing people to see things your way. Sounds *real* ethical." His voice dripped with sarcasm.

"War doesn't always follow ethics." Involuntarily, my voice hardened. He didn't understand what it was like being unfairly hunted. He was only seeing one side of the coin. There was too much at stake, too many innocents who could be hurt, if I didn't do the things that needed to be done. I was letting the hunters live. That was a lot more than others of my kind would do.

Jake leaned over his knees, regarding me. "No, it doesn't, which makes me wonder ... since you can't warp me into your twisted little army, and you say you've no desire to kill me or drink from me ... what *are* you going to do with me?"

Yes, that *was* the dilemma now. He'd tried to kill me and two other vampires. There had to be some sort of punishment for that. But what? In his eyes, he wasn't doing anything wrong. Not knowing the answer, I told him, "I honestly don't know what will happen to you. That will be up to the panel to decide. For now, my only intention is to speak with you a moment."

A sneer twisted his lips. "Well then, mission accomplished, you've spoken with me. Congratulations."

Ignoring his comment, I asked the question I really wanted an answer to. "Do you know why I wasn't able to affect your mind?" The man contorted his face, like he was digging a piece of food out of his teeth with his tongue. He'd already said once that he wasn't going to tell us anything. Guess he was sticking to that. I hoped to shock him into a response with my next question though. "Did you know you're part vampire?"

He stopped picking at whatever he was trying to get loose and gave me a blank stare. His eyes were wider, but I had no idea if he'd known that or not. I seemed to recall him being surprised by the fact that Julian had been immune to silver. That would suggest he didn't know about mixed vampires, so he probably didn't know what he was. Either that or he was faking it, because a vampire hunter with vampire DNA in him wouldn't go over too well in some circles.

As Jake straightened his stance, I leaned forward. "There are vampires in the world as alive as I used to be. They live, they die, and they occasionally give birth to other living vampires. Their children have fewer and fewer of the vampiric side effects and benefits. In fact, I know a man who appears to be a completely normal human being, except he can't be compelled. That was how we knew he wasn't entirely human. He's a mixed vampire ... same as you." Silence met my statement. "A tiny fragment of your blood is demonic, as you put it. That's how you avoided my compulsion. That's how you're protected."

"Lucky me," he growled. Jake clamped his mouth shut tight, and I still couldn't tell what he knew. His heartbeat was faster than a man's at rest, but calmer than when I'd first come in here.

Taking a shot in the dark, I asked, "You were already aware of your heritage then? You knew?"

"Does it matter?" His eyes narrowed to a glare.

Gritting my teeth, I bit back the comment I really wanted to make. Instead, I told him, "Maybe, maybe not. Either way, I'd like to know what you know." This runaround conversation was frustrating. It'd be so much easier to just compel the truth out of him.

"And I'd like freedom. Guess we'll see who gets what they want first." Jake smiled at me, a cold, cruel smile that made me want to hiss at him like Halina had hissed at Gabriel. Yep. Definitely easier to compel him.

CHAPTER SEVEN

Julian

TONIGHT WAS THE night the panel was going to decide the fate of the man who had attacked Hunter, Halina and my sister. The three vampires were completely healed from the silver they'd ingested, you wouldn't even know they'd been injured. The man, Jake, had been staying at the ranch for the past couple weeks while panel members had listened to the testimony of the people who'd been there, and then debated amongst themselves about what should be done with the guy. Several suggestions had been thrown around.

Rory, one of the converted hunters who followed Hunter around like a puppy dog, wanted the man dead. That seemed pretty harsh to me. I mean, Jake hadn't actually killed anyone—at the meeting, at least. I was sure he had the blood of quite a few vampires on his hands. But he'd been ambushed while doing his job. I couldn't sentence him to death for that.

One of the panel members had mentioned letting him go with one of the other converted ex-hunters, as a guard of sorts. He said someone could drive him hundreds of miles away, and make sure he never returned to Salt Lake. Almost everyone shot down that notion though. One, Jake could easily escape his escort and sneak back into the city. And two, Jake could warn other hunters about what we were doing here. The only reason it was working, was because we were taking hunters by surprise. If they came into the home aware of the trap awaiting them, it would mean a fight. And I for one had had enough of fights.

Some of the other converted hunters on the panel had suggested a lifetime of confinement. But that seemed cruel too. Weren't we trying to prove that we were fair and just? But what was fair and just—and *safe*—in this case? It gave me a headache whenever I thought about it.

"Dude? You want some? You look like you could use it?"

Trey held the end of a short joint out to me. It used to be that it wasn't very often when I sat with Trey while he got high, but now that school was out and Nika was asleep all day, I'd found myself watching him get baked more and more frequently. He usually didn't ask me to partake though. The last time I'd said yes, bad things had happened. Very bad things. I had no desire to repeat that night. I needed to keep my senses about me.

"No thanks." Shaking my head, I looked away toward the bright sun making its afternoon descent through the sky. "Besides, I think I'm getting loopy just taking in your fumes." I'd have to remember to shower as soon as I got home, so Mom and Dad didn't think I was the one smoking. I'd been doing that more and more often too. Showering to mask my activities. Seemed devious to me. Childish. And I was trying to be more grown up. Oh well, baby steps. And gigantic leaps, like tonight. Man, I didn't want to condemn a man to die.

"You sure? You look like stressed. Worried about Saturday?"

I dropped my head into my hands. "Saturday. Damn it … I forgot all about that." Saturday was the raging party that the school had decided to have at my house. The party that I still hadn't mentioned to my parents. The party that I was pretty sure was going to happen now, regardless of what I said to people.

Groaning, I stretched out on the picnic table behind me. The sunshine slipped under the edge of my sunglasses, momentarily blinding me. Overhead, I could hear birds chirping a merry melody in the leafy tree canopy. Somewhere else in the distance, I heard a lawnmower. Even though it was a typical, lazy summer day, I felt anything but typical. What fate should I choose for Jake?

Trey leaned back on the table with me. Even though it was hot out, he still paired his cargo shorts and light t-shirt with a tightly knitted stocking cap. It made me sweat just looking at him. He took a long drag of his pot-cigarette, held it a few seconds, and finally released it. "How did you forget your own birthday party?"

I rolled my head from side to side against the table; the ridges in the wood felt good against my scalp. "I don't know. Busy, I guess." I rolled my head completely to the left to look at him. "Besides, my actual birthday is Wednesday."

Trey nodded. "I know. I'm excited to hang with the Adams clan again." Trey smiled a lazy smile. "Your mom is so freakin' hot."

I just about gagged, but laughed and slugged him in the arm instead. My mom was pretty, but I didn't want to think about her in the way Trey was thinking about her. And he meant Starla anyway. Trey knew nothing about my real life. Halina had made sure of that. He only knew the fantasy. For a minute, I envied him.

The park we were resting in was teeming with dogs; Trey and I had seen more than a few meander past with their owners. They almost always stopped to sniff our way, thanks to my friend's odiferous habit. A couple of dogs snarling at each other on the other side of a shallow duck pond got my attention. Their owners were furiously pulling on the dog's restraints, trying to keep the creatures from killing each other. It was clearly a struggle for the owners. Whatever animosities the two canines had, it was bad enough that they wanted blood. It reminded me of humans and vampires, and the natural inclination they had to kill each other. And the league was like the owners, holding onto their leashes, trying with all their power to keep the two fighting mutts at bay. Would that tiny little strand of leather holding onto the beast be enough?

Trey was oblivious to the chaos nearby. While I sat up on my elbows to watch the struggle better, he asked, "You talked to Arianna yet this summer?"

One dog across the way bit into the flank of the other dog, but thanks to Trey's comment, I was the one who felt the puncture. Arianna. I hadn't seen or heard from her since the last day of school. And when I wasn't contemplating a man's future, I was thinking about her. Wondering what she was up to, how she was feeling, if she was happy … if she missed me too. She leveled my mood when I was down, and made me feel exhilarant when I was happy. She made me monstrously sad too. The loss of her was always with me.

"No," I whispered, sinking back down to the table. I didn't want to watch dogs maim each other anymore.

Trey exhaled a smoky breath, and then gave me an apologetic shrug. "Sorry, man. I'm sure she'll dig you eventually. Just don't give up."

I looked at him, smiled, then looked up at the cloudless blue sky that matched the color of my eyes. Eyes Arianna had loved looking into. "I don't plan on it."

As the day cooled and shadows lengthened, my thoughts firmly centered around Arianna. She'd been apprehensive but accepting when she'd first found out what I really was. I wondered if she'd still react that way, now that she no longer loved me. Now that we were just ... friends.

Trey hopped off the table, a lazy smile on his mouth and a reddish tinge to his eyes. "I need to eat. Catch ya later."

I nodded as he waved and left. I should leave too. I'd driven to the park to meet Trey—my parents were getting more comfortable with letting me drive places lately—so I leisurely walked back to my car. It was nine thousand degrees inside when I climbed in. Next time I'd have to remember to park in the shade. The oppressive heat made me clammy in seconds, and I couldn't stop the thought that Nika would probably love hopping into sauna-cars now—if she could. Sun-warmed cars were a bit of a problem for vampires.

Cranking up the AC, which thankfully still worked in this beat-up, old car, I backed up out of the stall. As I drove out of the park, I found that I couldn't go home yet. There was something I wanted—no something I *needed*—to do first. It had been ages since I'd seen Arianna, since I'd talked to her, and even though I'd probably see her Saturday at the ... party ... I just couldn't stand another second without seeing her smile. Yes, I'd just pop in really quick, say hello, then I'd go home ... and prepare for tonight.

The drive to Arianna's didn't take long, but with the way my heart was accelerating with nervous anticipation, it felt even shorter. Pulling up to the street in front of her house, I took a deep breath and shut off the car. I wasn't exactly sure what I could say to her that wouldn't sound creepy and stalkerish. Would she buy that I was just in the neighborhood?

While I tried to control my rapidly pounding heart, I looked over at Arianna's place. The white rambler was offset by the massive graveyard behind it. The eerie backdrop should have been disturbing, but I found it beautiful and calming. The myriad assortment of statues, crosses, flags, and headstones, made everything intriguing. And the grounds were bursting with bouquets of flowers in nearly every color under the sun. Even with the window rolled up, I could smell them.

Feeling more at peace, I focused on the front door. Time to go in. Even though my car was partially blocked by the mammoth tree in the yard, I had a decent view of the dining room window. When Arianna's mom came into the room carrying a stack of plates, I frowned. They were about to eat. I shouldn't bother them. And I didn't have a good excuse to be here anyway; I didn't want to scare her off, make her think twice about coming to the party.

Mind made up, I started the car. I was just about to pull back onto the road when I noticed something odd. Arianna's mom had set four plates on the table. Arianna was an only child. There should only be three plate settings. Shaking my head, I moved my hand to the shifter. So what. Her parents could be having a friend over for dinner, or Arianna could be having someone over. No big deal. My hand paused on the rectangular, leather knob. Unless ... she was sharing her table with her hot neighbor?

Even though I felt like my leering was crossing the boundary of politeness, I leaned over the passenger's side to get a better view. I stared without blinking at the window until my eyes felt like they were on fire. Mrs. Bennett set out four glasses and four sets of silverware. Then she started bringing out food. They were having lasagna, garlic bread, and salad. It made my stomach rumble seeing all of it, and I wished I could smell it too. Whoever this guest was, they were in for a treat.

Mrs. Bennett yelled that dinner was ready—I heard her loud and clear—and Mr. Bennett shuffled into the room. He sat down while Mrs. Bennett started dishing out servings. They were sort of in my way and I made a pointless shooing motion with my hand while cursing under my breath. Then Arianna's head of caramel gold entered my line of sight. I completely froze while I watched her. She was so beautiful. She was laughing and tucking a strand of hair behind her ear. I could hear the sound through the walls and it overjoyed me. Then a second laugh chimed in and my blood went as cold as my sister's.

The laugh belonged to a guy. The neighbor?

He came into view a heartbeat later. He was just a step behind Arianna, so close that he could have been touching her. Who was this guy, and why was he sitting down to dinner with my girlfriend? Oh God ... had she started dating the neighbor guy after school ended? I didn't think I could handle it if they were together.

He seemed to be around my age, with blonde hair, and light eyes. I didn't think I'd call him "hot" but I supposed ... to a girl ... he was attractive. All I knew was he was way too close to Arianna. *Please don't let them be dating ...*

He obliterated my view of Arianna when he sat down to eat in the seat beside hers. No one spoke a whole lot, so I didn't pick up any information on the newcomer ... couldn't determine just what he was to Arianna.

Moments later, they all began eating their dinners. They talked companionably, with a brief laugh here and there. It was relaxed and comfortable—not the first time he'd eaten here then. What did that mean? As I watched them enjoy each other's company, I suddenly felt out of place. *I shouldn't be here. I don't belong.* And if Arianna had moved on and she was happy ... maybe I should walk away and let her be happy. I mean, being with me had almost gotten her killed ... twice. Didn't she deserve a shot at a normal life? And normal was something I'd never be able to give her.

"Bye, Arianna," I murmured, pulling my car away from the curb.

My mood was sour when I got home. Arianna was seeing somebody. I was losing her. I'd lost her. What the hell was I supposed to do now? I choked back the tightness in my throat, blinked away the burning sensation in my eyes. Opening my car door, I stormed to my feet, then slammed the door shut behind me. I closed it so hard I heard something break. When the door opened a half inch on its own, I realized I'd broken the latch keeping it shut. Fabulous. Could my day get any better?

Leaving my car the way it was, since I couldn't do anything to fix it anyway, I trudged to the porch. Winning Arianna back was supposed to have been easy. I mean, she'd loved me once, she could love me again. Or did fate need a series of specific steps to happen for us to be in a relationship? And since those steps had already happened, did that mean I could never recreate them? God, I hoped not.

When I stepped inside the house, my bad mood hadn't lifted. I accidentally slammed the front door shut before I could stop myself. Luckily, no part of this door broke though. My mom blurred into the room in a heartbeat. "Hey, easy there, tiger."

While she inspected the wood around the frame, to see if I'd cracked anything, I murmured, "Sorry," and started heading for my room.

Sniffing the air, Mom asked, "How's Trey?" The frown on her face told me loud and clear that she could smell the pot on me, and she wasn't pleased.

Stopping at the bottom of the staircase, I shrugged. "He's fine." I didn't feel like defending Trey's habit again, so I left it at that.

Mom crossed her arms over her chest as she eyed me with suspicion. I had to force myself not to shift my weight, look away, or appear guilty in any other way. Other than break my car door, I hadn't done anything wrong.

After another minute of silent studying, Mom finally asked, "You okay?"

No. No, I wasn't. "Yeah, I just want to shower off this smell before dinner."

Mom nodded, but I knew she didn't believe me.

I continued to my room and showered just like I said I was going to. When I was finished, I debated calling Arianna, and asking her if she was seeing someone. But if she said yes, what could I say to that? We were friends. Just friends. And that was all we'd ever be now. Sitting on my bed, I stared at the ceiling until the sun went down.

My sister emerged from her underground rooms, greeted our parents, then made her way up the stairs to me. She knocked, even though she didn't need to. Her old bedroom shared a bathroom with mine, and both bathroom doors were wide open. She could have entered my room that way if she wanted.

My head swiveled to the closed bedroom door. "Come on in, Nick."

She entered with a small, knowing smile on her lips. Just by listening to me talk to Mom, she knew something was wrong. Sitting up, I wrapped my arms around my knees and studied her as she approached me. Just the couple of months of zero exposure to the sun had changed her appearance. This time last year, she would have had a golden glow to her skin, and her hair would have been highlighted with sun-kissed streaks of gold. Her hair was completely dark now, an even deeper shade of brown than it was during the winter months.

She sat beside me on the bed. "You seem down. Want to talk about it?"

I glanced at the floor, to where our parents were beneath us. They were putting the finishing touches on dinner, and not paying attention, but they couldn't help but hear us. "It's just ..." I sighed, and looked back up at Nika. "I miss her. I want her back, and ... I can't have her. It's so hard ..."

With a sigh of her own, Nika stretched her arms around my neck and pulled me in for a hug. "I know. I'm so sorry, Julie."

I accepted her sympathy in silence. It helped to let someone commiserate with me. Nika's arms stiffened around my neck so suddenly, that for a second I thought she was attacking me. I instinctively fought against her until I realized what the problem was. She was breathing heavier as she clutched at me for dear life: Hunter was approaching. I instantly shoved her away from me. "Nick! Please don't hug me when you're all jazzed up about him coming over."

Looking embarrassed and turned on, Nika squirmed as she sat on her hands. "I'm sorry! It's not like I can stop the reaction." She closed her eyes and laid her head back. Her chest was starting to heave.

I scooted off the bed. Watching her reaction to him was nearly as bad as experiencing it when we'd been connected. Walking backwards toward the door, I murmured, "I'll see you in the kitchen, after Hunter gets here."

Feeling lonelier than I had in a while, I twisted away from her. I'd never had to share my sister before, but now ... More often than not, Hunter was glued to her side, or rushing to her side. They were practically one person now. And watching their relationship just reminded me how alone I was.

"Wait!" she exclaimed. Pausing at the door, I looked back at her. Her breath was still fast, but her eyes were open. "Don't go. I want to talk to you about what happened." She bit her lip, and clutched the sheets underneath her fingers, like she was making herself stay put.

"Later," I promised, as I darted out the door.

Like I told her I would, I headed toward the kitchen to wait out the drama. It happened every night, so it didn't even faze me anymore. Nika held out as long as she could, then she darted after Hunter. Irritated, Dad took off after her to break up the explosive reunion.

When Dad predictably flew out of the house, I turned to Mom. "How long is Dad going to let this continue? You know he can't keep them apart, they're bonded." Sadness enveloped me. God, I even missed the bond. At least I'd felt connected to somebody then.

Mom reached over to grab my hand. "You're not okay. I heard you … you miss her. Arianna."

Lowering my eyes, I said, "Yeah. But there's nothing to be done about it. Wiped is wiped. She's gone …" I stared at my plate of roast beef, mashed potatoes, corn on the cob and apple crisp. None of it sounded good. Scooting my chair back, I told her, "I'm not hungry. I'm going to take a nap. Will you wake me when it's time to go to the meeting?"

I raised an eyebrow, silently asking permission to leave. Mom's face showed her inner struggle. The mother in her wanted to make me stay and eat something, wanted to make me open up to her. The friend in her wanted to let me have what I needed. Finally, she conceded to my request. "Okay. You can nap in my room if you want. It's quiet."

I nodded in thanks, then trudged upstairs to sleep away my troubles in my parents' sound-proof bedroom.

When I woke up, my stomach growled more fiercely than any vampire in creation ever had. I put a hand on the unruly beast, attempting to tame it with pressure. Maybe I should have tried to eat something earlier. I looked around my parents' bedroom with just my eyes. The décor in here was soothing, peaceful. The walls were tan, the furniture black, the accent pieces around the room—framed photos of Nika and me, a vase of flowers, pillared candles—were black, white or silver. The bedspread I was lying on was beige with huge circles in varying colors that complemented the room. It was both masculine and feminine. It was so dark now, though, that I could barely make out anything.

A horrible feeling knotted my stomach and I shot off the bed. It would be just like my dad to let me miss the meeting by not waking me up in time to go.

I blurred out of the room in a panic, but the second I opened the door, I heard my parents' voices. They were discussing the upcoming meeting, so at least I hadn't missed it. Scrubbing my eyes, I headed downstairs. Maybe I could get a quick bite before we left.

Mom and Dad were talking with Hunter, Gabriel and Ben, sans Tracey. She'd probably had her fill of vampire meetings after the last one she'd gone to. Everyone except Gabriel was on the "trial" panel. Gabriel said he had too many important things to work on, and didn't have time for what Halina referred to as "permanent jury duty," but he was coming tonight in case anyone had questions about why the man was impervious to compulsion. Truly, nobody should be questioning that anymore. It had been discussed ad nauseam over the past couple of weeks.

When I walked through the living room on the way to the kitchen, every voice stopped and every set of eyes followed me. Self-conscious, I froze. Pointing to the other room, I asked, "Do I have time to eat?"

Dad nodded. "Make it quick. We're leaving in a minute."

I zipped off to the other room, shaking my head. A minute, huh? Guess I woke up just in time. I opened the fridge looking for something, but now that I was starving, nothing was appealing. I just wanted food. I grabbed a pizza box from the other night. There will still a few slices left, and I could eat them cold. I downed one slice as quickly as if I were drinking it, and was starting in on another when Dad called out that it was time to go. I finished the triangle in my hand, then grabbed one last slice for the road. Thankfully, pizza was very portable.

It was a beautiful night out, so we decided to walk. The panel deciding Jake's fate was meeting at a community playground in the middle of our neighborhood. The gathering had originally been slated to meet at Hunter's old place, but there was some worry that a hunter who'd been told to wait there for instructions might show up and interrupt the party. So, to avoid that highly plausible scenario, our group was meeting by the jungle gym instead.

When we arrived at the playground, several humans were already there. Two of them were sitting on the swings, and a couple of them were perched atop the monkey bars. Given another set of circumstances, I might have found vampire hunters lounging around a playground humorous. Tonight was a solemn occasion though; nobody was even cracking a smile. The only purebloods in attendance were Hunter and Nika. Halina was with the prisoner. She'd wanted to watch his fate being decided, but she hadn't felt good about leaving the man alone in the house with her child and grandchild, even though Imogen and Alanna could take care of themselves, especially with Rory and Cleo there to help. Halina didn't want to take any chances though.

My dad shook hands with some of the other panel members, a big fat guy named Rob, and a tall skinny guy named Tom. The pair rocking side by side on the swings were Gloria and Karl. They were married, and had begun a life of vampire hunting when their son was murdered by an out-of-control pureblood. The group on the monkey bars was Jorge, Rocky, and Kat. The three of them all came about hunting in different ways than Gloria and Karl, but their stories were similarly tragic. Most people that I'd run into joined the life because a vampire had hurt them at some point. That made Jake seem right when he questioned what we were going to do about the purebloods. One problem at a time though.

Hunter stepped up to a large metal circle that the kids used to spin themselves sick. He sat on a hand railing with Nika, easily balancing on the thin cylinder. He'd been one of the rare vampire hunters—someone who'd been born into the life. His family had hunted my kind for generations upon generations. That was also a rarity—living long enough to raise a family while seeking out some of the most dangerous creatures on earth.

After the final members of the panel showed up, Dad raised a hand into the air to get their attention. "Folks, we come here tonight to make our first decision on what to do about a vengeance attack. I personally would rather all be meeting tonight for something a little more jovial, but if we're going to stop the chaos, then hard choices have to be made."

Karl hopped off the swings and stepped forward. "He attacked an innocent without provocation. He should be put to death."

Dad sighed as he looked Karl's way. "A few months ago you were part of the crew that attacked my family's home ... without provocation. And yet here you stand. Death is too harsh a punishment in this instance."

Gloria stood and walked to her husband's side. "Our minds were opened, and we were allowed to see the truth of your species." She bowed an acknowledgement to Hunter. "There is good among you, as well as there is evil. And it's not up to one man to decide which is which." Several hunters in the park agreed, and were nodding their heads with her. Gloria pointed toward the ranch, where Jake was being held. "But that man is protected, and his mind will never be opened." She flicked a glance at Gabriel and he nodded, affirming her statement. Gloria set her jaw, then continued, "Hate will rule his every decision, and innocents will suffer for it." Her dark eyes shifted to me and softened. I was roughly the age her son would have been. Now that she knew I wasn't inherently evil, she had a soft spot for me.

Mom and Dad followed her eyes to me. Mom frowned. She wanted to err on the side of caution, and remove the threat permanently, but she also agreed with Dad. What he'd done wasn't severe enough to warrant death.

Jorge jumped down from the monkey bars to land on the ground near Hunter and Nika. "Then we keep him holed up until the end of his days. Life in prison. There isn't another option besides death, and a most of us don't feel he deserves that." Rocky and Kat nodded in agreement with him. I inwardly sighed. Death or life in prison, those were the choices we were left with, and neither sounded good. I didn't want to force either of those fates upon Jake. I'd rather compel him to accept the truth about my kind. That was the best scenario, for everybody, but that wasn't going to happen.

Dad ran a hand through his hair, then exchanged a long glance with Mom. I sat up a little straighter on the slide I was sitting on. They had an idea, that much I could tell. I glanced over at Hunter and Nika, but they were looking at each other, and didn't seem to notice Mom and Dad were plotting something.

Dad cleared his throat, and all eyes swung his way. "There is ... one ... other option," he slowly said.

I frowned, along with half the other hunters. Gabriel was the only one who still seemed impassive. He was merely observing the proceedings, and probably didn't care too much about what happened to the hunter we were holding.

Dad glanced at Mom. "Emma and I have talked in length about this, and ..." His gaze swept over the crowd, "... we ask that the panel release Jake into our custody."

My jaw dropped nearly to the bottom of the slide. He *what*? Why would he offer to do that? The other panel members seemed equally confused by Dad's statement. Karl crossed his arms over his chest. "And what is it that you plan on doing with him, Teren?"

Dad shrugged. "All we've been talking about since the attack was whether we kill the man or lock him up and throw away the key. But that's not the point of this league. It's to change the way the hunting world thinks about us. To stop the unjustified attacks, on both sides. Yes, compulsion is the easiest way to make that happen, but it's not the *only* way." Dad's eyes shifted to Hunter. "Sometimes people can be shown a truth, and they'll come to the realization on their own." Hunter gave him a smile and a nod, and Dad returned his attention to the others. "What I propose is that Jake is taken under our wing, that he's allowed to be involved in the process, that he sees with his own eyes that we're not all bad, and that this group serves a purpose. We make it so he *wants* to join us, of his own free will, because he believes what we believe. He has to join us naturally, so, let's make him a member of the league."

The others seemed skeptical. "A league member? With *his* animosities? What if he never accepts that vampires are anything but soulless, bloodthirsty monsters?" Rocky asked.

Dad slowly shook his head. "If given enough time, it still seems his intentions won't change, then ... we'll let him go ... because we're *not* monsters, and we won't coerce someone into joining us by threatening them with death or life imprisonment if they refuse. But he'll be watched, guarded. I won't allow him to hurt anyone."

The group thought on that a second, and I raised my hand and asked, "So ... you want to make him a hostage?"

Dad cringed at my verbiage, but nodded. "For lack of a better word, yes, I suppose so, but he'd be as free of a hostage as we can make him. He'll continue to stay at the ranch with us, but not locked up in a room. He'll be a part of everything, and I believe, if he spends enough time with our family, he'll see that he doesn't need to be afraid of our species."

I rubbed my lip as I thought about that. Was Dad's suggestion really for us to watchdog a dangerous man for who the heck knows how long? Ben stepped forward, a scowl on his scarred face; he seemed to have the same fears as me. "Teren, your family—"

"Is strong enough to stop him from escaping, and quick enough to chase after him if he does," Dad said, cutting him off. Shaking his head, he added, "We can't risk him running off prematurely and warning people about what we're doing here." Dad locked eyes with Mom again, and she gave him a tight smile. They'd obviously talked about this, but it was still a hard decision for both of them. Above all else, they wanted to keep the family safe.

Turning back to the panel, Dad said, "We can hold him, and, by staying with us, he'll see that we're not as bad as he thinks we are. We'll convert him the old-fashioned way with time, patience, and understanding." He smirked at the end of that.

The panel members immediately started debated which course of action would be best. A pair of hunters in matching denim jackets thought that throwing him in a cell to rot was the way to go. Gloria and Karl were still leaning toward death, while Jorge, Rocky and Kat were clearly moved by my father's words. I was tired of debating. I wanted something to be done. I wanted action. Standing from the slide, I told the group, "I vote for my father's suggestion of making Jake an unwilling member of the league, and I agree that he should remain in my family's custody so he can see we're not all evil." I raised my hand for emphasis, then looked around at the others. "Who's with me?"

A breeze rustled the leaves in the tops of the trees, a couple of dogs bayed in the distance, but nobody moved and nobody said anything. For several long heartbeats, I felt completely alone and vulnerable. Oddly enough, I felt strong too. I'd made a decision, a decision I felt good about, and I was acting on it. It was time for the rest of them to do the same. Then, one by one, the others started raising their hands and murmuring, "I vote for Teren's idea," and "Make him one of us," and "Yes, he should be a hostage." I didn't care for the term, but a vote was a vote, and I was happy to see them make one.

Not everyone voted for Dad's idea. Karl still voted for death, and Rocky voted for imprisonment. The majority vote was with Dad though, so Jake was staying with us. Indefinitely. Man, I hope we'd made the right decision.

CHAPTER EIGHT

Nika

I WATCHED MY brother leaving the park with heaviness in my heart. Even though we were the same age, he seemed so much older than me now. Depression was wearing him down. I couldn't feel it, but I knew it. I could see it in the slump of his shoulders, the dimness of his eyes, and the weariness in his voice. He wasn't ever going to get over Arianna, not truly. The memory of her would be in his heart until the end of his days.

But even depressed, he'd done well today. He'd heard all the options presented, and he'd made a choice based on what he felt was the right course of action. I'd voted the same way as Julian, although, it had been harder for me to go along with it. Jake had attacked me, caused me a great deal of pain. And he'd come really close to killing Hunter. A large part of me wanted him dead, but somehow I'd shoved that part aside and voted for him to remain at the ranch with our family.

I wasn't thrilled about it though. Hunter would be around Jake every day now. Jake would be around *us* every day now. I wished there was another vampire family nearby to pawn him off on, but there wasn't. Salt Lake had visitors off and on, but we were the only permanent nest in the area.

Mom left with Julian, Dad stayed behind, maybe to watch over me, maybe to work out details with the other panel members, I wasn't sure. Ready to leave, I turned to Hunter. "Shall we go?" Hunter's dark eyes turned introspective. I didn't take that as a good sign. "What?" I sighed, already fearing I knew the answer.

Hunter's eyes flashed to my father, then hesitantly came back to me. "It's just ... if we're going to turn a hunter around, make him see vampires in another light, then, I don't think anyone else is more qualified to do that than me."

I stared at him blankly for a few seconds. "You want to go back to the ranch and get to work hanging out with Jake, right?" Hunter gave me a small smile and I knew I had it right. I shrugged. I didn't really care what we did, so long as we were together. "Okay, let's go."

The sudden guilt on Hunter's face spoke volumes. He opened his mouth to speak, but I knew what he was going to say long before the words came out. In fact, all he got out was my name. "Nika ..."

"You don't want me to go with you!" Some of the ex-hunters nearby turned to look. I hadn't said that quietly. They turned back around when they saw it was only Hunter and I having a spat. Whether vampire or human, fights were an inevitable part of a relationship.

"Nika," he tried again, "I just don't feel good about you being around him right now."

I crossed my arms over my chest and tapped my foot. "I'm a pureblood vampire, not some fragile, human little girl that you need to protect. I can take care of myself."

Maybe understanding how close he was to a major blowout, Hunter raised his hands. "I get that, and I know you can handle yourself, and I don't need to worry about you, but ..." he let out a weary exhale, "I still do. You're everything to me, and I had to watch you die. Do you know what that did to me?"

I swallowed and looked down. "Yes ... I watched you die first ..."

His fingers stroked along my jaw, lifting my chin. "Then you know why I can't lose you again. I can't. I won't get through it. You can call me old-fashioned, you can call me sexist, but really ... I'm just selfish. I can't cope with the thought of losing you, so until I know Jake has been safely declawed, I'm asking you to stay home with your brother and your parents."

I closed my eyes and turned my head away from him. There was no effective argument against "my world would end if anything happened to you." It was irritating, frustrating, and sweet all at the same time. And I also couldn't argue with the fact that Hunter was the best person for the job to turn Jake around, if turning him around was even possible. It all seemed so improbable.

Cracking an eye open, I asked, "Does it have to be tonight? He's been at the ranch for a couple weeks now, surely another night wouldn't hurt anything. And besides, it's past midnight, he's probably sleeping." I opened both eyes to plead with him. "Please? I don't want to part ways yet. It's torture."

Hunter's expression softened into a smile. "Nika," he whispered as he leaned down to kiss me. Like they always did, the softness of his lips stole my breath. As our mouths moved together, my hand came up to thread through his hair, pulling us together; I wished we were closer.

"Hunter," I murmured between our lips, "I want ..."

I felt a presence behind me that iced the molten desire rising in me. I pulled away from Hunter's kiss to look at Dad over my shoulder. His eyes were narrowed in irritation like he knew exactly what I'd been going to say. When he saw that he had my attention, he spoke before I had a chance to. "I'm going to head back to the ranch with Gabriel to let Great-Gran know what the verdict was, and come up with a plan for ... carrying it out." He sighed, like he also realized this task he'd volunteered our family for wasn't going to be an easy one.

Hunter stepped around me. "I'll go with you."

Feeling stubborn, I said, "So will I."

Hunter and Dad both turned to me and said, "No," at the exact same time. I glared at the pair of them. It was like I had two overprotective fathers now.

"If I was Halina, neither one of you would be able to—"

Dad cut off my pointless rant. "But you're not and we can. Go home with Julian." His stance softened and he leaned in to hug me. "Please, go home, sweetheart."

Irritated, I didn't return his hug. I knew I was being insolent, but I didn't care. They were both being ridiculous.

Turning around, I stormed off after Julian. When the painful tug of the bond with Hunter kicked in, I embraced the discomfort. If I was feeling it, then he was feeling it too, and I wanted him to feel a little misery. He deserved it. Okay, maybe not, but I wanted him to feel it regardless.

HUNTER VISITED ME the following night like usual, but his visit wasn't as long as it typically was. He was anxious to rush back to the ranch, uneasy about Jake being there "unrestrained". But Rory and Cleo guarded him during the day and Halina or Imogen guarded him at night. Hunter felt obligated to be there though, and so, after far too short a time, he ran back to Jake while I stayed home.

I went to bed alone and woke up alone, but that was nothing new. Not being woken up by my Mom and Dad singing "The Birthday Song" was new though. Every year before this one, Julian and I had groaned and smashed pillows over our ears when our parents had loudly interrupted our slumber to sing to us before they headed to work. Today though, I woke up to silence. Mom and Dad were still at work, and Julian was a couple of miles away, probably hanging out with Trey. A bit of melancholy seeped into me as I sat up and looked around my empty bedroom. I actually missed the embarrassing musical wakeup. Kind of funny how something so annoying could become something I longed for once it was gone.

"Happy Birthday to me," I muttered, slipping out of my lukewarm bed.

My boyfriend and my other relatives were away at the ranch; I was completely alone. I should have slept in today, so the odds of someone being here when I woke up were greater, but I'd tossed and turned all day long, waking and sleeping, waking and sleeping. I just hadn't been able to get comfortable.

Hunter's proclamation was still on my mind; I hoped he'd had trouble sleeping these last couple of nights too. He probably hadn't though. He'd probably taken his new mission to heart, and had spent the entire time with Jake, getting started on operation *Vampires Are Your Friends*. I already had to share Hunter with the meetings and with Halina, and now I had to share him with this project too. I knew it was important, and I knew he was doing it in part for us. I just … missed him. Maybe if Dad would allow us to live together it wouldn't be so bad, but I was pretty sure Dad would keep me holed up until my eighteenth birthday. Next year. Oh well, at least the countdown to my freedom had begun.

I turned on a nearby lamp, then pulled out some fresh clothes. Just as I slipped my T-shirt into place, I heard a sound that froze my unbeating heart. A noise from the kitchen—somebody opening and shutting a cabinet. I wasn't alone, but I couldn't go upstairs to investigate. I couldn't leave my room until the sun set. An intense surge of vulnerability washed through me, and I suddenly understood Hunter's desire to keep me out of harm's way. I might be a vampire, but I wasn't invincible. All the person rummaging through my home would need to do was set a fire, and I'd be gone. I'd have no way to escape it. Unlike the log cabin where Hunter had almost been burned alive, my bedroom was more of a basement than a crawlspace now—the floor was made of thick cement, I wouldn't be able to claw through it. Not in time anyway.

I used every enhanced gift I'd been given to track the person above me. They were moving into the living room now. Stopping my breath, I held completely still. Whoever was here wasn't a pureblood vampire since they were traipsing around in the daylight, but they could be a mixed vampire, like my parents and Julian. I eyed my cell phone, charging on the other side of the room. I could call for help, but that would alert whoever was above me that I was hiding out down here, and there was a chance they didn't know I was in the house.

The footsteps were light, but I could easily follow them. They were headed toward the closet that led to my secret entrance. That couldn't be coincidence. They knew I was here. Maybe it was Starla then, or Jacen? But whoever was here was being quiet. Starla was rarely quiet. She'd have yelled out that she was here, turned on the TV, started making out with Jacen, or something equally noisy. This person was twisting the knob to my door like they were sneaking out of the house and didn't want to wake their parents. Or sneaking into a lion's den and didn't want to wake the lion. Well, too late. This lion was already awake.

I considered blurring to my phone and calling someone, but that person wouldn't get here in time. Best if I just dealt with this myself. I quietly turned off the lights then crept toward the hall leading to the closet. It was pitch-black, and my eyes gave off a ring of phosphorescent light. When I came upon the door leading to the room directly below the closet, I closed my eyes; I didn't want my attacker to see me when they opened the door.

And I hoped and prayed that no stray sunlight followed them down. If they left the closet door open and the trap door in the closet open, some faint light might hit me. It wouldn't be enough to give kill me, but I'd seen vampires exposed to the sun before, and I knew it hurt. A lot. I couldn't worry about that though.

I heard someone drop down into the room. It was so strange having my heartbeat absent, so strange that my chest ached. If I were alive right now, my heart would have been pounding against my ribcage. It would have given me away. Its absence was actually a blessing.

The person right next door to me was making weird shuffling noises. I swear they were pulling the chair into position and grabbing something from the closet above. The intruder was breathing heavy, and letting out small grunts like they were in pain. Then the trap door in the closet closed. I couldn't smell my attacker, the door was sealed too tightly for that, but I could hear a faint crackling sound, like a fourth of July sparkler. I almost opened my eyes. Fire? Were they coming down here to set me ablaze? Well they might get me, but it would be the last thing they ever did.

I heard the knob of the door in front of me twisting, heard the seal swishing against the hard floor. Then I felt the scant bit of heat from an open flame, and smelled something that tugged at a memory, and something else that made me a little nauseous. Mainly, all I felt was fear though, and the need to protect my home and myself.

I knew I had the advantage. The person intruding on my space obviously knew I was down here, but they were in a lit room while I was in a dark hallway. They wouldn't see me until it was too late. When the door was opened to capacity, the figure stepped into the hallway with me. I had seconds to get the drop on them. In my mind, I said a silent goodbye to my family, then I opened my eyes and dropped my fangs.

The person in the hallway let out a high-pitched scream when my glowing orbs appeared out of nowhere. She dropped whatever inconsequential thing she'd been holding, and backed up a step. She wasn't fast enough though. I lunged for her neck and clamped my teeth onto her skin. I was just about to bite down on her jugular, ending her life in a matter of moments, when the last few seconds replayed in my mind and my brain screamed at me to stop. I put the brakes on my adrenaline and pulled back to look into the scarred face of a woman I loved very much. "Aunt Ashley? What are you ... ?"

She was shaking like a leaf, her face drained of color, and her deep brown eyes locked onto mine. They were wide, but they were fixated on the otherworldly glow emanating from my eyes in the dark section of the hallway. I quickly shifted positions with her, so my face was fully in the light streaming through the open door of the room beneath the closet. With my eyes no longer holding her entranced, Ashley blinked, and then shook her head. When she was herself again, she clutched a hand to her chest and exclaimed, "Nika! You scared the bejesus out of me!"

I gave her a wry expression. "You're not the only one. I had no idea it was you clunking around up there."

Ashley wrinkled her nose in apology. "Sorry, I wanted to surprise you."

"You definitely did that," I muttered. "You didn't have to come down here. I know it's uncomfortable for you." The fire that Ashley had been caught in when she was just a girl, had left her badly scarred. She'd been through several surgeries to repair the damage, but there were still obvious lines over her face and her body, and her joints were sometimes stiff and sore as a result. Coming down here had to have been a challenge for her.

Ashley only shrugged and said, "It's your birthday."

Sniffing the air, I smelled the wondrous aroma of blood, followed by the sickly sweet aroma of ... cake? Looking down, I saw that Ash had been bringing me a treat when I'd jumped out and surprised her. A miniature cake was laying on its side, broken into large chunks, the plate holding it was shattered into bits. Sparkling candles highlighted the words *Happy Birthday, Nika!* Beside it was a travel mug; the top had popped off, and deep, dark blood was staining the cement. Feeling really guilty for spoiling her surprise, I picked up the mug and tried to put the cake back onto the larger remnants of the broken plate.

Ashley stiffly knelt beside me, picking up shards of ceramic surrounding the ruined cake. I blurred back to my room to get a towel for the blood, a flat binder for the cake pieces, and a small garbage bag for the rest of the plate. "Sorry, Aunt Ash, I didn't mean to ruin your surprise." I lifted the half-full travel mug of blood. "This is very sweet, thank you."

Her lips twisted into a smile. "No, it's my fault. I should have known better than to break in on a sleeping vampire."

I shook my head. "You didn't. I was up." I frowned. *And feeling very lonely, and now I'm feeling very foolish.*

Ashley managed to get most of the cake onto the binder; the candles were even still intact, throwing small sparks into the air that faded with a faint orange glow. "At least we can still have a little cake," she brightly said.

I gave her a soft smile. "Aunt Ash ... I can't eat cake anymore, remember?"

Her smile faded as my words triggered a memory. "Oh ... right. I knew that ... how stupid of me to forget. It's just ... we always do black and white cakes for your birthday."

She sighed and I felt guilty again. Ashley always purchased a chocolate on chocolate cake for me and a white on white cake for Julian from this amazing bakery in San Francisco. It was our birthday tradition, but it was one I couldn't partake in anymore. "It's okay. This is new ... for all of us." I took a sip of what was left of the bloody treat she'd brought down for me. As much as I used to love those San Francisco cakes, the blood tasted better than any cake in the history of the world. I purred with the pleasure of it. "*This* is incredible though, thank you."

Her face brightened back up. "At least I did something right."

After we'd cleaned up as much of the mess as we could, I helped her to her feet. "Where's Uncle Christian?" I asked. No one else was banging around upstairs, so I knew she was alone.

Ashley wrapped her arm around me as I led her to my room. "He's out at the ranch with Mom and the others. We flew in this morning so we could be at the party tonight, but I wanted to come surprise you and Julian with your cakes before then. You guys always used to look forward to them ..." Sighing, she shook her head. "Julian was gone when I got here, but Emma told me where she kept the spare key." She laughed and tucked a strand of hair behind her good ear. "Em wanted to rush over here and let me in, but I told her to finish out the work day. No need to become a slacker on my account. Plus, I wouldn't want to get her fired." She winked and I cracked a smile. Dad was Mom's boss, so the odds of her being fired—for any reason—were pretty slim.

Aunt Ashley looked around my room with a frown on her face. "I can't believe you're still sleeping down here," she said, her voice incredulous. "I thought you would have been moved to a nicer place by now."

I cringed as I eyed my dungeon-like bedroom. "Yeah, well, it's the only light-proof room in the house."

Ashley turned to me. A scar down the middle of her forehead puckered as she pressed her brows together. "Why aren't you staying at the ranch with the others then? The underground rooms there put the finest hotels in California to shame."

I gave her a tight smile. *Because my father is afraid to let me grow up.* "Funny you should ask—"

She cut me off with a strange expression. "Is it because of that man staying there? The one with constant bodyguards? The one Hunter was watching like a hawk when I left this afternoon?"

Irritation swam through me at her innocent comment. So, Hunter really was staying up all day to play with Jake. I knew he would. He was going to burn the candle at both ends, just like my father was doing with me. Only, Hunter wasn't trying to protect my virtue like Dad was. Hunter was trying to convert a man who couldn't be converted. In my opinion anyway.

"In part," I muttered, not really wanting to talk about it. I sat on the bed with a wide, distracting smile on my face. "Tell me about work," I exclaimed, changing the subject.

Ashley gave me a curious expression as she sat down, but then she started telling me about some of the burn victims she was helping at the hospital, and our conversation about why I was here at home and not there at the ranch was forgotten.

Mom rushed downstairs to be with her sister the second she got home. Even Dad came down to visit, and suddenly my dour room was the happening place to be. Ashley gave my dad crap for keeping me locked up down here—one of the many reasons why I loved her. "This is no place for a seventeen-year-old girl, Teren. She should be staying at the ranch with the other purebloods."

Dad glared at me, like I'd coached Ashley on what to say. "It's ... complicated," he answered.

Ashley laughed. "Everything about the Adams is." She sobered, and her tone grew serious again. "But the ranch is where she should be, as I'm sure you know."

Dad gave me a look that almost broke my heart. I stayed firm in my expression though. The change would be difficult on all of us, but Ash was right ... I belonged with the others now.

Julian came home a bit later, and joined us in my room. Ashley told him where his cake was and he blurred back upstairs to get it. He had a faint pot smell about him that I could tell irritated my parents, but he was sober so they didn't say anything about it. When he came back downstairs with his white on white cake, Dad lit his candles and we all sang Happy Birthday to each other. While Julian ate his cake, Mom bugged Ashley about staying here at the house instead of the ranch.

"We've got plenty of room, and then I'll be able to see more of you," she begged.

Julian cast a quick glance in my direction. As far as I knew, the school-wide party was still happening on Saturday. Hunter had some plan to get my parents out of the house, but Ashley and Christian staying here would complicate matters. Of course, I wasn't sure if Hunter even remembered that he'd offered to lure Mom and Dad away. He sort of had more important things on his mind now, thanks to Jake. Saturday night could blow up in our faces. Julian should have put a stop to it ages ago. Maybe he still could.

Ashley sighed as she ate a clean section of my broken cake. "I know, Em, but Christian loves the ranch, and he asked to stay there." She smirked. "He's got a thing for animals. He can't get over the fact that there aren't any horses though. He says it's unnatural." She shared a look with Mom and Dad and they all started laughing.

I knew the purebloods were partly to blame for that, so I joined in with them. Horses were naturally skittish around vampires, even mixed blood vampires, but it was more that Halina had a taste for them. We'd tried having ponies when Julian and I were younger, but, they didn't last too long. Halina still apologized to us for eating them.

When Starla burst through the front doors with Jacen, everyone headed back upstairs. Dad carried Ashley like she was a child, making her giggle. The pesky sun was still up, so I had to wait downstairs and listen to everyone greet our "mother".

Trey showed up not too much later, and I listened to everyone greeting him. Trey was thrilled that the party had been moved to the ranch, and was eager to get going. I heard him tell Julian that he'd been dying to see it for forever. Funny thing was, he'd seen it several months ago and just didn't remember, thanks to Halina.

It was just last night that Dad had decided to move the party to the ranch; we'd always had it at the house in the city before now. But Dad wanted to start exposing Jake to friendly vampire behavior, so he could begin to see that we weren't evil, and it was easier and safer for all of us to go over there, then to risk removing Jake from the ranch to bring him here. I was eager for Jake to not hate us, so my boyfriend had more free time, so I wasn't complaining about the change of location.

While Trey joked around that our mom (meaning Starla) looked smoking hot tonight, I thought back to the ill-fated prom we'd all gone to. Trey had seemed kind of into me that night. I wasn't sure if it was just circumstantial on his part, or if there was something brewing there. I hoped not. I didn't want to hurt him, and my heart definitely belonged to Hunter.

Trey asked where I was and Julian told him I was still getting ready. Looking down at my worn jeans and frayed t-shirt, I decided I might as well spend the time I had making myself presentable. I found a cute, all-black party dress to wear, and paired it with some electric blue heels. Two inchers, since that was all my dad would allow me to wear. I curled my dark brown locks and expertly applied mascara, blush and lipstick. Maybe I'd look alive for once.

When I was done, mere minutes of daylight were left. Trey was starving, Starla was bored, but my family was waiting for me, so we could all go to the ranch together. It bothered me that we were getting such a late start thanks to me, but since I was one of the guests of honor, it wouldn't be much of a party until I arrived.

I went to my foyer, the room below the closet, when only a minute of daylight remained. After I instinctually knew the sun was down, I pushed the door in the ceiling aside, replaced the chair, and hopped up into the closet. I listened at the closet door to make sure no unsuspecting humans, i.e., Trey, noticed my arrival. From the way his voice echoed back to me, I knew he wasn't facing the closet door. Julian probably had something to do with that. Opening the closet, I slipped into the room. Mom saw me, and smiled a greeting. Then she cocked an eyebrow at my dress and gave me a subtle thumbs up.

Encouraged, I stepped into the center of the room. "Ready?" I asked no one in particular.

None of the vampires were surprised to see me, but I caught Trey unawares. He jumped a bit as he turned around, then he did a double take. "Damn, Little A, you do clean up nice." Extending his arms wide, he walked over to me. "Give us a hug, it's been way too long."

Familiar with his playful form of flirting, and glad that things between us weren't weird, I held up my hand to stop him from putting his arms around me. "Who exactly is this 'us' you're referring to? Have you finally gone crazy, Trey?"

He put his hands over his heart like I'd ripped it out of his chest. "Only with my undying love for you, sweet thing."

As I rolled my eyes and shook my head, a stab of pain went through me. If this were any other night, I'd share a look and a laugh with Arianna, and we would have bonded over how imbecilic Trey was. But Arianna was gone, lost to Julian and me forever. I suddenly felt like crying, but I pasted a smile on my face instead. "I have a sudden desire to stuff myself with cake. Let's hit the road."

Trey clapped his hands together. "Mmmm, cake. I'm so hungry I could eat a horse."

"Me too," I joked. I flicked a glance at Ashley and she snorted.

Trey pointed to me as he headed for the door. "You're sitting by me, Little A. You need to tell me the real reason why you ditched me and my awesomeness for homeschooling."

With a laugh, I shook my head at him. His awesomeness was hardly the reason I'd "ditched". As people started grabbing jackets and purses, a disturbing thought settled over me. Walking up to Julian, I placed a hand on his shoulder and whispered, "I can't ride in the car with Trey."

Julian half-turned toward me while keeping an eye on his friend. "Because of the homeschooling thing? Just tell him you got tired of going to class, he'll understand that."

I turned him all the way toward me. "No, because the minute I start heading toward Hunter ..." My voice trailed off as embarrassment surged into me. If my cheeks could still turn red, I was sure they would have. Hunter usually sped to me before we went anywhere, even if we were going to the ranch, but my family was already late, so I'd be meeting him there tonight. Flying to him was going to be ... interesting.

Julian's cheeks did turn red. "Oh ... right. Don't worry about it. I'll tell him you're annoyed with Starla and don't want to ride with her. He'll understand." Starla looked up from digging in her purse and frowned. Julian shrugged. Like it or not, sometimes we needed a scapegoat, and she was the best one we had. She shook her head like she really didn't care ... her perfectly styled coif didn't move an inch.

I ended up riding to the ranch with Dad in his car. Mom and Ashley followed behind us in Alanna's sedan; Ashley had borrowed it this afternoon to come over and surprise us with our cakes. Starla, Jacen, Trey, and Julian made up the final car in our procession. Trey seemed a little bummed that I wasn't riding with them, until he got into the car with my brother. Then he was all playful laughs and gentle teasing.

My bond with Hunter kicked in the moment we set off down the street. It always started out mildly, so I gripped my chair and breathed in and out as deeply as I could. Dad glanced my way every five seconds. "You all right?" he asked.

I nodded, slowly and calmly. "Yeah, I'm fine." I could do this. I could control the bond and not let the bond control me. I was going to win this time.

Unfortunately for me, the bond amplified the closer I got to Hunter, and it didn't take too long for the sensation to become unbearable. When we were halfway to the ranch, I was panting, squirming in the seat, and repeatedly running my fingers through my hair. I'd kicked off my shoes and was running the edge of my feet up and down my bare calves. I couldn't control anything I was doing, and it was only getting worse as the pull became stronger. The slow pace of Dad's car was only adding to the torture. If I were on my own two feet, I would have been with him by now.

"You still all right?" Dad asked, concern in his voice.

I unintentionally groaned. God, this was so embarrassing. "No," I finally bit out. "I can't do this. Stop the car."

"Nika, you have to learn to control—"

"Stop the car and let me run!" I snapped. The battle was lost. I had no control left to me, and if Dad didn't stop the car, I'd jump out of a moving vehicle.

Sighing, Dad turned on his blinker and pulled over. I was antsy watching the car change lanes. Starla's car was behind us, with Alanna's car making up the rear. Everyone in our caravan changed lanes too, like they were all going to pull over, but I didn't care. I needed out. My hands were clawing the door handle when the tires crunched along the pebbles beside the highway. I had the door open and one foot out before the car completely stopped moving.

"Wait, Nika ..." Dad grabbed my arm as I leaned out the door. I twisted back around to him and hissed in his face with fangs extended. My violent reaction startled him enough that he let me go. I was gone a split-second later, flying over small sharp stones that pricked the soles of my bare feet. In the breeze, I heard someone say, "Fix Trey before you go …" but I didn't care about Trey anymore. I didn't care if he'd seen my fangs or if he'd seen me streak from the car. All I cared about was the fact that Hunter's blood was calling to me, and I needed to answer him.

Now that I was unimpeded by my father's slow-moving vehicle, it took me no time at all to reach the ranch. I was tearing my feet to pieces on the rough terrain, but the tiny cuts healed with each step I took, leaving only a raw, aching sensation. I flew up the long gravel driveway to the main house, only stopping when I reached the ornate gate with the family name in giant letters above it. My hand reached out to smash the gate open, but it swung inward before I could. The hinges squealed in protest at the swiftness of the opening, but my heart soared because of the person who'd opened them—Hunter.

I leapt into his arms once the crack in the gate was wide enough. He staggered back with the force of me, then dropped us to the ground in the patchy, dry grass beside the gate. He was on top of me an instant later as our mouths ferociously attacked the others. His hands caressed my body, sliding up under my dress. My fingers raked down his chest, ripping the buttons holding his shirt closed. When it fluttered open in the breeze, Hunter ripped it off his body with a growl.

The lights above the looming gate next to us were facing the other direction, and Hunter and I were bathed in darkness. Our eyes glowed to their fullest, highlighting our bodies. Hunter's face was a mixture of pain and desire. My slow journey to him had been difficult on us both. We were equally out of control, and weren't going to be able to stop this. I worked on his jeans while his fingers tore down the straps of my dress, exposing my bra-covered chest to the air. He reached around the back and unzipped the dress while I shoved his jeans down his hips. Neither one of us spoke besides groans and grunts. That was all the use for words we had right now.

After he pulled my dress down my legs, I pushed him to his back and ripped off his jeans. Seeing how much he wanted me bumped my frenzy up a notch. My fangs dropped as I grabbed the waistband of his underwear. I needed him. Now.

After I pulled them off, Hunter flipped me to my back and ripped the rest of my clothes away. My body was pounding with desire I wanted him so badly. He moved into position and I nearly screamed at him to take me. It had been so long since our one time together. Just as he started, headlights flashed over our bare bodies. I instantly snapped out of my daze, and remembered where I was and what I was doing.

Pushing Hunter off of me, I grabbed my dress, holding it against me like a shield. Hunter grabbed his pants and placed them over his privates, just as a SUV rolled passed the gates. It jerked to a stop when the occupants noticed us huddled in the dark grass. Ben opened the driver's side door and ran around to where we were sitting. I groaned, mortified, and made sure everything on me was as hidden as possible.

"Nika! Hunter! Are you okay? What's ... ?" Ben slowed to a walk when he finally understood just what he'd stumbled across. His hands went to his hips as his eyes narrowed at Hunter. "What's going on here?"

Oh, God ... if he'd been just a little later, if we'd reacted just a little slower ...

As if my night couldn't get any worse, the rear passenger door closest to us opened. A youthful blonde jumped out, and her pale eyes widened by a foot. "Whoa! You're naked!" Ben's preteen daughter, Olivia.

I laid back in the grass, wanting to die.

CHAPTER NINE

Nika

BEN TRIED TO shove Olivia back in the car while covering her eyes at the same time. It was a losing battle, since Olivia could bob and weave like a professional boxer. I covered my eyes instead, wishing my life away and willing the tears to stay in my body. The last thing Olivia needed right now was to see blood-red streaks down my cheeks. She'd never understand what was happening, and thanks to her DNA, we couldn't compel her to forget.

Ben gave up on Olivia and tried his wife instead. "Trace, can you take Olivia and continue up to the house? I need a minute to talk to Hunter and Nika alone."

Tracey had been watching us with an open mouth the entire time, but she snapped her jaw shut and looked back at her husband, then her daughter. "Olivia! Sit down and buckle up!" Olivia obeyed her mom, but she asked questions the entire time. "Why are they naked? Were they having sex? Isn't Nika kind of young? I mean, don't you have to be old and married? That's what Ms. Wilson said, but I don't know if I believe her. Johnny told me anybody can do it. Can anybody do it, Mom? Do you and Dad do it? Am I going to have a brother or sister soon?"

Tracey was bright red by the time she scooted over to the driver's side and stomped on the gas.

When they were gone, Ben crossed his arms over his chest and glared at us. "Sex Ed was not a lesson I wanted to teach her about tonight." He turned around so we could get dressed. "What were the two of you thinking?"

Hunter had a scowl on his face as he yanked his underwear back on. "We weren't. It was the bond. It got kicked into overdrive."

I frowned at the look on his face, the harsh way he was getting dressed. Yeah, it was embarrassing getting caught, but ... up until then, it had been amazing. Feeling strange, I timidly tried to put my underwear back on. I couldn't. They were ripped beyond the point that I could wear them, and the hooks for my bra were completely torn off. Hunter had been a little impatient there at the end. A fact that saddened me now. We'd been so close.

"Sorry, Uncle Ben," I muttered, tossing aside my undergarments and slipping on my dress. There were slight tears and wrinkles in the fabric, and it was covered in grass and dirt, but at least it hid my nakedness for the time being. I could change once we got to the ranch. Great. How would I explain that to Dad? Oh well, Ben would probably tell him what happened anyway. Or Liv. She'd probably tell the entire house what had happened. Wonderful.

When I stood up, Ben risked a glance over his shoulder. Seeing we were dressed, he turned around. Hunter had his pants and shirt on, but he couldn't button his shirt and it hung open. He was scowling at the ground where my ruined undergarments were resting. I picked them up so he'd stop staring. So far, Ben hadn't noticed them, and I'd prefer it if it stayed that way.

Ben sighed and shook his head. Raking a hand through his blonde, highlighted hair, he told us, "I know it's not your fault. I remember what it was like when Teren and Emma went through it." He frowned, and a brief shudder went through him. "Anyway, we should probably get to the house. I'm assuming your parents are on their way?"

I nodded. Yeah, they were moving again, inching their way to the ranch at a moderate, human pace. Ben nodded and looked me over. Barefoot, rumpled, and covered in grass, I was sure I was quite a sight. With a smile and a shake of his head, he told me, "Happy Birthday, Nika. I'll hug you a little later, if you don't mind."

I managed a weak laugh. "Thanks."

As we trudged along to the house, Hunter's mood darkened even more. I grabbed his hand, trying to lighten his emotions, but it didn't help. Irritated, he muttered, "I shouldn't have left Jake alone in there."

I bit my cheek, but it wasn't enough to bite back the comment I felt coming. "He's not alone. He's with Gabriel, Rory, Cleo, and my grandparents. You're not his *only* bodyguard, you know."

Hunter's dark eyes swung down to me. "I know, but I still should have stayed close to him." His eyes returned to the gravel beneath our feet; the glow of his eyes highlighted every pebble. "This bond is getting ridiculous. It's distracting me from what I need to do."

Stopping on the driveway, I glared at him. "So, I'm a distraction now? Being bonded to me is annoying you? Are you wishing you'd left me for dead?"

I knew he didn't mean it like that, but his "duty" superseding me *yet again* was frustrating as hell. Plus I was doing the walk of shame barefoot and braless *on my birthday!* Holding my tongue was beyond me at this point. I jerked my hand away from his.

Hunter stopped with me and Ben slowed, but kept walking to give us some privacy. "No ... I didn't mean it like that." He cupped my cheeks. "You're everything to me. You're my number one priority, don't ever think you're not. It's not the bond I dislike, it's this obsessive ... pull ... that clouds my mind, makes me do rash, careless things, makes me ... lose control." He indicated the remains of my underwear in my hand. "I don't like losing control."

Hunter gave me a kiss on the cheek to take the sting out of his words, and we continued walking hand in hand. Ben looked back at us, saw we were following, and then turned back around. When the main home at the ranch came into view—the steepled points of the roof, the smooth, circular driveway with the massive fountain of a woman crying in the center of it—Hunter sighed.

"I don't like you being here. As I've told Teren and Halina multiple times, this party is a bad idea. They seem to think it will be fine with how many of us there are tonight, and they assigned Rory and Cleo to watch Jake like a hawk, but still ... this isn't the time to let our guard down. Not with Jake free from his room, walking around like he's one of us. He's a loose cannon. There's no telling what he'll do given the right circumstances." He looked back at me with a frown. "But we have to let him be free otherwise he'll never accept us, and Teren thinks a birthday party is the perfect way to show him how normal we are. I don't like it though. We're stuck in a damn catch 22. Damned if we do, damned if we don't. You and your brother shouldn't be here tonight."

We'd held hands again during our walk, and I squeezed his hard. I was still embarrassed, frustrated and sore, and the last thing I wanted to hear about was Jake the vampire hunter. An irritated huff escaped me. "Hunter, you're seriously getting on my nerves. First, you want me at the ranch so our bond doesn't kick in, and then you say I shouldn't be here because Jake is too much of a threat. Which is it?" I glared up at his sullen face. "Because it can't be both of those things."

Frowning, he released my hand and ran his fingers through his hair. "I don't know, Nika. I don't have all the answers. I'm not perfect," he muttered.

"Oh, I know that," I retorted. "I'm going upstairs to change." After that, I stormed off to the house at a fast walk that was nearly a jog. When I breezed by Ben, he glanced back at Hunter. I saw Ben give Hunter a sympathetic smile, and I nearly snapped at him too. I didn't need to see male camaraderie right now either. I wished I could blur and get away from both of them fast, but I knew I couldn't. Ben's car was parked right outside the triple front doors, and I could hear Olivia in the entryway, asking where Julian was, and regaling Alanna with her story about coming across Hunter and I in our birthday suits.

I gritted my teeth and walked around to the back of the house. I didn't feel like seeing anybody yet. Once I was sure I was away from prying eyes, I zoomed up to my room faster than light. In my frustration, I slammed the door shut. I knew Olivia wouldn't hear me, but Hunter and the rest of my family would. Good ... I wanted Hunter to know I was irritated with him.

I changed into fresh clothes—jeans and a T-shirt—then sat on my bed and waited for Julian and my parents to get here. Safety in numbers. I felt them in the driveway, so I cracked open my bedroom door. When I walked out into the hallway, just that brief step toward Hunter made the bond kick in. We weren't nearly as far apart as we usually were, so the pull wasn't nearly as strong, but it was enough to make me close my eyes and breathe heavier.

I tried walking to him at a human pace, but I couldn't. When I got to the nearest set of stairs, I blurred down them. I heard Olivia ask Hunter, "What's wrong with you?" and I knew he was feeling this too. I heard Hunter excuse himself, then felt his presence rushing toward me. We collided at the base of the staircase. Hunter shoved me against the wall, his lips on my neck. I hooked a leg around him and murmured, "I'm sorry. I know you're just looking out for me." I hadn't meant to apologize, but the glorious relief of joining up with him brought it out of me.

Panting, Hunter pulled backed to stare into my eyes. "I'm sorry things are so complicated right now. It won't always be like this, I promise. Someday we'll be together, and nothing will be able to keep us apart."

I cupped his cheek, wishing that day was today. "I can't wait."

"Me either." Just as he lowered his lips to mine, someone behind Hunter coughed. We both directed our attention that way, and I saw Jake standing a few feet away, watching us with his arms crossed over his chest. He was alone, unsupervised. He raised a hand in greeting when he saw that we'd spotted him spying on us.

"The sooner we get rid of him, the better," Hunter sighed under his breath. Hunter looked around for Rory and Cleo, but Jake's human bodyguards were nowhere around.

Jake understood what Hunter was searching for and pointed toward the entryway. "Your minions are greeting the new arrivals. I was too, but I slipped out." He crooked a grin. "Needed air."

Hunter's expression darkened. He looked about to zip off to collect Rory and Cleo, but just then they appeared. Rory's face was bright red, and Cleo looked frantic. They froze when they saw Hunter. Hunter pointed at Jake. "Lose something?" he asked, venom in his voice.

Rory grabbed Jake and pinned his arms behind him. "There was a moment of chaos when the young girl spotted Julian, and he got away from us. It won't happen again."

Hunter raised an eyebrow in warning. "It better not. He could have done a lot worse than run in here. Everything I hold of value is under this roof. Try and keep that in mind."

Rory and Cleo both nodded. Hunter indicated with his head for them to bring Jake back into the entryway, and the group of us went to meet up with everyone else. The room was packed when I got there, and I could easily see how Jake had managed to sneak away.

Julian was near the doors, trying to detach himself from Olivia, who had clamped onto his side like a barnacle. Christian was hugging his wife, Ashley. Christian was quite a few years older than Ashley, and in an ironic twist of fate, he had lost almost all of his hair while Ashley had gained hers. Grandma Linda was by Christian's side, ready to hug her daughter when her husband was through with her. Halina was standing by Ben and Tracey. Tracey's eyes were wide as Halina played with a long strand of her golden hair. Halina was laughing. I think she enjoyed making Tracey squirm. Intimidating people was a favorite pastime of hers, one she didn't get to partake in much anymore.

Trey was looking around the home slack-jawed. It was an expression I remembered seeing on him the first time he came here. If it wasn't already so late in the evening, I'd take him upstairs and show him the sauna, since he'd been so impressed with it before. "Whoa, dude ... why don't you live here all the time?"

Good question, Trey. For me at least anyway. Maybe curious to see how I was doing, Dad turned his head from where he was greeting Alanna and Grandpa Jack, and locked gazes with me. His pleasant smile leveled as he noticed my outfit. It was much plainer than the fancy dress I'd arrived in. I glanced at Hunter, but he'd changed his shirt, and from what I could tell, there weren't any noticeable strands of grass in his hair. There wasn't any physical evidence of our romp, but Dad knew, regardless.

I shifted my focus from him to Mom. Dad was partly to blame for the strength of the bond by keeping us apart. If he didn't like it, then he should let us live together. Mom was hugging Imogen, while Starla was throwing her arms around Gabriel. Jacen was standing by Starla's side, smiling up at his leader. Everyone important in my life was here. Everyone but Arianna. She was the only one missing, and her absence stung me as much as it stung my brother.

Hunter kept his eyes glued on Jake, but he didn't seem to be doing much of anything other than watching. I was sure his mind was going a mile a minute with plans of escape though. Or maybe he was planning an attack. That seemed foolish to me. There were too many of us, he'd never make it out alive. Someone I loved would probably get hurt if that happened though, so I prayed Jake was a smart, life-loving man.

After everyone was greeted, and Olivia was detached from Julian's body, we all headed outside, to the patio. There were pink and blue streamers around every piece of furniture, clumps of pastel balloons around the base of every flowerpot, and Happy Birthday confetti strewn about the tables, and the cement floor. Everyone's shoes were covered with the shiny metallic lettering in no time. It was a gorgeous night, the moon was full and bright, and there was a breeze that warmed my chilly skin. Citronella candles kept the bugs at bay, while recessed lighting around the deck kept the glow of our vampire eyes at bay. Popular music that Julian and I liked was streaming through outdoor speakers shaped like rocks. Aside from the lack of my best friend, and Rory and Cleo physically keeping a hold of the family prisoner, it was a perfect party.

Grandpa Jack made burgers for anyone who might be hungry, while Imogen set out a pyramid of pink and blue cupcakes. There was sherbet punch available for the humans and a "special" drink available for the vampires. That one was left simmering in the kitchen, since not every human in attendance knew our little secret.

When the party was in full swing, Alanna and Grandma Linda brought out armfuls of presents. I groaned as I looked at them all. I had practically everything I wanted already; I really didn't need anything else. Hunter's expression turned guilty as he eyed the gifts being put on the table. "I ... uh ... with your conversion and Jake ... I didn't have time to shop. I'm sorry, I didn't get you anything for your birthday. Is there something special you'd like?"

As I eyed a pink and white polka-dotted oblong box, I instantly thought of something he could give me that no one else could. It was something I really wanted too, and he didn't even have to shop for it. He had it with him everywhere he went. Turning to Hunter, I slung my arms around his waist. "As it turns out, there is something I want from you."

Hunter's eyes briefly flashed to Jake sitting on a bench with Rory and Cleo. "Oh? And what's that? Because if this is about earlier, I don't think—"

I cut him off before he could finish that thought. "No, it's not. It's something else."

I looked around the backyard, hoping no one was paying us too close attention. Starla and Jacen had already vanished. Trey was trying to convince Julian to talk "Teren and Emma" into going into the hot tub with them, because he wanted to see Emma in a bathing suit. Julian was trying not to gag, while my dad was trying not to laugh. Halina and Gabriel were having an argument, while Imogen, Alanna, and my mom were in the kitchen having refreshments. The rest of the guests were human and couldn't hear Hunter and me talking. And of them, only Jake was paying attention to us.

Leaning up to Hunter's ear, I whispered, "I want your blood. I want to share with you again."

When I pulled away to look at his face, I saw the conflict there—the desire, the uncertainty. "Nika, I don't ..."

I cupped his cheek. "You wanted to know what I want, and that's it. If we can't ... go all the way yet, and I really don't understand why we can't, then at least we can share that intimacy." He still seemed unsure, so I leaned up and kissed him. "Please," I murmured between our lips, "I want you so much."

Hunter's hand on my waist slipped just a bit lower to rest on my hip. As tightly pressed against him as I was, I could feel him stirring, hardening. He wanted me there was no denying that, it was just a matter of him giving into it. I was just about to kiss him again, maybe lower my fangs and let them graze his neck, when a young voice broke through my moment. "Are you going to get naked again?"

I looked down at Olivia. "It's rude to interrupt people when they're talking, Liv."

She cringed. "Sorry. Dad gets after me all the time for that. I was just wondering if I needed to cover my eyes or something. You know, if you guys were going to roll around without your clothes on again."

Olivia wasn't being nearly as quiet as I'd been, and I saw Dad's head snap my way as he heard her. I swallowed. Great. So much for keeping that little piece of information from him. Looking around, I saw that Julian had heard too. His eyes were much too wide and much too amused.

Before I could answer Liv's question, or drain her dry for squealing on me, she asked another string of questions—all centered around Jake, Rory, and Cleo. "Who are those three? Do they live here with your Grandpa? Why are they always touching? Are they all married? Can you marry more than one person? I didn't think so, but my friend Mary says a lot of people around here have more than one spouse. Is that true?"

I had a headache just listening to her. Julian was laughing at this point, and Ben finally caught on to the fact that his daughter was intruding on personal boundaries again. With my hands raised, I stepped away from her. And into Jake. He'd stood from the bench, and I'd backed right into him. Rory and Cleo immediately jerked him away from me as I spun around in surprise. Jake gave me a disarming smile. "Didn't mean to spook you, just stretching my legs."

Hunter was in front of me in a flash. "Not a problem," he evenly said.

Jake narrowed his eyes at Hunter. I had a feeling that even though this entire idea had been Dad's to begin with, Hunter was number one on Jake's hit list. Jake glanced at me, his face twisted in disgust. "Isn't she a little young for you? For the life you've given her? She's just a child ... might as well turn the chatty one next."

Sensing that inappropriate things were going to be mentioned, Ben hurried Olivia into the house. Before she vanished, I heard her ask, "What does he mean by turn? Do you think I'm chatty?"

Hunter glanced at Trey, but he wasn't paying attention to us. A swarm of gnats around one of the torches had him mesmerized. Ashley was distracting Christian by showing him a flower garden along the side of the house. Nobody not in the loop was listening. "I did it to save her life," Hunter said. "My only other choice was to let her die."

Jake snorted. "In case you hadn't noticed, vampire, she *is* dead."

I lifted my chin. "My body, not my soul."

Jake narrowed his eyes. "That's debatable. You are keeping me prisoner after all."

Dad stepped up to our group. "You're a guest, not a prisoner."

Jake snapped his eyes to Dad's. "Guests get to leave, and they aren't manhandled every second of every day." He lifted his arms for emphasis. I could see the bruises beginning to form from where Rory and Cleo had been clutching him all night. Dad saw it too. To them, he said, "Let him go." The pair were reluctant, but they eventually dropped Jake. He rubbed his arms. "Thanks. I guess I'll be on my way then."

Hunter put a hand on his shoulder. "You can't leave yet. I'm sorry, but this is the only way."

Jake clenched his jaw. "I can't stay. I have ..." he snapped his mouth shut, and bit back whatever he'd been going to say. Instead, he locked eyes with Hunter and murmured, "Like I said, prisoner. And if it's all right with my *warden*, I'd like to go back to my room."

Hunter glanced at Dad, who nodded once. To Rory, Hunter said, "Take him back."

While Rory led him away, Jake smirked and told Hunter, "Better give her what she wants, demon ... since you made her."

I ground my teeth to stop the angry retort from escaping my lips. The only comeback I had was *shut up*, and that really wasn't impressive enough to say. While I fumed, Trey came up and slung a hand over my shoulder. "What's going on, Little A? And who's the grumpy dude the blockhead's taking away? He drunk or something?"

Looking over my shoulder, I shrugged away from Trey's affection. "Yeah ... or something."

Trey nodded. Clearly not liking Trey being so friendly with me, Hunter pulled me into his side. He had a sneer on his face, and I almost thought a possessive growl was going to escape his lips. That confrontation with Jake had put him on edge. Really, the entire evening had. Trey frowned at Hunter. He still didn't much care for my boyfriend, since Hunter had broken my heart not too long ago. There had been good reason for the pain, and we were past it now, but I would never be able to convince Trey to forgive Hunter unless I compelled him to do it, and I didn't want to use my powers that way.

Ignoring Hunter, Trey said, "So, Nika ... what is it you want that only demon-boy here can give you?"

I cringed that he'd heard that, and was positive Hunter had a new nickname now. My dad crossed his arms over his chest. "I think this party is just about over."

Alanna and Imogen insisted we open our presents before we left, so Dad wasn't able to get us out of there as quickly as he would have liked. Forty-five minutes later though, we were all packed up and ready to go. Hunter held the rear passenger's side door open for me. "Well, that could have gone worse," he said, his deep voice completely serious.

"My dad called the party quits early, pretty much because of you and me." I glanced to the front door, where Dad was saying goodbye to his mom. "And I'm pretty sure I'm going to get a lecture about how I'm too young for a relationship as intense as ours, and I need to learn to control the bond better."

Hunter leaned on the door, resting his chin on his arms. "Jake could have tried to escape, or he could have attempted to fight his way out of the house, or he could have taken a hostage. All things considered, I think the party went well."

I smiled at him. At least he seemed to be in a better mood than before. Of course, that could be because I was finally leaving and he didn't have to worry about my safety. I struggled to keep my grin. "I suppose."

Hunter sighed as he watched me. Reaching out, he brushed a finger down my cheek. "I'm sorry your party wasn't what you wanted it to be." He looked around the parking lot. My parents were still in the house, and Julian and Trey were walking across the cobblestone toward us. In a low voice that would have been inaudible to a human, he told me, "I'll consider giving you what you asked for your present."

I was so surprised by that, my fangs almost released. "You will?"

He nodded, then leaned over the open door to kiss me. "Yeah." Pulling back, he frowned. "It seems unfair though. It would be a gift for me too."

My giddiness nearly overwhelmed me. I wanted to share that intimacy with him again so badly. While I struggled to control my excitement, I noticed the hollowness of his features. I ran my hand along his stubbled jaw. "You're tired. You should rest."

The seductiveness of his smile inflamed my dead heart. "I will ... later." I knew he wouldn't. I knew he'd stay up all night and probably all day doing his "duty," and I also knew there was nothing I could do or say to stop him. Hunter just needed to do this. For me. For our nest, because family was just as important to him as it was to my dad ... as it was to me. It was a pity Hunter couldn't have children anymore. He would have been an excellent father.

As Hunter and I were sappily staring into each other's eyes, Mom and Ashley walked out to the car arm in arm. "Are you sure you won't reconsider staying at the house? We could have breakfast together? And it's not like we don't have animals too. Spike may not move much anymore, but still ..."

Ashley laughed at my mom's attempt to persuade her. "No, we're going to stay here, Em."

I looked over to see Mom glance back at the house with a frown on her lips. "I don't like it, Ash. Not with ... not with our guest here." I looked up at Hunter, and I knew he agreed with my mom's concern. Ashley didn't. "He's fine. He's being watched around the clock. He won't do anything to me or Christian. And besides, maybe I can talk to him? Give him an inside scoop on what vampires are really like."

Mom stopped in her tracks. "No, you stay away from him."

While I watched Mom and Ashley, Julian shoved Trey into the middle of the car. I wasn't sure if Julian was paying attention to the conversation or not, but Dad was. He came up to them and put a hand on Mom's shoulder. "Em, it's important that we're as normal with him as we can be. He needs to see us as people. Avoiding him won't help anything, and Ashley's right, he's being watched. She'll be as safe as can be."

Mom lifted an eyebrow at him. "And that's why we're running back home with the children?"

Dad looked my way, a frown on his face. "No, that has nothing to do with Jake."

I hastily dropped my eyes, but continued listening. Dad was telling Mom, "Tonight was a good start, but I think he needs to see more of us being a family. I thought we'd come back up this weekend? We could all hang out together? Do some work around the ranch? I know Dad could use the help."

Julian snapped his head toward our parents. "No, I don't want to do that."

I blinked and looked at my brother. I guess he was paying attention. For a moment, I thought he just didn't want to help out around the ranch, but then I remembered the secret party. He must still want it to happen, so he could have one more chance with Arianna.

Trey also looked over at Julian. "Don't wanna do what? Sit by the window? Cause I already called the hump. Sorry." Trey smiled and looked back at me still standing in the open door. I knew exactly why Trey had called the middle seat. So did Hunter. The scowl on his face would have given Trey goose bumps ... if he'd noticed.

Dad glanced at Julian, then back to Mom and Ashley. "We can talk about it later. I think there are a few other things we need to discuss first."

I sighed, gave Hunter one last kiss, and then slunk into the car beside Trey. I knew that most of the things Dad wanted to discuss involved me. If he only knew about Julian's school-wide party on Saturday, maybe he would share the scolding. I wasn't about to tell on my brother though.

Trey scooted toward me when I sat down. Hunter opened the door wider and leaned into the car. "If you want to live to see tomorrow, you'll keep your distance from my girlfriend." I immediately frowned at Hunter. Threatening Trey wasn't necessary. Hunter glanced my way, but he didn't appear apologetic in the slightest.

Trey inched toward Julian. "Whatever, dude. I was just settling my butt cheeks." Hunter grudgingly closed the door on us. As my parents got into the front seat, Trey looked around for Starla. "So, your mom just up and left you at the party? On your birthday?" Mom and Dad exchanged a glance as they sat down. Sometimes Starla wasn't the most maternal person. Or reliable. If there was something she'd rather be doing than pretending to be our mom, more often than not, she'd do it.

Julian scratched the side of his neck. "Uh, well, I don't ... I'm sure she had a reason."

Shaking his head, Trey let out an annoyed grunt. "Yeah, I'm sure. And I thought my parents were dicks." He nodded up at my actual parents. "Cool of you guys to stick around. How are you related again?"

Dad cocked his head as he started the car. "It's ... complicated."

Trey nodded, already tuning him out. "Yeah ..." He raised his fingers at Hunter as we started to pull away. Hunter clenched his jaw, and an annoyed growl vibrated through the car. Being human, Trey didn't hear it.

"Knock it off, Trey," I muttered. Dad started down the driveway and I watched Hunter getting smaller and smaller in the rearview mirror. As his shape receded, the ache in my chest grew. I knew it would be a thousand times worse by the time we got home.

Trey scoffed and laid his head back on the seat. "Dude needs to chill. It's not like we're anything but friends anyway." Lifting his head, he asked, "Speaking of friendship, want to tell me—the best friend of your twin brother and therefore vicariously the best friend of you—why you left school?" He leaned into my side with his eyebrows raised. When my bare arm touched his, he added, "And why are you so freaking cold?" To my parents, he said, "Can you guys turn the heat up? She's a popsicle back here."

With an amused smile on his face, Dad did as Trey asked. As the car filled with warmth, I sighed and wondered what to tell Trey that wouldn't hurt his feelings. All I could come up with was, "I missed my family, so I wanted to go back to homeschooling." Locking gazes with my dad in the rearview mirror, I added, for his benefit, "The ranch is where I belong."

Dad averted his eyes, and his hands tightened on the steering wheel. I knew I was pushing it, so I clamped my mouth shut and didn't say anything else.

CHAPTER TEN

Julian

IT WAS SATURDAY. Tonight was the party. And I'd done nothing to ensure that my parents would be out of the house before the entire school showed up. I. was. screwed.

Even worse, my dad was still gung-ho about all of us heading out to the ranch to bond with our captive. Or "guest," as my family was calling Jake. Dad wanted him to see just how normal and unthreatening we all were. In that case, maybe Jake should come to the party too. Then when my parents inevitably broke it up and skinned me alive, he'd see just how normal a family we were. Crap, what the hell was I going to do?

To top it all off, I wasn't even sure when people were going to start arriving. High schoolers could start showing up as early as this afternoon, and I had no idea how I would deal with that if we were all still at home. Mom and Dad were having a debate about that very topic though. Mom wanted to head out to see her sister, Dad wanted to wait until the sun went down, so Nika could come with us.

Dad sipped on his blood while I slurped down a bowl of sugary cereal. I also had a cinnamon roll, glass of juice, and a bowl of fruit waiting for me. Mom hadn't eased up much on the meal making.

"We should have left last night," Dad was saying between sips.

Mom sighed. "I know. But Ashley and Christian wanted a night out on the town, and by the time we all got back, it was too late to wake Julian up and drag him out there. You know how he gets when he's woken up."

I flicked my gaze between the two of them. They realized I was right here, didn't they?

Dad smirked and nodded. He even went so far as to laugh a little. Feeling the need to defend myself, I muttered, "Hey, I'm a lot cheerier than Nika." That wasn't true, but it felt good to say it, and since Nika was sound asleep in her lightproof room, so she couldn't even defend herself. Double bonus.

Dad's amused eyes watched me from over his glass as he took a long drink. Stirring my bowl of strawberry colored milk, I tossed out, "Why don't you guys go up now? I'll stay behind with Nika, and we'll head up after sunset." I crossed my toes, since crossing my fingers would be too obvious.

Mom pursed her lips, considering. Dad looked like he was considering it too, but not coming to the conclusion that Mom was. "I don't know, Julian ..."

Setting my spoon down, I tore off a chunk of my cinnamon roll. "You don't want to leave Nika alone here because of Hunter, right? Because you're worried about what will happen when their bond kicks in ... if no one is around to stop it, right? Well, I can stop it." I shrugged. I really didn't want to physically pry my sister and Hunter apart when the two of them were acting like out of control maniacs, but I knew that was my dad's main hang up. If I could solve that problem, I'd at least have a few hours to solve the party problem.

Mom seemed sold. "We could head up now, and spend a little more time with everyone than we have been. Maybe we could even spend the night tonight, so we have all day on Sunday?" She leaned into Dad's side. "It's been a while since we've checked out the hot tub."

An intrigued expression crossed Dad's face and I shoved the cinnamon roll into my mouth in a vain attempt to distract myself with the sweetness of it. My parents were so embarrassing. Dad cleared his throat, then said, "I don't know, that's a large responsibility, Julian." Mom gave him a pointed glance and Dad tapped his finger against his lip like he was deep in thought; his extended fangs amplified his expression. "Well, I suppose you *are* on the panel now, and you *did* help determine a man's fate, so I guess it's time for me to let you be a little more responsible."

He sighed, like admitting that was hard for him. Knowing what was going down behind my parents' backs today, I immediately felt guilty and irresponsible. I still didn't entirely want to stop it though, if I even could at this point. Right or wrong, if all went well, I'd get to see Arianna tonight and I wanted that to happen ... even if she had moved on.

I felt like complete crap, but I smiled at Dad anyway. "Thanks, Dad. And don't worry, I won't let you down." I felt like I'd just taken a knife and stuck myself in the stomach with it. *I won't let him down?* If he knew about the party, he'd definitely feel let down. Oh well, I felt certain I could get the party broken up before Dad was clued in. Or die trying anyway.

Dad looked over at Mom. "I guess we're leaving. Grab your stuff."

Mom giggled she was so excited. Under her breath, she murmured, "I'll grab that little red bikini you like too."

Dad studied his glass of blood, but I saw the huge smile on his face. Gah! They couldn't leave quickly enough. As Mom left the room to go get ready, I set to work on my food. In between bites, I told Dad, "I'm gonna go hang out with Trey for a bit, but I'll be back long before the sun sets."

Dad acknowledged my comment, then told me, "Call if you need anything. And I mean anything. I'm only a few minutes away."

For the briefest second, I wondered if running out of ice for drinks was something I could call him about. I dismissed the errant thought as I popped a piece of watermelon into my mouth. "Sure thing."

Finishing his breakfast, Dad rinsed out his cup and then Mom's. Over his shoulder, he said, "I'll call Starla and Jacen, have them come over later and give you a hand."

Irritation and frustration ran up my spine, making me drop my fork. "Dad, I got this. I can handle Hunter on my own. And besides, you guys can help detain him on your end. You hold him there, I'll bring Nika to you, and by the time they explode, we'll all be in the same place." Dad and I grimaced at the same time, and I changed my wording. "I didn't mean explode ..."

Dad held up his hand. "I know what you meant. Your idea is a great one, but after the ... incident ... at the birthday party, Hunter is refusing to let Nika zoom out to him. He insists on meeting her here tonight, then running out to the ranch together. Seems like a waste of time to me, but I'm not the one struggling through a brand new sire bond, so ... whatever we can do to make it easier on them."

Because I couldn't resist, I muttered, "Besides letting them live together, you mean."

A definite scowl marred Dad's features and I backpedaled as quickly as I could. Damn it, I needed him in a good mood so he'd leave. "Never mind, I didn't say that. Nika and I will catch up with you later." Standing, I patted his shoulder. "Have a good time."

I started to leave the kitchen as hastily as I could, but Dad called my name. When I looked back at him, he indicated my half-eaten breakfast, and all of the dishes that had gone into preparing said breakfast. "Don't forget to clean up."

His grin was a little smug for my tastes, but I did what he asked without question or complaint. Maybe he'd remember that I'd been compliant when he killed me later tonight. No, I wasn't getting caught. Power of positive thinking.

Later at the park with Trey, I asked if the party was still happening. I was anxious and dreadful of his answer. It was short in coming. Keeping a small ball in the air with his knee, he animatedly told me, "Yeah! Everyone I talked to is still coming." He gave me a sly grin. "Even Arianna."

I frowned and considered flinging the cloth ball into the next county. "You talked to Arianna?" When did that happen?

Trey shook his head as he refocused on his game. "No, but Raquel did. She ran into her and a couple of her friends at the movies." I bit my lip and stopped myself from asking if Arianna's friends were male or female. Trey looked over at me when he missed the ball and it fell to the ground. "You ready for the party? Need help setting up?"

I raised my eyebrows at him. Was I supposed to decorate for this? I'd never hosted a party before. I just assumed all I had to do was provide the place. "Set up? Like do what set up?"

Trey looked at me, dumbfounded. "Uh, food? Soda? Jell-O shots? Don't tell me you don't have anything ready?"

I scratched the back of my neck. "Well, I uh ... I've been busy."

Trey shook his head. "Jesus Christ, Adams. I don't know about you sometimes. It's like your head is only partially screwed on."

Hearing that coming from Trey made me laugh. Trey grabbed his skateboard then started heading toward my car. "Come on, we'll go to my place. I've got everything we need."

I was both surprised and unsurprised. From everything I knew about them, Trey's parents were the type that were ready for a massive get-together at the drop of a hat. And they were also the type who probably wouldn't notice if half of their stash went missing.

Forty-five minutes later, Trey and I were loading up my car with bags of stuff: chips, dip, some trail mix thing made with cereal, peanuts, and caramel, cases of soda, boxes of frozen croissant-wrapped mini hot dogs—or as Trey affectionately called them, "Manna from Heaven"—a tray of Jell-O shooters that Trey just happened to have in his fridge, a gallon tub of vanilla ice cream, and a plate of "special" brownies that smelled suspiciously like Trey's clothes often did.

As I'd predicated, Trey's parents didn't notice him ransacking their kitchen. In truth, they barely even noticed he was home. Trey lived in a house that I would have sworn was a junkyard from the amount of crap on the lawn. There was a car buried under tall grass, and about five lawnmowers. By the front door, there was a toilet with flowers planted in the bowl; the back of it was being used as a dumping ground for various odds and ends. A skateboard, axe handle, and ski pole were sticking out of it now. It was the epitome of Starla's worst nightmare.

Trey shouted he was there and shouted he was leaving, but his parents never emerged and never answered him. I could hear them; they were in the back bedroom, giggling and smoking. Smoking what, I wasn't sure, but from the smell it wasn't cigarettes. When we were back in the car, I asked Trey if he was all right.

He gave me a blank, confused expression. "All right with what?"

I looked away, not sure how to answer that. Trey was used to being largely ignored. It was so opposite from my life, I could barely comprehend it. Even now, I knew my parents were monitoring my position. Trey could probably go wherever he wanted and stay out as late as he wanted and nobody would give him any sort of grief. I was jealous at first, but that faded pretty quickly. I'd rather have my parents care too much, than not at all.

When we got back to my house, Starla and Jacen were there. Starla was flipping through channels on the television. Jacen was massaging her foot while reading a book. Starla looked up when Trey and I walked into the room, and I cringed. I was carrying bags overflowing with food, Trey was holding the platter of Jell-O shooters. Trey didn't seem to be worried at all that Starla had caught us, and happily exclaimed, "Hey, Mrs. A. Looking good, as always." He winked at her and I wanted to smack him. She might not actually be my mom, but she was playing my mom and Trey flirting with her was just ... wrong.

Starla raised an eyebrow while Jacen narrowed his eyes. "Having a party?" she asked.

I felt my gut sink. I was busted already, and the party hadn't even started. Not knowing what else to say, I shrugged and told her the truth. "Um ... yeah."

She nodded, not surprised in the least. "Do the landlords know?" she asked, a smirk on her lips. I knew by landlords she meant my mom and dad.

I shook my head. "No."

Starla smiled as a chuckle escaped her, and she looked over at Jacen. "And just when I thought tonight was going to be boring." Returning her eyes to me, she held out her hand. "Give me something chocolate and salty."

Trey grinned as he set his shots on an end table. "I've got just the thing." He dug into a bag until he found some chocolate-covered pretzels. He tossed them at Starla and she effortlessly caught them. Smiling in approval, she started opening the bag. Trey picked his shots back up and told her, "And we've got brownies for later."

"Awesome," Starla told him, chomping on her treat.

While I walked into the kitchen with Trey, I heard Jacen whisper, "Starla, Teren wouldn't approve—"

She cut him off with a kiss. "He only told us to keep an eye on them; he never mentioned that we had to parent them."

"Yes, but—"

Starla again cut Jacen off with a kiss. "They're safe, and they're at home. I'd say we're doing a bang-up job at this parenting thing. Now stop worrying so much and kiss me."

The sounds of smacking that followed that remark made me cringe, but I appreciated Starla's devil-may-care attitude. Trey shook his head. "Your family's awesome and cool. I can't wait to join it someday." His grin was cocky, like it was a done deal already. I knew better though. Nika would never marry him, not in a million years. Not now. Starla knew it too, and she started laughing from the living room.

"Ah, this is going to be fun," she muttered.

It was a couple of hours before dark when people started showing up. I stressed out every time I opened the door to let someone in. Each new arrival was one more person I'd have to run out of the house if my parents started heading this way. And if Nika and I didn't go to the ranch when the sun set, then Mom and Dad would surely come get us. And with their speed, they could get here pretty quickly.

Starla wasn't concerned. Of course, she was on her third special brownie, so she wasn't really worried about anything. Trey acted as the host, showing people the food and drinks. He turned on some music too, nothing too loud and crazy, just loud enough that it could be heard throughout the house. Nika was singing along downstairs, since she couldn't come out yet.

I relaxed as much as I could, but I was a nervous wreck. On my tenth time of opening the door, I figured out why I was so nervous. It had nothing to do with my parents. It had nothing to do with feeling guilty about having a party behind their backs, or being worried about them busting it up. No, my anxiety was all around seeing Arianna. I realized that the second I opened up the door and Raquel walked through it.

My former crush was a sight for sore eyes. I nearly hugged her, I was so relieved to see her. "Hey there, Julian. Miss me?" she asked, a playful tilt to her dark head.

A genuine smile erupted on my face. "You have no idea," I murmured, throwing the door wide open for her.

She stepped in and looked around. She was wearing a short, frilly sundress, with a light jacket over her shoulders. A while ago, the thought of her standing in my home would have had me on my knees, but things weren't like that anymore. Her dark eyes inspected the people in the living room, and then shifted to the photos along the walls. As I shut the door, she pointed to a picture of Starla, Nika and me at Disneyland. My mom had insisted on all of us wearing mouse ears for the photo; she'd been the one taking the picture. Starla and I had "set-dressed" the house while Trey had been busy in the kitchen. We'd moved so fast, he hadn't even noticed.

"Cute," Raquel said, giving me an amused smile.

I let out a short laugh. "Yeah. Wanna drink?" I indicated the kitchen, where I could hear Trey rattling off the various beverages we had on hand.

Raquel shrugged. "Sure, thanks." I instantly wondered if Russell would show up to bug Raquel. He hadn't really let the breakup go, even if he claimed he was over it.

As I was walking away with her, the doorbell rang again. I gave Raquel an apologetic smile. "Be right back."

She nodded, unperturbed, then headed off to the kitchen without me. I skipped back to the door to let the new arrival into the house. My heart leapt into my throat when Arianna's hazel eyes met mine. I was so stunned, I couldn't even say anything. I just kept staring at her through the semi-open door. After an uncomfortable second, she softly asked, "Can I come in?"

Stupidity flooded through me. "Yeah, yes, of course." I opened the door all the way for her, and swished my hand toward the entryway.

Arianna was in a pair of super-short, khaki shorts. The top she was wearing was bright red, and it twisted into an X right at her cleavage. It was so intriguing that I couldn't stop staring at her chest; she was going to think I was a creeper if she noticed. Stepping into the house, she looked around just like Raquel had. It saddened me. Unlike Raquel, Arianna had been here before. Several times.

She turned in a circle, examining everything. When she was facing me again, I made sure my eyes were safely focused on her face. She gave me a breathtaking smile. "Your home is beautiful," she said. While her comment was nice, her voice made me even sadder. She was using her curt and polite voice, a voice she used with adults and strangers ... it wasn't the voice she used to use with me.

Still staring at her, I started shutting the door. "Thanks, we—"

The door bumped against a body walking through the opening and I redirected my attention to the doorframe. I hadn't realized someone else was here. I immediately opened the door a smidge wider again. "Sorry, I ..."

My throat dried up as I stared at the man who'd been haunting my mind. I had to struggle to hold my fangs up, to not hiss at the stranger like a ticked off cat. Or an irritated vampire. What the hell was Arianna's neighbor doing here? Oh God ... was he here because they really were dating? Somebody shoot me. Right now.

While Arianna's new guy gave me a strange expression, Arianna rushed forward. "Oh, Simon. You okay?"

The blue-eyed, blonde-haired jerk-hole in front of me looked over to *my* girlfriend and smiled. "Yeah, not a big deal." He laughed and lifted his foot. "He just caught my toe is all."

I laughed an obvious, fake laugh and both Simon and Arianna twisted to look at me. I flicked a quick glance at their hands. If he tried to hold her hand here, I'd lose my shit. I'd not only bare my fangs at him, I'd probably tear a small chunk out of his neck. Calm … I needed to stay calm. I didn't know for sure they were together. For all I knew, Simon could be stuck in the friend zone too.

Taking a preventative step, I extended my hand out to him. He couldn't hold her hand If he was holding mine. "Julian Adams. This is my house," I stated. *And my girlfriend*, I almost added.

He tilted his head like he'd heard my silent thought, then he grabbed my hand. "Simon Cutler. Hi."

I shook his hand for longer than was probably socially acceptable as I sized him up. He was of equal height and build to me, but I was positive he didn't have my enhanced abilities. I could take him if I needed to. No, I couldn't fight him. Not even for Arianna.

Maybe sensing that the tension in the room was starting to grow, Arianna cleared her throat and said, "Simon's the neighbor friend I told you about. I invited him to the party, I hope you don't mind. He needed a night out." She sympathetically rubbed Simon's back. I dropped his hand lest I accidently remove his arm from his shoulder.

"No problem. The more the merrier." My smile was tight, my words crisp. Neighbor *friend*? Was he truly just a friend? Or were they more now?

Seemingly uncomfortable, Simon murmured, "I'll get us some drinks," and slunk off toward the kitchen.

I tried not to drill imaginary nails through his back as he walked away, but I failed. After Simon was gone, Arianna shifted on her feet, like she was nervous. "You don't mind him being here, right? I figured it wouldn't be a big deal, since so many people from school were coming. He's a good guy, a good friend, and he's had it tough lately and he really does need to get out and … and I'm rambling, I'll shut up now."

She let out an embarrassed laugh as she tucked a honey-colored strand of hair behind her ear. I started relaxing in her presence—and at the fact that she'd called him a friend twice now. I had to resist the urge to hold her tight though. It was so hard to feel what I felt for her, to remember what she felt for me, but not be able to do anything about it. It was like looking at the thing I wanted most in the world, but not being allowed to touch it. Painful, wasn't an adequate enough word to describe the torture of being near her. But it beat being apart from her.

"Don't worry, it's fine. I'm glad you're here." I gave her my most attractive smile. A one-sided grin that I'd seen my dad give my mom half a million times.

Arianna had been nervously glancing around, but she paused and her eyes traveled to my lips. My heart started thudding in my chest. Maybe I'd finally get through to her tonight, make her see that I was a feasible potential boyfriend for her, not just a recently acquired friend. *You know me ... please remember.*

Breaking eye contact, Arianna glanced back at the kitchen. Hopefully Trey was keeping Simon occupied, so I could have a little more alone time with Arianna. Even if they were just friends, that didn't mean Simon wanted it to stay that way. He could want to date her just as much as I did. No ... not *just* as much as I did. "Your mom was okay with you coming to the party?" I asked her.

Looking back at me, she nodded. "Yeah, if Simon came with. My parents love him." Looking uncomfortable, she added, "He moved into the house down the road a couple months ago, but he's ... been going through a rough time lately, so my family has sort of adopted him. We all spend a lot of time together..."

Yeah, I know ... I saw. Not wanting to sound jealous or overbearing, I made myself say, "That's ... really nice of you and your family."

She nodded again. "Yeah, his dad is ... out of town, and he's kind of on his own right now, so he's staying with us. We look out for him." I gritted my teeth, but smiled. He was living with her? Great. Just when I was about to change the subject to something that didn't involve Simon, Arianna tilted her head and said, "Were you at my house the other night?"

My mouth popped open in surprise and fear. She'd seen me? "Uh, yeah, I ... um ..."

Pursing her lips, she frowned. "How come you came by? And why didn't you come to the door? I didn't notice you until you pulled away ... How long were you parked there ... watching?"

She was rambling again ... nervous. Sighing, I studied her shoes. They were cute shoes, with little bows at the top. I really should have complimented her on them at some point in our relationship. Too late now. "I'm sorry, I was just ... in the area. I was going to knock and say hello, but then I realized you were about to have dinner and it felt inappropriate, so I was going to leave ... and then I saw *him*, and I ..." With sheepish eyes, I looked up at her. "I got jealous. I couldn't move, so I just sat there like an idiot for way too long. I'm sorry."

Her expression softened as she regarded me. "You got jealous?" she asked. "Of seeing me with another man?" Feeling like I was practically admitting that I was in love with her, I nodded. Her only response was to whisper, "Oh."

Oh? As in, *Oh, I see you in a different light now*, or *Oh, I feel sorry that you care about me because I don't see you that way*? I was nervous to ask her what she meant, but not knowing was killing me. Could she see me as more than a friend?

I'd just worked up the nerve to ask her, when Simon rejoined us. He had a plastic cup in each hand. Arianna wrinkled her nose as she took one. "This doesn't have alcohol in it, does it?"

Glaring at Simon, I answered before he could. "No, it's just cherry cola," I stated.

They both turned to look at me. "How do you know that?" Simon asked.

Mentally kicking myself, I shrugged. "I have a really good sense of smell."

Simon accepted that and turned to Arianna. "Want to dance?" He indicated the living room where some of the other partiers were starting to form a group of swaying bodies. It wasn't exactly dancing, but probably would be in an hour or two.

I bristled at the idea of him dancing with her, but held my tongue. Before Arianna could answer, a high-pitched laugh distracted us. I looked over to see Starla sauntering my way. Jacen was walking behind her with a frown on his face; she wasn't walking in a straight line. I sighed as she came up to us and tossed an arm around me.

"Julian! What the heck are you doing over here? And who is your pretty friend?" She squinted her light blue eyes as she studied Arianna, then she inhaled a surprised breath. "I know you! You're the girl Julian can't get over." She turned back to me. "You slept with her, right? I sure hope so, otherwise there's no point in pining over her. Not that there really is a point in dwelling anyway. What's done is done, that's my motto."

I slapped a hand over her mouth to shut her up. Arianna gaped at her. "No! No we didn't ..." She twisted to me. "Who *is* this?"

Raising my eyebrows to Jacen, so he would remove Starla from the room, and hopefully from the house, I glumly told Arianna, "My mom ..." I felt like hiding in a hole as Jacen led her giggling ass away. My real parents had never embarrassed me anywhere nearly as bad as she just had.

Arianna wrapped her arms around herself. "How does she know me? And why does she think we ... ?"

She didn't finish her sentence, and I ran my hands through my hair, buying myself a few seconds of time. Simon felt the need to fill that silence with his own thoughts on the matter. "She's obviously wasted ... she can barely stand up straight."

His face and voice oozed judgment, and I suddenly felt very defensive about my pseudo-parent. "Hey, you don't know anything about her. Her life hasn't been easy. My dad left when I was a baby, and she had to raise my sister and me on her own. If she needs to unwind every once in a while, then she's earned the right." I couldn't believe that not only was I standing up for Starla, but I was doing it by spouting the completely BS fable we spun about our lives.

Seeing I was getting upset, Arianna put a hand on my arm. "He didn't mean anything by it. It's okay." Her smile was so calming, I instantly felt my anger fading. What I wouldn't give to wrap my arms around her and bury myself in her peace. What I wouldn't give to have her back.

What I wouldn't give for the doorbell to stop ringing. I grunted in irritation as another partygoer arrived. Backing away from Arianna with an apologetic grimace, I said, "I have to get that."

She nodded, then started following Simon into the living room. Not able to watch her go without saying something, I called out, "Arianna!" When she twisted back to me, I lamely pointed at her feet. "I like your shoes ..." *Oh God, did I really just say that to her?*

She bunched her brow like I'd completely perplexed her, but then she smiled. "Thank you, Julian."

Trey walked past her, heading toward me. He was gnawing on a chicken leg. That wasn't one of the snacks we'd brought from his house, so I could only assume he'd raided my fridge. And if he'd raided my fridge, other people probably had too. Crap. There was no way I could get all these people out, clean the house, and zoom out to the ranch in just a few minutes after the sun set. My parents were going to be suspicious, and then they'd become protective. And then they'd kill me.

Trey clapped my shoulder as he moved to open the door. "Good job on the compliment. I'm telling you, it works every time."

As four people I didn't know shuffled into the house, I asked him, "Really? When was the last time you had a girlfriend?"

Trey pointed to himself with his pinky finger. "I didn't say it worked for me, but it works ... or so I hear." As I smirked at him, he looked around my beginning-to-get-packed home. "Where's Nika?"

I discretely glanced out the windows to gauge the amount of time left in the day. I was surprised to see how dark it was getting. We didn't have much time. In another twenty minutes, it would be fully dark. Crap! There were at least forty people in the house already, and I knew even more were on their way. What was I going to do with all of them? And ... I hadn't spent nearly enough time with Arianna to call it quits now. Zero time alone with her. This sucked.

"She should be here soon." And then we would have to go. No ... I needed more time.

I left Trey manning the door, while I scooted into the living room. I wasn't much of a dancer, but my minutes were numbered, and I wanted to spend all of them with my former girlfriend. I found her with a pack of her friends from school. Simon was right beside her, of course. The group of them were standing in the center of the room, but they weren't really dancing. Just swaying while they talked. I could sway. I could sway like a madman.

I joined them, accidentally on purpose sliding in-between Simon and Arianna. Arianna looked back at me and gave me a shy smile before returning her attention to her friends. Like high school girls tended to do when they clumped together, they all stared at me and giggled, but I didn't care. Even if it only lasted for a few minutes, I was with Arianna again.

As I swayed slightly behind her, I noticed that she was getting closer to me, not farther. I hadn't moved in either direction, so she must have. My heart picked up as her body bumped against mine. Feeling bold, I let my hand brush against hers. She didn't pull away. I did it again, this time letting the backs of our hands rest against each other. Reaching out, I looped my index finger around her pinky. She still didn't pull away. She'd been concentrating on her friends up to this point, but with our hands joined, she twisted her head to look over her shoulder at me.

I gave her a soft, disarming smile while I begged her in my mind to remember me. *Just remember you love me ... then we can go back to the way we were, and all this pain can stop.*

My least favorite person in the world took that moment to make his presence known. Simon shoved his way past me, dislodging our fingers in the process. Giving Arianna a smooth smile, he asked, "Need another drink?"

Arianna frowned, glanced at our separated hands, then lifted her still-full cup to Simon. "No, I'm good, thanks."

Simon looked mildly defeated, which made me happy. I was just about to try to send him on a pointless errand, when over the music, I heard Trey exclaim, "Little A! About freaking time you got here!"

I felt all the blood drain from my face. If Nika was upstairs, then the sun had set, and if the sun had set, then Hunter would shortly be on his way to collect us, and we'd be expected to leave. Or else Mom and Dad would come collect us. Shit.

Leaving Arianna's side, I made my way to Nika. Once Hunter started toward her, their bond would kick in ... and then the entire party would know something was up. Try as she might, Nika just couldn't mask the effects of the bond. I'd have to hide her away so no one filmed her intense reaction.

Trey was already upon her when I got to her. He was asking, "Where the heck have you been?"

I wasn't sure what Nika would tell him, but surprisingly, she had an answer all mapped out. "Some of us have jobs, you know?" I raised my eyebrow and Nika winked at me. That was actually a pretty decent answer.

Trey made a pffft sound. "Job, schmob. You're missing out on the party of the year. Your mom's already stoned."

He started laughing while Nika looked around for Starla. I grabbed her arm to get her attention. "We need to go somewhere quiet, somewhere I can contain you, until Hunter gets here." Just saying it made me cringe.

Nika frowned while she gazed at me. She wasn't thrilled that she had to be restrained, but unless she wanted to have sex on the side of the road, or even worse, in the middle of the party, it was a necessary precaution. "We have time; he's still at the ranch."

Tuning in to Hunter's location, I could feel that she was right—oddly, he was still with the others. Nika seemed upset by that fact, while I was just relieved. Maybe Dad was keeping him held up, unknowingly buying us more time. Whatever. All I cared was that he wasn't on his way yet, so we didn't need to wrap up the party yet. Just like she'd said, we had time. Once we felt Hunter move, then I could take Nika some place private, maybe the shed in the back yard.

Looking around me, Nika noticed someone over my shoulder and waved. I turned around to see that Arianna had followed me over. That had to be a good sign. Like a shadow, Simon was a couple of steps behind her.

"Arianna! Hi!" Nika exclaimed.

There was such hope on Nika's face that my chest ached in sympathy for her; she wanted Arianna back too. We both missed her, just in different ways. But while Arianna knew and recognized me from school, she didn't know Nika at all. She'd been completely erased ... a total stranger. "You're Julian's sister ... right?" she asked, frowning.

Nika's smile faltered for a second, before she brought it back. "Yeah ... Nika."

Arianna nodded, tucking her hair behind her ears. "Pretty name."

Nika let out a disappointed exhale. "Thanks."

I was just about to ask Arianna if she wanted to go somewhere quiet, when Simon suddenly asked her if she was hungry. Grabbing her stomach, she told him, "Starved. Let's get some chips or something." Simon's smile as he led her away was triumphant. I wanted to strangle him.

When they were gone, I turned on Nika. "I don't suppose you can order him to stay away from Arianna?"

Her mouth pursed in disapproval, then twisted into concern. "Why isn't Hunter on his way? I should call him ..." She pulled her cell phone out of her pocket and I yanked it out of her ice-cold hands. "What are you doing?" she snapped. "Give it back."

I shook my head. "We're having a secret party. What do you think will happen when Hunter gets here and we can't leave? Our parents will show up, and we'll be busted."

Nika folded her arms over her chest. "This was your idea, Sherlock. I tried to broach the idea of a party to them, but you clammed up every time I did."

I sighed; she was right about that. "I know, but it's sort of too late now to do anything else. The longer Hunter takes to get here, the better."

"For you," she grumbled.

I was about to give her some witty comeback for that when her phone in my hand rang. Ice went through me. It was most likely a vampire on the other end, and a vampire would be able to hear the sounds of a party going on in the background. They'd know exactly what was going on the second we answered the line. I glanced at the screen, prepared to hit the end button, but Nika snatched the phone back before I could.

Smiling, she answered it. "Hunter, where are you?"

Hunter's answer was quiet, crisp, and curt. "I've bought you 'til midnight, longer if I can stretch it out."

I blinked, confused. "You ... what?"

Hunter heard me, even over the sounds of the party. "I owe you one, Julian, so consider this a payment on my debt ... one of many. I told your parents I wanted to talk to them alone, without the interference of the bond. I asked if the two of you could stay at the house until our talk was over ... and I'll make sure it takes a while to get over with." Sounding rushed, he added, "I also made sure it was me who called Nika to explain, and not your parents. I didn't want them to hear the raging party you've got going on in the background."

I almost didn't know what to say to that. As Nika smiled into the phone held to her ear, I muttered, "Thanks, man. I appreciate it."

Hunter let out a humorless laugh. "After everything that's gone down, I really don't think you need to thank me for anything. It was the least I could do."

Nika had a sappy, romantic expression on her face as she thanked him. He told her it was no big deal and that he had to go before our parents got back within earshot of him. I was torn as Nika hung up the phone. I guess I had Hunter to thank for not getting skinned alive tonight, and it was strange to feel like I owed him one. Honestly, I wasn't sure if I liked the feeling.

As I turned back to the door to see Trey letting five more people into the house, I let out a long, slow exhale. We might have more time on our hands now, but keeping this expanding party under wraps was still a long shot.

CHAPTER ELEVEN

Hunter

DISCONNECTING THE PHONE, I shoved it into my pocket and made a mad dash back to the house. I'd excused myself to make the phone call to Nika in private, explaining that she'd be hurt if I didn't show up to get her, and I wanted to reassure her without the oddness of everyone listening. Teren had understood, and let me run off. I wasn't sure how long he'd let me run away though, so I'd kept the call to a minimum.

A part of me hated leaving Nika on her own. It felt wrong not to be with her. And I had to be extra careful about which direction I traveled. Even though it was inconvenient at times, I tried to only move laterally to her position. Because if I moved toward her too much, this insane bond we shared would kick in, and I wouldn't be able to stop myself from phasing out the door to be with her. Which would defeat my diversion tactic. And I owed Julian as good of a diversion as I was capable of giving him.

Teren frowned at me when I returned. "I should really call Starla, give her a heads up that she'll be watching the kids longer than she planned." He rolled his eyes. "She'll be thrilled."

I plucked the phone from my pocket and showed it to him while I lied my ass off. "Already done, and yes, she was thrilled."

Teren nodded as he eyed me. "So … you said you had something of great importance that you needed to talk about. Something that you didn't want Nika to hear. What is it?"

Staring at the floor, I sighed as I wondered if I was making a mistake or not. It felt wrong, but it also felt incredibly right. We were in the spacious living room of the ranch. Long, plush couches were paired with solid comfortable chairs with coffee table before them and end tables between them. There were enough sitting areas for three or four groups of people to converse simultaneously. That would be frustrating for groups of vampires though, what with our advanced hearing. A wall of newly replaced windows highlighted the expansive back yard, the acres of fields waving with tall grass, the rolling hills sharpening into majestic mountains in the background. It was an awe-inspiring sight, and one I frequently enjoyed. Like the old windows, these new ones had been treated with a special formula that let full vampires experience sunlight for a few minutes a day. It was a perk I looked forward to every day. It paled in comparison to Nika though.

I indicated for Teren to sit on one of the many chairs clustered around a long, low table. The table was new, as well—a lot of the old furniture had been damaged in the raid. Teren seemed reluctant, but he eventually sat down. Emma sat on his right. Jake was hanging around too. He was currently playing chess with Teren's father, Jack. Rory and Cleo were standing behind them, watching the monotony. It was all part of the master plan to get Jake to gradually not think of our species as monsters. But he was watching and listening to us as much as we were watching and listening to him. That was fine. This conversation sort of had to do with him anyway.

I sat across from Teren, on a low chair that really wasn't all that comfortable. It seemed fitting that I fidget though, so I didn't change spots. Jake glanced at me from the corner of his eye. I recognized his awareness and tense posture. He was on full alert, ready to bolt at a moment's notice if the right opportunity presented itself. One of those "right opportunities" just might be a family member's life, and that was what made this conversation so important.

"Um, well, first off, I want to thank you both for taking the time to listen to me alone. I know you were anxious for Nika and Julian to join us." I glanced over at Jake just in time to see him dart his eyes back to his game board filled with clear and frosted glass chess pieces. I really wasn't anxious for the twins to join us, the further they were, the safer.

I frowned. Now I had to say something that totally contradicted what I believed, what I wanted. But I didn't see another way. Not right now. "I need your help," I whispered.

Teren and Emma both looked at each other in surprise. Clearly, that wasn't what they'd expected me to say. "With what?" Teren asked slowly, his expression oozing curiosity.

Biting my lip, I willed myself to stop this conversation before it got too deep. I couldn't though. It was already too late when I'd asked for them to speak with me. "The bond with Nika." When they didn't look any less clueless, I started explaining. "I wanted to speak with the both of you, because you, out of everyone, knows what Nika and I are going through. The bond is ... explosive. Maintaining control when it takes over is difficult, if not impossible. I've lost track of myself on so many occasions, sometimes I feel like a stranger. And ... adjusting to this life has made me feel strange enough. I can't take anymore."

Teren sighed, while Emma gave me a sympathetic smile. "We know it's hard, Hunter, believe us, we know." Emma turned to her husband. "When Teren and I were first bonded, I turned into a caged animal whenever he came near me. I thought I'd be torn apart by all the wanton need I had." She turned back to me. "But it gets better. I promise."

I nodded. I'd heard all this before. "Yes, I know. In a year or so, the desire to be near each other lessens, and we'll start to feel more like we did before. But in the meantime ..." I ran my hand through my hair in frustration. I knew they understood, but they didn't *really* understand. "You two were married at the time, you lived together, and you worked near each other. Your separation was generally within a couple of miles, at best. Nika and I are *dozens* of miles apart. The effect of the bond strengthens with distance. The ache you two felt is minor compared to the agony we feel ... every single day."

I scrubbed my eyes, suddenly exhausted. Of course, I hadn't been sleeping much, since I was keeping an eye on Jake whenever I could. "Every day is torture, and time is only making it worse. Even now without her my chest feels hollowed out, and I know that all I have to do to get rid of that feeling ... is run to her." Lowering my hands, I locked eyes with Teren. "She's the sweetest drug, tailor-made for me."

Teren scowled, but didn't comment on that. Perhaps he understood only too well how true that sentence was. Instead, he asked, "What can we do to help you? To help you both?"

I could hear the unhappiness in his voice. He knew exactly what I was going to ask. Or at least, he thought he did. I sighed just as unhappily. "The best thing to ease the bond would be for Nika to stay here at the ranch with me. It would prevent our impassioned nightly reunions. It would keep us mellower. She could finish high school here, being homeschooled by Alanna, Imogen, and Halina instead of the online courses you've been having her take. She'd have more room to spend her days. She'd have more people to talk to. In every way, it would be better for her."

"I know," Teren muttered before he looked away. I saw the debate in his eyes as he twisted his head to look at Emma. He must have had these thoughts himself, or else enough people had mentioned it to him that he'd considered the possibility. He didn't like it though. I didn't either.

"That's not what I want to happen. That's not the help I need from you."

Teren and Emma both snapped their focus to me. "What?" Teren asked, dumbfounded.

I shrugged. "It's true, not so long ago, that was exactly what I wanted … but things have changed." I slid my eyes over to Jake. He was blatantly watching us now. "Life here isn't as easy and carefree as it used to be. It's not as … safe." I returned my eyes to Teren's.

He flicked a glance at Jake, his father, and Jake's two bodyguards, then his gaze slowly returned to me. "I can understand why you feel that way," he quietly said.

I knew he didn't entirely agree on the level of danger Jake presented. He felt he was well guarded, and it was important to show Jake a normal and loving environment, one that included his children. But Nika was my entire world. I couldn't risk even the slightest bad thing happening to her. "I don't want Nika here, not right now, but I can't stand being apart from her either, especially with the bond amplifying everything I feel for her. I'm stuck."

Teren sighed and leaned back in his chair. "I see your dilemma. I … I could offer a room in my home to you."

Emma's eyes widened as she stared at her husband. I stared at him too. The only lightproof room in the house was downstairs … with Nika.

He was essentially okaying me to share a bedroom with his daughter. I was tempted, sorely tempted, but being with Nika wasn't the only thing I needed to be doing right now. "I appreciate the offer. More than you know. But ..." I changed my stare to Jake. "I'm needed here."

I saw Teren nodding out of the corner of my eye. "I thought you might say that. So, if you can't go, and Nika can't stay ... what other option does that leave you with?"

I inhaled a breath and held it. He wasn't going to like this. But his dislike was going to be mild compared to the two women in my life that this was going to affect the most. Luckily for me, neither one of those women were in the home right at the moment. With a sharp exhale, I told him, "Help me convince Halina and Nika that, for right now, the bond needs to be severed. I'll take Gabriel's shot. I'll keep taking it, until I no longer need to." I flicked a glance at Jake, silently blaming him with my eyes. But for him falling into our laps, I'd be asking Teren a much different question.

Teren and Emma both seemed equally stunned. Teren shook his head. "When you asked to talk without Nika here, I just assumed you'd be asking to marry her. I never imagined this conversation."

A sad smile escaped me. Marrying Nika, making her my wife. That was a dream I'd had more than one time. It seemed like an impossibility at the moment, and she was still so young but maybe, someday ...

"Ah, no ... I don't think we're ready for that. Yet."

Emma smiled at my word choice. Teren pursed his lips in a gesture that could have been pleasure or irritation. I wasn't quite sure. Rubbing his hands, Teren exchanged a glance with his wife. "Hunter, we can't ... breaking the bond ... Halina and Nika won't accept that as a solution. There has to be something else."

Teren looked over at Jake. Jake, no longer hiding that he was listening, leaned back in his chair and crossed his arms over his chest. "I got a real simple solution for you. Let me go, then your girl can move in, no problems," he said.

Teren shook his head. "So you can tell all your hunter friends what we're trying to do here? I don't see how that's going to help much." He returned his eyes to mine. "We'll all have bullseyes on our hearts for what we've done."

"Then maybe you shouldn't have done it," Jake snapped. "You're messing with people's free will. You're acting like gods."

Letting out a weary sigh, I turned to regard Jake with tired eyes. I really needed to get more sleep. "We're trying to forge peace between our species."

Jake smirked. "Forge peace? Interesting choice of words. But appropriate considering that you're shaping minds to your beliefs, just like a blacksmith shapes steel into a weapon of their choice. But tell me, vampire, who is shaping *your* species to not murder ours? Who fights for the humans in your negotiations?"

I turned away from him. I was getting really tired of his never-ending diatribe. And a tiny part of me agreed with him. "I don't see another way with Nika right now. Gabriel has already perfected the shot, I just have to ask him to—"

"No." A figure walked into the room, grabbing everyone's attention. I looked up at Gabriel's cool eyes as he stood a few feet away from me.

"No?" I blinked, surprised by his entrance. I'd assumed Gabriel was downstairs in his lab or outside with Halina. She was in the pastures, hunting some fresh meat before she went out to wait at the meeting site where more hunters would be converted tonight if they showed up. I should be going with her, but this took precedence.

Gabriel's jade eyes regarded Jake before returning to me. "I will not participate in helping you break your bond with Halina. I angered her once by doing that, and I have no intention of doing so again."

I clenched my jaw in frustration, but I understood Gabriel's reluctance. He was already on thin ice with my creator. "I promise you I won't be taking it without her consent and approval." I shook my head. "I'm not running away this time. I'm not going anywhere. I just want to make things easier. For everyone."

Gabriel frowned. "You will be hard-pressed to convince her. Nika as well. Breaking the bond between vampires is ... uncomfortable for each vampire."

My lip curved into a half smile. "Believe me, I know that. I just don't see any other option." I glared at Jake. "Any feasible ones."

Jake only smiled at my comment. Gabriel's dirty-blonde head turned to rest on the captive vampire hunter in the room. "I find you fascinating," he plainly stated.

Jake looked mildly uncomfortable being the ancient vampire's sole focus. "Well, that's great. I find you a bit creepy."

Gabriel tilted his head, like he didn't understand why anyone would find him creepy. "Your blood is quite different from any mixed vampire's blood that I've ever inspected. And I've inspected a lot of blood. It is sort of my specialty."

Jake returned his eyes to the chessboard. He fingered the bishop, like he was debating a power play. "Yeah, I'm sure you're a real expert on blood ... but I'm no vampire."

Gabriel blurred to Jake's side, startling him. Jake jumped to his feet, making us jump to ours. Tensions rose. Jack slowly stood and backed up a couple of steps while Rory and Cleo jumped forward like they were going to tackle Jake. Gabriel held up his hand to stop them. "I *am* an expert. And your blood is not natural. That much I'm certain of."

Jake sniffed and lifted his chin. "If I knew what that meant, I might be offended."

Stepping toward them, I asked Gabriel, "What do you mean? How is he not natural?"

Gabriel twisted his head to look at me. "I think our friend here is right. He's not a vampire, mixed or otherwise. The vampire blood in his system was given to him, but not through birth."

I didn't know what the hell that meant, but I didn't have time to worry about it either. Jake had a tempting target in front of him, a target who wasn't paying him any attention, and he wasn't about to let that opportunity go. Almost as fast as a vampire could move, he shoved the bishop clenched in his fingers into Gabriel's exposed neck. The sharp, glass piece punctured Gabriel's jugular, and fresh blood exploded into the room.

It only took me a split-second to react, but in that second, Jake made his move. He shoved Gabriel away from him and jumped over the table to get to Jack. Teren's father was an old man, and not nearly as nimble as Jake. The vampire hunter pulled him in front of him like a shield, just as the wolves descended. Teren and I were in front of him in a flash, Rory and Cleo were tense and alert behind him. He was surrounded.

Still holding onto his bloody chess piece, Jake held it to Jack's throat. "Nobody move." He gestured toward Gabriel, still on the floor. "He may survive his neck being torn open, but I have a feeling this one won't."

Emma was hunched beside Gabriel. He was fine, his wound had already closed, but he was clearly shaken. Teren and I were nearly brushing against Jack we were so close. I was sure we could yank him out of harm's

FAMILY IS FOREVER

way before Jake could do anything, but jerking him that hard and that fast might hurt him just as much as Jake stabbing him.

"You don't want to do this," Teren said in a low, cold voice.

Jake pressed the piece harder, so that Jack's neck turn red and splotchy around the point of impact. "Don't I?" he asked.

Teren shook his head. He had his hands out in front of him, but he was crouched for action. "You're a guest here, and so long as you're a guest, no one will harm you. But if *you* hurt anyone, all that changes. I'll put you down myself."

Jake smirked. "Doesn't that defeat the purpose of your little vampire protection agency? Aren't you opposed to vengeance killings, on both sides?" Teren clenched his jaw and Jake smiled even wider. "Now as your guest, I'm kindly asking to leave."

I opened my mouth to speak, but before I could, Jake was rapped over the head with a frying pan. I blinked in shock as I watched him crumple to the floor. Alanna was standing next to him, a greasy pan from dinner still clutched in her fingers. She'd been listening to everything in the kitchen, and had blurred into the room behind him, between Rory and Cleo, and taken him unaware.

"No one threatens my husband in my house," she seethed. Dropping the pan, she rushed over to Jack to make sure he was okay. He was shaken, but physically, he seemed all right.

Gabriel stood and looked down on Jake's slumbering form. The crisp, white dress shirt Gabriel had been wearing was soaked with crimson now. So was a good chunk of the rug around him. Blood dripped off his wet shirt, staining his slacks. It dripped off his fingertips, splattering onto the floor, adding to the horror.

Concerned for the old vampire, I asked, "Are you okay?"

He looked back at me, nodded, then returned his eyes to Jake; Jake's heartbeat was slow, but steady. He was fine. "The wound has healed. I will live." He said it calmly, but I knew for a fact that he was in pain—getting hurt still hurt.

Reaching down, Gabriel picked up the unconscious vampire hunter. "What are you going to do with him?" I asked.

Gabriel swung his gaze to me. His cheek and jaw were covered with arterial spray. It was a distressing sight. "I'm going to make sure he's all right, then I'm going to escort him back to his room where he'll be closely guarded for the remainder of the evening." He looked over at Rory and Cleo and the pair immediately nodded. With this lapse in security, they'd probably be even more dedicated to the task.

Gabriel and I didn't have the warmest relationship, but I patted his shoulder as he walked by me. Surprisingly, there were tiny drops of blood on my hand. Gabriel's wound had been messy. "I'm glad you weren't seriously injured."

Gabriel raised an eyebrow at me. "I am as well."

While Gabriel walked away with Jake's limp body, Teren made sure his father was okay. The unprovoked attack only strengthened my resolve. The ranch was no place for Nika. In truth, it was no place for any of the humans either. I'd never get Jack to leave without his wife, though, and Linda was equally reluctant to leave. Ashley and Christian weren't going anywhere until their vacation was over. There were way too many potential targets in this nest for my liking.

I walked over to Teren with images of Jake stabbing Nika in my mind. It sickened my already twisting stomach. "Teren, it may be time to rethink the panel's decision about keeping him here."

Teren sighed as he patted his dad on the back. "It was my decision ... and I know." His eyes were worn when he looked at me. "Life in prison or execution didn't sound like viable options either though. This is the only way ..." His eyes drifted back to his parents, and I could clearly see how much putting his family in jeopardy bothered him.

"Well, at least reconsider your children being a part of this. Nika ..." My words caught and I couldn't continue.

Teren's mouth hardened as he looked back at me. "You're right. Right now, the risk is too great. Julian and Nika shouldn't be here. I'll help you break the bond with my daughter. I'll help the two of you stay apart."

It felt like my gut had been punched in with his words. The last thing I wanted was to be apart from Nika. I'd much rather be wrapped in her arms. I'd much rather be in her tiny little cement box under her parents' home than here in this spacious, luxurious ranch without her. But, I had a duty to perform—keeping my nest safe—and it would never be safe so long as Jake believed we were soulless, bloodthirsty monsters.

My chin dropped to my chest as I bowed my head. "This isn't what I really want, but ... thank you."

Teren pressed his palm to my shoulder. "I know. You're a good man, Hunter." I peeked up at him, surprised that he would admit that. He shook his head. "I may not like the fact that you're my teenage daughter's sire, but ... I couldn't have picked out a better boyfriend for her."

A small smile lifted my lips. "Thank you. Your approval means a lot."

Teren lifted his finger to my face. "That does not mean I'm okay with you sleeping with her."

"Teren! Boundaries ..." Emma snapped.

Teren ignored his wife as he stared at me. I immediately averted my eyes. "We're not ... We don't ..." Not sure what to say, but knowing I owed him the truth, I returned my eyes to his. "I'm not sleeping with her."

The others in the room were studiously ignoring our conversation, which I had to assume was intentional. While Emma glared at her husband, Teren cocked his head. "Have you *ever* slept with her?" he asked.

Damn it. I wanted to be honest with him, but I was pretty sure he was going to stake me if I told him the truth. So much for being a great boyfriend. I opened my mouth to answer him and Emma slapped her hand over my lips. "Do not answer that," she said. Then she smacked Teren's shoulder. "You can't ask your daughter's boyfriend that question, Teren."

Teren twisted to face her. "I just want to know if our daughter is still a virgin or not. Isn't that my right, as her father?"

Lowering her hand from my mouth, Emma crossed her arms over her chest. "No, it's not. If Nika wants to talk to you about it, then she will, but you have to let her come to you." She raised an eyebrow at him. "Remember how intrusive your family was when we first got together? And how annoying and frustrating that was? You can't do the exact same thing to her." She shook her head, looking very set on protecting her daughter's privacy.

Teren pursed his lips, but didn't argue. From behind him, his mother Alanna, muttered, "Even though it's been said a hundred times ... we're very sorry about that."

Teren's expression eased as he laughed. The slight tension in the room dissolved with his sudden mirth. Looking over at me, he said, "All right, don't tell me." He raised his hands. "I really don't want to know anyway. She's my baby. I want her to stay that way."

I nodded in understanding. Teren's chuckles died with a sigh. "I suppose I should call Nika and explain that coming out tonight isn't going to happen. She's not going to like that." Frowning, he twisted to Emma. "Maybe I should run home, talk to her in person?"

Emma was already nodding, and saying that was good idea when I suddenly remembered the secret party I was helping to cover up. "Um, actually, I think this is a conversation I should have with her. I mean, I *am* the one about to sever our bond. She'll be even more upset over that."

Teren considered that, then nodded. "We'll all go. It should be a family conversation anyway, especially since it affects Julian as well as Nika."

Teren took a step forward like he was heading for the doors, and I shot my hands out to stop him. "There's no need for you guys to leave right now. There's a pretty big mess to clean up here." I indicated the bloody evidence of Gabriel's attack, then looked over at Emma. "And I know you want to spend time with your sister. If you go all the way home, you know you'll end up staying there and you'll miss out on time with her."

Emma glanced at Teren. "He's right. You go, I'll stay here with Ash."

I wanted to groan in frustration. If I could only just order them to stay.

Teren nodded, gave her a kiss, then patted my shoulder. "Shall we race?" he asked me. "I might be mixed, but I think I can take you."

I shook my head as I fumbled for a reason for him to stay. *Any* reason. "I can do this alone. You can stay with your wife. I'm sure she'd love to have some kid-free time with you."

Teren laughed once. "We work together. In a private office. With a locked door. We get lots of kid-free time."

Emma gasped and playfully pushed his shoulder. I wrinkled my nose, wondering what to say now. "Well, still. I've got this. You can stay here."

Teren shook his head. "I should run into town anyway. Check out the meeting spot with Great-Gran. See if any hunters showed up tonight. It's been a while since we've had any new arrivals, but ..."

I don't know if there was something in my expression that tipped him off, but he suddenly stopped talking and stared at me with curious eyes. "You keep trying to make me stay here ... is something going on?"

Smiling, I raised my hands. "No. What could possibly be going on?"

I swallowed the lump in my throat. Crap. Why did I agree to play defense for Julian? Right. Because I killed his sister and obliterated his girlfriend.

With shrewd understanding, Teren narrowed his eyes and said, "You asked to speak with us alone ... the twins are up to something, aren't they? They're still at home though, so ..." His eyes widened and he snapped his head to Emma. Hers eyes widened too. At the same time, they both said, "They're having a party."

I closed my eyes, wondering who was going to kill me first—Julian or Teren. Teren snatched his phone out of his pocket and immediately dialed someone. At first, I thought he was calling the house, but then I heard Starla pick up the line. I also heard blaring, thumping music in the background. If Julian and Nika didn't turn that down soon, they were going to get complaints from the neighbors.

"Vamp boy!" Starla's cheery voice proclaimed.

Teren's eyes narrowed. "Don't call me that, especially if you're at a party. Are you at a party?"

Starla started giggling. "Every day's a party, vampy."

Teren closed his eyes and looked like he was counting to ten. "Where. Are. You? And where are my children?"

"I'm at the house. And they're here too ... somewhere." To someone else, we all heard her yell, "Hey! You seen a couple of kids around here? Yay big? Black hair, blue eyes? Brown hair, brown eyes? Yeah, I know that could be anyone. Is that a yes then? Hey, where are you going? Ungrateful little twerp."

As she started prattling on about not being helpful, Teren let out a long exhale. "Starla ..."

Starla's voice returned more directly into the receiver. "They're here somewhere, I swear. No need to worry. Wait, you have trackers on them. Don't you know where they are? Why the heck are you asking me?" She started laughing again, and making a pinging noise like a submarine radar.

Teren clenched his jaw. "Are you ... drunk?" he asked her.

That only made her laugh more. "I don't know. Maybe. Gotta go, vamp boy. Chow!"

After that, she hung up. His cell still clutched in his hand, Teren pointed at me. "You're helping the kids have a secret party while we're gone? Forget everything I just said about you being a good boyfriend."

I started to lift my hands and protest, but he was already gone. Emma blurred away a second after him.

Great. Well, at least I was able to buy Julian a little bit of time. Hopefully it was enough.

Because I was a full vampire and Teren and Emma were only part vampire, I was able to overtake them. I blurred passed them like they were merely jogging at a leisurely pace. I'd set out for Nika's house with a desire to get there first, but as I flew across the pastures, another desire overrode that one. The bond kicked in, and all of a sudden, I needed to get to her simply because I needed her. Nothing in the world existed but her, and I couldn't move fast enough. My heartbeat quickened and I felt shaky all over. I pushed myself nearly to the breaking point of my abilities. To anyone looking, I'd be a momentary blur in their vision, something easily dismissible and forgettable. It still wasn't fast enough for me though.

I was aching, panting with desire. Things blurred passed me that I should have recognized, but I didn't. They were just smudges of green, brown, black, trace scents of pine, water, blood. None of it mattered, nothing but getting closer to the intoxicating presence of my mate. Her face in my mind superseded everything else in reality. The remembered smell of her pushed back the abundant nature between us.

She was too far from me to sense if she was pacing, but I imagined I could feel her anticipation of my arrival growing. I pictured her restless, breathing heavy, running her hands over her body, wishing it was me. I was completely ready to be one with her. It was all I wanted, all I needed ...

When I got to her street, I expected to see her, to feel her rushing toward me. She hadn't moved though, and the loss of her was painful. I rushed into her home, breezing past people entering and exiting the house. I couldn't wonder who they were or why they were there, I only knew, they were keeping me from my goal. I sensed my love in an upstairs bedroom, and shoved past the humans in my way. They didn't even see me. Fighting broke out behind me, as the simple-minded people started blaming each other for the jostling. I didn't care. Nika was all I cared about.

She was in her old bedroom. I burst through the closed door, halfway breaking it off the hinges. My love was being held back by two men I didn't recognize at the moment, although the scent of one stirred something deep within me. Other people were in the room ... two women, another man ... but I didn't care. One of the girls screamed as I came to a stop in the center of the room. It hurt my ears, but I couldn't pull my eyes away from Nika. Each man was holding back one of her arms, pinning her in place. Once Nika spotted me, she jerked free from one of her captors. She lunged for me, but the other man slipped his arms around her waist and restrained her.

Fangs lowered, I hissed at the man keeping us apart. Someone else in the room cursed, and I could sense movement by the doorway, but I didn't care. I wanted Nika, and nothing was going to stop me. I thought I heard my name, followed by the word, "No," but it barely registered with me. I blurred to Nika, pulling her free. The person behind her tried to grab her again, but I shoved him into the wall, cracking it. The other man who'd been holding her stepped forward, and I pushed him away with one hand. He flew, tumbling over the bed, and landing on the far side of it.

With everyone between Nika and me gone, we melded into each other's arms. Lips found lips, hands found bodies. We sank to our knees as the urge to be together overwhelmed us. I pushed her to her back, laid over the top of her. She was panting, moaning with desire for me to take her. Our mouths never stopping, I pulled at her jeans, tearing them in my desire to get them off. Her hands pulled at my shirt, ripping it.

Odd sounds pricked my ears—cheering, gasping, whistling, agitated voices yelling. None of it penetrated deep enough to stop me though. I was with Nika, and nothing would ever come between us again. As I yanked her jeans down her hips, a sudden unexpected sensation cracked through the bond's hold over me.

Burning hot water splashed over my back, neck, and head. I was soaked, but more startled than anything else. The surprise of it made me forget about Nika writhing beneath me. I snapped my head up to the person in front of me holding a bathroom-sized, plastic garbage can. I scrunched my brows, trying to understand what was going on.

"Julian? What the hell are you doing?"

Julian sighed in relief, then indicated the room we were in—a room packed with curious people watching. "Just stopping you from having sex with my sister in the middle of a party."

My eyes flashed down to Nika beneath me. She was soaked from the warm water and panting with the residual desire of our intense connection. A throat cleared in an authoritative way, and we both looked over to see a very irate Teren and Emma Adams. Teren's eyes shifted from me, to Nika, to Julian. "Everyone needs to leave. The party is over."

CHAPTER TWELVE

Julian

I FELT LIKE some weird, male-version of Cinderella, staring at the clock, waiting for it to strike midnight. Only I wouldn't be losing all my magic when the bell tolled, I'd be getting filleted alive by my overprotective parents. Somehow, I had to get everyone out of the house before that happened. And a part of me really didn't want to. Because, oddly enough, I was having a good time.

It was fun hanging out with kids my own age, even if I didn't know most of them. Sure, I'd seen them before at school, but Nika and I kind of kept to ourselves. We'd always known living in Salt Lake was temporary, and so was every friendship we made here. So why open up to people if it wasn't going to last? Why give yourself the grief of missing them later on down the road? Plus, Nika and I had to lie about so much in our lives, that it sort of took the fun out of socializing.

But tonight, none of that mattered. Being part vampire didn't matter. Being undead, as in my sister's case, didn't matter. And having a rogue vampire hunter chained up at the family ranch didn't matter … because I was passing out Jell-O shots. I was the King of the Kitchen, and all of my subjects were coming to me for a bright, cheery refreshment.

It had been Trey's idea. When he saw how stressed I was, he'd ushered me to the kitchen, set me up at the island in the middle of it, and proclaimed me the Lord of the Land, Ruler of the Fridge, and Doler of Drinks. I'd rolled my eyes at first, but eventually I'd started having fun with my bartending duties.

And people confided in me while I got them juice, water, pop, or something stiffer if they preferred. Sally told me that Ian was a jerk for cheating off her in chemistry. Ian told me that Holly had an unnatural obsession with teddy bears. Holly told me that Ryan was a conceited, self-absorbed asshole with no taste. And Ryan told me that his underwear cost forty bucks.

My favorite conversations were the ones that centered around Arianna and her circle of friends. Her friend Pam told me that Arianna wasn't seeing anyone. Her friend Liz told me that Simon was cute, and she was going to date him if Arianna didn't. I silently wished her well on that mission. Her friend Nicky said she thought Arianna and I would be a good match. I kind of wanted to hug Nicky.

Simon didn't seem to have any friends at the party. Nobody seemed to know him either. All I could get out of people was that he lived next to the high school, but he didn't go there. I already knew that much. He spent the entire night by Arianna's side, which irritated me to no end. It was the only part of the party I didn't care for. But Arianna only seemed to be respectful of him, not interested in him. I watched them like a hunting vampire whenever they wandered into the kitchen for drinks. Arianna would smile and shake her head every time Simon offered her a snack. I wanted to reach out, grab him, and yell at him that she wasn't hungry anymore. But I resisted.

Arianna smiled whenever she saw me. I was handing a guy named Scott a lime-green Jell-O shot when she approached me alone. I raised an eyebrow at her. "I've got four left ... want to try one?"

She bit her lip. It was adorable. "I don't know ... I don't really drink."

I handed her a pretty pink one, while I took an electric blue one. "I don't either. Together?"

Giggling, she nodded and took the small, plastic cup. We both tipped them back. Mesmerized, I watched her mouth as she swallowed. Then the alcohol hit me and I gagged. That made her laugh even more. "You're cute," she mumbled.

I thought I probably wasn't supposed to hear her say that, but my enhanced ears picked it up. I grinned into my cup. Over her shoulder, I saw Simon heading our way. Nika stepped in front of him, detaining him. He stopped short of running into her, then tried sidestepping around her. Trey popped up on one side to block his path; Raquel popped up on the other. My smile grew. I had the best friends.

Arianna chewed on the rim of her glass as she studied me. Tilting my head toward the archway that led out of the room, I asked her, "Do you want to go somewhere quieter?" I realized it sounded like a pickup line after I said it, but the music in the living room was thumping loud now, so it *was* a legitimate request.

I thought for sure she'd tell me no, but setting her cup down, she smiled and said, "Sure."

The room was packed with people, so I reached down to grab her hand. It was warm and familiar, and felt better than anything I'd felt in a long time. I pulled her through the living room toward the stairs. Bodies were all around us now—I couldn't believe how many people were here. I'd already heard a couple of things break, and garbage was everywhere. I was pushing that from my mind though. I'd deal with it later.

Arianna balked when she realized where we were going—to the bedrooms. I looked back at her innocent, angel face. Leaning in, I whispered in her ear, "It's the only quiet place in the house, but if you're not comfortable, we could go outside or something?"

She stared into my eyes, maybe judging how trustworthy I was. I dropped every wall I had, and let her see how much I cared about her. *I would never hurt you. I love you. Remember me ... please.* She smiled, like she'd somehow heard my silent plea. "It's okay. We can go upstairs." She poked her finger into my chest. "The door stays open though."

Laughing, I nodded. "Fair enough."

As we reached the steps, I looked around for Arianna's human-shadow. I didn't see Simon anywhere though. Trey popped his head out from the crowd, spotted me and where I was going, and gave me two thumbs up. I rolled my eyes. This wasn't going to be what he thought it was. Not tonight. Not when she didn't love me.

People were everywhere on the stairs. I sighed when I saw that they were all over upstairs too—in all of the guest rooms, in my room, in Nika's room, and even in my parents' room. Groups of them were huddled on each side of my parents' door, laughing and exclaiming, "Shut it! You'll see!" I cringed as I realized what they were doing—testing the vampire-worthy soundproofing. Great. If they somehow broke the seal, my parents would notice instantly. God ... I was going to have so much to clean up when they all left. Thank God for super speed.

I took Arianna into Nika's room. Somehow, taking her into a girl's room seemed less intimidating than taking her into my room. And ... I could hear the sounds of someone making out in my room. I was going to have to get new sheets.

With a stern voice, I told the three people lounging on Nika's bed to leave. When they didn't move, I told them there was a fresh plate of special brownies downstairs. They left pretty swiftly after that.

Arianna blinked when she saw the feminine décor. Flushing with color, I quickly explained. "It's my sister's room." I glanced at the bathroom separating Nika's room and mine. Nika's side was open, while mine was thankfully closed. "Mine's on the other side of the bathroom."

Smiling, Arianna sat on Nika's bed. "Oh ... I didn't even know you had a sister. Why doesn't she go to our school?"

I sighed as I sat beside her on the bed. *Yeah, you do know I have a sister. She's your best friend.* "Um ... she's homeschooled. She just ... prefers to be alone."

Arianna tucked her hair behind her ears. "Oh. I have an aunt who is agoraphobic, so I get it."

I widened my eyes like I didn't know that, but I did. I knew most everything about her. "Oh, wow. That must be hard on your parents."

Arianna's face relaxed as she nodded. "My mom, yeah. She doesn't understand why her sister won't go anywhere. She thinks she's being unreasonable, paranoid. Life is scary but ... hiding yourself away and not living it ... that's even scarier." She shrugged. "To me, anyway."

She gave me such a warm smile that I almost believed she knew me ... I mean, *really* knew me. But then her expression turned embarrassed and she looked away. "I can't believe I just told you that. I don't really talk about my aunt."

Needing to touch her, I lightly put my hand over hers on the bed. "You can tell me anything. You can talk to me."

I thought she'd pull away, but she looked back up at me instead. "I know. I'm not sure how I know ... but I know."

My grin was unstoppable. She might not remember me, but she instinctually felt safe with me. That was a good thing. A very good thing.

Bringing her legs up cross-legged on the bed, Arianna leaned forward over her thighs. "Okay, Adams. Tell me everything there is to know about you. Every single detail. Let's get to know each other, like you said."

I couldn't contain my smile, and, for the next several minutes, or maybe it was several hours, I proceeded to tell Arianna everything I could about my life. I loved it, and I hated it. Since she didn't remember who I really was, I had to tell her the lie we told everyone—Starla was my mom, my dad was dead, Nika was a 100 percent normal teenage girl. It gave me a lot to say to Arianna, and our conversation was light and breezy, but I felt guilty. I wanted to tell her everything we'd been through together ... good and bad. She'd only think I was nuts though. Once a compulsion was done, it was as if those wiped moments had never happened. Not even another vampire's compulsion could bring them back. They simply no longer existed; it was why Arianna had inexplicable holes in her memory.

Arianna had relaxed quite a bit during our conversation. Her demeanor was casual as she played with the strap of her shoe. Her laugh came naturally. It was easy to pretend that we were still together as we sat there talking. Our arms were even touching. It sent a jolt of electricity down my spine to feel my skin against hers again. It felt like we were finally shifting, finally moving in the right direction. It was everything I'd hoped tonight would be.

After a brief pause in talking about our summer plans, Arianna pursed her lips and said, "Why have we never been friends before now? We're in the same grade, and we must have had classes together before ... but I don't recall ever seeing you before a couple of months ago."

I sighed, not sure how to answer that. "I don't know ... We must have just kept missing each other. But I'm so glad that's not the case anymore. You ... there's just something about you. You're kind, warm, accepting. You see past people's faults, to the person they are underneath. You're patient, forgiving, and open to things that are a little ... different. But you don't take crap from anyone either, and you stand up for what you believe in. You're just ... amazing."

Her expression was blank. "You saw all that, sitting across the room from me?"

I peeked up at her with a small smile that I couldn't hide. "I see you, Arianna. I see the real you." Straightening, I met her eye and held her gaze. "And I really like what I see."

Arianna held her breath as we stared at each other. Her heart rate spiked, and I momentarily felt bad that I could hear it. She'd probably be embarrassed if she knew I could. But then her eyes drifted to my lips, and I really didn't care that I had a slight advantage. All I cared about was whether she wanted me to kiss her right now. Was she ready to see me as more?

I leaned in, tentative and unsure. Maybe I was misinterpreting this. Maybe, because I wanted it so badly, I was seeing something that wasn't there. My heart was thumping in my chest so loudly, Nika probably thought I was doing something much more strenuous than just sitting on a bed, staring at Arianna, and waiting for our second first kiss to happen.

When I got to the point where it would be obvious to Arianna that I was about to kiss her, I paused. I needed her to actively engage in this. I needed her to want this too. *Please, Arianna ... kiss me.* The hesitation as our mouths hovered just a few inches apart from each other felt like it went on for days. The energy in the room intensified with each second that ticked by. So did my breath. I was almost to the point of hyperventilating. Wouldn't that be romantic?

Just when I thought she was going to pull away, Arianna closed the distance between us, and our mouths connected. Hope and desire exploded throughout my body, pricking my skin like thousands of tiny insect bites. I felt dizzy, lightheaded, nauseous, like I was having heart palpitations. It was the best feeling in the world.

Cautious to not move too quickly with her, I didn't touch her except to lightly cup her cheek. It took a great deal of restraint on my part. What I really wanted to do was lay her down on the bed, and tangle our arms and legs together as I sprinkled kisses all over her body. It was *way* too soon though.

She made a familiar noise in her throat that went straight to the lower portion of my body. I had to struggle to keep my fangs in. After her passionate moan, her lips pressed even harder against mine. I thought I'd died and gone to heaven. She was responding ...

There was a gap in our lips, and I gently poked my tongue through, probing. She made another pleased noise, and her hand came up to fist in my hair.

A groan escaped me as I slipped my tongue in again. She was receptive, warm, willing ... it was just like it used to be. Even though the party was raging all around me, a party I needed to wrap up soon, I blocked out everything but her. She was my life, my air, my world. She scooted closer to me on the bed, and I ran my hand around her waist, pulling her tight.

Our lips never stopping, I gently started to lean her back. Her shoulders had just touched the mattress when a couple of partygoers crashed into the room, slamming Nika's door against the wall. I'd completely forgotten the door was even open. I snapped my head up to see it was my friends at the door ... and my sister. Trey and Raquel were each holding one of Nika's arms while she struggled against them with an anxious look on her face. I'd been so lost with Arianna, that I hadn't even felt her approaching me. Now that she was here, and looking like she was having some sort of attack, I could sense other family members on their way here—Hunter. And Mom. And Dad. Shit.

Arianna squirmed beneath where I was hovering over her. I looked back down at her, and she had an embarrassed smile on her face, like she was happy but mortified all at the same time. It thrilled me that she might feel that way, but I couldn't dwell on that feeling, because Hunter and my parents were going to be here any minute. I had to get everybody out. Standing, I immediately said, "Nika, we need to clear everybody out of here."

Nika shook her head. She was panting as much as I had been earlier. "I can't ... go down there ... he's coming ..."

Right. Her bond with Hunter had obviously kicked in, and she was either going to rush to him, or spontaneously combust waiting for him. I suddenly remembered my ingenious plan to hide Nika in the shed when this happened. Only in my plan, Hunter was supposed to be arriving alone, so I'd have plenty of time to clear out the partiers and clean up the trashed house. Why were our parents rushing home too? Did they know? Crap.

I jogged over to the door to close it. What Nika needed now was privacy. But before I could shut it all the way, Simon strode in. With narrowed eyes, he looked Arianna's way, then mine. "What's going on up here?" he asked, his voice haughty, like he already knew the answer and he didn't like it. He didn't know though. He had no clue what was *really* going on up here. I didn't have time to deal with him. Nika had shucked off Raquel's grasp, and was pulling against Trey. She was going to make a run for it. I grabbed her arm, holding her back. "Fight it, Nick."

"I can't," she moaned.

Everyone in the room was staring at Nika like she'd just grown a second head. Trey looked over my writhing sister to me. "She started wiggin' out, then told us to take her to you. She said no matter what, we had to make her stay in the house. What the heck is wrong with her, man?"

Great. Another question I didn't know how to answer. "Uh, panic attack," I muttered.

Arianna seemed to understand. Hope blossomed in me that she knew the truth, but it faded when she commented, "Too many people at the party?"

I knew she was referencing her aunt's illness, since I'd kind of told her that Nika suffered from the same anxiety. I smiled at her as Nika gave me a particularly good tug. "Something like that."

Simon crossed his arms over his chest. "I've never seen an anxiety attack that looked like this." He tilted his head as he studied my sister. "It's almost like she's ... turned on ..."

I felt my cheeks heat as my sister let out an erotic groan. Yes, that was exactly what it was like. Why I'd told my dad I could handle this, I had no idea. Watching Nika act this way was really disturbing, for both of us.

Raquel smacked Simon's arm. I adored her for that. "She is not. Don't be crude. Panic attacks are different for everyone."

Simon rubbed near his elbow. Raquel had almost hit his funny bone. Too bad she missed. "Whatever ... this isn't normal."

Nika looked over at me with embarrassment and frustration on her face. "Make this stop, Julie."

I sighed as I watched turmoil and passion twist her features. "I wish I could, Nick."

Eyes sympathetic, Arianna asked me, "What did she mean by 'he's coming'?"

I clenched my jaw, this was the worst possible timing for this to happen. There were way too many witnesses up here ... and my parents ... God, I was so screwed. "Um, I don't ..." I dropped it. I didn't know how to answer anyway.

Nika's struggling increased. I thought she was two shakes shy of shoving Trey and I away and jumping out the window. She didn't get the chance though. Her bedroom door exploded inward, the force breaking one of the hinges. Arianna screamed in surprise. Raquel and Simon both jumped. Trey squeaked like a little girl.

Nika, unsurprised, looked up to see Hunter in the doorframe. A crowd was beginning to gather behind him. Nika became uncontainable with Hunter right in front of her. She easily jerked away from Trey. She made a move for Hunter, but I wrapped my arms around her waist and held her back. She was stronger than I was now that she was a pureblood, but I could give her a run for her money.

Hunter was looking at me, but I was pretty sure he wasn't really seeing me. Lowering into a crouch, he dropped his fangs and hissed. I stared at him in disbelief. He was exposing himself. Everyone in the room could see his teeth. Trey's mouth dropped wide open while Simon cursed under his breath. The girls were too shocked to do anything. The crowd around the open door got even bigger as people nearby came to watch the showdown. *How do I stop this?*

"Hunter! No!" I yelled, hoping to get through the fog.

It didn't work. Hunter wanted Nika, and right now, I was the only thing in his way. He blurred over to me with inhuman speed and yanked her free from my grasp. Knowing what would happen if they collided, I tried to get her back. Hunter shoved me, and I felt myself flying through the air. Then the wall rushed up to meet me, and I crashed into it hard, cracking it, and my skull. I sank to the ground, stunned.

With hazy vision, I watched Trey nobly try to get Nika back. He had a slimmer chance than I did though. With one hand, Hunter tossed him across the room. He tumbled over the bed, landing on the other side of it. At least he hadn't hit a wall.

With no one left between them, Hunter and Nika melted into each other's arms. Arianna was by my side in a flash, helping me to my feet while I groaned in pain. Hunter and Nika sank to the floor, clothes ripping in their eagerness to be together. The assembled crowd cheered them on. Horrified, I quickly realized that my sister wasn't going to be able to stop this. Hunter either. They were going to have sex, right in front of a good chunk of the student body. Right in front of *me*. I couldn't let that happen.

Arianna was staring at Hunter and Nika with pale skin and red cheeks. Everyone else was watching them too. I didn't have much time. Blurring to the bathroom, I turned on the water as hot as it would go. Cold water worked well to shock humans, but vampires would barely feel it—they were too cold themselves. To get Hunter's attention, I needed the water to be scalding. The best I could do right now was to get the water mildly uncomfortable. That would have to do. And besides, he was so cold, it would feel like it was boiling.

Emptying the trash nearby, I filled up the bucket, then darted back into the bedroom, praying the whole while that my sister still had her clothes on. Luckily, she did, although, Hunter was tugging at her jeans by the time I got there. Without missing a beat, I dumped the bucket of searing water over them.

Hunter snapped out of it instantly. Gasping in surprise, he looked up at me. "Julian? What the hell?"

Letting out a sigh of relief, I looked behind Hunter to the crowd of amused and amazed guests who had watched the entire thing. Trey stood from the other side of the bed; he appeared to be too dazed to really know what the heck was going on. Simon was more aware, he was staring at Hunter like he'd just seen something that wasn't possible, which was exactly what he'd seen. I tried to lighten the mood by telling Hunter, "Just stopping you from having sex with my sister in the middle of a party."

Hunter looked down at Nika, and they both seemed chagrined. A voice nearby broke through the tittering and whispering. I didn't want to look at the door—I already knew who was standing there—but I didn't have a choice. Reluctantly, I lifted my eyes. Mom and Dad, both pissed, were standing just inside the room. Dad's hard eyes shifted from Hunter, to Nika, to me. "Everyone needs to leave. The party is over."

Hunter stood up, his shirt was torn around the neck from where Nika had tried to rip it off him. Standing in front of her, Hunter used his body to offer some protection from the prying eyes hovering around the door. He wasn't much of a shield though. My bedroom door was wide open now, and people were jostling for position in that doorway too. "Teren, I'm so ... I'm so sorry."

Hunter shrugged in a defeated way, like he had no idea what to do anymore. Even though I was mortified over what I'd just witnessed, I felt bad for the guy. Nika pulled up her pants, then stood as well. "We'll fix this. We'll fix everything."

Dad's eyes narrowed as he circled his finger to indicate all the lookey-lous watching. "Nobody remembers a second of this party. Got it?"

Both Hunter and Nika nodded. I sighed as I locked gazes with Arianna. Great. Now she wasn't going to remember our second first kiss either.

Arianna's face was an almost comical picture of confusion. She looked from me, to Dad, to Nika with her mouth opening and closing, like she didn't know where to begin asking questions. Eventually, she just said, "Julian? What's going on?"

Because I was feeling frustrated that Arianna was never going to remember me, because I was depressed that we'd never have what we'd once had, and because I was angry at the world in general, I told her something I shouldn't have. With everyone's attention on me, I said, "Hunter is a vampire. He turned Nika into a vampire, and whenever they start coming toward each other, their sire-bond kicks in and they start going at it. Oh, and I'm a vampire too, I just still have a heartbeat."

Mom, Dad, Hunter, Nika, Trey, Simon, Raquel, Arianna, and everyone crowded around the doors who'd heard what I just said, gaped at me. Eyes wide, Nika snapped, "Julian!"

Feeling embarrassed for my outburst, I shrugged. "What? You're going to wipe them all anyway, aren't you?"

I knew I'd crossed a line. I knew it with every single cell of my body. Concealment was something Nika and I had been taught since birth. There was no excuse for what I'd just done. None. And even if nobody remembered me saying it, I'd still broken the trust of my family by opening my big, fat mouth. So much for proving to my parents that I was a mature, responsible man who could handle adult decisions. But then again, I'd ruined that the second they'd found out about the party.

Trey slapped my shoulder. "Vampire? For real, or are you messing with me? Can I see your teeth?" Before I could respond, he slugged me in the arm. "Why didn't you tell me you were a freak? Well, at least more of a freak than I already knew you were."

Wanting away from everyone, I ignored Trey and tried to elbow my way past the people blocking the path to my joint bathroom with Nika. Dad wasn't about to let me escape though. "Stay here, Julian. I want to talk to you once everyone is gone." I frowned but stayed where I was. Seemingly satisfied that I wasn't about to sneak out the back door or leap out a window, Dad turned to Hunter and Nika. Beneath the thumping music from downstairs, he murmured, "Hunter, you start on the group downstairs ... I think some are already leaving. Nika, you fix the people up here."

Trey was muttering that he'd suspected what I was all along. The stunned crowds around us were debating whether or not I was crazy. Some believed what I'd said though; I could hear heated conversations traveling down the hall. Pretty soon the careless words I'd spouted would be downstairs and out the front door if Hunter didn't hurry. He gave Dad a stiff nod, then walked around him into the hallway.

As Dad stared Nika down, Mom whispered, "I'll go help make sure no one leaves before they're supposed to."

Keeping his eyes on Nika and me, Dad nodded at her. Mom left, and I forced down a swallow. Dad wasn't harsh or anything, but I'd still rather have Mom around. Nika seemed nervous as she turned to our classmates. "Everybody, can I have your attention?"

I twisted Arianna so she was looking at me, not Nika ... it wouldn't save her, but I wanted one last minute where she remembered our kiss. Her face was scrunched into a strange expression, like she was also wondering if I was crazy. To ease her mind, I hurriedly told her, "I was just teasing about the whole vampire thing, but ... I wasn't about that kiss ..."

Arianna bit her lip. "Julian ... I saw his fangs ..."

Nika's voice overpowered ours. "None of you will remember coming over to my house tonight. You're going to get into your cars, or walk, or ... well, however you got here ... and you're going to go home, to spend some quality time with your family. All you'll remember about the evening was that you *were* going to go to a party, but you decided to do something else instead ... bowling or a movie, or whatever you want. You'll forget about everything that happened here tonight and truly believe that you never came here, the second you step out the front door ... or the back door ... or however you choose to leave my house."

She sounded flustered, and I knew it was because she'd never done anything like this before. I'd probably be flustered too. The music downstairs stopped—Hunter was compelling his own group of teenagers. Without the music playing, you could hear a pin drop; everyone nearby was listening to Nika with rapt attention. She could tell them all to start line dancing and they would. Arianna had even twisted her head toward my sister. I turned her head back, then grabbed both of her hands.

"We can talk about that later, Arianna," I passionately whispered. "I just wanted to let you know that kissing you tonight meant everything to me. I'm here for you ... just know that." I knew she'd forget that the second she left my house, but I still had to tell her. Nika was still droning on with her instructions. She moved out into the hall to include the people who perhaps couldn't hear her.

"Nobody will remember a thing about this house, or about anything you might have seen or heard while inside it ... especially the vampire stuff. Everything Julian said about them, and the fangs you saw, and the super speed. And me making out on the floor! Definitely, no one will remember that ... and if you happened to take a picture or record it on your cell phone, take your phone out right now and delete it!"

Her voice grew heated as she erased a memory that was really embarrassing to her. A few people pulled out their phones and I briefly smiled at my sister. That was a good call on her part. Returning my attention to Arianna, since my time with her was running out, I said, "You don't remember this, but we used to date. No ... more than that. We used to be in love."

Arianna's eyes widened. "What? No ... that never happened. I would *remember* dating you. I would *remember* being in love with you."

I shook my head. "It *did* happen, but the memory was taken from you. That's why you have holes, gaps where you can't remember anything. It was erased, but I swear ... you loved me once. And I loved you. I still ... love you."

Arianna looked confused, bewildered, but at the same time, enlightened and ... relieved. She was staring at me like I'd just flipped on a light switch, and she finally understood why there were spots in her mind that were vacant—and it made sense to her. "Erased," she slowly murmured, like she was testing the word.

Gripping her hands tight, I nodded. "Yes, you were altered, and—"

I wanted to say more, but before I could, Nika gave her last command. "Okay, everyone needs to leave—right now." Smiling, she dramatically swished her arms toward the stairs. The people around us started dispersing, and Nika started giggling. She was enjoying her power trip a bit too much. Dad brought her down a peg by narrowing his eyes and crossing his arms over his chest. Nika instantly bit back her laughter.

Arianna started to move away from me, just like Trey, Raquel, and everyone else in the room. I wanted to physically restrain her, but that would only delay the inevitable. She was tranced to forget the minute she left the house ... a walking time bomb. I still grabbed her hand at the last minute though; it was so hard to let her go again. Her hazel eyes flashed to mine, frustrated and worried like she wanted to leave, but she didn't understand why.

I was about to release her, when someone pushed me away from her. "Let her go! She wants to leave."

Shocked, I looked over at Simon. He was staring at me, his mouth compressed with irritation. I glanced around at everyone else I could see. Besides me, Nika, and Dad, everyone was doing as Nika ordered and starting to leave the house. Everyone but Simon. He was just standing there, staring at me. "Why aren't you leaving?" I stupidly asked.

With pain in my heart, I noticed Arianna slipping around my dad and out the door. That was it. I'd lost her. Again. Simon caught my attention by shoving my shoulder back. "What the hell was all that?" he barked.

"What was what?" I seriously wished I had a better comeback.

Simon pointed at my sister. "Her. Commanding people ... and them listening." He looked around the room. "Where the hell are they all going?" His eyes returned to mine. "And what was all that about vampires? Are you guys insane, or do you really believe that stuff? And how did that guy move so fast!"

Dad walked up to Simon. "You don't feel the urge to leave?" he asked, his tone thoughtful.

Simon looked like he'd rather be anywhere but in this room with me. "Well, yeah, I'd love to go home now, but not because she told me to."

Brows bunched, Dad twisted his head to Nika. "Tell him to do something," he said.

Nika walked in front of Simon. Expression serious, she said, "Give me your wallet."

Simon raised an eyebrow. "Why?"

Nika frowned. So did I. Humans didn't question an order given by a vampire. They just did it. "Tell him to do something unusual," I offered.

Nika's expression turned sour. "I thought that's what I just did." Shaking her head, she said to Simon, "Okay ... cluck like a chicken."

I grinned. That was definitely unusual. Simon put his hands up as if to ward her off. "Okay. You guys *are* all nuts. I'm out of here." He started to leave, but Nika blocked his path.

"Don't move," she stated, her face dead serious.

Simon tried to get around her the other way while my eyes widened in disbelief. He shouldn't be able to do any of this. Worried, Nika looked over at Mom and Dad. "I can't compel him, Dad."

Simon seemed even more bewildered. "Compel me?" He looked at Dad. "You're her dad? No way. You're only a couple of years older than she is."

Dad's expression shifted into concern. "He's just like Jake and Ben …" He looked to me, then Nika. "We have to hold onto him, so Gabriel can test him."

Simon didn't like the sound of that one bit. "Screw you! I'm not being tested by you freaks." He tried to barrel past Dad, but that was like trying to slam through a cement wall; Dad didn't move an inch. His fingers clamped onto Simon though, and held him tight. Simon freaked out once he was trapped. "Let me go! You can't keep me here. This is kidnapping! Your ass is going to jail for at least fifty years! Let go of me!"

Looking like he was repressing a weary sigh, Dad ignored his comments. Stepping up to him, I said in a low voice, "He's right, Dad. We can't keep him … he hasn't done anything wrong." I thought about Simon moving in on Arianna and frowned. "Well, nothing bad enough to contain him. So … what do we do with him?"

Dad suddenly looked very tired. "I have no idea, Julian."

From downstairs, we all heard my mom say, "We take him to Gabriel and let him test him, just like you said. Then we'll decide what to do."

Simon started yelling and shouting for someone to help him. The last few kids walking past the room looked his way, but Nika merely told them to keep walking. Nobody was going to help Simon. His newly adopted family might wonder why he never came home though …

"Dad, we have to stop Arianna from leaving," I stated, panic in my voice.

Dad let out the sigh he'd been holding. "Julian, now isn't the time to talk about you and your ex-girlfriend. I'm very sorry about what went down, but you should be letting her go, not—"

Stepping forward, I cut him off. "No. Simon lives down the street from her. His dad is gone and her family watches out for him ... he's staying with them. She should be compelled with some story to tell her parents, so they won't come looking for Simon when he doesn't come home."

Dad looked at Simon. "The Bennett's are looking after you? Where is your family?"

"Hell if I'm telling you, freakazoid," he muttered through clenched teeth.

Ignoring him, my dad looked at the floor. "Hunter ..."

Hunter, having heard all of that conversation, immediately responded with, "I'm on it. She's almost to the door, I'll bring her back up." My heart started beating harder. She hadn't been erased yet. She still remembered me.

My parents' bedroom door opened, and the sound of giggling filled the hallway. I cursed. I'd forgotten about the kids playing with the soundproofing. By the way they were talking, it was clear they hadn't heard Hunter or Nika's commands. Of course, they probably hadn't heard me spouting about vampires either.

Dad groaned as he looked back at his room. "Our bedroom? Really?" Frowning, he returned his eyes to mine. "You and I are going to have a talk real soon."

CHAPTER THIRTEEN

Nika

KNOWING MY DAD was about to kill Julian, and therefore kill me, since I was as much to blame for the party as my brother, I blurred out of my old bedroom to deal with the people leaving my parents' bedroom. Julian and I were going to be in a heap of trouble over this. But, in actuality, it had proven to be a good night too. Well, not really. I'd nearly had sex with Hunter in front of a crowd. I was still mortified over that fact.

Hunter was in the entryway with Arianna. Even that short distance pulled at our bond. I wanted him to be so much closer. I ached with it. Sometimes I wanted to be free of the bond, of the stress and embarrassment. I just had to be patient though. It would fade over time.

I blurred to a stop in front of two guys and a girl. The guys gasped at my sudden appearance, the girl squeaked. "Stop," I told them. They stopped moving, the girl stopped making noise. The only sound now was Simon shouting at my dad to let him go. Hopefully, he stopped doing that soon.

The group in front of me heard Simon. The panic in his voice, plus me seemingly materializing out of thin air, had the group on edge. I immediately put them at ease. "Relax, I'm not going to harm you. I just wanted to let you know ... you won't remember a thing about coming here tonight the minute you step out of the house ..." With that baseline command given, I then proceeded to play around with their memories.

It was a heady thing to be able to alter people's minds, but I took it as seriously as I could. I was doing this for the betterment of my family, not for my own personal gains. And family was everything to me.

By the time I had them scurrying on their way, Hunter was returning up the stairs with Arianna. The bond kicked in, as it always did when he started approaching me, but since we weren't that far apart, it wasn't nearly as powerful as before. I wanted to be with him, but I didn't want to strip him, pin him to the floor, and make him mine. I breathed through the discomfort until it passed.

Our gazes locked when he appeared at the top of the steps. We both had goofy smiles on our faces that would have sickened anyone watching. But Arianna seemed like she was in a daze as she stood beside him, and my dad and brother were still in my old room with Simon. Mom was cleaning up downstairs, helping the last of the stragglers leave, and cursing about empty cups and broken picture frames.

Hunter and I walked toward each other at a brisk pace, and gave each other a brief kiss when we reconnected. Arianna trailed behind Hunter, looking confused as to why she was following him. She had no choice though. Hunter's command downstairs had been "Follow me," so that was what she was doing.

Not dwelling too long with our joyful rejoining, we headed to my bedroom. Simon was still struggling against Dad, but it was a futile effort. He just wasn't strong enough to break free from a vampire. Julian looked stressed, but the moment he took in Arianna, all of his turmoil faded and a smile exploded on his face. It was like he had a bond with her, just one she wasn't aware of at the moment. Walking around Hunter, Julian took Arianna's hand. She still seemed a little out of it.

"Arianna, are you okay?" he asked, his voice soft with concern.

Her brows scrunched together as she considered what she was feeling. Since my compulsion had told her to leave, and Hunter's had told her to stay, I was sure she was mainly conflicted and confused. "I ... I don't know. I think so. Why am I back upstairs, Julian? I was leaving ..."

Julian smiled even wider when she said his name. He swished a hand at Simon. "We need your help," he stated.

Arianna's eyes went to her friend's. "Simon?"

Simon started shaking his head and spouting, "Run, Arianna! They're monsters! You need to run!"

Arianna couldn't though, the order Hunter had given her made her want to stay close to him. Her eyes widened and she started shaking. "What's going on? Why are you holding him?" she asked.

Dad altered how he was holding Simon, so he could slap a hand over his mouth. His loud complaints shifted to muffled ones. "You know this boy?" Dad asked her.

Arianna nodded, but she didn't say anything more. Dad turned to Hunter. "Ask her to tell us everything she knows about him." Simon struggled, and I could tell he was still beseeching Arianna to leave, but Hunter turned and spoke the question, and she couldn't do anything but comply.

"He's my neighbor. He's been living with me and my family for the past few weeks. His dad is a traveling salesman. He was out on a job and never came home. We helped Simon file a missing person's report, but his dad hasn't turned up yet. The state is letting Simon stay with our family since he doesn't have anybody else. Simon is sad, and scared. He doesn't think his dad is still alive. It's really tragic …"

Her voice died off as her summary of her relationship with Simon ended. Julian's face was a mixture of sympathy and irritation. I'm assuming the former was because he didn't like the fact that Simon was living with his ex-girlfriend.

Dad turned his head to look at Simon. He was red-faced, huffing against Dad's hand as he struggled to free himself. "Traveling salesman? I don't suppose you want to elaborate on your father, do you? Maybe we can help you find him?"

He released his hand so Simon could talk. Simon immediately said, "I'm not telling you anything. Let me go!" Dad returned his hand to Simon's mouth, cutting off his demands, just as Mom joined our group. Mom didn't look happy about any of this.

Arianna seemed even more confused by the exchange. She looked between Mom, Dad, Simon and me, then whispered to Julian, "What's going on? Why is that guy holding Simon? What does he want with him?" She turned to face my brother. "Is this some sort of hostage thing? Are you a part of it? You've got to stop this, Julian. Let him go."

Julian looked heartbroken as he searched her face. "I wish I could, I really do ..."

Arianna shook her head. "Julian, I don't understand ..."

Julian cringed and glanced at me. "I know ... I wish I could explain ... but it doesn't really matter, because, well ... Nika needs to tell you something."

Arianna instinctually looked at me. I wasn't sure what to tell her. Remembering her story, I told her the only thing that seemed feasible to me, "You and Simon were out together. You ran into Simon's father, and Simon left with him. Simon's father said he found work in another city, and they are leaving to start their new life. You're thrilled that Simon is happy, and with his family again. Oh, and you'll forget all about this conversation, about ever coming to this house tonight, the minute you step outside the house."

I looked over at my dad to see if that story was good enough. Dad nodded, and I let out a sigh of relief. Julian seemed sad as he looked back at Dad. "Can I walk her to her car?" he asked.

Dad pursed his lips. "You can walk her to the door, Julian. Any further than that, and she might get confused."

Julian slowly nodded, accepting his answer, and then he turned to Hunter. "Can you tell her that she doesn't need to follow you anymore?" Hunter nodded, and then gave the command so Arianna would no longer feel compelled to stay near him. Julian left the room with her soon after.

Mom gave Dad sad eyes. "I guess we should take the boy to Gabriel now."

Dad let out a low sigh as he nodded. "I hate having to do this, but I don't see another way."

Hating the look of pained resignation on his face, I put my hand on Dad's arm. "It will be all right, Dad. Julian and I will go with you to keep him company so he doesn't feel like a hostage."

Simon glared at me through narrowed eyes, and I was pretty sure he was slaying me in his mind. I thought I could turn him around though, once I showed him that my family and I weren't the bad guys. Much to my surprise, Dad shook his head. "No, you and Julian need to stay here. You can't go out there anymore."

My mouth dropped open. "What? Why not?" I twisted to Hunter. "What did you tell him?"

Hunter's face was bleak, to the point of despair. "We should talk, Nika. Alone."

A chill went down my spine. There was no situation in the world where that combination of words was a good thing. None. Mom and Dad exchanged a look, then left the room with Simon. I nearly begged the three of them to stay; I suddenly had no desire to be alone with my boyfriend. I didn't know what he was going to tell me, but I had a feeling it would hurt. I reflexively crossed my arms over my chest. Sighing, Hunter ran his fingers up and down them. His skin was bone-chilling to people who were alive, but to me, he felt lukewarm.

"Nika," he murmured. Just the sound of his voice made me want to bolt, but I somehow stayed put.

"Don't say it," I bit out.

"Say what?" he said, his voice soft. "You have no idea what I'm going to tell you." The sadness in his face grew with every word he said.

I swallowed, and my eyes felt thick with tears, my vision hazed with red. "I know whatever you're going to say is going to keep us apart, so I really don't want to hear it."

Hunter squatted down to look me in the eye. "Something happened at the ranch. Jake ... attacked, and people were hurt." My eyes widened as fear punched through my trepidation. Seeing my question, Hunter immediately added, "Everyone is fine. They healed." I relaxed a little and nodded. Thank God. I couldn't handle anything bad happening to my family. Not now. Not after everything we'd already been through.

Hunter ran a hand down my hair. "Your father and I ... we both feel ..." He stopped, forced down a hard swallow, then continued. "The bond is dangerous right now. It distracts us, overwhelms us, clouds our judgment. It's going to be the death of us—"

I agreed with him, so I interrupted with, "And that's exactly why we shouldn't be kept apart. It's worse when we're apart."

A sad smile crept into Hunter's lips. "The ranch is too dangerous right now ... but it's where I'm needed. And you're needed here with Julian, with your family."

Not understanding, I raised my hands. "So, your solution is what? Because it sounds like you want to keep staying at the ranch and you want me to keep staying here. I don't see how anything is being resolved that way."

Hunter cupped my cheeks as he let out a weary exhale. "Gabriel's shot. I'm going to start taking it again. I'm going to break the bond ... break *our* bond."

I felt like he'd just ripped out my stomach. "But ... we ... I thought ... You really don't want to be bonded with me." Heavy, blood-red tears dropped to my cheeks.

Hunter brushed them away with this thumbs. "No, no that's not it at all. I love being bonded to you. I love knowing where you are. I love the feeling that comes over me when you're around. But ... I need to keep you safe. That's more important to me than any of the good feelings the bond brings with it. And right now, the bond isn't keeping you safe. It might pull me away from a situation I need to be a part of. It might pull you into a situation you need to stay away from. And ... nothing else matters once it's kicked in. Only you." He looked down, guilt all over his face. "And as much as I love you being the only thing that matters to me, I can't stomach the idea of you getting hurt because I was blind to the danger. I'm sorry, Nika. I just can't handle that."

I wanted to object with his assessment of our bond's power, but everything he said had merit. We'd narrowly escaped exposing ourselves in a very public, embarrassing way. I swallowed a knot in my throat, then whispered, "I know."

Hunter drew me into his chest for a quick hug. I wrapped my arms tight around him, wishing we could stay like that for a million years. Hunter quickly broke the moment by saying, "And we should be honest about our relationship. Everything happened so fast ... and you're so young."

I looked up, about to object to that comment but he silenced me with his next statement. "We were thrust together by some pretty traumatic circumstances. It's like our feelings have been put on overdrive instead of naturally growing at a slow, steady pace. And now, the bond is ramping up every sensation we have ... How much of what we feel for each other is because we really feel it, and how much of it is from the bond?"

I blinked at his question. My feelings for him were something I'd never worried over. I loved him, with every fiber of my soul. But he had a point. We'd been thrust into a dramatic, live-or-die situation, where every moment was intensified. Then the bond had taken over our lives, skewing our feelings. If we put all that aside, would we still have the same warm, loving relationship we had? I felt positive we would but we'd never really know our true feelings if we didn't explore them. I didn't want to wake up ten years from now, when our lives had settled and the bond had lessened, and realize that my feelings for him had never been real. Or vice-versa. That would be incomprehensible. I didn't think I would feel any differently years from now, but … if we didn't take this opportunity to find out now … how would we ever know?

Even though I felt like my dead heart was cracking open, I told him, "You're right … we should break the bond. We should see if this is real." More tears dropped to my cheeks as I admitted defeat. Although, it wasn't necessarily defeat. It could quite possibly be what strengthened us. Yes, I preferred to think of it that way.

Hunter nodded, then his eyes started glazing over. "Don't think this is easy for me, because it's not. The thought of no longer being connected to you..." He closed his eyes and a shiver washed through him. "I'd rather drink a vial of pure silver than do this, but I really don't see another way."

I cupped his stubbled jaw and he opened his red-tinged eyes. "I know. Will you do it tonight?" I asked, feeling a phantom heart thumping wildly in my silent chest. *Was I losing him right now?*

Under my fingertips, Hunter shook his head. "No … I need to talk to Halina before I do anything. I need her to understand. I won't do it behind her back again."

I nodded as I felt the tension in my body marginally relax. I had time, at least one more night. I wasn't sure what good a brief amount of time really did me, but delaying the inevitable felt wonderful. Letting go of his face, I whispered, "I want to be there when you talk to her. She might take it better if it comes from both of us."

Hunter smiled, the guilt lifting from his expression. "Thank you. I really appreciate that and I think you're right." He looked down, to where my parents were struggling with Simon in the kitchen. He was still trying to cry out for help. "I should help them get Simon back to the ranch first." He returned his eyes to mine. "We'll have to take a car, since we ran here."

I frowned as I considered all of the things keeping me from my family home. "The ranch is turning into a prison. I'm really not thrilled about that."

I heard my dad sigh downstairs, and I knew he agreed with me. Hunter did too. "Nobody likes it, but it's just how things are right now. We need somewhere to put the hunters we can't compel, and the ranch is the safest place for them."

"And what if there are more than two? What if there are a *lot* more than two? How many people are we going to contain? And for how long?"

Hunter's face darkened with every question I asked. "I don't know ... but I doubt there will be any others. This is rare ... a fluke. And Gabriel will figure out why they're immune and once we understand, we'll be better prepared." He stroked my cheek. "We'll fix this ... soon, and then we'll be together."

I refrained from showing my disbelief at that statement and gave Hunter an encouraging smile. What they were trying to do seemed improbable and unending, but what choice did they have? If they didn't do something, then the hunters would pour down on us en masse, just like they'd done a couple months ago. But Simon wasn't a hunter ... he was just immune. Locking him up with Jake seemed wrong. All of this seemed wrong.

Grabbing Hunter's hand, I blurred downstairs with him. Dad was holding Simon's arms behind his back while Mom clamped a hand over his mouth. Simon was breathing heavy as he tried to jerk away from my parents. He reminded me of a wild stallion resisting being broken. Even though I knew Simon was privy to all our secrets and could easily expose us, I didn't want this for him.

I put my hand on Dad's arm. "Leave him here. Julian and I will watch him. Starla, Jacen, and even Uncle Ben can help us keep an eye on him."

Dad shook his head. "Gabriel needs to test him. We need to know why he can't be compelled."

I raised an eyebrow at Dad. "Gabriel needs his blood. Take a sample back with you, but leave him here. He's innocent. He's not a hunter like Jake. He's just a kid, Dad." I added. "He's just like us."

Dad hesitated before he answered, and I could see that he agreed with me on some level. He looked over at Mom. She pursed her lips, shrugged, then nodded. Dad looked over to me again. "All right. He's just a teenager, not a threat. For now, he can stay here with you and your brother. But I'm calling Ben, and letting him know what's going on." He pointed at Hunter. "And I want you to stay here with them, at least for tonight."

Hunter blinked in confusion. "But we talked about this ... I'm needed there ..."

Dad nodded while I squeezed Hunter's hand. He was needed here too. "I know," Dad said as he shook his head, "but that was before this ... complication." He sighed. "Emma and I need to go back ... I need to get my car, give the sample to Gabriel, check on Jake ... Just watch over them tonight, okay? Then you can return." Dad's eyes flicked to me, and then over to Julian who was shuffling into the room with his head down. I didn't need the emotional bond in place to know that Julian was heartbroken. Again. He must have said goodbye to Arianna. Again.

Hunter straightened as he took Dad's assignment to heart. I wanted to roll my eyes. I was a pureblood vampire. I could handle one freaked-out teenage boy all by myself. I resisted the snotty behavior and attempted to act mature. Dad was ordering my boyfriend to stay with me all night. I didn't really want to argue him out of that.

While a surge of excitement went through me at the thought of Hunter staying here, a surge of panic went through Simon. He fought against my dad, and then pulled away from my mom. He managed to get his mouth free long enough to shout out, "You're not getting my blood! No way, no how!"

Mom grimaced, clearly not liking the idea of puncturing his skin. "Teren, how do we take his blood out? I'm pretty sure we don't have any syringes lying around the house. And it feels wrong to take it against his will like this."

Dad inhaled a deep breath, then shook his head. "I don't know, Em, but we need a sample. We need answers."

Thinking we were going to slice him open, Simon started freaking out in earnest. I felt bad for him, but we really didn't have a way to subdue him, unless we wanted to knock him out, and I didn't want to do that. Maybe there were some of Trey's special brownies left ...

With a burst of adrenaline, Simon broke away from Dad, and made a dash for it. Unfortunately, since Julian, Hunter, and I were blocking his escape, the only direction Simon could run was around the island. A hallway on that side of the kitchen led to the laundry room and a mudroom, with a door that led to the side of the house and to freedom. My super-fast family wasn't about to let that happen though.

Dad blurred the opposite direction, beating Simon to his retreat. Hunter moved in right after Dad, stopping a few feet behind Simon, so he couldn't escape that way either. Seeing Dad seemingly appear out of thin air in front of him, Simon pulled up short. Unfortunately for Simon, the kitchen was an absolute mess. Spilled drinks, broken chips, and empty plastic cups were all over the ground. Simon slipped on the remnants of a Jell-O shooter near the fridge. He lost his balance and started to fall.

Hunter and Dad reached out for him, but Simon grabbed the counter beside him before either vampire touched him. Proving that nothing was going right for Simon tonight, the spot where he'd grabbed to steady himself was home to a small collection of sharp ceramic pieces—remnants of a decorative plate that hadn't survived the party. When Simon smacked his hand down, a thick piece cut deep into the meat of his palm. Jerking in pain, he pulled his hand back and continued falling to the floor.

The smell of blood was fresh and heavenly. Simon groaned as he clutched his bloody hand to his body. He'd been so afraid of us taking his blood, that he'd inadvertently given it to us himself. Dad and Hunter were kneeling bedside him in a flash. Dad examined Simon's wounds, then lifted his eyes to Julian. "Quick, get a container. Something with a lid." When Julian scampered off, Dad swung his eyes to Mom. "And get some bandages."

While Mom zipped away, Julian came back to Dad and gave him a shallow bowl. As Hunter held Simon in place, Dad grabbed his wrist. Simon, scared and in pain, jerked and bucked so wildly against Dad that I was sure he'd get away again. Hating what we were doing, I blurred to Simon's side, and helped to hold him steady. Between Hunter and I, Simon was now being held almost perfectly still.

Simon's eyes were wide as Dad brought his injured palm to the bloody bowl; the large piece of ceramic was still stuck inside it, staunching the flow. If Simon wasn't suffering from shock, I was sure he'd be screaming again. I wished I could compel him to make this easier. But if I could compel Simon, we wouldn't have been in this mess in the first place. I tried again anyway. Attempting to hold his gaze, I told him, "Relax, you're okay. We're going to help you. You'll be fine. Just relax." I repeated it over and over, but it didn't matter. Simon wasn't relaxed.

Not wanting to torment him any longer, Dad pulled out the piece of plate and squeezed Simon's hand. Simon cried out in surprise and pain, but he was firmly stuck. A small pool of blood collected in Simon's palm. Tilting it, Dad poured the blood into the bowl, filling it with the dark, red liquid. In just a few seconds, the bowl had a small collection of blood in the bottom of it.

"Is that enough?" Mom asked, returning with a bandage.

Dad gave Simon a remorseful expression. "It will have to be. I want to get him cleaned up and calmed down."

He handed the bowl back to Julian, so he could put the lid on it. Once the blood was secure, Dad stepped away from Simon, and Mom kneeled down to tend to his hand. Simon was shaking in my arms, his teeth chattering. His chin was lifted and he was trying to be brave, but I could tell he was terrified.

Mom murmured gentle words as she cleaned his palm with a wet rag, checking for stray ceramic pieces as she went. She sort of sounded like I had earlier, when I'd been trying to compel him to calmness. It worked better with Mom saying it, and Simon minutely relaxed under her touch. Once Mom was finished bandaging his palm, she patted his hand and helped him stand up. When he was on his feet, she let go of Simon and nodded at Hunter and me to follow suit. When we did, Simon stared at his palm, then to the hallway leading to freedom, then back to his palm again.

Simon was somewhat calmer now that he wasn't restrained, but he still seemed to be on the edge of a nervous breakdown. "I want to go home. Why are you holding me against my will? And ... what *are* you people?" His eyes were wide as he stared at Dad.

Dad held up his hands. "We're not going to hurt you, but you need to stay at the house. So long as you stay put, nothing will happen. No one will hurt you. I promise."

Simon straightened his stance, but he didn't look at all relieved by Dad's words. Lifting the bowl of blood, Dad turned to Mom. "We should get this to Gabriel."

Mom nodded, but Dad seemed hesitant to leave us with Simon. I was just about to tell him he was overreacting, when Hunter spoke up. "I've got this. Go, get the blood to Gabriel. Get some answers."

Dad patted Hunter's shoulder. "I have a feeling all I'm going to get are more questions." He gave Julian and me a hug, then Mom did the same. Grabbing Mom's hand, Dad told us, "I'm going to call Ben and Starla on the way, although, I doubt Starla is going to be of much use right now." He sighed and shook his head, then narrowed his eyes in seriousness as he stared at Julian, Hunter and me. "You call us if anything, *anything* goes wrong."

Grabbing my hand, Hunter told him, "We will."

Dad gave him a grateful expression, then turned his eyes to Julian. "When we get back, we're all going to sit down and have a discussion about this 'party' the two of you were having." Julian let out a pained sigh while I bit my lip. That conversation wasn't going to be fun. With one last look at Simon, Mom and Dad blurred out of the house. I could feel them down the street in the blink of an eye.

Once they were gone, Simon seemed a touch more relaxed and a touch bolder. He took a step toward the exit. "I'm sure whatever sort of babysitting plan you guys had in mind for me was great and all, but I think I'll just be going now. Thanks for the hospitality."

A low growl escaped Hunter. "You'll never make it, kid. I'm a hundred times faster and stronger than you. I really don't want to hurt you, so stay put."

Maybe realizing that not all of the threats had left, Simon froze. Julian suddenly looked very nervous and antsy. I wasn't sure why, or if I was really reading his emotions correctly, but he seemed preoccupied as he bit his nails and shuffled from one foot to another. I studied him while Hunter asked Simon, "Do you have any idea why Nika couldn't trance you?"

Simon's face went completely blank. "What the hell are you talking about? What the hell are any of you talking about?" Gently touching the bandage over his palm, he muttered under his breath, "I'm surrounded by lunatics."

Ignoring his comment, I looked up at Hunter. "He doesn't know anything." Returning my eyes to Julian, I finally asked him, "Got ants in your pants, Julie? What's with you?"

He removed his thumbnail from his teeth, gave me a pondering onceover, then walked over to me. Nodding his head toward the garage, he said, "I've got to show you something ... but I don't want you to get mad."

I instantly frowned. "What did you do?"

Not answering me directly, he grabbed my hand from Hunter and started pulling me toward the garage. I watched Hunter grab Simon's arm, pulling him along to follow us. I wasn't sure what I was going to find in the garage. I kept my mind open to anything, but I was sure I was still going to be surprised. Julian and Dad weren't done organizing the space, and boxes of junk to be tossed or sorted were scattered here and there. I was pretty certain that after this fiasco, I'd be out here helping Julian finish. Maybe Hunter would have to help too, since he'd been a part of the cover-up. That seemed only fair.

Julian pointed over to a couple of camping chairs in the corner and my mouth dropped. Gaping in disbelief, I stared over at Arianna sitting on one. Julian had hidden her away in here instead of making her leave the house. Unbelievable. I smacked Julian's arm with every ounce of my enhanced strength. He cringed away, holding his arm. "Ow, Nick!"

"You're gonna think ow," I snapped. "What is she doing here? She's supposed to be on her way home, blissfully ignorant of everything that happened here tonight."

Julian's face went from irritated to embarrassed. "I couldn't send her away again. I couldn't make her forget again. She kissed me, Nick. We had a moment, a *great* moment—and I want her to remember that we had it. And you didn't give her the desire to leave the house that time, so all I had to do was convince her to stay. And so long as she stays in the house, she remembers, and the garage is still technically part of the house."

I felt like smacking him again. "Julian! She can't stay in the garage for the rest of her life."

Thanks to my shrieking, Arianna noticed us. Her features were a combination of confusion and concern as she stood and started walking our way. While we watched her approaching, Hunter joined us in the garage, a struggling Simon in tow. Hunter frowned when he spotted my brother's ex. "Why is she still here?" he asked.

"Because my brother's an idiot, and he's trying to get us into even more trouble," I muttered.

Julian gave me pleading eyes. "Arianna isn't a problem, Nick, and you know that. Just erase the memory trap you implanted, and I'll make sure she gets back home."

I stared at my brother like he'd just told me he'd purchased the moon online. "What? I can't—"

By this time, Arianna had reached us. "Julian? You told me you'd explain, so ... what's going on? What was all that upstairs? And why are you guys holding Simon like he's ... dangerous or something?" Her eyes flicked to Hunter and his unwilling captive. Her gaze fell on Simon's bandage and eyes widened in concern. "Oh my God, are you hurt?" She hurried over to him and grabbed his hand with both of hers.

"Arianna, you should ..." Simon cut off on his warning when Hunter squeezed the spot on his arm right above his elbow. Flinching, Simon changed his sentence to, "It's nothing. I was just clumsy, slipped in the kitchen."

Arianna seemed to believe him, but she also didn't like Hunter hanging on so tight. With a scowl, she yanked Simon's arm free. Frowning at all of us, she crisply bit out, "Will someone please tell me what the hell is going on?"

I debated wiping her memory right then and there, but Julian was still begging me with his eyes. He wanted her to remember their time together so badly. He wanted to avoid having to start over. And a part of me wanted that too. I wanted Julian and Arianna back together, and they'd taken a huge step toward reforming their relationship tonight. With a sigh, I nodded my head toward the kitchen. "Come with me, and I'll tell you exactly what's going on."

I supposed it wouldn't hurt anything to tell Arianna, yet again, what my family was, and what predicament we were currently in. It wasn't like she would remember for long anyway. Julian could wish for her memory to remain intact all he wanted, but it wasn't up to him, and since Arianna didn't remember being in love with him, it didn't make much sense for her to remember that he was a vampire. At the very least, I'd have to wipe that part of the evening. But then how would I explain the fact that none of her friends remembered the party? Crap ... I *had* to take it all.

Julian reached out for Arianna's hand. She hesitated as she stared between his palm and his eyes, but then she held her fingers out. I couldn't help but wonder if some intrinsic part of Arianna knew that Julian and I were safe, that she could trust us. I liked that thought, that somewhere deep down in her subconscious, she knew us.

With a small smile on his face, Julian led Arianna back into the main part of the house. Simon's eyes turned into deadly daggers as they left. Not thrilled with what I was about to say, I turned to Hunter. "Stay out here with Simon. He knows too much already, no need to tell him everything."

Hunter glanced at Simon, then leaned in and gave me a kiss on the cheek. "What are you going to tell her?"

I shrugged. "Everything I can. Then I'm going to send her home, and she won't remember any of it." The sadness of Arianna forgetting about tonight was almost too much to bear. Julian was going to lose the connection they'd made, but what else could I do? I couldn't leave the good segments of the evening without leaving large chunks of the rest—like the fact that she was here because of a massive party. At least Julian would get a few more minutes with her this way. At least he would get to say goodbye.

Hunter nodded. "I'll give you a few minutes alone ... but don't take too long. I don't like being apart from you."

He kissed my cheek again and I sighed. "I know. I don't like it either." I knew that what Hunter really meant was that he didn't like being apart from me right *now* when we were watching somebody, even though the person we were watching was a harmless teenager, but my mind leapt forward and a flash of pain went through me. Not too far from now, Hunter was going to sever the bond and we'd be apart for an indefinite amount of time while he worked on Jake at the ranch, and I stayed here with Julian. Maybe it was for a good reason, but the idea of being separated still sucked. I had a newfound appreciation of my brother's misery.

CHAPTER FOURTEEN

Hunter

I WATCHED NIKA leave with hollowness in my heart. I might put on a brave face, but I really hated the idea of no longer being bonded with her. It gave new meaning to the word torture. I halfheartedly kept an eye on Simon while I listened to Nika in the kitchen. She was telling Arianna everything that she shouldn't be telling her. Everything about vampires, everything about their parents—their *real* parents, everything about Arianna and Julian being a happy couple until fate had torn them apart and Halina had erased Arianna's mind. Nika was explaining it all.

Simon was examining the garage while I listened. Sitting on a cooler, he was flipping through the camping gear. I kind of felt bad for the guy. He hadn't done anything wrong, he just couldn't be forced to forget. Somebody else who we couldn't fix like we wanted to. Frustrating didn't even begin to describe it.

Simon cleared his throat and I looked back at him. He was holding a coiled bracelet that I believed was supposed to keep mosquitoes at bay. I had a feeling it didn't work very well. "So, I couldn't help but overhear that you're holding another captive. Hostage taking a new pastime of yours?"

I frowned at his assessment. "You're not a hostage ... and no, it's not a hobby." Although it was starting to become a problem.

Simon tossed the bracelet aside and picked up a square lantern. "But you do have somebody else, right?" He turned the lamp on and stared into the fake flames glowing through the frosted plastic panels.

"Yes," I simply stated. Anything else would either be a lie, or too much information.

Simon nodded as he turned the light off. "Jake?" he said, as he put the lamp away. He rummaged through the box at his feet, stopping when he found metal pie plates. "And how old is that kid?"

"He's an adult." Oops, I probably shouldn't have told him that. Clamping my mouth shut, I twisted toward the door leading back to the house, so I could focus on that conversation and not give Simon any more information.

While I listened to Arianna asking Julian why she couldn't remember him, even though Nika had already explained that already, I heard Simon dink around for something else in the myriad amount of camping gear. "Interesting," he mumbled. A little louder, he added, "And where do the adult hostages get to stay? Some place more luxurious than the Land of Forgotten Camp Supplies, I'm assuming?"

When I looked back at him, he raised a cast-iron pot into the air. I frowned as I answered him. "As I said before, neither one of you are hostages." I twisted my lips as I thought about what we were doing, and how wrong it was. What other choice did we have though? "You're more like temporary prisoners."

Simon gave me an angled smile. "Awesome. That's so much better."

I crossed my arms over my chest as I turned to face him. "Sometimes life doesn't give you what you want. Sometimes you just have to accept what is, and move on."

Simon's face darkened as he continued digging around the box of odds and ends. "Trust me, I know all about things not being fair." Before I could comment on that, Simon asked me, "So, who is that Gabriel guy, and what's he gonna do with my blood?"

I really wasn't sure how to answer that. Being vague seemed best. "He's a friend. He's just running a couple tests."

Simon stopped rummaging and looked up at me. "To find out why you can't boss me around? Because you're all...vampires?" His expression was dubious, like he didn't believe a word of it. It was best for everyone if he didn't.

"Vampires aren't real. Julian was joking earlier. What we suffer from ... could be called vampirism in some cultures, but we're not the mythic variety." I shrugged. *That sounded good, right?*

Simon still looked like he was surrounded by halfwits. "Yeah ... okay. Anytime you loonies want to let me go, I'm more than ready to leave." His expression turned thoughtful. "Or is that why you're really holding me and this Jake guy? So you have something to eat. Or drink, or whatever it is your kind does? Is Jake already dead, and that's why he's not here?" While his tone was still full of disbelief, there was bitterness in it now too.

I rolled my eyes at him. "Of course he's still alive. We're not as bad as you seem to think."

"So ... where is he then?" he asked, forced casualness in his voice.

I narrowed my eyes as I studied him. "Why do you want to know?"

Simon gave an unimpressed shrug. "You said you found someone else in the world that you can't control. I find that interesting, and I'd like to meet the guy."

I was about to tell him that that wasn't going to happen anytime soon when I heard an odd sound outside. A continuous grinding sound, like wheels rolling over concrete. A skateboard. I held my breath, waiting to see if the sound was going to stop or keep going. To my dismay, the sound started moving up to the walkway. Then I could hear someone stepping off the board, and walking up the front steps. Simon asked me, "What?" but I ignored him as I honed in on the slow, calm heartbeat right outside the front door.

"Now what?" I murmured. It wasn't Ben, he would have driven here. It wasn't Jacen, he would have walked. I supposed it could be someone here for the party? They were just arriving really late.

As a light knock filtered through to me, I crooked my finger at Simon. "Come with me." His eyes narrowed, but surprisingly he didn't object.

Once we were back inside the house, I could see Arianna staring in disbelief at both Nika and Julian. Everything they'd been telling her was frazzling her mind. The bond was filling me with a light, but pulling sense of joy. Ignoring the need to be with Nika, I locked eyes with her. She smiled at me as Julian glanced my way. Another knock rang through the hard wood and Julian blinked. Guess he'd missed it the first time. He stood up, but I raised my hand. "I got it," I said, walking to the front door.

Putting my hand on the knob, I looked over at Simon, still following me. "You make a break for it, and I'm just going to run you down and tackle you. And I won't be gentle. Something will probably break."

Simon clenched his jaw, so I figured he believed me. I opened up the door a crack to see who was here. When I saw who it was, I swung the door wide in surprise. Holding his skateboard in one hand, Julian's friend Trey was standing there with a bored expression. "Trey? What are you doing here?"

He sniffed when he saw me. "Oh, hey ... Nika's BF. Julian here?" He looked over my shoulder, spotted his friend, and walked into the house without even waiting for permission. "Hey Julian, Little A. I'm glad you guys are here. I thought for sure you'd be out at the ranch." He nodded at a still-stunned Arianna. "Hey, Arianna. You finally going to give Julian a chance?" He held his thumb up to Julian and mouthed, "Awesome."

Julian's face filled with color. If the night had been going better, I might have found it funny. Looking around me, Simon asked Trey, "I'm sorry, did you say ranch?"

Trey glanced over at him. "Yeah. The Adams family ranch, a magical, mystical place that makes me question my friend's sanity, since he chooses to live here instead of there." I wanted to slap my hand over Trey's mouth, but he was on to something else before I could. "Wait, who are you?" Before Simon could answer, Trey seemed to notice the devastated condition the house was in. His eyes snapped back to Julian. "Dude ... the party ... I was totally going to come, but then I changed my mind ... and went to a movie." He scrunched his brows, like he didn't understand how'd he come to that decision. "Wow ... I'm so lame. Sorry. How was it?" he asked, looking like he was angry at himself.

Julian moved forward to greet his friend. "Trey? How are you here?" Julian seemed baffled by Trey's presence. I was too. Nika had told him to go home. He shouldn't be here.

Trey shrugged as he took in the carnage. "*How* am I here? Uh, I rode a skateboard?" He pointed outside for emphasis. "I had this weird urge to chill with my family tonight, but, uh, my family is lame, and you guys are more like family to me, so I thought I'd hang with you."

Julian opened and closed his mouth while I realized the problem in Nika's compulsion. She'd told everyone to hang out with their family. Trey's family was apparently the Adams. He must have gone home, then turned around and come right back. As I took in the group assembled before me, a sense of foreboding filled my stomach. The last time I'd hung out with Julian, Nika and Arianna, it hadn't ended well. And now with Simon and Trey in the mix ...

I stepped forward to stand in front of Trey and Simon. Seeking Nika's eyes, I said, "Nika, I think it's time that the guests go home." I frowned as I looked over at Trey. "And stay home."

Trey blinked at me, then shrugged. "Why are you looking at me like that?"

Rolling my eyes, I ran my hand back through my hair. "No reas—"

I didn't get to finish my sentence. Pain exploded all over my body, starting from a point just under my shoulder blade. I gasped as I fell to my knees, and my vision swam as I felt the wetness of blood running down my back. I instinctually reached behind me, but I couldn't get whatever was hurting me. Shouting and screaming filled the air, then someone kicked whatever was in my back even further into my body. I cried out in pain as I crashed to the floor. Maybe I was imagining it, but I could have sworn I felt the object touch my heart. I couldn't move, I couldn't breathe. I was positive that anything I did would shift the weapon and puncture the only thing that was keeping my dead corpse somewhere near the realm of the living.

Nika was beside me a heartbeat later. "Hunter!"

She tentatively touched the object and I hissed out, "No!" She could inadvertently kill me by trying to move it. "Simon," I whispered. He was the only one who could have done this. The only one with a desire to hurt me.

Nika stroked my forehead. "He's gone. He took off after you hit the floor. Jesus, Hunter. He shoved a knife in your back."

A knife? A sharp, serrated knife. That explained a lot. "Go ... get him," I muttered, blackness encroaching on my vision. The pain was so great, it was about to knock me out.

"I'm not leaving you," she bit back. "And Julian won't leave Arianna. Trey ran after him ... but he'll never catch him. Simon stole his board ..."

I strained my ears, listening for the sound of Trey's skateboard, Simon's heartbeat, but I was in too much agony. I couldn't focus. All I could hear was Arianna asking Julian over and over, "Is he okay? Is he okay? Jesus, will he be okay?"

Nika's hand flittered around the object protruding near my spine. It felt like I was on fire around the area of impact. "What do I do?" she asked, her voice high and nervous.

I didn't know how to tell her that it was resting against my heart, that if she pulled it straight out, she'd slice my heart open, essentially staking me. And with as badly as it hurt to make the small movement needed for speech, I didn't want to think about how excruciating its extraction was going to be.

"Don't pull it straight out. Push it away first. Along my ribs." I patted my side with my fingertips, so she would know which direction to go.

I heard the panic in her voice when she answered me. "You want me to cut you even more? I can't … I can't do that."

I inhaled a quick breath so I could speak. It burned. "Have to. You'll cut my heart if you don't."

"Oh God," she muttered. "I'm gonna be sick."

"You'll be fine," I whispered. I was the one who was going to be sick.

I heard Julian approach her, a sniffling Arianna beside him. "I can do it, Nick."

With a determined voice, Nika told him, "No, he's my sire, my boyfriend. I'll do this for him."

My eyes were closed, but I could clearly see the defiant set of Nika's jaw, the blaze of determination in her eyes. Her never-give-up spirit radiated around her, giving her dead body life and vitality. She was an amazing gift, and I was grateful every day for her. Even when she was about to cause me tremendous pain.

I felt her fingers wrap around the object inside me. It sent tremors of agony through me. Knowing what was coming was horrific. I wanted to cringe away, I wanted to run, but all I could do was wait. Wait for her to hurt me, to help me. She pulled down on the blade until it hit a rib bone, then she shifted her position and slid along the bone until she was well clear of my heart.

I'd never felt anything more painful in all my life. Ten times worse than the initial cut. Twenty times worse than Simon shoving the blade in deeper with his boot. I'd rather be knifed a hundred times over than ever be carved again. I screamed out with the pain until I lost all coherency. I thought I heard someone crying, but it could have been me for all I knew.

Once the knife was out, the pain subsided but not by much. I curled into a ball, then felt Nika position me onto her lap. Hands pressed against my back, holding my torn skin together so it could heal. And even as I recovered, I could feel my body knitting back together. I knew I should get up and go look for Simon, I just didn't have the energy or will power to do it. I needed to rest, I needed to heal, and I needed the last remnants of pain to fade. Right now, I was completely worthless.

The front door banged against the wall, and I looked over to see Trey standing in the doorframe, panting and shaking his head. Holding his side, he told us, "He was too fast. I couldn't catch him." Hands on his knees, he started inhaling deep breaths. When he noticed me, and the amount of blood on and around me, he barked out, "Jesus! You all right? I was sure you were a gonner."

Wanting to do anything but move, I shifted to my hands and knees. My head swam as an electric zing of pain rippled across my torso. "I'm fine. He missed." I glanced down at the knife on the floor. It was a long serrated knife that looked to be about twenty years old, and had seen much better days. It was sharp enough to cut through me though, and that was all that mattered.

Fingers shaking, Arianna shook her head. "No, he didn't miss. He got you. The blade was up to the hilt."

I looked up at her pale, but stoic face. "Yeah, he got me, but he missed what was important."

Arianna swallowed and looked over to Julian. "It's all true? Everything you just told me?"

Julian nodded as he took her hand. "Yes. Every word."

Arianna's eyes drifted to Nika's, then mine. "You're all vampires," she whispered.

From the door, Trey muttered, "Vampires? Holy shit ... that explains so much."

Sighing, I tried to stand. Nika immediately ducked under my shoulder to help me. Surprisingly, Arianna hurried under my other shoulder. She was trembling like a leaf and too weak with her human strength to really support me, but I appreciated the gesture nonetheless. "Thank you," I told them both. "I just need time. Then I'll be fine."

Trey clapped his hands then walked over to Julian. "Seriously? You're a vampire and you never told me? Why the hell would you keep that from me?"

Julian gave him a tired, wry expression. "I've actually told you a few times, you just don't remember."

Trey's mouth dropped open. "You made me forget?" He smacked Julian's arm like Nika sometimes did. "What the hell? Whatever happened to the Bro Code? You don't erase your best friend's memory." With a pointed finger, he indicated Nika and me, then he tapped his knit cap. "None of you get to touch this masterpiece."

Nika pursed her lips, and looked about to speak when I stopped her with a look. "He's not the problem right now. Simon is. We need to find him."

Nika turned her gaze to me. "He's a kid. Yes he knows, but what damage could he really do?"

A slice of pain went through me and I swallowed. "Taking me from the back, he nearly punctured my heart with a rusty hunting knife that he found in the garage. That's not as easy a task as you'd think. He knew what we were and how to get rid of us, before we did or said anything. He played dumb so we'd drop our guard. He's a hunter's son, just like me. I'm sure of it."

Nika's eyes searched mine, then she looked over to her brother. "If that's true ... then his being immune and Jake's being immune isn't a coincidence. They're related. Jake is his missing father."

Trey let out a low whistle. "Wow ... that's ... well, actually, I have no idea what any of that means."

Julian elbowed Trey while I pieced together my conversation with Simon in the garage. "Simon will try and get Jake away from us." My eyes drifted to Trey as I recalled him telling Simon about the ranch. "And I'm pretty sure he knows exactly where Jake is. We need to get to the ranch as soon as possible."

I tried to take a step forward, but my strength wasn't up to par yet. Nika was the only thing keeping me standing. Arianna struggled with her side of me, and Julian rushed over to switch positions with her. While Arianna rubbed her sore shoulder, Nika said, "You're in no shape to run. We'll have to drive."

Trey stuck a finger in the air. "Shotgun!"

Julian shook his head as he gave Trey a stern look. "You're not going, dude."

Trey mimicked Julian's stern expression as he crossed his arms over his chest. "Hell if I'm not. My friend's sister's boyfriend just got stabbed by my friend's wannabe-girlfriend's neighbor, because my friend, his sister, and his sister's boyfriend are all bloodsuckers, and they're holding my friend's wannabe-girlfriend's neighbor's father hostage at their ranch fortress." He lifted his eyebrows, the arch of them disappearing under his hat. "That's hella confusing. How in the world am I gonna keep all of that straight if I don't tag along?"

Julian seemed unsure how to answer that. While he stumbled for words, Arianna piped up. "I'm coming too."

Sadness washed over Julian's face. "You can't, Arianna. You need to stay here. The second you leave … you'll forget everything that happened … again."

Arianna looked over at Nika. "You said we were best friends, right?" Nika nodded remorsefully. With a stubborn set to her jaw, Arianna told her, "So, as my former best friend, I'm asking you to remove whatever it is you did to me, and let me keep my memories. They're mine anyway. You don't have the right to just take them or change them whenever you want to."

Nika cringed. "It's for your protection as well as ours, Arianna."

Arianna shook her head. "Trey and I are human beings, Nika, not science experiments. If we want to remember this, we should be allowed to." In a softer voice, she added, "And I won't tell anyone. I promise."

Nika looked to me, then Julian. A clear question was in her eyes—*What do we do?* My gut told me we should just wipe them clean, send them home, and be done with it, but these two were just kids to me. I had no personal attachments to them. Nika and Julian though … they mattered to them. "You guys decide," I whispered. "But do it quick. We should get going."

Julian thought over my words while he stared at Arianna. After a long moment, he finally said, "Are you sure you *want* to remember this?" He indicated the dark pool of blood on the entryway floor.

Arianna peeked at it with the corner of her eye. Her face was an unhealthy shade of white, but she nodded. "It's my right," she said. I smiled at her answer. The girl had guts.

Nika locked eyes with her friend, then her brother. After another moment of contemplation, she finally said, "Arianna, when we leave the house, you'll keep your memories of everything that happened tonight."

Arianna let out a quick exhale of relief and resignation. Julian looked over at Nika. "Can you make her remember everything she's already forgotten? Everything about us?"

Nika scrunched her brows together. "I don't think so, Julian. Once it's gone, it's gone."

"Just try," he pleaded.

Nika sighed, but turned back to her friend. "Arianna, you now remember everything you knew before about you and Julian being in a relationship."

Arianna looked like she was thinking really hard as her hazel eyes concentrated on Nika's face. After another moment, she let out a heavy breath like she'd been holding it in. Turning her eyes to Julian, she gave him a sad shake of her head. "I still don't remember. I'm sorry."

Julian nodded as he swallowed. "It's okay. It's just not there anymore." Overwhelmed with disappointment, Julian looked away. I felt bad for the kid. My nicked heart still ached a little, but that pain was nothing compared to the shambled state of his heart.

"Let's go," I murmured, feeling a little steadier on my feet.

Nika drove us out to the ranch, while I sat in the passenger's seat recovering. Julian and Arianna sat next to each other in the back of the station wagon, holding hands. Trey pouted as he sat on the other side of Julian. His pouts quickly turned to questions, though, and I swear, in a span of twenty minutes, he asked Julian every vampire question known to man. "Do you really drink blood? Are you dead? Were you bitten? How do you walk around during the day? Does silver hurt you? Garlic? Holy water? Crosses? Can you fly?"

I found it very hard to not tell him to shut up. Instead, I kept my eyes closed and concentrated on blocking out the irritating nonstop talking. I'd started out the evening trying to keep everyone away from the ranch, and now here I was, bringing even more people back to it. Time was of the essence though. Simon was going to try to break his father out, and someone I cared about could get hurt in the process.

My phone rang, and before I even answered it, I knew I was about to have an unpleasant conversation. Digging into my pocket, I pulled it out. "Hello?" I asked, my voice finally no longer laced with pain.

"I thought you were staying at the house with Nika? Why are you all on your way here?" It was Teren's voice on the line. He wasn't happy. "I thought we agreed that the ranch wasn't a good place for the kids."

I sighed as I answered him. "We had a bit of a situation at the house. Simon got away. He's more than he led on to be …" I massaged my chest, where a phantom ache still lingered.

"He got away?" Teren asked. "How?"

I didn't want to go into details of my superb screw-up, so I changed the subject as best I could. "Simon may be a problem. You need to make sure Jake is being well watched." I knew he would be, there was no way Rory and Cleo weren't all over him after what he did to Gabriel, but better safe than sorry.

"Jake? What does he have to do with Simon? And how would Simon know where he was? Did you tell him?"

I sighed again and glanced over my shoulder at Trey. Julian had a hand over his mouth, so Teren wouldn't know he was in the car. A lot of good that precaution would do once we got to the ranch and the family spotted him. "He was informed unintentionally. We aren't 100 percent sure, but we think Jake and Simon are related somehow. Father and son maybe. And we're fairly certain Simon is coming for his father, and he most likely won't be alone. We're expecting you to have company soon."

That was met with a long moment of silence. "This is getting more complicated than I'd originally anticipated."

In the background, I heard Emma say, "Teren, we should talk about this. Maybe we should just let Jake go."

In answer to her and him, I said, "We'll be there within the hour. Gather everyone, but don't do anything yet. Okay?"

Another quiet moment of contemplation, then, "All right. Hurry though." Nika stepped on the gas in answer.

She looked over at me while she flew along. "You okay?"

I nodded as I hung up the phone and tucked it back into my pocket. "I'm tired, but much better."

Nika frowned. "You need to drink. You should have had something before we left."

I peeked in the rearview mirror. Arianna's eyes were wide as she listened, her face pale. Trey was too busy telling Julian that his hand smelled like Cheetos to hear Nika's comment. I returned my gaze to Nika. "There wasn't time." My eyes drifted to the window. "There still isn't ... drive faster."

I could feel the car's speed increase as Nika pushed the station wagon to its limit. I hoped the car held together, and that we made it there in time. I wasn't sure what was going to happen but in my gut, I knew it wasn't going to be good. Like the markers flashing by me, my anxiety grew with every mile.

When we got to the ranch, I was a bundle of nerves. I half expected to see a dozen hunters surrounding the home, wearing all black and scurrying up the walls on thin ropes suspended from grappling hooks, loaded down with enough weapons to take on a small country. But when we pulled up to the triple front doors, the gargantuan home was quiet, the steepled roof empty. No one was attacking us. Yet.

Trey let out a low whistle. "Damn, I still can't believe you don't live out here all the time. I'd refuse to leave if I were you. Just bolt yourself to one of the bedrooms. There's gotta be like fifty thousand of them."

I rolled my eyes at Trey's comment as I got out of the car. There were a lot of rooms, but not nearly that many. It was definitely nice though. For a time it had felt like a prison to me, just like it must feel for Jake, but I viewed it differently now. It was home. And I would do anything to protect it.

Nika had stopped the wagon right in front of the doors, instead of driving around to the garage. As she walked around to help me out of the car, the center set of front doors burst open, and like a swarm of agitated bees leaving the hive, a stream of concerned vampires emerged from the house.

Halina was first. She rushed over to me, while I extended a hand to Nika. Her eyes were huge, the whites of them faintly highlighted with a phosphorescent glow as she took in the bloody evidence all over my shirt. The back of it was ragged from where Nika had ripped it, and it was sodden with blood. Even after the time it took to drive here, it was still wet, still clinging to my body.

Grabbing my hand, Halina yanked me forward. "You need to eat. And rest. I need to make sure you heal properly."

I resisted her tug. "I'm fine, and we don't have time for that now."

She arched a brow at me. "Because a *child* knows where we are? I have no fear of children."

I shook my head. "You'll fear him if he leads an army our way."

Nika clenched my hand as she looked up at me. "Do you think it will come to that?" She looked over to the home, and I knew exactly what she was thinking. Our family had just survived an attack. It was too soon for another one. Not that time would make an onslaught any more pleasant.

"I hope not," I told her, trying to sound optimistic. My eyes returned to Halina's. "But just in case, we need to be prepared."

Sighing, my sire finally nodded. "At least let me bring you something to eat?"

My fangs almost dropped at the thought of a meal. I wasn't eating enough. I wasn't sleeping enough either. I wasn't killing myself, but I certainly wasn't doing my body any kindness either. "That would be wonderful, thank you."

She beamed at me like a proud parent, then rushed back into the house, but at a human speed, since innocents were watching. By the time her jet black hair was gone from sight, everyone was out of the car, and everyone was out of the house. Well, everyone but Jake and his bodyguards. I assumed they were still downstairs.

Teren was eying me with concern. "What happened?" he asked. His eyes flashed to Trey and Arianna, but my wounds taking precedence, he held off his questions about them.

I kept my expression even as I admitted how badly I'd messed up. "Simon got a jump on me, stabbed me in the back with a hunting knife. Nearly nicked my heart," I admitted in a low voice.

Teren's gaze switched to his children. Alarm and fear was clear in his features. I shared the same feeling of horror. If Simon had gone for one of the others ... Nika ... I didn't know what I would have done if she'd been hurt like that. Again. "He's coming for his father," I told Teren. Knowing the question was coming, I supplied the answer about Trey and Arianna. "These two were there when it happened. They saw everything."

Frowning, he responded with, "You should have erased them and sent them on their way."

I couldn't explain how I'd been too tired and Nika had been having doubts about playing with her friends' minds, so I simply said, "It was easier and faster to bring them along. And time is of the essence. He could be here any moment."

I looked around at all the easy-to-hit targets roaming around the driveway. Emma was examining her daughter, making sure she was fine, even though Nika kept repeating that she was. Alanna was hugging Julian while Jack looked on. The older man still appeared a little frazzled from his earlier incident with Jake. Imogen was explaining who she was to a still-stunned Arianna. Halina's daughter had an affinity for Julian's paramour, and maybe hoping that Arianna was going to be allowed to remember the evening, she was telling her the truth. Gabriel was giving Trey an impassive stare down, like he cared little who he was or why he was here. Knowing Gabriel, he probably wasn't even paying attention to Trey or his endless questions. Hopefully, he was stewing over the mystery of Simon's blood. Linda was standing on the other side of Gabriel, Emma's scarred sister, Ashley standing by her side. Ashley's husband, Christian, was standing next to her, looking very tired, and very confused; he was clueless about all of us.

Returning my eyes to Teren, I told him, "We need to get everyone in the house. Now."

Sensing my urgency, Teren nodded and turned to his mother. "Get everyone back inside."

"They would be safer in the rooms down below," I added.

Alanna looked from Teren to me, then nodded. With Imogen's help, they started herding the humans indoors. All I saw as I looked around the people I cared about was casualties. Casualties of a fight I'd inadvertently started when I'd tried to compel a man who couldn't be compelled.

After the last of the humans were ushered into the house, Christian looking even more bewildered by the late-night commotion, I heard a sound that froze my blood near solid. It was the distinct noise of car tires turning into the driveway. I tensed. It couldn't be Simon. He wouldn't be stupid enough to drive straight up to the house. Would he be desperate enough though?

A low growl rose from my throat as I crouched into a defensive position. I looked around for a strategic place to hide, somewhere that I could get the drop on Simon, if it was indeed him approaching. I could only hear one vehicle in the driveway, so if it was him, he was alone. That could be a good or bad thing. If others were with him, they might be making a stealthier approach while Simon had us distracted.

Picking out a good spot near a dark clump of trees before the driveway split into a wide circle, I dropped Nika's hand. Sensing my intentions, she clutched my shoulder. When I looked back at her, she was shaking her head. "Stay here with me."

"It could be him," I answered, removing her fingers from my shirt.

Teren tilted his head, listening. "No ... that's Ben's SUV." His brow scrunched together in confusion. "What is Ben doing here?"

I didn't know, and I didn't care. All I cared about was getting everyone together and safe. "Are you positive?" I asked, listening to the vehicle's progression down the road.

Teren nodded. "Same tread pattern, same engine noise. It's him."

I relaxed my stance as I waited for him to arrive. I could deal with Ben. Halina returned, a travel-sized, stainless-steel coffee mug in her hand. I could see steam rising from the small hole at the edge of the lid. The scent of fresh blood wafting from it nearly dropped me to my knees. I was much thirstier than I'd realized.

I grabbed it from her without a word and immediately began drinking. Nika rubbed my back while I pounded it down. The metallic sweetness of fresh blood was still somewhat horrifying to me but it was so good, and so necessary to my strength and survival, that I ignored the barbarism of the act. This was how I lived now, and Nika, Halina, and the rest of the Adams, were what I lived for.

By the time I handed Halina back the mug, Ben was approaching the home in his car. His wife was with him, which surprised me some. I looked in the backseat for their little girl, but I didn't see her. Ben pulled to a stop by Nika's station wagon, then hopped out. Teren was by his side a moment later, clapping him on the shoulder and asking him what he was doing here.

Ben looked over to Nika; Julian had gone into the house with his girlfriend. "I went to the house to check on the kids after you called. They were gone, but Jacen was there. He said he wasn't sure where everyone had run off to, but we both decided it had to be here. I figured something was up, so I left Olivia with Jacen. Tracey is still a little freaked about that, but she wanted to come with me." With pride in his eyes, he indicated his wife with his thumb; she was talking to Emma, but flashing nervous glances at Halina and me.

Ben's eyes slid to my shirt. "What happened?" he asked, mirroring Teren's earlier question.

"That's what I'd like to know," I responded. "And there's really only one person here who has the answer." Without waiting for a response, I turned on my heel and headed toward the house. Nika immediately followed me. The others were only a couple of steps behind.

Heading toward the secret passageway in the living room, I listened for the family. I couldn't hear anyone though, so I had to assume they'd followed my directions and were all in the lowest, soundproof level. I could only imagine Trey's animated responses to all the wonders he was seeing tonight, and I wondered if Arianna had stopped shaking.

Once I was on the lowest level, I stepped through the main soundproof doors on the way to Jake's new home here; he'd been moved to a room at the end of the hallway. Even without already knowing which room he was in, I'd have found it right away. Rory and Cleo on guard outside was a dead giveaway, as was the heavy iron bar latched into place across the door. While we'd been allowing him certain freedoms during the day, he was always locked up at night. I passed by a large common room on the way there, and found almost everybody. As I'd predicated, Trey was dumbstruck by the underground layers he'd never known existed.

"Okay, as your best friend, tell me the truth ... is the Bat Cave down here too?" While Julian rolled his eyes and stroked Arianna's hand, Trey exclaimed, "Come on, it makes perfect sense—vampires, bats, Bat Cave. It's a no-brainer."

I continued on past Julian and Trey, with Nika beside me, and Teren, Emma, Halina, Ben and Tracey on my tail. I looked up at Rory when I got to the door. The large man didn't have an ounce of humor on his face as he stonily stared straight ahead. It was clear he was exhausted. Cleo too. We all were. Having to guard someone twenty-four-seven was draining, even if we did take shifts.

"Open it," I told him.

Without hesitation, Rory unlocked a padlock on the outside of the door, and lifted the iron bar. It was excessive to use that kind of a lock on a human and normally we didn't, but after today, everyone was on high alert. Especially me. After Rory unlocked the door and opened it, I stormed through. Rory's eyes took in the condition of my bloody shirt, but neither he nor Cleo said anything. Fearing failure, they might have been too afraid to know the answer.

With a death grip on Nika's hand, I walked over to where Jake was lying on his bed, staring up at the ceiling. He didn't bother looking at me as I approached. He knew we wouldn't hurt him. He had nothing to fear from us, but we had something to fear from him. That was what his message today had been about.

"Who is Simon?" I asked, my voice calmer than I felt.

His head snapped to the side, his eyes instantly glued to mine. "What?" His voice was casual, but in a strained sort of way.

"Simon," I repeated. "Roughly sixteen. Blonde hair, blue eyes. About this big." I indicated his size with my hand. "Good with knives," I added, a small twist to my lips.

Like he couldn't care less in the world, Jake returned his eyes to the ceiling. "Doesn't sound familiar," he grumbled.

Tightening my grip on Nika's hand, I said, "Good. So when he comes down on this ranch, guns blazing, you don't mind if we fight back? You don't care if he dies? Because the odds are really good he won't survive." Odds were good some of *us* wouldn't survive either, not that I was going to mention that fact.

Jake's eyes returned to mine and he sat up. "What? He's coming here? Why? What did you tell him?" His eyes were blazing with genuine concern now, as I'd known they would be. No one wanted to see a family member in trouble. And there was no doubt in my mind that Jake and Simon were related.

"Who is he?" I repeated.

Jake rubbed his lip as he looked at Teren, Ben, and me—the three he saw as threats in the room. Little did he know Halina could probably decapitate him with one hand. Eyes washing over all of us, Jake pleaded, "Please, let me go. I have to stop him."

Teren frowned as he stepped forward. "So he is coming here? To bust you out?"

Jake shot up off the bed and ran both hands through his hair. Face frantic, he shook his head. "No, he wouldn't come here, not alone. He'd get help, and the only person he knows who can help him is …"

His sentence trailed away. Reaching out a hand, he grabbed Teren's arm. "I'll do anything you want. I'll say anything you want. I'll believe whatever you want me to believe. I'll protect your nest and your family as if it were my own, and I'll take your location and the knowledge of what you're doing with hunters to my grave. Just please ... I need to get to him, I need to stop him. If I don't, he's going to die. And he's just a kid ... please don't let him die. Help me save him, before it's too late."

My eyes were wide as I listened to his impassioned speech. I'd expected him to say several things, most of them derogatory and unhelpful, but I'd never expected him to say anything like that. The fear on his face and the concern in his voice made an electric zing of anxiety zip up my spine.

Who—or what—could frighten a seasoned hunter who was surrounded by vampires?

CHAPTER FIFTEEN

Nika

THE AIR WAS thick with tension. My vampire eyes could almost see it hanging in the room, like a light fog shrouding everything in mystery. Hunter was staring at Jake with a dumbfounded expression. He had no idea what he was talking about. I didn't either. The vampire hunter had done a complete one-eighty in a matter of seconds, and all because of the kid we'd just met tonight...Simon.

While my father gently removed Jake from his arm, I asked a question that had already been asked several times. Maybe we'd finally get an answer though. "Who is Simon?"

Jake's tired eyes turned to mine. "A kid. Orphaned, but I've raised him since he was in diapers. I showed him how to protect himself, but he's never …" His eyes flicked back to Dad's then Hunter's. "He's never been alone this long. And now that he knows I'm in danger he'll do whatever it takes to get me out of it."

"You're not in danger," Dad quietly told him. "No one here is going to hurt you."

Jake shook his head. "Simon won't know that. I've raised him to think the worst of your kind. Right now, he probably believes I'm being shackled and drained. Just a little at a time, until my body finally gives out. He'll be in a state of panic, and he'll do something stupid." He clenched his hand into a fist. "Because of me."

Dad met eyes with Mom. No words passed between them, but I knew what they were saying regardless. *We have to help him, Teren. I know, Em.* Help the helpless, defend the weak. It was just the way my parents were. But family trumped all, and they wouldn't do anything if it would put us in too much danger.

Mom shifted her eyes to Jake. "What trouble is Simon in? What do you think he's going to do?"

Jake fell onto the bed, his body suddenly as exhausted as his eyes. "Normally, he'd call up a hunter friend of mine and ask for help, but ... hunters have been acting weird lately, almost preaching against hunting. I wasn't sure why until I went to that stupid meeting ..." He glanced up at Hunter, guilt, knowledge and irritation in his eyes. With a sigh, he looked at his hands resting on his knees. "Anyway, before I disappeared, the last thing I told him was to stay away from hunters, so there's only one place he'd go for help now. My grandfather ... Henry."

Jake's eyes hardened in a way that was nearly as vicious as when he spoke about vampires. Feeling nothing but love and adoration for my own grandfather, I didn't understand Jake's expression. "Why is that a bad thing?" I asked, hoping I didn't sound young and naïve.

Turning to me, Jake studied my face, then my hand clenched in Hunter's. "Henry is a brilliant man. Too smart for his own good actually. He came upon a ... vaccine of sort. Telling us it was necessary to protect the family, he gave us each a dose. We weren't even sure what it did at the time, but we trusted him."

Jake sighed, his eyes taking on a faraway look. "When the first of us showed to be immune to vampire compulsion, he admitted what he'd done. The vaccine infused vampire blood into our blood. He'd injected us with a little bit of the demon ... to keep us safe. To keep us protected." Clearly not happy with that fact, Jake's face momentarily hardened. When he spoke again, fear softened the heat in his eyes. "When that proved successful, he got greedy. He thought, if a little bit of blood would protect us from compulsion, then maybe more would give us some of the vampire attributes. If we had vampire strength and speed, we'd be better soldiers, better fighters. He started introducing vampire blood into people, little by little, hooking up volunteers to IVs that would drip vampire juice into them for hours at a time. When that did nothing ... he had the idea to balance the blood. Remove half of the human blood, and replace it with a vampire's, to create a being that was the 'best of both worlds' as he called it." Jake smirked on the end, like he didn't really believe that.

My mom gasped while my dad muttered, "He was trying to make mixed vampires? With transfusions?"

Jake calmly met his gaze. "Yes. We didn't know about you at the time, but that's essentially what he was trying to do. Make living vampires."

Dad shook his head. "It doesn't work like that. Mixed can hardly ever make more mixed. And full vampire blood ... it wouldn't make a mixed vampire. It would make another pureblood, or it would ..."

Dad let his thought trail off while Jake nodded. "Or it would kill them. I know." He stared at his feet. "My father was one of the volunteers. He didn't survive the process. None of them did."

Hunter squeezed my hand while Jake lifted his chin and returned his eyes to Dad's. "I told Henry he needed to stop with the experiments, that it couldn't be done, and his own son was dead because of it. Maybe it was his grief talking ... maybe it was just pure stubbornness, but he refused to stop. He said he had to keep trying, especially after Dad's death. 'Otherwise, it was all for nothing,' he said. Only problem was, once word got around that the experiment never worked, and wasn't ever *going* to work, people stopped volunteering. The day he tried it on an unwilling participant, was the day I took Simon and left. That was six years ago, and I haven't talked to Henry since."

"Is he still doing the experiment?" Hunter asked with a furrowed brow.

Jake ran a hand down his face. "Yeah. A buddy of mine told me a few months ago that he was."

"You think he'll force Simon to go through with it if he shows up?" I asked, hating the sudden mad scientist vision in my head.

Jake pressed his lips together as he shook his head. "Honestly, I have no idea. Simon is family, not some easily missed transient that Henry found on the street. But ... my fear is that ... if Simon thinks I'm locked up in an impenetrable fortress full of bloodthirsty vampires ..."

"He'll volunteer," Hunter finished, glancing down at me.

Jake's eyes were watery when he looked up at Hunter. "Yeah. He'll volunteer so that he'll be strong enough to bust me out, and he'll die before he even has a chance. Or worse ... Henry will accidently change him into a pureblood. If that happens, he'll stake him the second he wakes up ... just like he does with all the others he accidentally converts. Just like he did to my father, his own son."

The sudden pain in Jake's face tore my heart. Reaching into my pocket, I pulled out my cell phone. "Call him. Tell him you're fine and you're safe. Invite him out here, so he can see for himself." I shrugged and looked at my parents. They didn't seem opposed to the idea, and surprisingly, neither did Halina. She pursed her lips, but nodded in approval.

But with a grieved expression, Jake told me, "That won't work. Simon will just assume it's a trap. I taught him too well," he murmured, his voice drifting off.

I didn't know what other suggestion to make, other than, "Let's go get him then." All eyes in the room shifted to me. I met every pair with stoic resolve. "Jake's family is in trouble. Family is everything, so ... we need to help him."

Julian had wandered into the room at this point, holding hands with Arianna. He looked unsure about what we should do, but after a moment of consideration, he nodded in agreement. Even though Simon wasn't his favorite person—or mine, he *had* tried to kill Hunter, after all—right was right, and Julian knew that.

Mom and Dad shared a prideful look, then Dad nodded. "We'll take you to him, Jake. Show him you're fine." Dad clapped Jake's shoulder. "Everything will be okay. You'll see."

Jake looked hopeful for the first time. "We have to hurry. Henry doesn't live far from here, a couple hours north, in Blackfoot. If Simon found a ride or was able to get a bus at this hour, he could be close. But knowing him, he probably hotwired a car and is already there." Obviously impressed, Hunter smiled at that comment. Even Julian looked amused. I rolled my eyes. Men.

My father looked around the room, examining the members of his family and choosing which ones would stay, and which ones would go. Releasing Hunter's hand, I took a step forward. "I want to go, Dad."

Both Dad and Hunter turned to me, and almost unanimously said, "No."

I frowned at both of them. "It's one teenage human and one old man. I won't be in danger."

Jake gave me a parental once-over. "Henry won't be alone. He'll be surrounded by hunters who are immune to compulsion. Hunters who routinely trap vampires, so Henry can drain them dry and use their blood for his pointless experiments. They'll attack any vampire they encounter, provoked or not, just for their blood. Trust me girl, it *will* be dangerous."

Hunter furrowed his brows in an expression of I'm-your-sire-listen-to-what-I-say. "Stay here with your brother and the humans."

I narrowed my eyes at him. "I'm not afraid. I'm strong, I'm fast, and I can help."

Hunter seemed unimpressed with my argument. He was about to provide his rebuttal, when my father put a hand on each of our shoulders. "You *are* strong, and you *are* fast, and we can't leave the nest unprotected. It could be that we're wrong. It could be that Simon went to hunters, found some we have yet to compel, and has formed a hunting party to retrieve Jake. If so … here will be the most dangerous place of all." True concern washed over his eyes, and I knew a part of him really believed that.

He had a point. We couldn't be certain where Simon had run off to. If we made the wrong assumption, and all of our strongest fighters left, the rest of the family would be in danger. I couldn't let that happen. I nodded at my father. "I'll stay. I'll protect the home."

A smile full of pride touched Dad's lips. "I know you will." Looking around again, Dad said, "Hunter, Ben, Jake and I will go get Simon. The rest of you stay here." Halina cleared her throat and crossed her arms over her chest. Dad flicked a glance at her, then lifted the corner of his lip. "You can come too, of course."

Halina rolled her eyes. "Like I need your permission to leave, child."

Dad grinned, then turned to Jake. "Let's go get your son."

A ghost of a smile brightened Jake's face. "He's not my son. Not really."

Dad clapped him on the shoulder. "Close enough."

Julian swallowed so loudly, we all turned to look at him. "I'm coming with you."

Arianna's face went a ghostly shade of white. She clutched at his arm and whispered, "No … he said it was dangerous. I don't want anything bad to happen to you."

Julian gave her a sad smile. "I'm sorry, Arianna, but I *have* to do this. It's my fault Simon found out about my family. I screwed up by throwing that party, by telling everyone in that room what I was, and I need to make things right." He kissed her cheek, and she suddenly flushed with color. Her eyes sparkled with multiple emotions—fear, confusion, desire. I knew she wouldn't be allowed to remember this night, but if she somehow could … I knew she'd choose to be with Julian. She'd always chosen Julian. She just didn't remember.

Arianna still seemed worried, but she didn't comment further. My dad had the same argument ready for Julian that he'd had for me though. "It's too risky. You're staying here with the others."

Julian lifted his chin. "It's not your call to make, Dad." He shifted his gaze to Halina, the true authority in the room. "I created this problem, and I want to be a part of the solution. *I* need to fix my mistake … not let others do it for me."

Dad immediately objected. "No, you're staying here and that's final."

Halina appraised Julian for a few moments, and then turned to Dad. "If he wants to come, he may."

Dad's eyes flared in warning. "No offense, Great-Gran, but you're not his parent. No matter what he said, it isn't your call."

Halina didn't look intimidated or ruffled by Dad's words. "He wants to make amends, and he's old enough to do so. And I happen to agree with him … he should fix his own mistakes." She shrugged. "Besides, it's not as if we're sending him into battle alone. He'll be perfectly safe tucked between you and me."

Dad seemed at a loss. He looked at Ben, me, then Mom. None of us had any helpful advice, so we stayed quiet. Finally, Dad tossed his hands into the air. "Fine. He comes." Dad pushed his finger into Julian's chest. "But you listen to everything we tell you, and you obey what we say without hesitation. Understand?"

Julian nodded, and I could see the fierce determination on his face. And the guilt. He truly did want to fix this.

Dad indicated the door to Jake. Jake glanced at it tentatively, like he was nervous to walk through it. He did though, and Rory and Cleo immediately grabbed him. Tired or not, they weren't about to let him walk past their defenses. And unlike the rest of us, their human ears hadn't heard the conversation. They had no idea what was going on.

Hunter stepped forward to intercept the vampire hunters, but Gabriel beat him to it. Facing Rory, Cleo, and the captive they were firmly holding between them, Gabriel coolly intoned, "Let him go. He's coming with us."

Even standing behind him, I could tell that Gabriel made Jake uneasy. Hunter had told me that Jake had attacked someone, someone who had healed. By Jake's reaction to Gabriel, I was pretty sure I knew who Jake had targeted.

Rory and Cleo immediately let Jake go. He shrugged away from them, then nodded a thank you to Gabriel. Gabriel raised his arm, showcasing the hallway, and Jake moved past him, his eyes still wary. Halina walked through the door next. She stopped beside Gabriel. She didn't touch him, but her tone was soft when she spoke. "*We're* taking him. Are you coming with?"

Gabriel tilted his head as he studied her face. "I wish to go with you, to help keep you safe, but I realize that you may not want me around, so I will do whatever you want, my love."

Halina was stone still for a moment, while Mom, Dad, Ben and Tracey brushed by her as they exited the room. When Hunter and I squeezed through the doorframe, Halina glanced over at Hunter, perhaps remembering what Gabriel had momentarily taken from her.

"My apologies are eternal," Gabriel whispered.

Halina's eyes returned to his, and her fingers reached up to lovingly stroke his neck. "Are you all right?"

Gabriel nodded once. "Physically, I am fine."

Her fingers shifted to cup his neck. "And emotionally?" she murmured.

Gabriel closed his eyes and pain clearly flashed over his features. It felt intrusive to be watching them, so I averted my eyes and followed my parents down the hallway. I heard Gabriel's answer though. "I miss you," he told her. There was so much raw emotion in his voice that I couldn't stop myself from peeking a glance at him. Emotion of any kind was rare from Gabriel, and therefore, so much more powerful when it surfaced.

I saw Gabriel lower his head in apparent agony, then I saw my grandmother wrap her arms around his neck. "I miss you too," she whispered in his ear. She started nibbling on his earlobe and I turned back around. Some things I didn't need to see.

My parents had stopped Jake in the common area where Trey was hanging out with my grandfather, aunt, uncle, and all of my grandmothers, besides Halina. Mom and Dad were talking strategy with Jake and Ben. I was sure Hunter would want to join them, but instead, he stopped several feet away and looked down at me, then back at Halina still hugging Gabriel.

When he returned his eyes to me, the dark brown depths were torn. "We should ... before I go ..." Pausing, he let out a heavy sigh. "This probably won't be as dangerous as Jake made it sound, but I can't afford to be ... distracted while I'm gone. You and I ... we need to ..."

He looked down at his feet, and I could tell he didn't even want to say it. I supplied the answer for him. "We need to break the bond. Now, before you leave?"

Pain in his eyes, he looked up at me. "Yes. For your safety as well as mine."

I felt my throat closing up and tears stinging my eyes. I'd known this was coming, and he was right, we needed to do it. But it still hurt. Just thinking about doing it was painful, the actual act would be torture. And I wasn't the only one who would be affected by the bond being broken. The shot Hunter was going to take would sever his bond with everyone he was attached to.

Even though she was still wrapped in Gabriel's arms, Halina overheard us. She was immediately at Hunter's side. "What? You're going to sever the bond again?" she asked, disbelief in her voice.

I felt bad that there wasn't more time to ease her into the conversation. To really explain why it needed to happen, and give her some time to deal with it. But if I was staying and Hunter was leaving, and neither one of us could afford the risk of being drawn to each other at an inopportune moment, then this needed to happen right now.

Dropping my hand, Hunter grabbed Halina's shoulders. "I'm sorry. I wanted to sit down with you, explain why I needed to do this and give you time to prepare, but there just isn't any time."

A red sheen moistened Halina's eyes. "You said you wouldn't do that to me again. You know how awful it was."

Hunter nodded as he smoothed her hair. "I know. And if things were different, I wouldn't do this. I don't want to, but I have to. It's the only way I can keep Nika safe. It's the only way I'll be able to stay focused while we're apart. You know what the bond does to us. If we're at a critical moment in Simon's rescue, and the drive to rush to Nika kicks in … I could get you all killed. And I won't risk that. I won't put my family in danger like that."

Halina gave him a small, sad smile. "Your family?"

Hunter wrapped his arms around her, bringing her into his embrace. "My family," he told her, kissing her head.

My eyes misted, and I had to look away. Jake was watching the tender exchange with a strange expression on his face, like he was seeing something he didn't know how to process. I hoped he was beginning to understand that being a vampire didn't necessarily mean you were a monster. We had lives, feelings, families … aside from being undead and living solely off the blood of other animals, we were just like everybody else.

After Hunter and Halina parted, Hunter looked past her, to Gabriel. "She's given her permission. Can you bring the shot to my room, please?"

Gabriel nodded, then turned to go to his lab. Halina frowned. "I don't know if I would call that my permission. I still don't like this … but … I understand."

Hunter nodded, then kissed her head again. Dad broke apart from Jake and the others to walk toward us. He put his arm around Halina, leading her to the circle plotting a potentially deadly mission. Dad must have figured that would make Halina feel better. He was probably right too. Hunter led me away, to his room. Normally, going to my boyfriend's room would have given me delightful goose bumps, but not today. Today Hunter's room was the last place I wanted to be.

I was practically dragging my feet by the time we got there. Hunter looked equally glum. He halfheartedly opened the door and pushed it inward. Even with no effort involved, the door still banged against the far wall. I stepped inside with a heavy sigh. I'd rather be doing something far more interesting in this room than temporarily removing our bond.

That delightful thought instantly set fire to another one. I was fairly certain I wouldn't be able to talk Hunter into sex before he left, but I might be able to convince him to do a different intimate act with me. Hunter turned on the light and we waited a few, brief moments until Gabriel arrived with a small, stainless steel suitcase. He handed it to Hunter, inclined his head in a respectful manner, and then left the room, shutting the door behind him. Quiet descended on us once the wooden door was closed. Like all of the bedrooms down here, Hunter's room was soundproof.

The still in the air was both natural and unnatural. It had been a long time since I'd heard so little. Like I was standing next to a freeway, there was usually a constant stream of background noise around me. The absence of sound amplified everything else. My skin felt on fire with anticipation, and I was overly aware of where Hunter was in the room. His light breath was behind me while I scanned the art on his walls, the odds and ends on his bookcase, the rumpled sheets on his bed.

Without a word, Hunter headed to his dresser and placed the suitcase on top of it. Unclasping the latches, he lifted the lid and exposed the handful of syringes tucked inside. I wanted to sigh again, but I held it in. He had to do this. I understood.

With sure, steady hands, Hunter grabbed one of the vials and removed it from the case. Walking over to him, I grabbed his arm. He turned to look at me, and there was no hiding the sadness in his eyes. He didn't want to do this any more than I wanted him to. Swallowing a lump in my throat, I said in a low voice, "Before you take it ... can I have my birthday present?"

A confused expression passed over him for an instant, and then he understood. His mouth dropped open and the pain in his eyes shifted to desire. "Nika ... I don't think now ..."

I pressed a finger to his lips. I didn't want to hear his excuses. We both wanted this, and there was no reason to deny ourselves anymore. I replaced my finger with my mouth, and worked my lips against his. A deep noise of satisfaction escaped his throat, and he shifted to set the syringe down.

One of his hands came up to cup my cheek, the other reached behind me to pull my body tight against his. Our slow breaths quickly increased, and I felt a phantom heartbeat pulsing in my chest. Hunter's tongue slipped between my lips and a groan escaped me. I was instantly grateful for the soundproofing. I also started to wonder if we had time for more than what I'd originally planned. I knew we didn't though. He had to leave me soon.

As his fingers drifted from my cheek to curl around my neck, mine ran up his broad chest. Every muscle was defined under my fingertips, and I could easily picture the curves and valleys of his skin. It only made me want him more.

Pulling my mouth away from his, I breathed across his cheek, "Please, bite me …"

I felt a growl rumble through his chest as his grip around me tightened. His hand on my neck shifted to pull my shirt down my shoulder. I hissed in a breath as my skin was exposed. His lips dragged across me, sending shockwaves of sensation through my body. I could feel the indentation of his teeth extending as his mouth pressed against me. My own teeth, no longer containable, dropped of their own accord.

I bunched his shirt in my hands. Feeling lightheaded, needy, and so full of love I thought my heart might burst, I moaned, "Yes."

I hiked my leg up his thigh, needing to feel more of him. His free hand grabbed my leg, holding me tight against him. His desire for me was almost overwhelming. I could feel all of his straining muscles. It made me feel weak, wanton, and lustful. I couldn't reach his neck from my position, so I told him, "Lift me." He instantly reached down with his other hand and scooped me up.

Wrapping my arms and legs around him, I settled my lips at the base of his neck, over his jugular. Hunter found the same sweet spot on me, and I ground against him in delight. "Now … I want you …" I murmured, before pressing my fangs into his skin.

Hunter let out a deep groan, then pressed his teeth into me. With my lips still firmly attached to his body, I cried out and grasped him even tighter. I almost couldn't take the heady, erotic rush of drinking from him while being entangled with him. It reminded me of our first electric time together. It made me want to make love to him, but we couldn't. This was it for now. And it was enough.

Our bodies moved together in a teasing, stimulating way while we drank, and I felt like I'd been transported to another world, one where nothing else existed but Hunter. It was a fabulous world, one I never wanted to leave. I felt strong in his arms. And loved … cherished. I never wanted to let him go.

Hunter released me first. With a gasp, he pulled his mouth away. His hands helped my hips rock against his while I continued to drink. With longing in his voice, he murmured my name. I felt a familiar ache building as his life poured into me. I knew I should stop. I should let him go so he could leave with the others, but I was past the point of being able to. With a few more frantic rubs against him, a powerful wave of ecstasy washed through me. I released him as I rode out the sensation with a series of light moans. It had been too long. For the both of us. Hunter's body was still ready to go. I wished I could help him as I came down from my high, but I knew he'd say no. Now wasn't the time, here wasn't the place. Just the fact that he'd let it get this far spoke volumes about how much he'd needed me.

When my breath was close to normal, Hunter released my legs. I stood, but I was a bit wobbly. When I giggled, Hunter furrowed his brows. Steadying me, he asked, "Did I take too much?"

Biting my lip, I shook my head. "I don't think it was the blood."

Hunter's lip curved into a half-smile. "Oh."

His fingers wiped away the remnants of blood on my neck. I knew I'd already healed. He had too. He seemed stronger as he stood before me. Even though I'd taken some of his blood, just the act of drinking had been good for him. I loved that I could help him in some small way.

"Are you okay?" he asked me, still concerned.

I nodded, feeling a little drunk. "I'm perfect."

By his corresponding grin, I could tell that he agreed with me. Flicking his eyes over my face, he sighed, then placed a light kiss on my forehead. "I should ..." He indicated the forgotten syringe with his head.

My happiness faded. "Yeah ... you probably should."

With slow fingers, he reached down and picked the syringe up. By the way he lifted it, you would think it weighed a thousand pounds. He squeezed a bit of the liquid out of the top. It was an unnecessary precaution, since an air bubble trapped in the vial wouldn't hurt him, but being cautious was a human trait that was hard to shake. His eyes were locked onto the syringe while he straightened his other arm. Where he shot himself didn't matter ... it just needed to be in his body. And it would hurt going in. I knew. He'd given it to me once.

I squeezed the fingers of his extended hand, giving him strength. He gave me a brief smile, but his eyes were still focused on what he was doing. With precision care, he brought the needle to the inside of his elbow. Seemed as good a spot as any, I supposed. He inhaled deep, then held his breath. I was a nervous wreck while I waited for him to push down the plunger. When he did, I flinched. He screamed.

He sank to his knees as a torturous cry escaped him. I sank down with him, holding his hand now. He clasped me with all his strength. If I were human, he would have crushed my hand. When the syringe was empty, he tossed it away and slapped his hand over the wound on his elbow. Rocking back and forth, he massaged the area.

I couldn't feel his pain, but I could feel the bond breaking. It was like a sharp crack up my spine. A dull ache started radiating in my chest, growing stronger with each surge. Then the pain faded and all that was left was an empty hollowness. The loss of our connection was so great, tears rolled down my cheeks. Hunter looked up at me then, and I saw the same loss reflected in his eyes.

It was gone. The part of him that resided within me, giving me peace, comfort, hope … was gone. Even though the torment he'd just gone through was so much worse, I couldn't stop myself from crying and my soul wept right along with me.

CHAPTER SIXTEEN

Julian

MY SISTER WAS in Hunter's room, saying goodbye. I could feel my own goodbye to Arianna approaching, but I was pushing that moment away for now. I wasn't ready. I probably wouldn't ever be ready. For now, I was busying myself with watching my family split in half.

Mom and Dad were saying their quiet farewells, each wishing the other to be safe. Since we didn't really know which direction the danger was coming from, it kind of felt like both parties were heading off to war. It made me wish Arianna and Trey had stayed at my house. Then they'd be safe with Starla, Jacen and Olivia. Maybe Nika and the others should abandon the ranch and go back home. That wouldn't really solve anything though. Simon knew where we lived.

Ben and Tracey were on the other side of my parents. Tracey looked like she was having a hard time with Ben leaving. Clutching his arm, she asked him, "Are you sure you have to go? Can't you stay here with me and Emma?"

Smoothing her hair, Ben told her, "You'll be safe here with the others. Being with Teren is where I'll be able to do the most good." Pausing, he examined his wife's face for a moment, then added, "But I was serious about doing anything to make our marriage work. If you want me to stay, then I'll stay."

Tracey's eyes went wide with surprise. Ben usually did what he wanted, especially when it came to our family. She glanced around at the couples separating. Looking distraught, probably because Hunter had just severed their bond, Halina was hugging Imogen. Alanna was squeezing Dad. Everyone here was accepting the risk of losing someone they cared about. Tracey's eyes were wide when they returned to Ben's. "No, you're right, I'll be safe here. You should go where you're needed."

Ben beamed as he smiled down on her. "I love you, so much."

Tracey nodded, swallowed, then told him, "I love you too. I must. You brought me into a house filled with vampires and I've yet to run away screaming."

Ben laughed and I looked away. My gaze settled on Trey. My best friend was frowning as he took in the exchanges around him. Walking his way, Arianna's hand firmly in mine since I wasn't letting her go until the last possible moment, I asked him, "Hey Trey, what's wrong?"

His frown deepening, Trey tucked his hair behind his ears. "I heard that dude over there telling that scarred chick that they were going on a rescue mission, and you were going with them. I should be going with you, dude."

I smiled at his courage, then frowned at his suggestion. "It's too dangerous, you're better off here with the others." Glancing over at the group he'd indicated, I said, "And that dude is my father, the scarred chick is my aunt."

Halina's eyes flashed to Trey. There was a deadly glint to them, and I knew she didn't approve of Trey's choice of words. He didn't mean anything by it, but with the mood Halina was in now, it was best to move the conversation along. Returning my eyes to Trey, I told him, "I need you to stay here and protect Arianna for me."

I wanted to laugh a little at how familiar this conversation was. I'd asked Trey to be her bodyguard before, but neither of them remembered it. Trey looked over at Arianna and his back straightened. Inhaling a deep breath, he stood from the small couch he'd been sitting on. His expression completely serious, he clapped my shoulder and said, "You got it, man. I'll die for her if I need to." With a cringe, he added, "I won't need to, will I?"

Laughing, I shook my head. "I hope not. Thank you though."

I looked between the girl of my dreams and my best friend, glad to have both of them in my life, even if they only recalled bits and pieces of it. I remembered it all though, and I loved them for their loyalty and acceptance. While only moments ago I'd wish that they were gone and safe, I now wished Raquel was here among them too. She'd shown herself to be a good friend recently, and I suddenly felt the need to have all my good friends and loved ones under the same roof while I was gone.

Jake was anxious to leave, I could tell by the way he paced and kept looking down the hall. I thought he might make a run for it at any moment, but not to get away this time. No, now it was to save Simon. Rory and Cleo were watching him like hawks. I supposed they would come with us, just to keep an eye on him. I didn't see Jake being the problem this time though.

Arianna tightened her grip on my hand and I focused my attention on her. Soft, luscious lips were curved down in displeasure. I hated seeing that expression on her face. "I don't like this."

I wasn't sure which part of *this* she meant, but I was hoping she meant the two of us going separate ways. That was the part I hated, and I wanted her to be on the same page. "I know," I told her, "but it's important, and … it will be over soon, I'm sure." Stroking her thumb, I whispered, "You should call your mom, tell her you're spending the night at a friend's. And … tell her something about Simon too, just so she won't worry."

Arianna sighed, then nodded. "Why do I get the feeling we've lied to my parents a bunch of times?"

I leaned into her as I laughed. "Only a couple dozen times. No big deal."

Arianna laughed with me, then she let go of my hand and tossed her arms around my waist. I froze with the shock of it at first, then I melted into her touch. Being in her arms was the single most amazing feeling in the world, and I'd missed it more than I'd truly understood until this moment. I clutched her tight, breathing her in. Without my consent, the words, "I've missed you," slipped out of my mouth.

After a quiet moment, she whispered, "I wish I remembered being with you."

An ache went through me. God, I wished that too. "Yeah, I know. Me too."

My sister reemerged from Hunter's room then. Her cheeks looked freshly scrubbed, but my sharp eyes could see the tinge of red left on her skin. And there were also droplets of blood on her shirt. She'd been crying. A lot. It pained me to do so, but I left Arianna with Trey and walked over to Nika. She needed me.

Nika gave me a blank stare, then a small sob escaped her. I wrapped my arms around her, remembering how it felt to be disconnected from our family. It was hard, and we weren't bonded like Nika and Hunter were bonded. Theirs was a deep, penetrating sire-bond. I could only imagine how lonely Nika felt right now.

"Is it bad?" I whispered in her ear. Over her shoulder, I watched Hunter walk out of his room. He was wearing a fresh, clean shirt, but he seemed just as glum as my sister. Determined, yes, but depressed too.

"I feel like a part of me is missing, Julie." She held me tight, savoring the fact that *we* were still connected.

I rubbed small circles into her back, hoping what she was feeling right now wouldn't last for the entire duration of their bond being severed. While I comforted Nika, Halina approached Hunter and comforted him. The three of them looked so desolate, it was as if someone had died in that room. Hunter gave Halina a quick hug, then pushed her back. "We don't have time for this. We need to leave now if we're going to save Simon."

Jake immediately perked up at the mention of heading out. "Yes, please. We need to go now. Every second we waste could be the one second we needed." His eyes were begging everyone in the room to hurry.

I pushed apart from Nika. "Let's go," I told my dad and Hunter. They both nodded. Hunter gave Nika a quick kiss on the head, then turned and started walking down the hall. Dad, Ben, and Jake followed him. I took one step after him, then turned back to Arianna. Knowing it might be the last chance I had, I reached out and pulled her into me.

I pressed my lips against hers with an almost frantic need to make her remember this moment. I knew it could be cleansed from her the same as every other moment we'd shared together, but I still tried to force it into some unreachable part of her brain.

When I pulled away from her, she was just as breathless as I was. I saw a spark of something in her eyes, something reminiscent of the way she used to look at me—like I was the most important thing in her world. I memorized the look, tucking it away in my head where I knew it would be safe.

I turned away and she grabbed my arm. "Julian!" When I turned back around, she grabbed my cheek and brought her lips to mine. The warmth and passion in her kiss almost dropped me to my knees. *She cares.* I was putty in her hands when she pulled back. "Come back to me," she murmured.

All I could do was stupidly nod.

I said a quick goodbye to my mom, and everyone else who was staying, and then I started walking away. My body might be leaving the ranch, but my heart was firmly fixed in this room. Dad, Ben, Hunter, and Jake were already out of sight. Halina, Gabriel, Rory, and Cleo were just leaving. I followed Cleo with a numb feeling in my chest. Why was leaving so hard? I resisted looking back. If I looked back at Arianna's big hazel eyes, I'd probably stay. And I couldn't. I had a wrong to right.

I heard feet running but I knew it was my sister, not Arianna. When she caught up to me, I glanced her way. "Dad said you have to stay here," I told her.

She smirked at me. "Dad said the same thing to you, but you don't seem to be paying attention to him." She nodded ahead of her. "I'm just seeing you to the exit. I need to watch …" She swallowed, and her eyes remoistened. "I need to watch Hunter leave the house."

We were silent for a moment, and I put my arm around her again.

Everyone in the rescue party was gathered in the living room by the time we got there. Dad turned to Roy and Cleo when they appeared. "One of you needs to stay here, protect the others."

Rory and Cleo exchanged a look. Cleo raised her eyebrow and Rory sighed. "Fine." He looked back at Dad. "I'll stay."

Dad nodded and looked at everyone else. "We'll take two cars. Hunter, Great-Gran, Gabriel, and Cleo will go in one car. Julian, Ben, Jake, and I will go in the other." Dad's eyes moved to Nika's. "And you're staying here, remember?"

Nika pursed her lips as she raised her chin. "I know. I just wanted one last goodbye."

Jake groaned while Hunter smiled. He shared one last tender kiss with Nika, then Jake grabbed his arm. "Come on. We've wasted enough time already."

Hunter snapped his head around to Jake and I halfway expected him to drop his fangs and growl. Surprisingly, he didn't. He simply shrugged him off. "We're leaving."

Everyone started heading for the garage. Not wanting to be left behind, I gave Nika a swift hug, whispered, "Keep an eye on Arianna for me," and hurried after them.

The drive to Blackfoot took a couple of hours, and Jake was antsy the entire time. He kept bouncing his knees, tapping his fingers, and looking around the barren landscape like the view was actually interesting. Dad's car was leading, with Gabriel driving his sedan a few paces behind us. I was getting really nervous about the upcoming mission, but I kept it to myself. Or tried to anyway.

The miles between Utah and Idaho were eventually eaten up. When it seemed like we'd been on the road forever, Jake leaned forward and told Dad, "We're getting close. Take the next exit off the freeway, then turn left onto the highway. Once you cross the river, take a right on 350th."

Dad did as Jake told him. It was dark outside, but the city lights made it pretty easy to see everything. I looked down at the water as we passed over the bridge; the Snake River was a roiling swath of black tumbling away into the night. Following Jake's directions, we traveled north along a road that paralleled the river. When we got close enough to our destination, Jake told Dad, "Okay ... pull over here. The road ahead is blocked off, and I don't have the code. It will be stealthier if we walk from here. Maybe we can get in and out without alarming everybody in the place."

Dad looked at Jake in the rearview mirror as he pulled over onto a gravel road beside a circular field. "He's your family. Can't you just knock on his door and ask for Simon back?"

While Gabriel pulled his car over behind him, Jake told Dad, "Let's just say, things didn't end well between us. He wouldn't intentionally hurt Simon, not directly anyway, but me ... he'd probably shoot me on sight." I kept my face even, but I couldn't help but think there were a couple of people in my family who felt the same way about Jake.

When I got out of the car, the soft gurgle of the river sharpened in my ears, and the smell of the countryside filtered through my nose. Preferring the scent of nature to the stale odor of the car, I inhaled deeply.

I turned to watch Cleo, Hunter, and Halina emerge from Gabriel's car. Hunter still looked dour. I wondered if he'd be morose the entire trip. He glanced up at the moon, then turned to Dad. "We've got a few hours before we'll need to head back. Let's make them count."

Dad nodded, then looked to Jake. "Where to?"

Jake nodded to the north of us. "There's a junkyard up the road. Henry has a place there. That's where we'll find Simon."

I frowned. "Junkyard? Does he have dogs?"

Jake gave me a wry smile. "Is the vampire afraid of dogs?"

Afraid? No. I didn't mind dogs so long as they were friendly pets. Guard dogs however ... that was a different story. Feigning confidence, I crossed my arms over my chest and lifted my chin. "Of course not. I just ... want to be prepared is all."

Jake's smile didn't lessen any. "Yeah, he has dogs, among other things. Just watch your step, kid."

I rolled my eyes at him. Like I wasn't going to be extra careful in the middle of the night, sneaking into a scary-ass junkyard that a possibly crazy vampire hunter called home. A trace amount of fear slipped into me at that realization. I felt the world compress in on me, making breathing painful and difficult. But then Arianna's love-filled eyes clouded my vision, and the momentary panic attack vanished.

Dad gave me a strange look, but I waved away his concern. I was fine. Dad accepted my silent gesture of assurance and patted Ben's arm. "Stay close to him."

Ben nodded but gave Dad a sly smile. "But then who will watch over you?"

Dad gave Ben much the same look I'd just given Jake. Hunter indicated the road we'd just pulled off of. "After you," he told Jake.

Jake started trudging up the dark road, Cleo barely a step behind him. Gabriel and Halina spread out to watch our sides. Hunter kept pace with Cleo while Dad and Ben each flanked me. I felt useless and out of place. Maybe I should have stayed home after all; both Dad and Ben were going to be distracted trying to keep me safe. It was too late to turn back now though. And ... I needed to do this.

Every crunch of rocks under my shoe heightened my senses. I could hear the heartbeats around me, could smell the different laundry detergents everyone used. Small animals skittered in the fields. Things were blooming. Things were decaying. And somewhere up ahead, the pungent smell of rust was on the breeze.

Moments later, we came to a miles long fence that looked to be circling heaps of garbage. Well, I supposed it wasn't technically garbage, but that was how it looked to me. Twisted metal, broken machinery, forgotten appliances. None of it seemed of value, but there must have been some point in keeping it all. The heaps of trash would provide decent cover though.

There was a metal gate in the fence barring the road we were walking down. It was sealed with an electronic lock that could be opened with a code, and twin cameras with bright red power lights were perched on either side of the gate, recording every visitor. There was also an intercom box beside the gate, so people who didn't have the code—like us—could ask for admittance. I was pretty sure our group wasn't going to do that though. We were trying to be sneaky.

Avoiding the cameras, we walked to the side of the road so we could scale the fence undetected; well, those of us who couldn't leap over it in a single bound, that was. Hunter, Halina, Gabriel, and Dad silently and effortlessly hopped over it like it was no more an obstacle than a baby gate. Jake watched them sailing through the air with a smirk on his lips. "Show offs," he muttered, as he grabbed the chain link fence and started climbing. Cleo and Ben followed suit.

Knowing I probably wouldn't successfully make a jump that high like the other vampires—I'd probably tangle myself in the fence if I tried—I started climbing up the links with the humans. It bucked, bent and made a lot of noise as I clambered up the side, and I was certain that a swarm of hunters would be waiting for us when I hopped off it on the other side. But thankfully the night was still quiet when I landed on solid ground again.

When we returned to the gravel road trailing through the junk piles, the road spilt. Dad, Ben, Halina, and I took one path. Hunter, Cleo, Gabriel, and Jake took the other. I had every confidence in Dad, Ben, and Halina, but it made me nervous to be in smaller groups.

Our group took the left side of the drive, while the other took the right. My eyes darted everywhere, looking for trouble. It was quiet among the piles of junk though. After a while, I could begin to see a pattern in the seeming randomness of the heaps of metal. A group of pipes, a stack of car doors, a pile of tires. It made me feel a little better that there was order here, and not just pure chaos.

When we got to the center of the junkyard, we spotted a building in the mess. It was long and wide, with a dark open sign in the front window. No lights were on, and it looked completely deserted. This must be where the junkyard conducted business during daylight hours. I found it interesting that Jake's grandfather had a fulltime job outside of experimenting with mythical creatures. It made him seem a little less frightening. Very little.

Beside the building, I could see a kennel running along the length of the office. It was empty, and the kennel door was wide open. "Great," I whispered, "The dogs are out." Halina smiled, like that was great news.

Dad pointed at the parking area in front of the building, where a small sedan was sitting. Jake was running over to it, exposing himself in the process. He must believe it was the car Simon had stolen to get here, if he was willing to break cover to check it out. Dad started to make a move toward Jake, but Halina grabbed his elbow and pointed to the building. There were cameras along the eaves. If Dad stepped out there with Jake, he'd be recorded and our cover would be blown too. With our backs to the piles of junk around us, we watched Jake open the car door and look inside for clues. He immediately popped back out. Turning in a circle, he shouted Simon's name.

"Idiot," Halina groaned. "He'll bring the entire junkyard down on top of us." Just as she finished saying it, two Dobermans ran around the corner from the backside of the house. They were on Jake in an instant; he only had time to raise his arms in defense. I heard shouting in the distance and knew Halina was right—they knew we were here.

Dad ordered me to stay put, then dashed out into the lot to help Jake. Halina and Ben were right behind him. I felt completely useless as I stood there with my heart racing. On the other side of the junkyard, I saw Hunter speeding off toward the voices coming from the back of the building. Gabriel and Cleo ran off with him. While I watched, Dad and Ben tackled one dog while Halina grabbed the other. Two more joined the fray, and the parking lot was soon a mess of snarling, growling, and biting ... and not all of that was from the dogs. Jake was sitting on the ground, dazed. He started scooting away from the dogs and vampires, and I whispered his name so he'd come to me where it was relatively safe.

Jake turned to look my way, then shouted my name in warning. I twisted just in time to see a pair of burly guys raising a gun at me. Jesus, I did *not* want to get shot again. My heart in my throat, I bulldozed into the first guard. I managed to knock him down, but I lost my balance and tumbled to the ground with him. The guard didn't get up, and laid there unconscious. *One down, one to go.*

I sprang to my hands and knees, but the second guard was faster. He hit me in the head with the butt of his rifle, and stars exploded in my vision, while blackness ringed my sight. My entire head hurt, all the way down my spine. Unable to fight, I slumped to the ground again. I was sure I was a goner, sure the guard hovering over me was going to finish me off. I'd never see my family again. I'd never see Arianna again. Just as her name passed my lips, the sound of someone being punched entered my ears.

When I could lift my head, I saw Jake duking it out with the guard. He clocked him in the jaw, then grabbed his head and rammed it into his knee. The guard fell to the ground, just as listless as the first one. Jake looked down at me; he had scratches on his face from the dog's teeth, and his clothes were bloody. "You okay, kid?"

Standing, I nodded. Just the act of moving my head made it throb. What I wouldn't give for super-healing powers. Looking past Jake, I saw that Dad, Ben, and Halina had subdued the dogs. Dad was carrying two of them in his arms—both looked knocked out. He placed them in the kennel, and then came back for the other two. He had to pry one away from Halina, who was taking a quick drink from the beast. Jake scowled, but didn't say anything. They *had* saved his skin after all.

We disarmed the guards at our feet, then walked over to the others who were locking up the rest of the dogs. From behind the building, the sounds of people scuffling were clear. Hunter and the others were still fighting. Halina looked between the noise and us. "Go," Dad told her. "We'll grab Simon, and meet you at the gate."

Halina nodded, then blurred away to help the others. Dad pointed up to the cameras along the building. "We destroy the feed before we leave. And any research we come across. Whatever is going on here, needs to stop."

Ben nodded and began walking up the steps to the building. I moved to follow him, and Dad pushed me behind him. "Stay behind us," he whispered, motioning for Jake to follow Ben. Frowning, I fell in line behind him. I supposed it was smart to be the last one in, but the building was completely dark. It looked empty. Remembering the guard who'd given me a massive headache, I reconsidered. This place wasn't completely abandoned.

Jake gave Ben one of the guard's guns, and the two of them flanked the front door like a professional S.W.A.T. team. Ben tried the knob, but it was locked. He looked over at Dad, pointed two fingers at him, then the door. Dad nodded, grabbed the knob, and yanked it out of the door. The chunk of wood around the knob broke off in his hand. Ben and Jake swarmed inside, weapons raised. Dad and I followed close behind.

The room smelled musty, but there was something in the air that made my heart thump even harder. I glanced at Dad and by his expression, I knew he smelled it too. Blood. Human blood. Dad gave Ben a sigh-language message that Ben apparently understood. He darted off in the direction of the blood scent, with Dad close on his tail. Jake was circling the empty room, looking for clues. He stopped and stared at a photo of a man with long, shaggy gray hair and beard wearing a Hawaiian shirt. Henry, I assumed. I let out a soft whistle to get Jake's attention, and indicated for him to follow us.

With Jake watching our backs, the four of us ventured deeper into the building. It was larger than I'd expected it to be, and any second I just knew someone was going to whip around the corner and cream us all. But every corner was clear, every room was empty. No sounds, no heartbeats—except for my own, Ben's, and Jake's. Whoever had been here wasn't here anymore. For some reason, that made me very uneasy.

When we reached the room where the blood was strongest, Ben kicked in the door and stormed inside. Emergency lights softly lit a room that reminded me of Gabriel's lab. Albeit, a poor man's version of his lab. A padded hospital table was in one corner, with a strange machine next to it. The contraption was a confusing mess of tubes and IV bags full of blood. It reminded me of some medieval torture device and looked just as old, but it had to be the machine he was using for the transfusions. The rest of the room was filled with vials, beakers, Bunsen burners, computers, carts of medical equipment, supplies, bandages, cleaners, medicines, and refrigerators that hummed in the silence.

The blood that we were smelling, was dripping from a tube hanging off the transfusion machine, collecting into a bucket underneath the machine. After sweeping the room to make sure it was empty, Dad knelt beside the blood. Sticking his finger into the bucket, he coated it with blood, brought it to his lips, then tasted it. His fangs were down when he looked up at Jake. Jake's eyes were wide, either in panic over his son's fate, or disgust over what he was witnessing.

"It's fresh, not from a bag," Dad told him. "And it's human."

Jake scanned the room, looking for some sort of hope that his son was here. "Is it Simon's? Is my son hurt?"

Standing, Dad shook his head. "I don't know. I've never tasted your son's blood, so I have nothing to compare it to."

Jake shot Dad a dirty look and Dad raised his hands. "I'm not saying I want his blood, I'm just saying ... I don't know whose blood this is. Your guess is as good as mine."

Running a hand through his hair, Jake cursed. "Where the hell is he? I was sure he would be here ... I was sure he would go to Henry. He must have ... Where would he take Simon?" He turned in a circle, scanning the room again, then he stopped. "Simon must have told him we might come here looking for him. He warned him, and Henry fled." His face fell as desolation overtook him. "He could be anywhere now."

He fell to the bed like he had no strength left in him. I sympathized. If it was one of my family members who were missing, I'd be a wreck. Walking over to him, I put a hand on his shoulder. "I'm sorry ... we'll find him." Simon might not be my favorite person, but I didn't want him to get hurt because of us ... because of *me*. And if that blood *was* his, well, there was a lot of it in that bucket.

Jake looked up at me with watery eyes. "How? How will we find him?"

I didn't know what to say, so I didn't say anything at all. Dad turned on the lights while Ben started rummaging around the room. With a sigh, Dad said, "We need to destroy all of this. Besides protecting people from compulsion, what he's doing here ... trapping and killing vampires for their blood, so he can attempt to make some sort of hybrid between the two species ... it's wrong, and innocents on both sides are being hurt because of it." He looked over at Jake. "We need to permanently put a stop to this."

Firming his jaw, Jake stood and nodded. "You're right, vampire. We need to level this place."

Dad swung his hand around the room as he locked eyes with Ben and me. "Make a pile of anything that looks like research. We'll torch every bit of it. It won't be all of it, of course, since I'm sure Henry took some with him, but it will be a start."

Ben and Jake immediately started tossing things into the middle of the room. Before long, there was a decent pile in the center—papers, laptops, blood. Anything and everything that had to do with vampires went into the burn pile.

I began milling about the room, adding things to the pile with the others. Coming across a locked cupboard that looked promising, I forced the doors open. What I saw inside nearly made my heart stop. The makeshift label on the front of it read *Compulsion-X*—it had to be what Jake and Simon had taken, the thing that was making people immune to vampire trancing.

Oh God ... immune to vampire trancing ...

A thought struck me so hard, that for a second, my vision hazed and my knees buckled. I was currently holding in my hand the key to Arianna keeping her memories *forever*. All I had to do was slip one in my pocket, and give it to her when I got back to the ranch, and she'd get to remember this night. She would always know exactly what I was, and there would never again be a shadow looming over our relationship. We'd never have to start over.

Of course ... to make Arianna immune, I'd have to completely betray my family. They'd be furious, and they'd never see me as the adult I was trying to be. Halina—and my father too, in a way—had seemed proud of the fact that I'd wanted to correct my mistake. Doing this, stealing this ... it would ruin everything I was trying to set straight.

But goddamn it, I hadn't expected the solution to all my problems to land in my lap like this. It wasn't why I'd come out here, it hadn't even been on my mind—not consciously anyway. Maybe some part of my subconscious had known this could happen, but I hadn't come here for this temptation. I'd come here to right a wrong, to stop a teenager from doing something stupid that was going to get him killed.

My body began to tremble as I stared at the canisters. Duty, family ... or love? Which one was more important? I knew even considering this was wrong, irresponsible, dumb ... but I missed Arianna so much ... She'd kissed me, she'd wanted me to stay with her, to be safe with her, she was starting to care about me, *really* care about me. I didn't want to lose that. I didn't want to lose *her*. I couldn't stomach the thought of her waking up tomorrow and not remembering the closeness we'd shared tonight. I couldn't handle going all summer long without seeing her, and then going back to school in the fall and just being ... friends.

And besides, Arianna *wanted* to keep her memories. She'd told Nika we didn't have a right to take them, and a part of me agreed with her. I should at least talk to Arianna about the vaccine. Offer her protection from compulsion, if she wanted it. Because wasn't that what a good boyfriend would do?

Feeling like my heart was being torn in five million different directions, I slipped one of the small canisters into my pocket. Guilt and shame filling me, I twisted around to show my dad the cupboard. "Dad ... I think I found the vaccine." My heart was surging as Dad turned my way. I immediately tried to calm myself down. I was just going to show it to Arianna, ask her how she felt about taking it. Then, once she'd decided what she wanted, the two of us would sit down and talk to my parents. I wouldn't use it without their permission ... and somehow, someway, I'd get their blessing. I had to. I couldn't lose Arianna, but I also couldn't do this without their support.

Dad swung his eyes my way. "Good job, Julian," he beamed.

Walking over, Dad examined what I'd found. Picking one up, he frowned. "This is a strange way to deliver a vaccine." He was right. The container didn't look like a shot. It looked more like a tiny bottle of hairspray, or a breath freshener, like Binaca. Dad experimentally pressed down on the top, and a cloud of horrible smelling mist erupted from the can. Dad's mouth dropped open and he locked gazes with Jake. "What is this?"

Jake walked over to examine the container. With a frown, he looked up at Dad. "It would seem Henry has improved the vaccine. He found a way to aerosolize it." Shaking his head, he handed the can back to Dad. "He can vaccinate people without them even being aware of it now. With a big enough delivery system, he could probably protect entire crowds, maybe even small towns." His lips twisted as he shook his head. "Sorry, vampire, but your days of controlling humans are coming to an end."

CHAPTER SEVENTEEN

Hunter

GABRIEL AND I sped after the group of humans guarding the junkyard, with Cleo running at a human speed behind us, while Teren, Ben, and Halina took care of the dogs. I wasn't sure how many humans there were, or if they were armed, but I figured silencing them before they could call for help was a good idea.

Jake had given away our element of surprise by running into the open and shouting his head off for his son. I wasn't sure if he'd done that intentionally, or if panic had momentarily turned him into an idiot. I was hoping it was fear, and he wasn't trying to screw us over. It really didn't make much sense for him to betray us though. He needed our help almost as much as we needed his. Maybe more so.

Once the dogs had started in on Jake, their human counterparts had made an appearance. When I caught up to the first one, he'd seemed surprised. Of course, I'd been moving at a vampiric pace and I'd seemingly materialized right in front of him; that would stun even a seasoned hunter. The man recovered quickly though, and was raising his gun to my chest even as I knocked him out.

Gabriel subdued his partner while a few more shouts carried along the breeze. Gabriel and I shot off in opposite directions while Cleo dealt with the man I'd knocked out. I searched the mounds of junk as thoroughly as I could, but I only found two more guards. From what Jake had been saying, I'd been expecting an army. It seemed too easy.

I dragged the guards back to the building, and dropped them in a heap beside the guard I'd clocked. Halina joined us, helping Gabriel carry a couple of men to add to the pile. I gave Halina a curt nod while Cleo went to work using zip ties to hold everyone's wrists together. The guards were alive, and would inevitably wake up before we were done here. We didn't want to fight them again, and didn't want to kill them, so we attached them to a rusted car frame. They would eventually be able to work themselves free, but we'd be long gone by then.

Halina zipped off to the front of the building, to grab a few unconscious guards who had bothered the rest of the group. Spotting a rolling door near the back of the building, I decided to investigate. The sooner we found Simon and Jake's grandfather, the sooner I could get back to Nika. I was trying to ignore the absence of our bond, but it was like trying to ignore a strained ankle or a muscle that was cramping. I ached.

Gabriel joined me while Cleo and Halina worked on the humans. The two of us each grabbed one side of the door and yanked. We ripped the entire contraption from the wall. Throwing it to the ground, we stepped over it to get inside. The room we were in was by far the oddest room I had ever seen. There were cages lining the walls, but unlike outside, these weren't kennels for dogs, these were cells … for humans, or I supposed, for vampires. Each one had a small, bare cot that was attached to one side of the cage, but nothing else. No blankets, no pillows, no comforts of any kind. And no real way for the caged vampires to escape the sun. While the walls around the room were made of thick, windowless concrete, the area around the rolling door wasn't entirely lightproof. During the day, whatever creatures were trapped in here would suffer from the trace amount of light that seeped through it. The entire space gave cruelty a new meaning.

Infuriated at the horror I was witnessing, I cautiously approached the cages. The room was dark, but my enhanced eyes could see that there was a metallic gleam to the bars that shimmered in the moonlight. Silver. A full vampire would have difficulty escaping these cages, especially if they were starved and half drained of blood. There were nine cages in the room, three along each wall. There were blood stains in every cell, from where the vampires had been drained, and there were heavy manacles looped around the cell bars, awaiting new prisoners to fill them; the chains were also silver. Yet another way to torment the captives being held against their will.

It sickened my stomach to think of all of the vampires who had probably been trapped in here, who had probably died in here. It was a sick science experiment gone horribly, horribly wrong, and I had a newfound appreciation of Gabriel and his methods. Science didn't have to be nasty.

As I glanced over at Gabriel, I saw that he was scowling. He didn't approve of this either. Halina joined us with a hiss of disapproval. "When we find Jake's grandfather, I say we rip him into tiny little pieces," she growled.

While I sort of agreed with her, I knew we couldn't. The entire point of the League was to stop the never-ending cycle of revenge. "I've seen enough," I muttered. "Let's go find the others."

Just as I turned to leave this place of death, I heard a faint voice whisper, "Wait ..." My gaze snapped to a cell in the far corner of the room. That cage wasn't empty, and something lying on the cot moved. Whatever it was, it was so frail and thin that it almost seemed like it was part of the small bed.

I blurred over to the cage while Gabriel found the lights. A frail man was lying on the bed. He groaned when the light hit his eyes, and when he raised his arm to shield himself, I was shocked at his appearance; he closer resembled a skeleton than a man. I instinctively grabbed the bars to yank the door open, forgetting that they were toxic to me. With a howl of pain, I pulled my fingers away. It felt like I'd dipped them in acid.

The man's sunken face turned to me as I held my fingers to my face; I almost expected to see smoke rising from them. "Help ... me ..." he squeaked. His voice sounded like two pieces of sandpaper rubbing together. I had gone through severe hunger once, but I had a feeling my turmoil was nothing in comparison to this man's.

He was completely naked, and the narrow bars of the cage formed a perfect box. The only place he was safe from the silver surrounding him was the worn cot he was lying on. Whoever had thought up this trap, hadn't wanted a clever vampire to shield their body from the silver so they could break out. Well, luckily enough for this man, while I couldn't hold the bars to pull them free, I could kick the door in.

"I'm going to get you out of there," I told him. "Stay back." He turned away from me, and I brought the heel of my boot against the weak portion of the door. It buckled under my strength, but didn't entirely break free. Well-constructed. I struck out again, and this time the door caved inward. I toed it open, then made my way into the cell coated in silver. Even though there was an exit, I hated being in there. Every fiber of my being was telling me to get out, and I had to fight the instinct to run with every step I took.

When I picked up the vampire, he weighed no more than a small child. He murmured a thank you as I carried him to safety outside the bars. Even though I'd never really been in danger, I exhaled a sigh of relief once I was free.

Cleo ran into the room, and her eyes widened when she spotted the ragged man in my arms. "Grab some clothes from the guards," I told her. Nodding, she ran off. I turned to look over at Halina and Gabriel. "We should take him somewhere safe, then rejoin the others and keep looking. Jake's grandfather could still be here somewhere." I could hear the others deeper in the building beside us; it sounded like they were trashing the place, and I could hear Teren ordering the others to make a burn pile.

"No," the emaciated vampire whispered. "He left ... took the boy."

All three of us looked down at the man in my arms. "The boy? Simon? Was the boy named Simon?" I asked.

The vampire nodded as he closed his eyes; he seemed so tired, barely alive, and I knew he needed to eat. Soon. "Yes ... he called him Simon ..."

We walked outside and Cleo approached us with pants and a jacket. "These will probably hang off him, but it was the best I could do." She jerked her thumb back at the assortment of tied-up guards. Most of them were awake now, and the pair missing items of clothing didn't look happy. The one missing his pants was sporting a black eye.

I set the weary vampire down. He was wobbly on his feet, so I helped him stand while Halina and Cleo helped him get dressed. He inhaled a deep breath when Cleo wrapped a jacket around him. A low growl rumbled out of his chest, but he made no move to attack her. I knew it was best not to tempt him though. Hunger had a way of making even good people do bad things.

After he was semi-dressed, I picked the vampire up again, before he fell over. To Halina and Gabriel, I said, "Let's find Teren and the others, let them know we missed Simon and his grandfather." I looked down at the man we'd saved. "Then let's get you something to eat, so you can tell us what you heard."

The man closed his eyes and Halina motioned to the front of the building, to where she could feel Teren and Julian. The loss of my connection to Halina wasn't as unsettling as my blocked bond with Nika, but it was still unnerving. I was standing right beside her, but I still couldn't feel her. It was ... unnatural.

Our small group wound its way through the abandoned building to where the others were. I could hear them talking, hear glass breaking. Following the noise, we came upon a room that was almost as odd as the vampire holding cells. It was clear from the medical equipment, vials, beakers, refrigerators and whiteboards covered with cryptic writing that we'd stumbled upon the "lab."

Jake, Ben, Julian, and Teren were here, throwing items onto a huge pile in the middle of the room. I figured when they set that heap ablaze, the fire would be big enough to burn down the entire building. Good riddance. It seemed to me that just torching the building now would be quicker, but I knew Teren. He wanted to be thorough, to make sure all of the research was incinerated. And he also wanted to search for clues, which was why what I was carrying was so important. If there were any clues to be found here, the vampire barely clinging to life had them.

Teren and Julian looked up at me when I entered the room with the others. Teren's face darkened when he saw that I was carrying someone. "Who is that?" he asked.

"A vampire who was being held captive here. He overheard Jake's grandfather talking to Simon earlier."

That got Jake's attention. "Simon?"

The man in my arms nodded, but it was all he had the energy to do. That wasn't good enough for Jake. Storming over to him, he demanded, "Where did he go? Did Simon leave with him? Was he okay?"

He began shaking the man's shoulders and I growled in warning. "He's been starved and tortured. Let him eat, then you can question him."

When Jake realized he was antagonizing a half-dead vampire, he backed away. Just when I was wondering what I could possibly feed him, the smell of fresh blood hit me. Ben was tearing apart some contraption that had tubes of blood running around it. On the ground below the machine was a bucket; the smell was strongest there. Blurring over to it, I set the vampire down. He smelled it too, and immediately struggled with picking up the bucket. As I helped him bring it to his lips, Jake screeched, "What the hell are you doing?"

His eyes were wide, his face pale. Encouraging the vampire to eat, I tossed Jake a look. "Either he drinks this, or he drinks *you*. Your choice."

Jake narrowed his eyes, but shut his mouth. Halina shot me an amused glance and I knew exactly what she was thinking. *You've not only accepted vampires, you're feeding them now ... look how far you've come.* I wasn't sure how to feel about the sudden change my life had taken, but I did know that denying a starving man a meal was wrong. And it was too late to help whoever had donated this blood anyway.

While the hungry vampire ate, Teren approached Gabriel. "We have a problem," he stated, his face grim. Gabriel tilted his head in question and I watched Teren hand him a small aerosol can. "It's the vaccine. He's made it airborne."

Gabriel's expression darkened as he examined the container. "That ... is quite unfortunate for us." He looked up at Teren. "He can protect numerous people at one time now. He could share it with others, vaccinate pockets of the populace up and down the countryside. And I have no idea if what he's done will be passed on to the next generation or not. If he's found a way to fuse it into the DNA ... the entire human race could be protected within the next millennium."

That sounded like a long way off, but to a vampire, it was still something we had to worry about. And hiding from technology was bad enough. How much longer could we stay off the grid? It was something I didn't want to think about.

Teren swept his hand over the dozen or so containers that were on the burn pile. "This can't be his entire stock. He wouldn't have left it all behind."

Ben crossed his arms over his chest. "It's just one more reason for us to find this guy. And fast." He shifted his gaze to our new vampire compatriot. He'd finished his bucket of blood, and was running his finger around the rim, like he was trying to get every last drop. Since I knew how hungry he was, I didn't blame him. I probably would have tried to lick the bucket clean. "You wouldn't happen to know where they went, would you?"

With a content sigh, the vampire set the bucket down on his lap. "God, I needed that ... thank you."

Squatting beside him, I extended my hand, "My name is Hunter. What's yours?"

The vampire took my hand, his caved face intrigued. "Hunter? Kind of ironic."

I shook my head. "You have no idea."

The vampire let out a soft laugh; the dryness in his voice was mostly gone. "My name's Malachi. I've been down here for ... well, what year is it?" I exchanged a glance with Teren as Malachi shook his head. "Well, doesn't much matter. It's been a while at any rate."

The group of us formed a half-circle around Malachi. We were all hoping he had some direction for us, otherwise we had nowhere to go, but back home. And too much was at stake to just give up.

Impatient for answers, Jake barked out, "Do you know where my son is?"

Malachi looked up at him with a sigh. "No, I'm sorry. I don't know where they went. I only heard them talking about needing to leave." He swallowed a rough lump and flicked a glance at the empty bucket before returning his eyes to Jake. "The kid, your son, he caused quite a commotion when he showed up. He said his dad was being held hostage by vampires, and he needed to have a vampire's strength to break him out. He was really worried. Terrified, I'd say. He sounded like he'd do just about anything to help you."

Jake ran his hands through his hair. "Simon ... What the hell was he thinking? He knew the experiment never worked. Why would he ... ? Did he do it? Did he let Henry drain him?"

Malachi stared at Jake a moment, then shook his head. "No. Henry wouldn't let him. Said there wasn't enough time to do it here. He said the kid had probably led the entire vampire nest right to him, so they needed to get the hell out of town. The kid was none too happy about that."

Jake let out a long exhale and closed his eyes. "He's okay." His eyes snapped open and narrowed into pinpricks. "For now. Whenever they get to where they're going, he'll set up shop again and Simon will be his first volunteer."

Malachi shrugged. "I don't know. Henry said he'd recently made a breakthrough. He said he knew why it wasn't working before, and he knew how to fix it."

Gabriel suddenly grew very interested in the conversation. "How was he going to fix it? Did he say?"

Malachi scrunched his brows as he remembered. "He said he needed a ... naturally born vampire's blood." He looked confused after he said it, like he had no idea what that meant.

I did. I locked eyes with Teren. "He knows about mixed vampires. He might know about your family."

Teren gave me a brief nod; his expression was dark. "Let's hurry up here so we can get back to the ranch."

I loved the sound of that idea, for more than one reason. Teren had Julian help Malachi to his feet while Cleo and Ben went outside to question the guards. The rest of us went about destroying anything in the lab that could be used to hurt us. When the pile was ready, Halina found a can full of gas to pour on it. She cocked an eyebrow at Gabriel as she doused everything with the pungent liquid. "I do love a good arson." Gabriel's lips cracked into a smile and she blew him a kiss. At least the two of them had bonded through this whole mess.

Before a match was struck, everyone was ushered to the relative safety of the junkyard. Teren stayed inside to ignite the pile, then blurred out to us a millisecond after we heard the whoosh of flames roaring to life. Cleo and Ben said the guards didn't know where Jake's grandfather had gone. All they had been told was to stay on the property and protect it from intruders. As we left them tied to the rusty car frames, I wondered if they were telling the truth. They were protected from compulsion, so, unless we wanted to torture it out of them, we had no choice but to take their word for it. And after seeing what had been done to Malachi, torturing them didn't feel like a viable option.

The vampires in the group grabbed those who couldn't run as fast as we could, and together, we raced back to the cars; we smashed right through the gate this time. When we were all beside the vehicles again, multiple small explosions rang through the night as the flames found the compressed cans of the vaccine. Julian murmured that he hoped the dogs locked in the kennel next to the building were all right. Licking her lips, Halina told him they were excellent. Jake looked disgusted by her response, but I knew she was joking. I'd seen her opening the latch to the kennel before she'd blurred away. She might find dogs tasty, but she wasn't cruel.

We all watched the sky lighten with flames for a moment, then Jake said, "Let's go. Every second we wait, is a second we've wasted."

Halina studied him a moment, then nodded. "We reconvene at the ranch. We need to make sure the nest is secure, and dawn will be here soon …"

I glanced at the dark sky above us, and knew she was right. The ticking time bomb that kept us buried beneath the earth was a few hours from going off. For some of us, searching for Simon would have to wait.

We all watched the sky lighten with flames for a moment, then we ducked into the awaiting cars and sped away. I couldn't wait to get back to Nika, to make sure she was safe. The ache I'd been ignoring all evening deepened as we drove toward her. Under normal circumstances, the bond would have kicked in by now, and I'd be tearing the car apart to get to her. While it was nice to have control over my actions, I missed the intensity.

To redirect my mind from missing Nika and worrying about my family, I focused on Malachi sitting beside me in the back seat. To make the trip easier on the still-starving vampire, Cleo had given up her spot in the car and was now riding in the other one with Teren, Ben, Jake, and Julian. The humans and the living vampire were too appealing to force Malachi to sit next to them for the long journey. Their heartbeats were as mouth-watering to a vampire as the sound of bacon sizzling was to a human. It wasn't all that long ago that admitting that would have had me hunched in a corner, resisting the urge to vomit. But the truth was the truth. Denying it didn't make it any less so.

Putting my hand on Malachi's shoulder, I told him, "As soon as we get to the ranch, we'll get you more to eat … as much as you can handle."

His eyes fluttered like he was having difficulty keeping them open. "Thank you … thank you so much for saving me. I wasn't sure how much longer I could take it …" His eyes closed and he leaned his head against the window with a sigh. I let him rest; I couldn't imagine how awful his imprisonment had been. Well, I suppose I could. I just didn't want to.

When the main home at the ranch came into view, the knot in my stomach finally eased. Everything looked peaceful—no crazed, mad scientist knocking down the door trying to kidnap naturally born vampires.

Family members poured out of the house as we pulled up beside Teren's car. Jake was just getting out of Teren's vehicle as Gabriel shut off our car. I was a little surprised Jake had willingly returned with us. A part of me had thought he would try to take off once he'd learned Simon wasn't at the junkyard. I guess he'd figured he would have more luck finding his son if he stuck with us. Maybe he was finally coming to see that we weren't all that bad. Sometimes the people you thought were evil, were actually the best people to know. And vice-versa. I'd learned that lesson the hard way.

Everyone was still awake, waiting to see the outcome of the raid. Nika rushed into my arms the second she spotted me. "I couldn't feel you coming. I felt everyone else, but I couldn't feel you. I hated it ..."

I kissed her hair as I squeezed her tight. "I know. I hate it too." I didn't add on that it was necessary. We both knew it, and we were accepting it. For now. Because as nice as feeling her presence was, it was nicer to be able to greet each other around family with a hug instead of ripping each other's clothes off.

After I separated from Nika, she hugged her father, and then Halina. Ben hugged Tracey while Julian greeted Trey and Arianna with an awkward wave. It was obvious that Julian was wishing to be more alone with his ex-girlfriend, so they could begin to reconnect. It was pointless though. After tonight, she'd be wiped and he'd be back at square one. Best just to leave it alone. Easier said than done though.

Emma scanned the crowd as she walked up to her husband. "Where's the boy? Where's Simon?"

Jake ran his fingers through his hair. "He wasn't there. We were too late."

Emma raised her finger to the gaunt vampire we'd rescued. "Who's this?"

Teren wrapped an arm around his wife's shoulders as he gestured to the newcomer. "This is Malachi. He was being held captive, used as an experiment. He's been starved, drained ... and who knows what else. He was the one who told us we were too late to save the boy. Simon and Henry had already gone." Jake let out an annoyed grunt, and kicked one of the car tires in frustration. Ignoring him, Teren looked through the crowd for someone. "Gran, could you take him inside, get him something to eat?"

Imogen rushed forward to help Malachi, while Jake turned to Teren. "We're wasting time. We need to figure out where they went, before Simon does something stupid."

Teren raised his hand in the air. "I'm all ears. If you have any idea where they might have gone, I would love to hear it. Especially since Henry is now targeting mixed vampires."

Emma gasped at the news. "He knows about us?"

Teren looked over at her with a sigh. "He knows about our kind, and, thanks to Simon, I'm sure he knows about *us* specifically. And he wants us ... wants our blood. Henry seems to think that's the key to making successful transfusions ... to making *living* vampires."

Emma looked over at Gabriel. "Would that work?"

Gabriel shook his head in answer to Emma's question. "Honestly, I do not know. A mixed vampire turning a human in the traditional way rarely works, as you know ... but a perfectly calibrated transfusion ... well, that is altogether different. It still depends on the human host of course, but ... it may be possible. I could not know for certain without running some tests."

Jake snapped, "We don't have time for tests. My son could be hooked up to that damn machine at this very moment!"

I was about to tell him that panicking wouldn't get him anywhere and he needed to calm down, but Trey said something that got my attention. "What you got there, Julian? Body spray?"

The second he said it, I knew exactly what Julian had. And like I was suddenly omnipotent, I also knew exactly what Trey was going to do with it. I was already blurring toward him when he snatched the cylinder from Julian, but I wasn't fast enough. He released a large stream of the compulsion resistance vaccine into the air, then leaned in to smell it.

As I rushed into the circle of Julian, Trey, Nika, and Arianna, the cloud of vaccine hovered in the air. My superior eyesight could see each individual droplet as it floated upon a sea of oxygen, and I could only watch in horror as the air current from my movement, caused the droplets to move. They settled on Arianna, then moved past her to the crowd of people now intently watching us. Ashley's eyes widened as it moved past her. Tracey sneezed when some settled on her. I had no idea how much was needed to make a person impossible to trance, but I knew at least some of the people here were now "vampire proof".

Halina blurred over to Trey, snatched the cylinder from his hand, and then turned all her fury on her grandson. "Julian! What did you do?"

With a sigh, Julian muttered, "Shit."

CHAPTER EIGHTEEN

Julian

I WAS SCREWED. My family was going to kill me, if I didn't die from shock first. Trey had released the vaccine, and odds were good he and Arianna were immune now. I hadn't planned on it happening like this. I was going to explain Arianna's options to her and then if she wanted to be immune, we were going to sit down with my parents. And while the chances of them saying yes to the vaccine were probably … slim … I'd still wanted to involve them in the decision. But now … now it was too late. Holy hell … my friends were immune.

Once we'd gotten back to the ranch, I'd wanted nothing more than to have a private conversation with Arianna. To explain to her what I'd done and what it could mean for us. Before I could get her alone though, Nika had walked over to us. She'd eyed me up and down, then immediately said, "What's going on?"

Glancing around at all of the super-hearing vampires in our midst, I'd shaken my head, silently telling her, *"Nothing, now be quiet."* Nika had crossed her arms over her chest and I'd almost groaned in irritation. How she'd even known something was up was frustrating. We'd been emotionally bonded for too long; even with the bond severed, she could read me like a book.

While Arianna had looked between us confused, Nika had mouthed, *"What is it?"*

Nika and I were good at lip reading; it was an essential part of maintaining secrets when your family had supernatural hearing. Making sure none of the adults were looking directly at me, I mouthed to her, *"I want to give Arianna a choice."*

Reaching into my pocket, I'd pulled out the cylinder and shown it to her. And that was when Trey had stepped in and taken the choice away from Arianna—away from all of us.

"What you got there, Julian? Body spray?" Before I could stop him, he plucked the cylinder from my hand and released a puff of it into the air.

I was so shocked I hadn't been able to react. Hunter must have seen Trey reach for it—he was inside our circle in a flash—but he was too late; the cloud of vaccine had drifted along the wind, settling over vampires and humans alike.

Halina was a split-second behind Hunter. She yanked the container from Trey, then turned to me with fire in her eyes. "Julian! What did you do?"

As I cursed, the only thing I could think to answer her with was, *I just got myself grounded for eternity.* I didn't say it though, this wasn't the time to be a smartass. My heart started thudding as I wondered how many of the humans nearby were now immune; I didn't know how potent the vaccine was. None of us did. That one squirt could have immunized everyone.

"What did you do?" Halina repeated. I swear I could feel the heat in her eyes on my skin. It gave me goose bumps.

"I … I didn't mean … This wasn't my plan, but he …"

I pointed at Trey, and he immediately held up his hands. "I was just testing your nasty-ass body spray." He stuck his tongue out and leaned into me. "Dude, if that was your plan to win Arianna over, I'd reconsider. That crap is foul."

Gabriel stepped up to Halina. He put a comforting hand on her shoulder and she moderately relaxed. Grabbing the cylinder from Halina, Gabriel examined it. "Young Master Trey here has released the vaccine it would seem." Glancing up at him, he murmured, "Interesting." Turning to Halina, he murmured, "Love, would you mind running an experiment for me? Could you please compel Master Trey to do something?"

Trey smiled and nudged Arianna in the side. "He called me Master."

Arianna and Halina rolled their eyes at the same time. "What would you like him to do?" Halina asked Gabriel.

Gabriel gave her a small smile. "Whatever you see fit, love."

Halina's grin grew tenfold and I quickly raised my hand to her. "Nothing that will hurt him."

Her smile dropped a little, but she nodded. "Trey ... go into the house and scrub the kitchen floor with one of Julian's toothbrushes."

"Hey!" I told her.

She only gave me a blank expression. "What? That won't hurt *him*."

Trey's eyes were wide as he looked over at me. "Is she serious? Do I really have to do that?"

Halina, Gabriel, and Hunter all exchanged looks. Trey shouldn't have asked me that. He should have just done what she'd commanded. Nika tried a different approach. "Trey, you don't remember how you got here. The last thing you recall is being at home with your family." After she let that sink in a second, she said, "Tell me how you got here."

Trey looked confused, but not for the reason he should be confused. "Uh ... do you want me to play along and tell you I don't remember, or do you want me to tell you that I got a ride here with you guys ... after that whole you're-a-vampire-and-I'm-gonna-kill-you mess with Simon? Not sure how I'm supposed to answer here ..."

Nika sighed and looked over at the others. "I think he's immune."

I locked eyes with my sister, and my heart started pounding against my ribcage in an unrelenting rhythm of hope. "Nick ... test Arianna." This was it ... the moment of truth.

My sister sighed again, and looked over at Arianna. "Arianna, I want you to passionately despise my brother. I want you to hate, Julian."

I smacked her arm. "Nick! What the hell?"

She merely shrugged at me. "You want to know if it works or not, don't you?"

My once hopeful heart stuttered in my chest. What if she'd been too far away? What if it hadn't worked on her for some reason? I'd placed love over duty for this. *Please let it work.*

Arianna bunched her brows as she looked between Nika and me. I couldn't tell what she thought of me by her expression. Just as I was beginning to believe anxiety was about to permanently damage my internal organs, Arianna let out a long sigh and shook her head. "Sorry, Nika. I don't hate him. I think he's ... sweet."

She thinks I'm sweet. Her words echoed in my mind, but moments later, they were completely obliterated as a new fact settled over the top of them. *She can't be tranced.* I would never lose her again, not like I had at any rate. She could still choose to leave me, but she couldn't be *stolen* from me. Oh my God ...

A low growl burrowed from Halina's chest. Over everyone's heads, she intoned, "I want all of you to hop on one foot and quack like a duck." Most of us simply stared at her, but then Christian and Grandma Linda, in the very back of the group began hopping and quacking. Halina let out a long sigh of relief. "At least some people still listen to me," she quipped.

Ashley eyed her husband with wide eyes. She was only standing a couple of feet in front of him, but it had been close enough to grant her immunity. Rory, Cleo, Jack, and Tracey as well. Tracey seemed nervous as she swallowed and looked over at Ben. "Guess I don't have to worry about you having my mind wiped anymore."

Ben shook his head. "I told you I wouldn't do that again, but ... yeah, I guess you won't have to worry about it now."

Halina threw her hands up into the air. "Well, this is fabulous. Guess we're just going to have to kill them all," she dramatically sighed.

Arianna gasped. Trey just looked offended. Grabbing Arianna's hand, I told her, "Don't worry, she's joking." Reconsidering, I turned back to her. "You *are* joking, right?"

Halina smirked in answer, but Dad quickly intercepted. "No one is killing anyone." Turning to Halina, he added, "Can you please make them stop quacking now?"

With a frown, Halina turned back to Christian and Grandma Linda. "Stop hopping and quacking." They immediately stopped, which made Halina grin. Even though she was responsible with her powers, she liked people being obedient to her.

Jake grabbed Dad's sleeve. His expression was tight, and he seemed unnaturally pale. Except for under his eyes. Deep circles lingered there, making him look more like a mythical monster than the rest of us. He was barely keeping it together. "We're wasting time, Teren," he growled.

Dad frowned at him as he removed his hand, but he didn't comment. Indicating Trey and Arianna, I told my father, "I'm sorry, Dad. This wasn't how I wanted it to happen. I was going to talk to Arianna first, ask her if she wanted to be immune, then we were going to talk to you and Mom together." Turning back to Arianna, I let out a sad sigh. "You were supposed to have an option. I'm sorry."

Arianna gave me a soft smile as she squeezed my hand. "It's okay, I would have chosen this. I want to remember. I don't want any more ... holes that make me feel crazy."

I smiled at her answer, my heart on cloud nine. Then I twisted back to Dad, swallowing the lump in my throat as he raised an eyebrow at me. "You were going to talk to us before you did anything?"

I emphatically nodded and opened my mouth to explain my plan more, but Dad raised his hand, cutting me off. "Then why didn't you say something at the lab? Why didn't we talk about it then?"

Shame coursed through me as I looked around at all the adults I'd disappointed. Needing to remind myself why I'd risked their respect, I looked over at Arianna, soaking her in. Turning back to Dad, I told him, "Tensions were so high, and everyone was so focused on the mission ... I didn't think you'd listen. I didn't think you'd hear me out. I didn't think you'd give me—give *us*—a chance." As I lifted Arianna's hand in mine, showing our solidarity, I couldn't stop myself from stealing a quick peek at Halina. If she'd just given Arianna more of a chance a couple months ago, I wouldn't have had to go to these extremes. Not that that was an excuse. I shouldn't have caved to the temptation. I should have talked to my dad.

Sighing, I told him, "You're right ... I should have talked to you then. I was just ... scared you'd say no. I'm sorry."

Dad sighed, and I could see his anger fading. "I get it, Julian. I'm not happy, but I get it."

With a shrug, I asked him, "So ... what do we do now?"

Dad's pale eyes shifted to the sky. "We've kept everyone up far too late. We go to bed, then we take the children home in the morning."

Jake's grip tightened on Dad's arm. "Sleeping won't help us find Simon."

Dad locked eyes with him. "Neither will being too exhausted to think. We rest, then we start again at daylight." Dad shifted his eyes to Halina and Hunter. "But we'll need to be cautious, just in case Henry decides to pay us a visit."

Halina and Hunter nodded while Ben interjected, "I should go get Olivia, bring her here so we're all together. As powerful as Starla and Jacen are ... I'd feel better if my daughter was with me."

A soft smile graced Dad's lips as he glanced at Nika. "I know the feeling." Dad's eyes shifted to Hunter and he sighed. Even though he didn't want to do it, Dad was going to have to give Nika up one day. And probably much sooner than he would have liked.

Gabriel looked over at Ben. "I'll call Starla, and have her bring your daughter to the ranch. So long as Henry is actively searching for mixed vampires, she and Jacen should be here as well." His brow furrowed as he thought of the safety of his nestmates. Halina sighed, but Gabriel ignored her.

Ben nodded and Gabriel pulled out his cell phone. While he dialed our house, where Starla and Jacen were watching Olivia, Tracey whispered to Ben, "Are they good drivers?"

Ben assured her that everything would be fine while Halina sniggered. Once we were all inside the house, clumps of people started branching off. Grandma Linda headed upstairs with Ashley and Christian, who was naturally confused about all the recent commotion. Luckily, Halina, Hunter or Nika could still clean up his memories before he went home.

Alanna and Grandpa Jack went into the kitchen to check on Imogen and Malachi. Rory and Cleo stayed close to Jake, who started pacing the entryway; I was certain he wouldn't sleep tonight. Mom urged Nika and me to go to our rooms. Nika was reluctant to part with Hunter and hovered close to her sire. Me ... I was eager to talk to Arianna alone, so I motioned for Trey and Arianna to follow me up the stairs.

My heartrate increased as I started walking. What would I say to Arianna? Really, most everything had already been said. All that was left was for me to listen. To hear how she felt, and more importantly, to hear what she wanted.

As I trudged up the steps, I pictured all the different scenarios that could happen—from Arianna rejecting me, to Arianna wanting to be my girlfriend again. I desperately wanted us back, and hoped she would give us a chance. In between visions of possible futures, I listened to the sounds of the house. Arianna was silent, lost in her own thoughts. Trey was oohing and aahing over every little detail he spotted. He hadn't come upstairs during the birthday party, and he didn't remember coming up here once before. Thankfully, this would be the last time the ranch would be "new" to him. Dad was telling Jake that if he would stop wearing a hole in the floor, they could stay up and brainstorm places to check for Simon. Gabriel was still on the phone, and, from the sounds of it, he wasn't getting anywhere.

"Sorry, Ben. I've tried several times, on their cell phones as well as their home phones, but no one is answering. They must all be sound asleep."

I heard Ben softly sigh in answer. "That's okay. I'll just go get her. Them too. I'll be back in a bit."

"Wait, I'll go with you." That was Tracey. I thought she was handling all of this pretty well, all things considered.

As Ben and Tracey left the house, Trey, Arianna and I reached my bedroom and Nika's old bedroom. "Well ... here we are ..." I opened my sister's door for Arianna. "This was Nika's, before she ... before Hunter turned her. Now she has to sleep downstairs, away from the sun."

Arianna's eyes were wide as she looked around the room. As I looked with her, a part of me hummed with regret. I missed hanging out with my sister during the day. Being on opposite schedules sucked. When Arianna's eyes returned to mine, they were soft with compassion. "Is that why she stopped coming to school? Because she was ... turned?"

I nodded, and looked down to where I could feel my sister. She was still on the first floor. Presumably, keeping a watch on things with Hunter, until the sunrise forced her underground. At least she didn't have to go back to the cramped basement she'd been calling home. The underground floors here were just as plush as the aboveground rooms. "Yeah ... that's why she's homeschooled now."

Arianna and I locked eyes. I felt like hers were magnetic, pulling me in. I was helpless against those golden orbs; like the warmth of the sun, they were calling me to her ...

Trey let out a loud yawn, breaking the hypnotic spell. "Dude, I'm gonna crash before I pass out." He slapped me on the shoulder, then turned the knob and disappeared into my room. He left the door open, but I didn't follow him. I wanted to follow Arianna into Nika's room, but I knew that wasn't a good idea.

Arianna held up a hand as she gave me a shy smile. "See ya tomorrow, I guess."

I didn't want to leave her, but she'd been up almost all night; it wasn't fair to keep her up even longer. Even still, I needed to know where her head was. "How do you feel? I mean ... with knowing you'll remember everything. With knowing what I am?"

Biting my lip, I hoped she really was okay with my family's revelation. She had been before, but a lot had changed since then. Arianna swished her caramel hair over her shoulder as she thought. It shone in my vision; I'd never seen anything quite so beautiful. "Well ... I'm not sure. Honestly, I'm still absorbing. But I am glad I understand you better, and I'm glad my memories are mine to keep now. They never should have been taken in the first place." Her voice when she said it came out a little hot, and I smiled. My old girlfriend was still in there.

Wishing I could kiss her again, I whispered, "Goodnight, Arianna," and turned toward my door. It was surprisingly hard to turn my back on her.

"Wait ..."

Just the one soft word from her lips instantly froze me in place. I turned when I felt her hand on my arm. Her eyes were wide when we locked gazes, and I saw the conflict brimming near the surface—the desire, the confusion, the hope and the uncertainty. She started moving in my direction and I swear I was about to have my conversion. My blood was racing through my veins, my heart was pounding in my chest, and every nerve ending on my skin was tingling in anticipation.

She brought her lips to mine with a suddenness that spoke volumes about her own nerves, but once we touched, we lingered in a long, slow, heartfelt connection. My anxiety settled as our lips moved together. It was so familiar, so wonderful. I'd missed this so much. Cupping her cheek, I deepened our kiss. A soft groan escaped Arianna, and the sound ignited so many memories so fast, I felt dizzy.

When we broke apart, we were both breathless. Arianna's eyes were burning with the need for more, and I knew mine looked the same. "Wow," she panted. "That was just ... wow ..."

A small smile and a relieved laugh escaped me. "Yeah ... it was always 'wow' with you."

Arianna grinned, then looked up and down the empty hall. I almost told her it didn't matter if we were being watched or not, we still being monitored. "Have you and I ... back when we were a couple ... did we ever ... go all the way?"

I knew my cheeks had just turned bright red, and I also knew that all the vampires had just tuned out whatever conversation they'd been engaged in to listen to my answer. I even heard Hunter let out a soft laugh and Nika tell him to stop it. Damn it. Why did Arianna have to ask that here, now?

Knowing my parents would love this, I shook my head. "No ... we talked about it, but we never ... we never took it that far."

"Oh, well, I guess that's good. It would be really weird to not remember losing my virginity." She let out a laugh, and I suddenly didn't care about any of the eavesdroppers. Even Halina snorting didn't faze me. Arianna was so beautiful. I leaned in to kiss her again, grateful that I could now. I would cherish every minute with her.

When it started to get intense again, my mom's voice broke through my fog of bliss. "Julian, I think it's time you and Arianna parted ways for the night."

Breaking apart from Arianna, I chewed on my lip. "Ummm, my mom wants us to go to bed now. In separate rooms." I added that last part for Mom, so she'd know I knew the rules.

Arianna looked confused as she searched the hallway. "Your mom ... ?" Her cheeks flushed with color when she realized how I knew that. "They can hear us?" I nodded. "All of them?" she asked, clearly stunned.

I again nodded. Damn our supernatural hearing. It was annoying being spied on all the time.

"Oh wow," she quietly intoned. "Guess I better keep my steamy thoughts to myself." My jaw dropped, and I instantly wanted her to ignore my family and tell me every single thought in her brain. Arianna laughed at my expression, then tilted her head. "Can you hear as well as they can?"

I nodded, then shook my head. "I can hear ... a lot, but the rest of my family can hear much better." Even now, I knew some of them were having conversations but they were being too quiet for me to make out the words. Like not having glowing eyes, that was a side effect of my generation. We were just a little more human than the rest.

With a curious smile, Arianna barely breathed the words, "I'm glad I'm going to remember that kiss."

I was grinning like an idiot when she finally slipped inside Nika's room and shut the door. When I trudged into my room, I was still smiling like a person who needed psychiatric help. It worked. I saved her. No one could ever separate us again.

Trey was sprawled across my bed, snoring, so I grabbed a blanket and walked over to a stiff chair in the corner. It was going to give me a crick in the neck to sleep there, but I didn't care. I doubted I'd even sleep tonight. I was too wired. Closing my eyes, I replayed Arianna's kiss over and over and over.

I was lost in the memory, listening to Arianna's light breaths as she slept, when I heard a commotion downstairs. I didn't want to be pulled from my fantasy, but something serious was going on and every vampiric nerve in my body went into overdrive as I concentrated on my family.

"Slow down, Ben ... what?" My dad was on the phone with my pseudo-uncle. I couldn't hear what Ben was saying, but Dad's words were coming through loud and clear. While other vampires gasped, I heard Dad asking, "Gone? What do you mean they're gone?" Another pause as Dad listened to Ben, then Dad said, "Did you check Starla and Jacen's?" Dad was silent again and I sat up straight in the chair. Ice started filling my veins. Gone? Who was gone?

I blurred from the room and down the stairs. When I stopped in the entryway, I could hear Ben's frantic answer, and I suddenly wished I hadn't. "Yes, I checked everywhere, even the meeting place for the League. Starla, Jacen and my daughter are gone! They're gone, Teren! They're just ... gone ..."

CHAPTER NINETEEN

Nika

MOM AND DAD headed back to our house after Ben's frantic phone call, but it was no use. There was no scent in the air they could follow, no clue in the home that gave them any indication where Starla, Jacen, and Olivia might have gone. There was nothing left behind but more questions, although, it was pretty clear to everyone that Henry had taken them.

While I waited out the sun with Hunter and Halina, the search for our missing family members began. I prayed that everyone was okay, Olivia especially. Ben and Tracey would never recover if she wasn't. None of us would.

When the sun finally went down, Hunter and Halina joined their futile search. Mom and Alanna went with them. I wanted to go as well, but I was asked to stay behind to guard the ranch with Julian, Imogen, Grandpa Jack, and Malachi, who was well on his way to being fully recovered; the worn vampire had become nearly inseparable from Imogen since she'd started taking care of him.

All I heard all night long was Tracey crying, and begging us to go to the police, to start a statewide manhunt. We couldn't though … not with Starla and Jacen being a part of the search. We had to keep this as contained as possible. Low-key, even. But Tracey didn't understand, or else she just didn't care about the exposure risk. Her daughter's life was on the line, and there was nothing she wouldn't do to get her back. If only my imbecilic brother hadn't snuck a vaccine home, and Trey hadn't accidentally set it off near Tracey, then we could have eased her mind. And it would be really nice if one mind in the house was at peace.

Everyone was freaking out in different ways. Mom had made Ashley take Christian back home. She'd also made Ashley take Grandma Linda with them, to keep her safe from this latest round of unpredictable chaos. Arianna and Trey were taken home to their parents as soon as they woke up, but they both returned not long after nightfall. A fact that overjoyed my brother.

"What are you guys doing back here?" he said, swinging the front door open wide.

Trey shrugged as he entered the house. "We want to help find all the missing people. Seems wrong to just sit at home while they're out there … somewhere." By the look on his face, he seemed as clueless on how to find them as we were.

"What about your parents? What did you tell them?" I asked.

Trey just shrugged again. He didn't have the most attentive parents. Arianna turned to Julian. "I told them I was hanging out with my boyfriend for a few hours …" She blushed after she said it, and Julian grinned like he'd just won the lottery. If the situation weren't so dire, I would have found it cute.

A sigh escaped me as I looked between my willing-and-able friends. "Thank you for coming out here, but there really isn't anything to do. We have no idea where they might be …" No one was bonded to either Starla or Jacen. We had no way to track them. Tracey heard me say that, and started crying again.

VARIOUS MEMBERS OF the search party came and went over the next three days, and every one of them had the same dejected looks on their faces when they returned. Nothing. Not a trace, not a sound, not a word. Hideouts had been ransacked and every lead had been followed, but to no avail. It was like they had all vanished into smoke. Our only hope was

Jake. So long as Simon wanted to rescue him, odds were good that *they* would come to us. Eventually. But what state our friends would be in when Jake's rescue attempt finally happened … well, that was something none of us knew.

"Tracey, she's fine. He wouldn't hurt a child."

Tracey and Ben were fighting again. It was almost a constant thing now whenever Ben was at the ranch. Tracey wanted the National Guard called in, but Ben wouldn't let her call for *any* outside help.

"How do you know she's okay?" she screeched. "He could be making her a vampire right now!"

"It wouldn't work on her," Ben said in a soothing voice. "She's already a partial vampire. A very, very small part … but's it's already there."

None of us were sure if that was true or not, but Ben had decided that the possible-truth was better than the alternative, and he was clinging to it with everything he had. Personally, I thought he was wrong. I'd been a mixed vampire once, but that hadn't stopped me from being transformed into a pureblood. If I'd been able to be turned from a mixed to a pure, then it made sense to me that a slight vampire could be transformed into a mixed … assuming the procedure really worked, of course.

While Ben and Tracey verbally duked it out, Gabriel paced the living room. "There must be something we haven't tried," he murmured to himself. "I contacted Jordan at the L.A. nest, but no one he knows is bonded to either one of them. So far as any of us know, all of their family is deceased. There's no way to find Starla and Jacen with the blood bond." He said that with a mournful sigh.

I'd never seen him look as completely lost as he did. It was disconcerting, to say the least—as was thinking about Starla and Jacen's fates. While Olivia was probably just being held captive, the two obvious vampires in the group were most likely being tortured. Like Malachi, they were being held, drained, and starved. Being undead, Jacen would probably survive what was being done to him. Starla though, she might already be dead.

As Gabriel had explained to us before, Starla's blood was flawed. She had to take Gabriel's shot every day to stop the conversion from happening. She didn't have a choice. She wouldn't survive a conversion. If she'd been taken without a stock of shots on her, then she was already gone. If she did have some, but ran out before we could find her, then she would die. Her heart would give out, her human side would fade away, and she wouldn't rise again. She'd be gone forever. That thought had Gabriel constantly on edge—as did the knowledge that if Henry's crazy plan worked, and he successfully made mixed vampires with Starla's blood, then they would also share her fate. They would die the second their hearts gave out. Gabriel didn't want anyone else to die.

"This is all my fault," Gabriel muttered as he walked a line to and from the slider. "I should have called them and had them take the girl here, to the ranch. I should have kept us all together. Together we are strong ..."

Halina came up and stepped in front of him to break his unending pattern of movement. "You didn't know. None of us did." Wrapping her arms around his neck, she gave him a squeeze. "I am so sorry. We so often get caught up in my family's problems, that yours are forgotten. Please know that I understand your pain, and I am feeling it with you."

Gabriel closed his eyes as he embraced Halina. "Thank you, my love. I needed to hear that. I am so worried ..."

Despair, dejection, and desolation were beginning to be familiar feelings in the house. Trey and Arianna were the only bright spots, and even though my family was still irritated that my friends were compulsion-proof, they perked up whenever they were around. The levity never lasted long though and as the days stretched into weeks, even their visits didn't alleviate the gloom.

It didn't help anything when our family pet, Spike, finally passed away. Even though the dog was ancient, and had lived well past his prime, his dire fate somehow seemed to foreshadow our friends' futures. Dad brought the collie out to the ranch, to be buried in one of the pastures. The entire house was somber as Dad thanked his canine friend for years of love and comfort. I couldn't stop the tears as Dad began hiding him with soil, and there wasn't a dry eye when the last heap of dirt finally covered our beloved pooch.

The next night, everyone resumed the pointless searching. Mom was in the kitchen with Tracey when the sun finally set and I was able to escape the underground levels and join the rest of the family. Dad, Ben, and some of the others were already out looking for clues. Hunter was currently making plans to leave with Halina. I hated that he was leaving, and I hated that I couldn't go with him. Everyone seemed to think the house was going to be sieged one day, so a few vampires always stayed behind to protect the nest. And more often than not, that included me. But I wasn't an idiot, I knew that the real reason I was being left behind was the miniscule chance that the search would be successful and they would find Henry. Neither my dad nor Hunter wanted me or my brother anywhere near him. It was a ridiculous precaution if you asked me. I wanted to help.

"Tracey, maybe you should ease up," my mom was saying.

When I walked into the kitchen, I understood why. Tracey was drinking vodka ... straight from the bottle. From the way she staggered and the sweet, antiseptic smell coming off her, I'd say she'd been drinking it for a while. "No, what I should be doing is flashing my daughter's photo over every news station in this country."

She started to cry, then she hiccupped, then she started to laugh. It quickly shifted into a sob. Mom rubbed her back as she looked over at me. Her eyes were warm with compassion, but they held a look of unsure bewilderment. No one knew what to do for Tracey besides tell her to not give up hope, which wasn't accomplishing anything. Tracey was quickly turning into a basketcase.

Behind them, Imogen and Malachi were having a quiet conversation at the table while they waited for the blood that Alanna was simmering on the stove. Imogen and Malachi had been spending more and more time together, which was sweet and strange. Imogen had been single for as long as I'd known her. But the shy smiles she gave Malachi were self-explanatory. She liked him. He had filled out a lot since being rescued, and he looked healthy and vibrant now ... for a dead man. His hair was a dark shade of chocolate-brown, cut and slicked in a style that reminded me of old-time 1940s and 50s actors. I wasn't sure how long ago he'd been turned into a vampire, but from his look and his demeanor, I had a feeling it had been a while.

Hunter and Halina came into the room behind me. Hunter gave Tracey a pained smile before stepping up to my side. "We're going to leave. Check out the lake."

I sighed in response. "The lake? We've checked the lake five dozen times already. They're not there."

Tracey started crying harder and Hunter glanced at her before looking back at me. "It's better than nothing."

A flash of guilt ran up my spine, but I forcefully shoved it back. I was stuck doing "nothing" because they were making me stay here. I would be more than happy to *not* be doing "nothing." I told him as much, and he sighed. "I'd feel better if you stayed here with the others." He looked over at Tracey again. "Keep Tracey company. You know how hard this is on her."

I almost wanted to smack him for saying that, but I refrained. "It's hard on everyone. And the more eyes in the field, the better."

Hunter and I had had this conversation so many times, we could practically skip to the end, where I got commanded to stay behind. "Nika ..."

I held up my hand. "Fine. You're just as bad as my father," I said, rolling my eyes.

Leaning forward, he kissed my fingers. "Thank you. We'll be back before dawn."

While Halina prepared some to-go cups for them, I grabbed his elbow. "Be careful."

He nodded, then gave me a long, lingering kiss. "I love you," he whispered as he pulled away. Staring into his dark eyes, for the millionth time, I ached with the loss of our bond. I hated not feeling his presence, hated not feeling that delicious pull. But so long as Henry was still out there, Hunter was going to keep taking the shot. He felt it was safer. I ... kind of agreed.

Moments later, he and Halina were gone. I sighed, then helped Mom make dinner for Julian, Grandpa, Arianna, and Trey. Those last two weren't here yet, but they would be soon. They came out to the ranch almost every night. Julian was trying to hide his joy, especially around Tracey, but he was failing. We all knew he was deeply in love and high on life. And thankfully, Arianna was reciprocating his feelings. Even though the situation sucked, I was happy for them.

Julian slid into the room in his socks. Clapping his hands, he exclaimed, "Guests should be here soon!" Mom gave him a pointed look then raised her eyebrows at Tracey. Julian's expression immediately leveled. "Oh ... um, well ... the day crew will be arriving soon, is what I meant. Hopefully they have good news." Arianna and Trey had been keeping their ears to the ground, talking with kids our age to see if anyone knew anything. It seemed like an even longer shot than Halina and Hunter searching the lake for the umpteenth time, but they wanted to help. I understood the feeling.

Coming up close to Mom, Julian frowned. "I still say I should be able to go out and search stuff with them."

Mom's lips compressed. "We've discussed this before, Julian. Several times. So long as Henry is out there searching for mixed vampires, you need to be here where you're safe."

"He doesn't need to search for mixed vampires, Mom. He already has some …" I knew I shouldn't have said it the minute it left my mouth, but I was tired of being babied. I was a full-blown vampire for God's sake. And nearly an adult. They couldn't keep sheltering me forever.

Mom's eyes snapped up to mine. But instead of lecturing me, she pointed to her right. "Go set the table."

I held up my hands, but did what she asked. Sometimes arguing was just as futile as what we were arguing against. We could be five hundred years old and Mom and Dad would still treat us like little kids. With blurring movements, I set the table. The doorbell rang just as I finished. Good timing.

Julian sped to get it, but I was a step behind him, and since I was faster now, I beat him to the door. It seriously irritated him whenever I did that. "Show off," he muttered as I pulled the door open.

Trey stepped inside the minute he had enough room. Honestly, I was a little surprised he'd even rung the doorbell—he acted like he lived here. Arianna must have rung it. "Dudes, we have good news."

Arianna stepped in behind him, and wrapped her arms around Julian. Like he was freezing to death and she was the only source of heat in the room, Julian immediately melted into her. The affectionate display made me miss Hunter. "What news?" I asked, melancholy in my voice.

Mom wasn't so ambivalent, and she rushed into the room with hope on her face. "Did you find out something about Starla and Jacen?" Olivia's name hung heavy in the air, but we were all avoiding saying it out loud. Tracey usually became hysterical when she heard it. And we were pretending Starla was alive and well, because thinking of her any other way was too painful.

Trey lifted a finger of victory into the air. "We … were invited to a party."

Everyone's shoulders slumped. Expanding our social life wasn't the goal right now. Mom immediately turned away from Trey. He looked a little hurt that we weren't all jumping for joy over the news. "Dudes?" he said in question. "A par ... ty. With a bunch of kids. Kids who might know something ... ?" He held his hands out, like he was waiting for an explosion of adulation.

Mom gave him a tired smile. "It's better than nothing," she told him, mimicking Hunter's earlier words; they were practically our family motto now. "Good work, Trey." She turned away from him again with a noticeable heaviness around her shoulders.

Trey dropped his hands. "Yeah ... and there's this rumor that some hot new drug is going to be there..." He met eyes with me. "They say it's ... *unforgettable*." He said that last part with air quotations, just so we'd be sure to pay attention. And I certainly was now. Mom too.

"Unforgettable ... as in, the compulsion vaccine unforgettable?"

Arianna removed herself from Julian's embrace far enough to look at me, but she stayed glued to his side. "That's what we're thinking. Henry must have mixed it with something kids would like ... to up the exposure."

I twisted to Mom, who was watching us with a shocked expression. She honestly never thought Trey and Arianna's day missions would amount to anything. "We *have* to go, Mom. This could be it! A solid, undeniable lead!"

Mom was nodding and shaking her head. "Yes ... but it's too dangerous. Your father and I will go with you."

I scoffed at her answer. "No offense, Mom, but you and Dad, well, you look like a mom and dad. The kids will instantly know they've been busted, and the drug will vanish. If we're gonna catch the distributor, then *we* need to go. We're the only ones who will fit in at a party like that."

Mom bit her lip, struggling. This went against every parental precaution she had. "Nika ... I don't know."

From the doorway leading to the kitchen, a soft voice said, "Em ... let them go. Please."

Tracey was standing there, eyes red and bloodshot, and for the first time, hopeful. Mom couldn't resist her best friend, and she let out a heavy sigh. "Fine." She quickly twisted back to us. "But Hunter and Halina will go in with you. *They* can still pass for teenagers."

Smiling, I nodded. Finally, I was going to be able to do something. It was about freaking time. Looking over at Trey, I asked, "When's the party?"

He grinned. "Starts at nine ... so we shouldn't get there until eleven." He winked at my mom. "That's called being fashionably late."

Mom smirked at him. "Just be fashionably careful ... and find out something we can use. They've all been gone for far too long."

A somberness fell over the room. Yes, they had been. God, I hoped this party led us somewhere. I hoped the drug was what we thought it was. I hoped they were okay ...

Mom called Hunter and Halina, to get them to come back so we could all leave together. Tracey was a nervous wreck, but it was a different sort of anxiety than before. Now she was eager and full of hope. Now she was nearly bouncing off the walls, like we'd already found Olivia, and going to the party was just a formality to pick her up. I had a feeling that if we didn't come back with Olivia, Tracey would have to be locked up somewhere.

Even though the party was hours away, Tracey helped Arianna and me get ready. "Wear something short ... show lots of skin. That will get the dealer's attention."

Mom smacked Tracey in the shoulder, gently so she didn't break her arm. "Stop encouraging my daughter to dress like a skank, Trace."

Tracey rubbed her arm anyway. "I'm not. I'm just giving her the right tools for the job, and if she's going to a party and wants to attract attention, well ..." She shrugged, like the rest of her argument was obvious. The older woman was still very attractive, with plump lips and bright blue eyes, and I could easily picture her and Mom turning on the charm for the boys. Considering my father and Ben were the boys in question, that was a slightly disturbing thought.

"We'll be fine," I assured Mom, putting on a short, flirty red dress. I wasn't typically a party girl, and generally preferred staying at home with a good book, but I was eager to get out of the house and do something. Anything.

Mom pursed her lips, but didn't comment on my outfit. Arianna's dress was similar to mine, but in a dark blue color that she was hoping Julian liked. I didn't bother telling her that she could have worn a paper bag and he would have liked it. Mainly I didn't tell her that because I was also stupidly hoping my man liked my outfit. It seemed reasonable that he would, but I was still hoping.

I was in the middle of curling my dark brown locks when Hunter and Halina returned. I couldn't feel my boyfriend, but I could feel Halina and I knew they'd be close together. After hurriedly finishing my hair, I rushed from the room to tell him the good news—that we'd be spending the evening together. I was sure that had already been relayed in the message, but I wanted to tell him too; I could be just as ridiculous as Arianna sometimes.

Hunter was in the dining room with Halina and the others when I got downstairs. I could hear his deep voice just as clearly as if he was whispering in my ear. He was asking Trey details about the party: where it was, where he'd heard about it, how many kids were expected to show up. Trey's answers were vague at best. "This one place. I don't know. A lot."

Like we were still bonded and he'd known I was coming, Hunter stopped questioning Trey and turned to look my way when I entered the room. A peaceful look came over him, a look that clearly said, *I missed you, and I'm so glad to see you.* But he stayed where he was near the table, something he never would have been able to do if our bond was still in place. His eyes lit up when he noticed my dress though. I knew he'd like it.

Julian watched me enter the room with an intense expression, and I knew he wasn't really watching me. He was listening to Arianna, calculating how long it would be until he could see her all decked out. I didn't need to tell him she was almost done, he could hear that she was on her way down.

Mom turned to Halina while I stepped up to Hunter and grabbed his hand. "Teren and the others want to keep searching the streets, but they'll shadow the party once the kids arrive," she told her.

"Remind them to stay out of sight, Mom. The quickest way to end this party is to have a bunch of adults lurking around outside, acting like cops." By the look on Mom's face, it was clear she didn't like that I knew enough about partying to make that suggestion. I didn't, not really. It was just common sense to me. Holding up my hand, I told her as much. "Just saying."

Hunter turned to Malachi, sitting beside Imogen. He looked so much better now that he was fed and rested. "What can you tell us of Henry's operation? What should we expect?"

Malachi sighed. "I'm sorry ... there's not a whole lot I can tell you. I was delirious with hunger, pain, and fatigue at the time. To me, there were hundreds of men working for him. I doubt that's true though. Maybe it was just dozens. Maybe it was just a couple. Impossible to say." He sighed again and Imogen stroked his back in a compassionate manner. He smiled at her in thanks, and a spark of something bright and hopeful flashed between them.

It felt intrusive to keep watching, so I turned away. Hunter's hand tightened around mine. "We'll just have to stay sharp then."

When we finally took off a few hours later, it was a relief to be leaving the ranch. It was a relief to be by Hunter's side. It was a relief to be doing something useful. Tracey argued that she should come with, so she could be there for Olivia when we found her, but Mom told her it would be best if she waited at the ranch. She'd told her she would only be a liability if she went—that she'd rush out in a mad attempt to get her daughter, and somebody would get hurt. Or even worse, the bad guys would get away. I think that was what finally convinced Tracy to stay. Her last words to me were, "Find my baby." Nope. No pressure at all.

The party was taking place at an abandoned building in the middle of nowhere. The place had been sold recently, and was in the process of being remodeled—part of the roof was torn off, and the skeleton of the building's framework was exposed to the night air. In the interim of its renovation, the place had become party central, and my sensitive ears heard the deep throb of bass as we found an inconspicuous place to park the station wagon.

"I don't know about this," Hunter murmured, looking over the sea of cars parked between clumps of trees. The tall trunks looked like ghostly claws in the moonlight.

Knowing this was our best lead in a while to find our missing friends, I placed my hand on his knee. "Regardless, we have to go."

He met my eyes, with a steely resolve that I knew very well. There was nothing on this Earth that would keep him from checking out this party. "Yes, I know."

We met up with Dad, Ben, Gabriel, Rory, Cleo, and Jake before we went inside. Jake, like Tracey, wanted to come inside with us. It took a little more convincing than it had with Tracey, but eventually we got him to see that he would stick out like a sore thumb, and scare whomever Henry had sent here away. If Henry had even sent anyone here. Like everything else we'd been trying lately, this could all be a gigantic waste of time.

As Julian and I turned toward the building vibrating with music, Dad grabbed my elbow. Julian stopped with me, and we met Dad's gaze together. "Be careful, you two." His hypnotic eyes were softly glowing in the moonlight, same as mine and Hunter's, but his held a look of concern. The arch of his brow and the crease of his forehead further emphasized his unease. It was clear he'd much rather be checking out the place himself.

I gave him an unworried smile. "It's just a party, Dad. We'll be fine." A party with a bunch of kids who might be on a drug laced with a compulsion-proof vaccine, and crawling with vampire hunters who wanted us for our blood. No problem. "We'll text you if we find anything."

Dad nodded and the six of us started heading for the building—Halina leading the way, Trey right behind her. Julian was next, holding hands with Arianna, and Hunter and I were last. Even though we were on a mission, I held his hand tightly in mine. There was no rule that said this couldn't be a mission *and* a date.

Inside the room, the bass slammed against my chest like it was a hollowed-out drum. The volume of the music was excruciating to my sensitive ears and even though I tried to school my expression, I knew I was wincing. Hunter was cringing too, and I wondered if the intensity of the music was specifically designed to chip away at our advantage. Either that, or kids just liked loud music.

The teens assembled were all dressed like they were at some popular club in New York or Vegas, and not dancing in a rundown building in the middle of a grove of trees. Someone had brought in containers of dry ice, and a spooky layer of mist shrouded everyone's feet. Girls ran their hands seductively up their bodies while guys ground their hips into the girl's backsides. The whole thing was alarmingly erotic, and that was exactly why Mom and Dad would never have let Julian and me go to something like this before. It made me want to grab Hunter and feel his body all over mine ... but we had a job to do.

As we reached the outskirts of the gyrating kids, Halina turned to us and said above the music, "We should split into groups, with one pureblood per group, so we can ask around." I hated the fact that Hunter and I couldn't be together, but I nodded. It made sense. We wouldn't know if these kids were resistant to trancing unless we tried trancing them.

Halina immediately took Arianna, which I found an interesting choice. Arianna looked a little uncertain about being next to her, but she bravely held her chin up and allowed Halina to pull her straight into the masses. Hunter took Trey, and the two of them disappeared into the left side of the crowd. I looked over at my brother and smiled. "Guess it's just the two of us again."

He gave me a bright, charming in-love-with-life smile that warmed my chilled heart, and reminded me of better days. My smile faltered. A critical part of our "better days" was missing, and we needed to find her. "Let's go get Mom," I told him. He understood my reference to our fictional mother, and his smile faded into seriousness.

We took the right side of the group, and I immediately got to work telling kids to do stuff. Since kids could sometimes be jackasses, I made sure what I was asking them to do was something they wouldn't want to do. "Get out your phone and call your mom." Every time I said it, I was met with a blank expression, but then the person reached into their bag or pocket and grabbed their phone. Half of our side of the room was calling home; I took that as a good and bad sign. None of them would do it if they could resist me, so the vaccine wasn't here.

I was nearly to the back of the building when I finally found someone who didn't do what I said. "Bite me, bitch," was his slurred response.

I glanced at Julian, and then snapped my gaze back to the man. His eyes were focusing and un-focusing, and he swayed a bit on his feet—obviously on something. "Do you have any more good stuff?" I asked him. "All we've had tonight is crap."

The guy shook his head of long, black hair. "Nope. Used it all." He smiled as he showed us a very familiar canister, holding a very potent and fast-acting vaccine. Not that this kid knew it. All he was feeling was whatever drug Henry had recently added to the mixture.

"This stuff is amazing," he murmured as he held his hand in front of his face and slowly moved it back and forth, entranced.

I contained a groan. It would be so much easier interrogating him if he wasn't stoned. Or if I could simply compel the truth out of him. I needed to know where he'd gotten it. "Did you buy it here? Maybe I can still get some?"

The guy shrugged. "Yeah, maybe. Some dude handed it to me. Said it beat everything else. He was right too …"

The guy started zoning into his own personal la-la-land, and I resisted the urge to shake him. Looking around, I saw that the clump of people around him all had the same glazed expression. They were probably all immune. "What did he look like? Where did he go?"

The guy pointed off to the left. "There somewhere. He was a scrawny blond kid, that's all I remember."

Julian stepped forward. "Kid? Not an adult?"

The stoned guy shook his head. "Nah, he was our age."

I locked gazes with Julian. "Do you think it's Simon?"

Julian looked hopelessly confused. "I don't know. Why would he be at a party, spiking kids? I thought he'd be going after Jake as soon as he could. What the heck is he doing here?"

Good question. I grabbed Julian's arm and started pulling him toward the direction the guy had indicated. We needed to solve this little puzzle. Now.

CHAPTER TWENTY

Julian

AS NIKA AND I made our way over to where the partier had told us the "kid" had gone, Nika tested every person she came across. We quickly began to see a pattern in the vaccinated kids. Behind us was a path of destruction, a trail that had started in the back corner of the room and was quickly heading to the center.

Halina and Arianna were interrogating the middle section of kids, and we joined up with them before we ran across the mysterious dealer. He had to be nearby though. "Find anything unusual?" Halina asked. By the way she said it, it was clear everything had been typical on her end. Guess the vaccine hadn't made it that far yet. It would soon though.

"Yeah, actually. We've been finding a lot of strange stuff." I quickly filled her in on the compulsion-proof path of stoned kids that had led us this far.

Halina crouched and spun in a circle, like the dealer was right next to her, and she just didn't know it. Arianna's mouth dropped in such an adorable expression of disbelief, that I was momentarily distracted from the importance of our assignment. She filled me with a euphoria that no drug on this planet could surpass.

"Do you really think it's Simon?" she asked. "I just can't believe he would drug kids …"

Personally, I didn't think there was much Simon wouldn't do at this point … but I kept my tone neutral as I answered her. "He's not trying to get them high … he's trying to make them immune. Question is … why? How will doing any of this help him get Jake back?"

Nika pursed her lips, like she'd been wondering the same thing. None of this made any sense, but … if it *was* Simon, then we had a chance to end things, right here and now. Because we had what he wanted. His father.

I was just reaching for my phone to text Dad and tell him to send Jake inside, when Arianna grabbed my arm. When I looked up at her, she pointed over to a clump of kids thirty feet away. "Julian, look! Over there … Simon."

I studied the cluster of kids all hovering around another kid with his back to us. It was hard to tell through all the bodies around him if it was Simon or not, but then the bodies separated, leaving a crack that we could see through. And like he'd heard Arianna's exclamation, the kid in question turned to stare at us. My breath caught in my throat. It *was* Simon. We could end this. Tonight!

Narrowing his eyes, Simon gave us a cold, hard stare … then he blurred from the room, like only a vampire could.

The kids around him let out surprised shouts, and looked around at each other like they'd all just mass hallucinated. That was nothing compared to our reactions though. "Oh my God … he's …" I couldn't even finish my thought. Simon was a vampire. Jake was going to have a coronary.

Halina growled, "He doesn't leave," then took off in the direction he'd fled. She walked quickly, but at a human pace. We'd practiced self-restraint for far too long to break it now, even when the task at hand was of the utmost importance.

Nika dashed away after Halina. Grabbing Arianna's hand, I hurried after them. I knew we should text Dad, Jake and the others, but we were so close to Simon that I didn't want to take the time to do it. We had to stop him from leaving. It was our only hope.

As we pushed our way through the room to another door in the far corner, I spotted Trey. He was dancing. I let out a shout as we passed by, and hoped he heard me. He didn't appear to, but Hunter was a few feet behind him, and he turned my way. When we met gazes, I yelled out, "Simon!" and pointed toward the exit. He immediately grabbed Trey and started moving there.

By the time I got outside, Halina was nowhere around. Neither was Simon. Nika was on her phone, talking to Dad as she spun in a circle, trying to get a lead on where Simon had fled. Halina was to the east of us, but knowing her, she'd just taken a stab in the dark, hoping she got lucky and found him.

"Dad, Simon is here! He spotted us inside and took off. And Dad ... he blurred. He's not human ..." Nika bit her lip, and even though I couldn't read her emotions anymore, I knew she felt bad for Simon. Jake too probably. If we'd only better explained what we were, if we'd only held on to Simon tighter, if I'd only never had that damn party to begin with ... Simon would still be alive, and Starla, Jacen, and Olivia wouldn't be missing.

Hunter burst from the loud building into the chilly night air just in time to hear Nika tell Dad Simon was a vampire. His expression darkened as he met eyes with Nika. Arianna tugged on my hand, asking, "What does she mean he's not human, Julian?" but Ben's voice in the phone stopped me from answering.

"He knows where Olivia is. He does not get away again!"

Dad told him that of course he wouldn't get away, then gave us orders to systematically search our side of the grounds. They would get to work on the other half, and meet us in the middle. When Nika shut off her phone, I shook my head. "He's long gone, Nick. If he's really a full vampire, he could be two counties over by now."

Arianna gasped as she understood just what had happened to her friend. Trey scoffed. "He hates vamps. Tried to kill him." He jerked his thumb at Hunter. "Why would he want to turn into one?"

Hunter sighed. "To save someone he loves." His eyes drifted to my sister, and the two of them shared such a pained expression, I had to turn away.

After a second, I asked Nika, "Can you smell him? Give us an idea where to go?"

Both Nika and Hunter stepped forward and started inhaling the air. I fidgeted while I waited. The longer we just stood there, the longer he had to get away. Maybe Halina had the right idea, and we should have just dove in without a plan.

Nika paused with her face to the west. "I think I've got something."

Hunter paused with his face staring straight ahead. "Me too."

I threw my hands up. "There's only one of him. How can there be two trails? Three if Halina smelled something too." I pointed to the east, where I could feel her presence.

"There's more than one out here," Hunter said. His voice was a low rumble that gave me goose bumps. After his pronouncement, Hunter minutely lurched toward Halina's direction before stopping himself. I knew he wanted to be with his sire, bond or no bond, but with Nika beside him and Simon potentially in front of him, he couldn't. He'd have to trust that she was fine, that she could handle whatever she'd smelled out there. Hopefully, we could too.

Nika let out a weary exhale as she turned to look at Hunter. "We'll have to split up again, to keep the scent." They looked back at me, and I felt more useless than ever before. My far inferior sense of smell couldn't grasp the faint aroma of vampire on the breeze. Right now, I was about as human as Trey and Arianna.

Like she was thinking the same thing, Nika said, "You should stay here with Trey and Arianna."

I crooked a smile at her. "Fat chance of that. If we can end this tonight, I'm all in."

Arianna stepped forward; she was vibrating a little, but her chin was held high. "I am too. Simon was my friend. He stayed with me in my home. He won't hurt me ... vampire or not."

I squeezed her hand after her statement, loving her even more. Trey looked around. "Well, hell if I'm staying here alone. I mean, I am the only one of you who thought to bring a stake after all. I say that automatically gives me front line status." Opening his jacket, he pulled out a wooden dowel that had been whittled to a sharp point on one end.

"You brought a ... ?" Shaking my head, I let it go. He'd probably been carrying it around before he was even aware vampires existed.

Hunter nodded, then looked over at Nika and pointed straight ahead. "I'll check out this one, you and the others check out the other."

Trey smacked Hunter's arm, startling all of us. "Screw that, dude. We're partners, remember?"

Hunter sighed, then shrugged. "Whatever. Let's just go." He smirked back at Trey. "Try and keep up." Then he was gone so fast it was almost like he'd vanished.

"That's cheating, jackass!" Trey shouted before jogging after him.

Nika pursed her lips and shook her head before looking over at Arianna and me. "I guess it's the three of us."

She zipped off lightning fast, and I scooped up Arianna so I could follow her ... almost as quickly.

By the time we stopped, we were at least a mile away from the party. Quite a distance for humans, next to nothing for vampires. Nika had her hand out, warning us to stay back. She had her nose scrunched and she was breathing deep, like she was sniffing the air for clues. I held Arianna close to me as I watched her. We were surrounded by woods on every side of us, but directly ahead, there was an older-looking car parked in the woods. If there was a vampire out there, this was his ride.

Twisting to me, Nika muttered under her breath, "I think there are two—" Just then, Nika was slammed into the ground by a force moving so quickly it was hard to track them.

I set Arianna down, stepping in front of her to keep her protected. Nika sprang to her feet and hovered in a crouch, searching for her assailant. I spotted a blur of movement approaching from her left, and shouted out a warning. Nika spun, grabbed the guy, and threw him to the ground. She was on him in a flash, pinning him with her legs pressed close against his arms and her hands on his throat. Her fangs were fully bared, and a low growl escaped her chest. I'd never seen my sister so confident and powerful. Even I could admit she was a little intimidating. Party dress or not, she was a force to be reckoned with.

The guy beneath her seemed to think so too. His eyes were wide and his fangs were long as he struggled to break her grasp. He couldn't though. He was clearly no match for my sister, and I began to wonder if he truly was a pureblood.

"Where is Simon?" Nika snarled.

From behind me, Arianna quietly whispered, "She said there were two. Where's the other one?"

Good question. My eyes kept a steady lookout as my sister interrogated the prisoner. Since he hadn't answered her question, she lifted his head, and then smacked it into the earth. "I said, where is Simon?"

The vampire beneath her growled, but didn't answer. On the other side of them, another vampire broke through the cover of trees. This one didn't bother with brute force football tactics. He just raised a gun at Nika and fired. Arianna screamed as the muffled shot rang out. I felt Dad's form immediately start streaking our way, and figured some of the others were coming too, unless they were entangled in fights of their own.

Nika leapt off the vampire beneath her, and the bullets struck him instead. A circle of dark red blood stained his white shirt around each bullet hole, turning him into a horrifying work of art. He didn't move; one of the bullets must have pierced his heart. I couldn't dwell on it though, because vampire number two had shifted his gun to Arianna and me. I picked her up again, and dashed to the side, just as he fired. I felt the difference in the air pressure as the bullets whizzed past me, and the fully healed wound in my thigh started throbbing with phantom pain. Too close. Much too close.

My heart thudded in my chest as I debated how to stop this armed madman. He had the aim of a hunter and the reflexes of a vampire: ruthlessness laced with deadliness. His arm followed my movement, blurring as he tracked me. I could tell that he knew how to compensate for my speed, and when he fired, he was gonna hit me. But then Nika ran in front of him, and he switched targets. I wanted to scream at my sister to not be stupid; I also wanted to thank her for possibly saving my life.

The guy fired at Nika, and I watched in horror as she stumbled and fell to the ground. Arianna screamed again, and I forced the worry for my sister from my mind so I could save my girlfriend. Several feet away from the shooter, I ran into Dad carrying Ben. He set Ben down and streaked off toward Nika. He'd heard her yelp when she'd been hit, same as me.

Setting Arianna down, I handed her to Ben. "Protect her," I exclaimed, before turning to follow Dad. Arianna screamed my name, begging me to stay, but I couldn't. My sister was hurt and alone.

Well, not quite alone. When I got there, Hunter was wrestling the shooter for the gun. Dad blurred over to help him, while I rushed over to Nika. Sliding to my knees beside her, I searched her body for clues. All I could see and smell was the blackish blood covering the front of her dress ... and I swear it was heaviest right over her heart. I started hyperventilating. I couldn't lose my sister right after getting my girlfriend back. The universe couldn't possibly be that cruel.

Scooping Nika into my arms, I debated what to do. I couldn't give her CPR, I couldn't bandage her wounds, try to stop the bleeding, the wound had already healed shut. I couldn't even check her pulse to see if she was weak or steady. She was already dead, so none of those human techniques would help me.

The gun went off three more times. I cringed each time the muffled blast pierced the air. It would be almost silent to humans, but to me it was like thunder and lightning cracking apart the night sky. When the gun finally went silent, I couldn't look to see the aftermath, to see if any more of my family was hurt ... or dead. All I could do was focus on my sister.

"Nick? Nick, wake up. Snap out of it." She had to be dazed ... that had to be it.

Hunter blurred to us, and brief exhale of relief hit me. He was okay. He didn't look okay though. He looked frazzled, scared out of his mind. Eyes rimmed with blood, he grabbed Nika from my arms. "Baby? Baby, please, talk to me." He held her close to his chest. "Talk to me ..."

When she didn't, a sob escaped him, and he started repeating, "No, no, no ... not like this. I just got you back ..."

"Oh God ..."

I looked up to see Dad staring down at the three of us. His face was an expression of disbelief, horror and confusion. His shirt was sprayed with blood spatter, but he didn't seem injured. A quick glance showed me the crumpled body of the second vampire. Guess they'd gotten him. Good. Nika's murder should be avenged. Jesus ... she couldn't be dead. Not dead-dead.

Dad took a step toward Nika's body. "Nika ... ? Can you hear me? Please say yes." That last part was said in a reverent whisper that was clearly a prayer.

"Dad, how do we know if she's ... ?" I couldn't even bring myself to say it.

Hunter's tortured gaze snapped to me. As a tear of dark red blood trailed from one eye, he snarled, "She's not. She's fine."

I was about to tell him that clearly she wasn't fine since she wasn't responding, when she gasped and her eyes sprang open. Hunter looked both relieved and smug that he was right. I didn't care, I only cared that she was okay. Rushing forward, Dad squatted beside Hunter. "You okay, Nika?" He examined her chest like he could see the bullet through her skin.

Nika shook her head. "No ... that really freaking hurt!" Her trembling fingers came up to touch what must have been the entry point. When she pulled them back and saw the blood coating the tips, she groaned, then cursed. "Damn it. I'm never going to be able to wear this dress again."

A nervous laugh escaped Hunter, then he pulled her tight. "Don't ever do that again, okay?"

Nika nodded as she cuddled into his side. "Yeah, I think I've died enough for one lifetime."

When Hunter finally relaxed his grip on her, I slugged her in the arm. Hunter growled at me, but I ignored him. Hitting my sister when she was acting foolish was well within my brotherly rights. "And don't ever step in front of a bullet for me again. Although ... thank you for doing that. I really don't ever want to be shot again."

Nika laughed as Hunter helped her to her feet. "I had to, Julie. I'm more resilient than you."

"Don't be all braggy 'cause you're dead," I scoffed.

She swayed on her feet, and both Dad and Hunter helped steady her. She assured them she was fine, just in shock, but Dad shook his head. "You have a bullet resting near your heart. It needs to be removed before it does serious damage." He cringed. "Sorry, sweetheart, but your pain isn't over yet."

If my sister hadn't already been pale before, Dad's words would have made her ghostly white. As it was, her eyes widened, her mouth parted, and she started breathing heavier. Dad squeezed her arm. "It's best not to think about it."

I was positive that not thinking about your chest being cut open wasn't a possibility, and as selfish as it sounded, I was glad our bond was broken and I wasn't going to have to feel her torment. Just looking at her anxiety was bad enough.

Ben and Arianna trotted into our section of the woods while we comforted Nika. Ben immediately started searching the dead vampire with the gun. Arianna ran to my side, tossing her arms around me. "I was so scared," she breathed into my skin.

I held her close, savoring her warmth and comfort. She went stiff in my arms. When she pulled back, her eyes were locked on Nika. "Are you ... okay?"

Nika gave her a small smile. "Nothing a little open heart surgery won't fix." Arianna's look of concern didn't change any, and Nika put a hand on her arm. "I'm fine. I'm already dead, bullets don't hurt me."

That wasn't entirely true, but none of us were about to tell Arianna that.

A couple of minutes later, Rory, Cleo, and Jake joined our group from behind. They were all winded—clearly having run the entire way after Dad had vanished with Ben. I instantly felt bad that they didn't have a reliable way to move at our speed.

Dad was filling them in on what had happened, when I heard a rustling sound coming from the woods in front of Ben. A moment of panic washed through me, until I remembered Nika saying that she'd only smelled two vampires in this direction. It was probably Trey. Maybe he'd gotten lost following Hunter, and he'd shot past us. That was possible. Or it could be Gabriel. Halina's form was still streaking to the east. I'd assumed he'd gone after her, but there was always a chance he hadn't. Ben wasn't taking any chances though. Gun raised, he stood his ground like he could take on anything that emerged from the woods … like he could take on the world.

A figure emerged just as Ben cocked the gun. Olivia stumbled out of the woods, brushing away twigs and branches as she walked. Fearing that Ben would shoot her, I just about had a coronary. He had quick reflexes for a human though, and he disengaged the gun and tossed it to the ground before running to scoop up his daughter.

He didn't make it to her, though, because she blurred into his arms first.

Ben was so ecstatic to have her back that he didn't seem to notice her speed. While he swept her into a giant bear hug, her feet leaving the ground, I looked around at everyone watching. Had they seen that? By the shocked expressions, I was guessing they had. "Dad … she's …"

Dad's lips pressed into a firm line, and he responded before I could finish. "Yeah, I know."

With a sigh, Dad started walking up to Ben and Olivia. The rest of us followed him. My mood was twisting from relief to revulsion so fast, it would have made Nika nauseous if we were still connected. How could anyone turn a girl that young into a vampire? It wasn't right, and it definitely wasn't fair. She hadn't even reached her teens, and now she was frozen in time. Tracey was going to flip, and she'd already been hovering on the edge of madness.

Ben was laughing, crying, and kissing her head when we approached. He'd set Olivia back down on her feet and was kneeling in front of her; he still hadn't seemed to notice her changes. And he should have—her fangs were dropped.

Dad put a hand on his shoulder. "Ben ..."

Ben glanced up at Dad with euphoria on his face. "She's alive, Teren. We found her!"

Dad grit his teeth, glanced at Olivia, and then returned his eyes to Ben. "Look at her, Ben."

Ben was confused, but he did as Dad said. He shot to his feet when he finally noticed what we already had ... that she wasn't human anymore. "No ... She's a child ... No!" There was heat in his voice, and I knew if Henry were here right now, Ben would have choked the life out of him barehanded. "How could he—?"

Olivia knew what he meant and interrupted him. "I volunteered, Daddy. I had Henry make me a vampire so I could find you. I'm not a full one, though. None of us are, so I'm still pretty much just like you, but with these cool pointy teeth! Feel 'em!" She opened her mouth wide so Ben could touch her very sharp canines. He didn't though, he was still processing what she'd just said. Olivia was a chatterbox on a good day, and now she had super speed to make her speech almost imperceptibly fast.

"You volunteered? Not a full vampire ... ? I don't understand."

Nika stepped forward then, her head tilted. "She's right ... her heart is still beating." She looked over at Dad with scrunched eyebrows. "I was too preoccupied during the fight to know for sure, but I think those vampires had heartbeats too." She blinked in astonishment. "He did it, Dad. Henry made mixed vampires."

Shock was the first thing I felt. Then relief. Olivia could still grow up, she wasn't stuck. Dad's hands curled into fists as he processed the news. "He made mixed vampires ... with Starla and Jacen's blood. And who knows how much he used ... how weak they are now." Dad turned back to Olivia. "Is Starla ... is she okay? Is Jacen?"

Olivia nodded. "Last I saw, yeah." She cringed, like she knew she wasn't being entirely truthful.

Dad exhaled in relief. "Thank God. We weren't sure Starla would still be ... We were worried about her. She has ... a medical condition." Olivia opened her mouth, then closed it. She looked like she wanted to say something, but was scared to say it. Dad asked another question before she gathered her courage. "Do you know how many vampires he's made with their blood?"

Olivia shook her head. "No, I'm not in the inner circle yet, but they're starting to trust me." She shifted her gaze back to her dad. "See, I told them you guys had kidnapped me too, like Simon and that guy," she pointed at Jake. "I told them I was immune to vampire compulsion same as them, and you guys wanted me locked up because of it. I even said Starla and Jacen were my captors." She frowned. "I felt bad lying about that, because I love Starla and Jacen, but I needed Simon and Henry to trust me. And they did believe me, but not right away. I volunteered to join their *army*—" she snorted with a laugh when she said army, like the entire concept was ridiculous to her, "—so they would trust me and I could escape, to get back to you and Mom."

Ben seemed flabbergasted that she'd done all that. I was too. And confused. Because the faint amount of vampire blood in her system made her naturally immune to compulsion, we'd been extra careful to make sure she was always left out of the loop. "How did you know what to say to them? How did you know about vampires? About compulsion? About Simon and Jake? How did you know ... anything?" I asked her.

Olivia put her hands on her hips as she gave me an insolent glare. "I'm not stupid, and you guys aren't as clever or as quiet as you think. I've known for a while what you guys were. I think it's awesome, and now I'm one of you!" She pointed at her teeth, just in case we'd missed it. Beaming, she looked back at her dad. "Pretty smart, huh?"

Ben smiled, then pulled her into him. "Yeah, pretty smart, kiddo."

Jake's patience had worn thin by this point. "Why is Henry building a vampire army? For what purpose?"

Olivia didn't seem sure how to answer him. "Well ... most armies are built to either defend or attack. I don't know which one he's planning on doing, but I do know his first mission is rescuing you. Well, that's Simon's mission anyway, and Henry is going along with it. Mainly because Simon brings him volunteers, I think."

"Simon ... brings him people ... to turn ... ?" Jake was more stunned about this than the fact that Olivia was a vampire.

She shrugged. "Yeah. He goes to parties like this with some beefy vampire backup, hands out that drug with compulsion-be-gone in it, then tells the kids to meet him somewhere when they want more. The ones who show up get convinced to be turned. Or they will be convinced, I guess. This is only the second party we've done." She crossed her arms over her chest. "And I was supposed to help, but Simon made me stay in the car with that asshole." She pointed to the vampire who'd shot Nika.

Ben looked pissed, but Jake was suddenly excited. "So Simon really was here! Where did he go?" He grabbed Olivia by the shoulders. "Where is he?" he screeched.

Dad and Ben moved to get him off her, but Olivia shoved him away. He landed on his butt, three feet away from her. While Jake sprang to his feet, Olivia looked at her hands like she was surprised. "Please ... where is he? He's my son ..."

His voice was so strained that Olivia's expression softened. "I don't know. He didn't come back this way."

Jake sighed and looked at the dead vampire on the ground. "Is Simon ... ? Did he do the procedure? Is he like *that* now?" He pointed to the vampire, his face twisted in disgust.

Looking offended, Olivia raised her chin. "Yeah. He was the first volunteer. That's how I knew it worked."

Letting out a soft curse, Jake closed his eyes. "Stupid kid," he muttered under his breath.

"He just loves you ... wants you safe," she said, her voice quiet.

Jake's eyes flashed open. "I *am* safe!" All of us turned to look at him in surprise. This was the first time he'd admitted that we weren't spawns of evil. Meeting our eyes, he amended his statement. "Well, I'm safer than he is, hanging around Henry."

Olivia nodded, and rubbed her arms like she was cold. "Yeah, that guy freaks me out. Which is why I have to go back," she said, locking eyes with Ben.

He immediately told her, "No."

Olivia's face scrunched into an expression of parental annoyance. "I have to, Dad. It's the only way to save Starla, Jacen and Simon."

Ben crossed his arms over his chest in a stance that clearly said, *This isn't happening.* "No. You're going to the ranch, and I'm never letting you out of my sight again."

Jake held his hand out to Ben. "Don't be stupid, she's the only one who knows where their lab is."

Olivia started dragging her toe in the ground. "Well ... actually ... they blindfolded me, so I don't know exactly where it is, but I can go to the meeting point and join up with everyone." Thinking of something, she sighed. "Actually ... those two knew the meeting point. They hadn't told me yet. I guess I can't rejoin Simon. I can't save Starla and Jacen ..."

That admission clearly bothered her. Her eyes started misting, and then a clear tear rolled down her cheek. Not a full vampire's blood-red tear, like Hunter and Nika, but completely normal, like a mixed vampire. It made me wonder who had sired her, and if the bond was in place, or if the transfusion had messed that up. "Who made you?" I asked her.

She seemed confused. "Henry?"

I shook my head. "No, whose vampire blood? Starla or Jacen? Can you feel either one of them? Do you know where they are?"

Jake had grown disheartened while she'd been explaining her limitations, but he was excited again as he waited for her answer. Olivia glanced at all of us with eyes that suddenly looked very guilty. "I was one of the few that they made with Starla's blood. They'd take a little bit from her each day, so she didn't bleed to death ... but that was before..." She swallowed. "I can't feel her now. Not since the transfusion."

Dad looked around the group, but none of us knew what she was talking about. "What transfusion?"

Olivia inhaled a deep breath, then let it out with slow resignation. "Starla told Henry that she had to take a shot of medicine every day or she wouldn't convert ... whatever that means. She told him that was why she was still alive, still aging, but Jacen was dead and would always look young." Her eyes widened. "I had no idea that was why she looks so old and the rest of you don't."

Ben sniffed, and I heard him mutter, "She's not *that* old." I wasn't exactly sure, but I had a feeling Ben had a few years on Starla.

Swishing her hand, Olivia continued, "Anyway, Henry said she was no use to him dead, so he let her take the shot. Luckily, she had a bunch in her bag when we were taken. They did my transfusion while she was still on the shot. But eventually, she ran out of medicine ..." Olivia shuddered as she remembered what had happened. "Starla freaked out, and she was already freaking out ... and cold, hungry, weak ... It's awful what they're doing to them, Dad."

She gave her dad helpless eyes, and they shimmered with tears again. I tried not to visualize what Starla and Jacen were going through, but it was difficult to keep the images out, especially when I started drifting into memories of a cold, dark, lonely place ... I squeezed Arianna tight to block out the fear trying to surface, and made myself focus on Olivia.

She looked ten years older than she really was when she started speaking again. "Henry didn't want her to die, but he didn't know how to save her without the shot, so he ... he transfused her blood with Jacen's. She didn't die that night, and it's been a week or so since then, but ... Starla is positive that any day now she's going to die, and never wake up."

With fear in her eyes, like she'd suddenly realized something, Olivia said to her dad, "They used her blood to make me ... so ... am I going to die? Is this blood going to kill me, and I won't wake back up?"

That was a legitimate question, and one we didn't have an answer for. Ben sighed and pulled Olivia into him. "You'll be all right, honey." He met eyes with Dad, and I could see he wasn't sure. Regardless, he patted her back and told her, "Everything is going to be just fine."

Dad sighed, and then said, "We should go find Great-Gran and Gabriel. They'll want to know about Simon and Olivia ... and Starla."

Ben nodded, and Dad turned to Rory and Cleo. "Stay here and make sure the bodies aren't discovered. We'll take care of them when we get back." They nodded and Dad let out a tired sigh. "Let's go."

CHAPTER TWENTY-ONE

Hunter

MY MIND SPUN as I watched Teren pick up Ben and blur away; Olivia immediately followed him. I couldn't believe what I'd just heard, what I'd just seen. Simon, Olivia, and a bunch of Henry's hunters had volunteered to become mixed vampires. Sure, that kind of advantage—the speed, the strength, the hearing—was desirable, but back when I was hunting, mixing my blood with a demon's was something I never would have considered. It was almost hard to imagine someone like that wanting that kind of life. Didn't they understand that all living vampires eventually turned into undead vampires? Guess they didn't care. Or perhaps they didn't know. Mixed vampires were rare, and many people, myself included, hadn't known about them until I'd encountered some of them.

Julian picked up Arianna and blurred away after his father. Huffing and puffing, Trey emerged from the section of the woods that we'd been searching. He looked around, his face a mask of disbelief at the carnage before him. "Stay here with Rory and Cleo," I told him. "We'll be back in a minute."

Nodding, he sat down. "I'm tired of running anyway."

Jake glanced at Trey, and then took off after Teren and Julian on foot. Nika was a split second away from following her father and brother, but I grabbed her elbow and stopped her. She looked back at me with bunched eyebrows. "What? We have to go!"

I gave her the sternest expression I had in my repertoire. "You still have a bullet lodged in your chest. You don't need to be running around, jostling it. We can't risk it puncturing your heart."

Nika crossed her arms over her chest, defiance written all over her face. "But we need to tell Grandma and Gabriel what's going on."

"True," I told her. "But if we're going to go, then you're going to have to let me be chivalrous."

Even though there was a lot going on, even though Trey was gagging as he examined the dead vampires, the look Nika was giving me was laced with seduction. Dead or not, my body instantly responded. "Chivalrous? How?"

I swept her into my arms, and held her close to my chest. "You're going to have to let me carry you."

Nika let out a noise that was somewhere between a groan and a giggle as she laced her arms around my neck. I tried to ignore the splotches of wet blood smeared over her chest. She had healed, she was fine. That had been too close though, and for a few seconds, I'd been sure that I'd arrived too late and she was forever gone to me. I never wanted to experience that level of pain again. I'd rather have a second conversion, starve again, or eradicate my father's memory again ... than lose Nika.

As we sped after the others, at a slower pace so I could be sure Nika was stable, she asked me about what I'd found in the woods. "Was there anything on your side?"

I frowned as I remembered. "Just a couple of newly-turned teens who obviously had never seen any real combat. They ran the minute they saw me. I was about to chase after them when I heard the gun go off."

A surge of pain filled my stomach. I hadn't known at the time who had been involved in the gunfight. Just the thought of Nika being in danger had turned me into a nearly deranged maniac, but any of my new family being hurt or killed was unthinkable. I'd attacked the armed vampire with a vengeance, and hadn't stopped until he'd been incapacitated. While he was the one who had ultimately pulled the trigger, I wasn't mourning the fact that he was dead.

We came across Teren and the others so fast, I almost shot right past them. Halina was with Teren, and she called my name as I ran by. Careful not to shake Nika too much, I slowed and returned to where Teren was telling Halina and Gabriel everything he knew.

Teren pointed at Olivia, who gave Gabriel a friendly wave. "He did it," Teren said. "He found a way to create mixed vampires. And he found a way to make it routinely work ... we just fought several of them."

While Gabriel stared at Olivia with obvious astonishment, Halina gestured to some bodies lying in the tall grass—nearly hidden in the darkness, but for the smell of blood wafting from them. One of Halina's vampire assailants appeared to be disarmed, while the other had a sword. I scanned my creator for any sign of injury, but she didn't seem to have a scratch on her; not even a strand of hair was out of place.

"As did we," she told Teren, her expression grim.

"This shouldn't be possible," Gabriel murmured, clearly stunned by all he'd seen. "The blood ... finding the right balance of human and vampire, finding a way to override the human immune system, so it *always* accepts the foreign material ..." His hand came up to touch Olivia, and his finger pulled down her lip to study her teeth. "What he's accomplished ... it's masterful, poetic. Pure genius."

"You mean pure evil genius, right?" Ben grabbed his daughter, and pulled her back from Gabriel. "She's eleven, and he did some crazy experimental procedure on her that luckily turned her without killing her. But he used *Starla's* blood to make her." He emphasized Starla's name, so Gabriel would grasp the danger without him having to say it in front of Olivia. Gabriel was too worried about his nestmate to catch the subtlety though.

His hopeful eyes locked onto Olivia. "Starla! Is she alive? Did she have her medicine with her? Did she have enough? Does she need more? I can ... I can get some, and you can take it to her. If we just ..."

He started looking around, like he was plotting how to go about doing that. Ben stepped forward to get his attention. "She doesn't need the shot anymore, Gabriel, but Olivia will."

Olivia immediately turned to her dad. "Whoa ... what shot? The one Starla had to take every day? Am I gonna have to do that?" She put her hands up before Ben could even answer her. "Nuh-uh, no way! I hate needles."

Gabriel caught the important part of her comment, and his expression relaxed. "She had medicine on her then ... good girl." Then his mouth firmed and his gaze swept over Ben. "What do you mean she doesn't need it anymore? She'll always need it, unless she ..." His eyes widened as he turned his face back to Olivia. "She's dead, isn't she?"

Halina put a hand on his shoulder in sympathy, and Gabriel reached back to squeeze it. Olivia shook her head in answer. "Nah, she's still kicking. Henry transfused her with Jacen's blood. They're like, bonded now, which is really amusing when they get separated and reunited." She made an explosion with her hands, followed by a bomb sound.

Halina let out an amused snort, while Gabriel looked intrigued. "I'd never considered something like that. Of course, I'd never considered transfusions at all. Brilliant," he murmured, genuinely impressed by the madman's skills.

Tenderly setting Nika down, I snapped, "Yeah, brilliant. He's creating compulsion-proof, super-hunters to capture vampires for our blood, or to just flat-out kill us. The bullet in Nika's chest is proof of that."

Halina growled and snapped her gaze to Nika. Her eyes narrowed as she examined the streaks of blood over her pristine skin. By the intensity of Halina's gaze, you would think she could see the bullet, and she was obliterating it with the power of her mind. I was sure Nika would prefer it if removing the bullet was that easy. Me too. Knowing the level of pain she was going to experience made me nauseous. Watching her go through it was going to be difficult.

Halina was about to say something when Jake finally caught up to us. He ran into the clearing full-bore, like a psychopathic axe murderer was on his heels. When he spotted us, he slowed to an easy jog. His chest was heaving and his breath came out in explosive exhales and sharp pulls. What had been a brief jaunt for us, had been a decent run for him.

Hand on his side, he strode up to Halina and Gabriel. "Did you see him? Did you see Simon? Did he come this way? Where did he go?" He looked around the woods, then spotted the mound of a body in the darkness and froze. "Is that ... ?"

Even in the moonlight, I could see his face paling. Halina shook her head. "That was a problem, one we took care of, but it was not your son." I didn't mention the fact that Halina had never actually seen Simon before, so she wouldn't know him by sight, and she could have possibly killed him. I was sure she hadn't though, and I didn't want to freak Jake out. He was holding together surprisingly well, considering.

Just after I thought that, his face clouded. "So ... Simon was here, but he somehow slipped past us ... and every lead who might have told us where to find him was killed? Is that what just went down?"

Olivia raised her hand and pointed at me. "I heard that guy say that the kids he faced ran away, so technically, they're still alive." When Jake threw a glare her way, Olivia shrugged and muttered, "Just saying."

Nika matched Jake's glare. "They were going to kill us. We did the best we could, but we're not sacrificing anyone for information."

Jake gave her a level look. "No one but Simon, Starla and Jacen, right?"

Nika's jaw tightened as she looked away, and I pulled her into me. "We all know what's at stake. You don't have to remind us," I said.

Jake took a step toward me. He was still breathing fast, and every word was punctuated with a heavy exhale. "Apparently, I do, because we're back at square one, with no leads, and no way to find my son!"

Olivia raised her hand again. "Actually, that's not entirely true." Everyone turned to look at her, and she gave us all a small smile.

Ben put a hand on her arm. "What are you talking about, sweetheart? Do you have a blood-bond with someone who might lead us to them? Someone else created with Starla's blood?"

Olivia scrunched her face. "No ... I can't ... Most everyone was made with Jacen's blood, since he could be drained faster ... The rest of us who were made with Starla's blood ... must all be dead. I'm the last one ..." She frowned, then brightened. "But we do still have a lead." She pointed in the direction of the building, where I could hear the music thumping into the night like a gigantic heartbeat. "The kids at the party. When Simon hands out the drug, he tells them where to meet him if they want more. It's probably somewhere easy to find. Simon wouldn't want the kids forgetting."

We all looked back to the party. Of course. Simon was recruiting volunteers that he could juice up for his rescue mission. Once he had enough of them, he'd descend on the ranch in some crazy attempt to get Jake back.

Jake slowly shook his head. "I wish I could get a message to him, let him know I'm all right, that he doesn't need to do this, but even if he believed I wasn't under duress, Henry would have confiscated his phone right away. He probably destroyed it. Crazy, paranoid, manipulative old man." He looked back at the group of us with hope in his eyes. "But at least we have another lead to follow."

Teren turned to Julian. "You and Arianna go back to the party and see what you can learn."

Julian looked ecstatic to be given such a big responsibility, and he straightened his shoulders as he nodded at his dad. "We'll find out where the meeting is. I promise."

He picked up Arianna, and the two of them sped away. Jake looked like he was going to follow, but Teren held up a hand to stop him. "Leave the kids to talk to the other kids. We have cleanup work to do." He indicated the corpses on the ground. Jake sighed, longingly looked back at the party, then finally nodded and got to work covering our tracks.

"I'd like to take one back, to study the blood," Gabriel told Jake as he passed by. Jake made a face that was two parts disgust, one part resignation. Whatever might help his son.

Teren turned to me while Halina, Jake and Gabriel began gathering the vampires. "Ben and I are going to help clean up the other site. Why don't you take Nika to the ranch? Mom, Gran, and Emma can get started on her ... injury." He frowned at the thought of his daughter being dug into. My stomach twisted.

I was just about to tell him that was a great idea, when Nika stepped forward. "I'll be fine a little longer, Dad. I'd like to go help Julian. No ... I'm *going* to go help Julian."

Teren clearly didn't like the tone of defiance in her voice, but I thought I saw a flash of pride in his smile. "Nika, you have a bullet in your chest. It could be near your heart—"

"And Starla could die any second. The longer we waste, the less time she has. She needs Gabriel's medicine. And they both need to come home." Her voice choked on the word home, and dark red blood welled in her eyes.

Teren looked moved by her tone, by her face. He opened his mouth to speak, then closed it and nodded. Nika looked back at me, a challenge in her eyes. I wasn't going to challenge her though. She made a good point, and the risk to her was minimal, so long as she was careful.

Instead of answering her unasked question, I scooped her into my arms. "Ready to dance?" I asked, a playfulness to my tone that really wasn't appropriate given the circumstances.

Nika let out a soft giggle, but then stopped herself with a sigh. "Let's go find Simon."

The task diminished the brief moment of levity, and I took off after Julian. Hopefully, we'd be able to find someone who would willingly help us, since we couldn't compel answers from these compulsion-proof kids.

When we got to the backside of the building, I gently set Nika down. She frowned as she stepped away from me. "I'm not made of glass, you know. I'm not gonna break." Some clouds drifted past the moon, casting a shadow across Nika's face. It was ominous, seeing her enshrouded in darkness.

"Maybe not, but I might if something happens to you. Trust me, keeping you safe is purely self-preservation on my part."

The clouds passed and the moonlight brightened the smile on her face. Or tried to. The moon could only do so much to enhance perfection. "I love you too," she told me, leaning in for a kiss.

I opened the door when we pulled apart, and was instantly assaulted by the thunderous club music; it gave me a headache. Grabbing Nika's hand, I entered the building with her. There were strobe lights everywhere, and buckets holding dry ice in sporadic clumps around the gyrating bodies. Combined with the sound, I felt like my senses were on overload. The quicker we got out of here, the better.

Nika was cringing too, but she indicated with her head where we should go. Whatever clumps of people Simon had managed to drug and immunize when he was here before had most likely spread out. Some had probably even left, forever taking their secrets with them. Wherever we started seemed as good a place as any.

Holding my hand, Nika pulled me toward the center of the masses. The more time we spent in the roar of overwhelming noise and movement, the more I was able to block it out. I even started picking up a few heartbeats, which was both miraculous and odd. My body was attuned to blood, though, and like a sweet fragrance in the air, I could almost always pick it out.

That was it though. I wasn't hungry, and the thought of ripping open the young throats around me was an unappealing as it would have been if I were still human. Teren and Halina were right. Being a vampire didn't alter who I was. All it had done was heighten my senses and change my menu.

Nika started commanding the people around her, asking them to do things they wouldn't normally do, looking for someone who could resist her. I followed suit. "Tell me your deepest fear," I asked a girl beside me.

Her eyes glazed over, as she immediately replied, "Losing my family."

I smiled at her answer, and then moved on to someone else. "Tell me your deepest fear," I asked a guy wearing a sideways baseball cap and enough gold chains to buy a small village food for a year.

"Snakes," he told me, his expression bland. Then he shivered, like just saying the word was disturbing.

Nika and I were almost to the other side of the room, having no luck finding someone who could refuse our questions, when I suddenly stumbled across an asshole. He was tall and lanky, with thick dark hair that fell over his eyes. I almost compelled him to get a haircut, but instead, I stuck to my normal line of questioning. "Tell me your deepest fear."

He eyed me up and down, or I assumed he did, since his head made a surveying motion, then he pushed me back and said, "Screw you."

I snapped my head to Nika, and called her name. Her sharp hearing heard me above the chaos, and she instantly turned to look. I pointed at the guy who'd turned me down—he shouldn't have been able to do that. Understanding my gesture, Nika smiled as she stepped the few feet over to where I was.

She tapped him on the shoulder, while I wondered what we should say. Since we couldn't make him tell us anything, we'd have to be charming and schmooze it out of him. That was not my strongpoint.

"Excuse me," Nika said over the thumping music. "We heard there was some amazing stuff going around the party. We were wondering if you knew where we could get some?"

The guy smirked. "I have no idea what you're talking about."

Just as I was wondering if pummeling answers out of the guy was acceptable, Nika shrugged and said, "That's too bad. I heard it's supposed to be an amazing ride. I'd do just about *anything* to try it."

She started turning away from him. His mouth popped open and he grabbed her elbow. My mouth dropped open too. Just what was my girlfriend promising him? "Wait ... mine is gone, but I know where to get more."

Nika looked back at him with a smile bright enough to knock a grown man to his feet. The teen in front of us surely felt the impact. He even backed up a step. "Really? That's great! Thank you! Where do we go?"

That was when the stoner seemed to remember she wasn't alone. He looked over at me with a frown. "Howard's Market, tomorrow at midnight."

Nika patted the guy's cheek. "Thanks! You're the best!"

She immediately moved away from him and he held up his hands. "Wait! We can still party!"

I put a hand on his shoulder. "No ... you can't." I wanted to bare my fangs at him, just a little ... but I refrained. Damn. Being responsible sucked sometimes.

Leaving the forlorn partier to his thoughts, I followed Nika. Like she could somehow still sense Julian, she found her brother in the swarm of bodies. He was asking a couple of girls if they had any good stuff. Both girls laughed at him, then walked away. Without being able to trance people, finding kids who were compulsion-proof was tricky. Nika put a hand on his shoulder and Julian spun around with wide, startled eyes. It was hard to surprise a vampire, even a mixed vampire, but Julian was several generations down the line, and his senses weren't as acute as the others. Plus, it was really damn loud in here.

Leaning forward, Nika shouted, "We got it! Let's go get Dad!"

Julian nodded and pulled Arianna toward the exit.

When we were finally on the way back to the ranch, I laid my head back on the car seat and let out a long exhale of relief. Not having that chaos assaulting me from every direction was bliss in and of itself, but having a location—an actual, physical location—was an answered prayer. We were one step closer to Simon, which was one step closer to Starla, Jacen, and stopping the science that would ultimately lead to our undoing if left unchecked. Everything hinged on that goth-boy's memory. Howard's Market. There was only one in the city, and it was sort of a landmark for locals, or so Nika told me. I hadn't been here long enough to know. But all the kids knew it, which was why Simon was using it. Even a kid blitzed out of his mind would know where to meet him.

"Do you think we should go there tonight?" Trey asked. He was hyper, bouncing in his seat, eager for another adventure. It was the exact opposite of how I felt, and I wished he was sitting in the front seat beside Julian, instead of right next to me so I wouldn't have to feel his energy; he was practically vibrating.

"The kid said tomorrow night, and Nika is hurt. She needs attention first," I told him, for the umpteenth time. And also for the umpteenth time, Nika cringed. She probably wouldn't mind a detour before going to the ranch. The others were meeting us though, so we couldn't deviate.

Trey started in on a recount of tonight's activity. I would have given anything for him to shut up so we could have some peace and quiet. Like Nika knew I was teetering on the edge of slapping my hand over his mouth, she grabbed my fingers and softly pressed them to her lips. Just like that, I didn't much care about Trey's incessant babbling anymore.

When she brought our fingers down to her lap, I cupped her hand with mine. "We'll get you taken care of as soon as we get there. Then you can rest."

She suddenly looked ill, and she peered down at her chest like a creature was about to burst out of it. "I'm sure it's fine ... we can wait a little longer."

Knowing she was just scared, I brought my fingers to her chin. "No, we can't, and you know we can't." She bit her lip, then laid her head on my shoulder. Ignoring Trey, we spent the rest of the car ride wrapped in each other's arms.

The ride to the ranch seemed to take forever, but when we got there, I heard Nika mutter, "That was fast." Time really was all about perception.

Everyone was outside when we pulled up, and I could see Tracey craning her neck, looking for her daughter. I instantly wished Olivia had ridden back with us. Ben hadn't wanted her to leave his side though, and they were following behind us in Cleo's car. Halina and Gabriel had decided to head out on foot while we all drove. Gabriel wanted to immediately study the mixed vampires we'd fought. Halina was waiting next to Emma, and both women smiled brightly at seeing their children return.

When we stepped out of the station wagon, Tracey seemed disappointed to see us. I was certain Ben had called her on the drive home, to let her know Olivia had been found. I wondered how much he'd told her. If she hadn't been informed already, she was in for a big surprise.

Stepping forward, Tracey asked, "Are Ben and Teren right behind you? I know Olivia is with them ... I want to see my daughter." She fisted her hands like she was commanding me. I didn't have the answer she needed though. The shot I was taking blocked me from everyone.

I opened my mouth to speak, but Julian beat me to it. "They're about ten minutes behind us, Aunt Tracey. They'll be here soon." His tone was calm and supportive, but he was clenching Arianna's hand. He knew what this was going to do to Tracey.

Halina smiled at me with approving eyes, then turned to Emma. "Nika was shot, she should have the bullet removed immediately."

Everyone snapped their gaze to Nika, and everyone's expressions suddenly went from relief to concern. "Shot?" Tracey asked, recovering first. "Who shot you?" Her hands went to her throat. "Was Olivia involved in a gunfight? Is she okay?"

Nika let out a reluctant sigh as Julian assured Tracey that Olivia was fine. He didn't mention she was a vampire, but I supposed Tracey hadn't asked that. Imogen, standing very close to Malachi, came forward. Her eyes scanned Nika, spotted the lingering bloodstains on her skin and dress, and asked, "Were you hit in the chest, dear?"

Nika sighed again, and her eyes guiltily drifted to her mother. "Yeah. One of the guys had a gun. He was gonna shoot Julian ... I distracted him." She rubbed her chest, like the wound still ached.

Emma's face went stark white in the moonlight, then there was a flurry of movement as women rushed around Nika. We were driven apart as searching fingers entangled her. While Emma and Imogen looked for signs of an entry point, that was almost impossible to see now, Alanna said to her husband, "Jack, we're going to need lots of towels and a sharp knife."

Arianna tossed her hand over her mouth while Trey looked confused. "What are they gonna do, dude? Cut her open and dig it out?"

Face sympathetic, Julian's eyes never left his sister as she was swept into the house. "Yeah ... that's exactly what they're gonna do," he murmured.

My own face grim, I nodded at him, then followed Nika. The women were taking her to the kitchen. Nika was shaking, and I could tell she was forcing herself to keep moving forward, when all she wanted to do was run away. My stomach was twisted into a knot so tight, I wasn't sure how I could let this happen. I knew it was necessary—the bullet needed to come out—but the pain she was going to endure … I couldn't take it.

"Is there anything we can give her? A drug? Alcohol? Anything to numb the pain?" I asked, panic in my voice.

Halina shook her head. "She's a pureblood now … her body would absorb most everything before it took effect, or it would just make her sick. Gabriel might be able to cook up something she could handle, but that would take time. It's best to just get it over with." Looking over at Nika, she brushed her knuckle down her cheek and said something in Russian.

Nika exhaled a slow breath as she nodded. The table was cleared off and Nika laid down on top of it. Jack was working on gathering a bunch of towels. He set a pile down next to his wife, then he went to get a knife. When he returned and Nika saw the sharp blade, she gagged, then covered her mouth and looked away. I squeezed her hand, wishing I could do more.

"We need to undress her," Imogen stated. From her voice, it was clear that was a cue for all the men to leave the vicinity. Malachi, who had been watching from the edge of the room, left with Jack. Eyes defiant, I squeezed Nika's hand tighter. If they wanted me to leave, they would have to pry me off her.

Maybe seeing that I was glued to her side, none of the women tried to remove me. They started removing Nika's party dress, and Nika started freaking out. "No, no, it's fine … it's not hurting me. Just leave it. Please, leave it."

She was frantically looking between her mother and grandmothers, but they were all avoiding eye contact with her. Knowing panic when I saw it, I brought my free hand to her chin, and turned her face to me. Hoping she would let me soothe her, I lowered my lips to hers. She was stiff with fear at first, but then she slowly began relaxing into my touch. She even brought a hand to my face, and for a second, I think we both forgot what was going on as we took a moment to enjoy each other.

Then she screamed.

She instinctually fought against the object causing her pain, and Imogen immediately told us, "Hold her down." I didn't want to, but I knew the end would get here sooner if we did. I held one side while Alanna held the other. Halina secured her feet.

Nika's cries were unbearable. So was her begging for us to stop. I don't think she was even aware of where she was or what she was saying.

She was just in pain. Bloody tears rolled down her cheeks nonstop. Seeing her torture brought tears to my eyes. I couldn't hold them back, and the blood-red drops dripped off me and onto her lips. She licked her lip without thinking, and her fangs instantly released. She stopped screaming and snapped her gaze to me. She wasn't really seeing me though. She had a feral, hungry, pained, scared look in her eye, and I suddenly knew what would ease her suffering.

Letting her go with one hand, I brought my wrist to my face and tore it open. The pain was searing, but nothing compared to what Nika was going through. I brought my wrist to her mouth, and she hungrily took it. She sucked down long draws of my free-flowing blood, and I started to feel lightheaded as she gulped down swallow after swallow. I didn't care. I'd let it all go if it helped her. If I didn't have to hear her scream anymore.

Just when I thought I was about to pass out, I heard Imogen say, "There ... I found it." Seconds later, she exclaimed, "Got it!" I glanced over to see her hand, drenched in dark red blood, holding a tiny bullet. My vision swam, then everything went dark.

CHAPTER TWENTY-TWO

Nika

I NEVER WANTED to be operated on again. I thought it had been awful when I was human, but without the benefit of anesthesia or painkillers, it outright sucked as a vampire. The only thing that had kept my sanity intact was Hunter's blood. His cool, refreshing, mood-enhancing blood. But thankfully, the bullet was out of me, and if the fates were with me, I'd never have to go through that again.

As I laid on the kitchen table panting, my body stitched itself back together. That part was actually enjoyable. It was like an itch being scratched, the pain fading into tingles of pleasure. I'd heard it said that some vampires cut themselves just to feel that tingle. I wasn't that addicted to the sensation, but after what I'd just gone through, it was heaven.

A low rumble of delight left me. So much better than jagged bolts of electrifying pain. Hunter's face loomed on the edge of my vision. He seemed pale and sickly, like he'd just been the one operated on. I immediately felt bad for how much blood I'd consumed.

"Are you all right?" he asked, his eyes tired, but happy.

"Yeah," I murmured. My tongue felt thick in my mouth. My fangs were still dropped from feeding. I hadn't had the energy to pull them back up yet. Weakly, I started bringing my wrist to his mouth. "You need to eat ..."

His hand reached up, grabbed mine, and returned it to my chest. A kitchen towel was draped across my skin, giving me a little modesty. "Imogen is making me some. Save yours, you need it."

I inhaled, and the scent of fresh blood tantalized my senses. I closed my eyes and another growl escaped me. Hunter laughed. "She's making you some too. And your mom is getting you clean clothes."

Opening my eyes, I nodded. "Thank you, for what you did."

"There isn't anything I wouldn't do for you, Nika." Leaning forward, he added, "I can't wait for this to be over, so we can be bonded again. So we can be together, day and night." There was fire in his eyes when he said it, and I had no doubt that even my parents wouldn't be able to keep us apart after this. We would be lovers, sire-bonded, nestmates ... no, soul mates, and no force on this earth would ever rip us apart again.

Sitting up, I pulled his mouth to mine. *Yes. That's all I ever wanted.*

A soft voice clearing their throat interrupted us. Imogen was standing there, holding two thermoses of blood. "Drink up, you two. You'll need your strength for the argument that's about to be heading your way." She smiled at us and winked.

I laughed as I took the mug. Yeah, Hunter's and my plans would not go well with my father. He'd fight us every step of the way, but I wasn't backing down this time. My place was at the ranch, with my partner for eternal life.

Tipping back the thermos, I let the hot blood flow into my mouth. I gulped it down in greedy swallows, and heard Hunter doing the same. I paused as I felt a familiar presence cross the property line. "Dad and the others are here," I said to Hunter.

He finished his drink, then handed the thermos to Imogen; she immediately walked over to the stove to refill it. "We should go, Tracey will have questions." He sighed. "*I* have questions."

I thought his cheeks looked a little fuller, but he still seemed like someone who'd been bed-ridden for three months. "You stay here and rest and eat. I'll go."

Feeling sprightly, and pretty much back to normal, I hopped off the table. Or tried to anyway. Hunter grabbed my wrist. "Nika ... your clothes." The meager kitchen towel covering my chest had fallen away, and Hunter's eyes were glued to the newly exposed, freshly washed skin. It made a different sort of tingle go through me.

His hand slowly started coming forward to touch me, and I held my breath. But then, all of a sudden, Hunter was whacked in the back of the head with a wooden spoon. "Not in my kitchen, you don't." Imogen handed me the towel while she gave Hunter evil eyes.

As he rubbed his head, Mom dashed into the room with clean clothes. She glared at Hunter too, like I hadn't been the one at fault, hopping off the table nearly naked. I blurred my clothes on while Imogen gave Hunter another thermos. Mom studied me after I was dressed. I supposed she'd heard our stubborn declarations to be together. She didn't say anything to me though, she merely raised an eyebrow.

I pointed outside. "I'm gonna go ... talk to Dad ..."

Mom grabbed my hand before I could blur away. "What did the two of you mean by 'Tracey will have questions'? Questions about what?"

I looked down, to where I could feel Halina under the earth. She was probably in Gabriel's lab, helping him collect samples from the body they'd carried back. The body of a man who had been turned into a mixed vampire. A feat that, up until now, had been rare and risky. My mom having been successfully turned was a miracle story in our house, but now, the miracle was a scientific procedure that anyone could have done, for a price.

"Jake's grandfather figured out how to make living vampires..." My voice trailed off. I couldn't bring myself to say that he'd turned an eleven-year-old. Just having seen it with my own eyes was bad enough.

Mom seemed confused, but then her eyes widened. "Olivia ..."

I nodded. "And Simon. And the men we fought. Things are different now, Mom." And they might not ever be the same again. Anyone could become a human/vampire mix now. It was a whole new world.

We heard a woman screeching outside, and I knew Tracey had finally been reunited with her daughter. While Imogen handed Hunter a third thermos of blood, Mom and I blurred outside. Everyone returning home from the rescue mission looked mildly defeated. Dad stared at Mom with somber eyes. Ben wouldn't meet his wife's gaze as she hugged her daughter with every ounce of strength she possessed. Jake looked frustrated, yet hopeful all at the same time. And Rory and Cleo looked like they were going to drop from fatigue any minute.

"Oh my God, you're okay! I was so scared. I felt like I was going out of my mind." Pushing Olivia back, Tracey stared her in the eye. "Don't ever get yourself kidnapped again! You hear me?"

Olivia smiled, and it was the smile that clued Tracey into the fact that something about her daughter was different. In her emotional turmoil, or maybe just in her newness, Olivia had forgotten to keep her teeth up. Her fangs were fully visible in her grin, and all of the blood drained from Tracey's face.

"What ... what's wrong with your ... ?" She took a step back from Olivia, then snapped her gaze to Ben. "What's wrong with her teeth, Ben? Why does she look like that?"

Ben exhaled, and his eyes studied the cobblestone. "Maybe we should go inside."

"No!" Tracey shouted. "I want an answer, right now! An honest to God, truthful answer. You can't make me forget stuff anymore. You have to let me in now, and I want to know." She inhaled a deep breath, then let it out slowly. When she spoke she seemed calmer, but her words trembled. "I want to know what happened to my daughter."

Olivia raised her hand. "It was my decision, Mom. You can't be mad at Dad."

Tracey's eyes returned to Olivia. "What was your decision?" Her voice was so quiet, I wasn't sure if she really wanted an answer to that.

Olivia held her head up when she spoke, and she suddenly didn't seem like a little girl at all. "I chose to be turned into a vampire."

Tracey took another step back. She ran into Mom, and Mom put a supportive arm around her. "It's okay, Trace," she told her. "It's going to be okay."

Tracey looked back at Mom with tears in her eyes. "She's just a little girl, and he made her into a ... a ..."

She struggled to say the word, so Olivia supplied it for her. Arms crossed over her chest, she snapped, "I'm not a monster, if that's what you're thinking."

Tracey returned her gaze to her daughter. "No, of course you're not, sweetie. You're fine ... we'll fix this." She looked over at Ben. "We can fix this, right?"

Ben finally met her eye. "There's no way to undo vampirism, Tracey. I'm sorry. This is just ... the way she is now."

Tracey became unglued. Breaking free from Mom, she stormed over to her husband. "You promised me she'd be fine here! You swore she'd be safe! She's just a little girl, and you got her killed!" She shoved against his chest, but Ben didn't move.

Everyone tensed, ready to spring into action, but Olivia made the first move. Blurring vampire-fast, she stepped between her mother and father, and gently pushed her mom back. Dropping into a protective crouch in front of Ben, she let out a menacing growl. "I'm not dead! Nobody has killed me."

Tracey staggered back a few feet. When she regained her balance, she looked at her daughter in confusion. "Not dead?"

Olivia shook her head. "No ... my heart is still beating, I'm still aging. I won't always be eleven." Seeing her mom calmer, she straightened. "I just have these teeth, and crazy-fast speed." She smiled, like it was all no big deal.

Tracey tried to smile, but it came out forced. "I need a drink," she muttered, then she turned and walked back into the house. She passed Hunter, who was finished with his blood and coming out to join me, but she didn't say a word to him.

Olivia looked back at her dad, and Ben sighed. "Is she mad at me, Dad?"

Ben shook his head. "Of course not. She's just ... overwhelmed. We'll give her a minute, then go talk to her."

Jake stepped forward. "What we should be doing is formulating a plan for tomorrow night, for getting Simon back."

My dad clapped him on the back. "He's safe, and he survived the process. He's going to be okay for one night, so we should rest up. Tomorrow is going to be a busy day."

Jake looked like he wanted to argue, but instead he nodded. "All right, I'm going to my room then." Once we'd started helping Jake instead of keeping him hostage, he'd started sleeping in the upstairs "daylight" rooms. I think he was more comfortable being above ground. Friendly or not, being around pureblood vampires was still a challenge for him.

Rory and Cleo started to follow him into the house, and frowning, Jake turned to Hunter. "Mind calling off your guard dogs? I'm not going anywhere."

Hunter turned to Rory and Cleo. "Why don't you guys take off? Go home for once—rest. You must have lives outside of all of this?" He indicated the family ranch with a sweep of his hand.

Rory and Cleo exchanged a glance, then shrugged. "Not really," Cleo told him. "We've been hunting your kind for so long now that everything else kind of ... fell apart. If it's all the same to you, we'd rather stay here, protecting your family."

Rory scratched his head. "It's the closest we've had to one in a while."

Hunter smiled, then shrugged as well. "I can't compel you anymore. You're free to do what you like."

Both hunters gave him a formal, stiff nod. Jake rolled his eyes, then wearily stumbled into the house. Hunter's bodyguards shuffled after him. Mom and Dad hugged while Ben and Olivia went to go find Tracey. As they entered the house, Julian, Trey, and Arianna exited it.

"Thanks for your help tonight, and for telling us about the party. I think you sort of saved the day," Julian was telling Trey.

Trey was beaming. Looking over at me, he puffed out his chest. "Hear that, Little A? I'm a hero."

Smiling, I shook my head. "Yeah, I know." Trey had been helpful on more than one occasion, he just didn't remember.

Trey gave me a nod, then Julian a brief guy hug. "See you tomorrow night, dude."

Julian shook his head. "No, you guys should sit this one out. It might be dangerous." His eyes flicked to me. "Even more so than tonight was."

Trey swished his hand. "Playing-with-Fire is my middle name, man. I live for this shit." Eyeing my parents standing a few feet away, Trey quickly amended with, "Err, stuff ... I live for this stuff."

Dad smirked at Trey, then clasped Mom's elbow and started walking to the house. Hunter grabbed my hand to lead me away, but I wanted to say goodbye to my best friend first, even if she didn't remember when we were best friends. Approaching Arianna, I wrapped my arms around her in a quick hug.

Dropping Julian's hand, she hugged me back. "Goodnight, Arianna. Drive safe."

"Thank you, Nika." Her voice was sweet, but there was still some distance there. While Julian had gone to school with her every day, and had been slowly rebuilding some sort of familiarity with her, I hadn't had as much time with her. We'd eventually rebuild what we'd had though. I was sure of it.

Stepping away so Arianna could say her goodbyes to Julian in peace, I grabbed Hunter's hand. As Julian and Arianna stared at each other with moons and stars in their eyes, Hunter pulled me back toward the house. "You've been through a lot tonight," he said. "You should rest."

His eyes were warm, soft, and concerned but shaking my head, I told him, "There's too much to do. We should talk to Grandma and Gabriel, see if they found anything important, anything we can use tomorrow."

His smile turned appreciative and amused as he led me through the entryway. "There are a million people in this house, Nika. Or it sure feels that way sometimes. If anything is discovered, they'll tell us before we go. In the meantime, the best thing we can do for Starla, Jacen, and ourselves, is to rest."

Even though I didn't want to agree with his logic, even though I wanted to keep moving, keep pressing forward, keep fighting, I nodded. "Okay ... fine. Let's go hole up somewhere." By my tone, it was clear I meant for us to go somewhere together. I waited for my father to voice his objections, but surprisingly, he didn't. Maybe he understood that it was pointless to keep denying the inevitable. Or maybe he was just giving me a free pass tonight ... since I *had* just had my chest cracked open. Or maybe he trusted that Hunter wouldn't try anything with me under his roof ... not until I was eighteen.

Whatever the reason was, no one objected when Hunter and I disappeared into his bedroom together. He closed the door behind us, disconnecting us from the rest of the house, and I was grateful and relieved that we would be in each other's arms tonight.

Leading me to his bed, Hunter pulled back the covers and murmured, "Lay down, love."

The term of endearment made me smile. It was similar to something Halina would say, and I wondered if he'd picked it up from her. As I crawled into bed, Hunter walked over to the dresser to take his daily shot. It still hurt him to take it, but he tolerated the pain much better now. It was sort of amazing what the body could get used to.

"You could skip a night," I told him, laying my head down on his pillow.

He looked back at me, and for a moment, he seemed entranced by what he saw. After a silent second, he shook his head like he was trying to regain his focus. "It's better this way. For now. If I let the bond come back, I don't think I'd have the strength to shut it off again. Being connected to you is too ... intoxicating to resist twice."

I wanted to remind him that he'd been resisting me for a while now, but I refrained. Now wasn't the time, we both knew that. With a sympathetic cringe already in place, I watched as he prepared a needle and jabbed himself with it. As soon as the liquid was inside him, he hunched over in pain. Tossing the needle aside, he clamped onto his arm and squeezed his lips together, stopping himself from making a sound. A muffled cry still escaped him though, and it tore my heart to hear it. I pulled back the cover to run to him, but he lifted a finger to stop me. As I hesitated, his expression softened, his body relaxed.

With a pained smile on his face, he looked back at me and shrugged. "It's really not so bad."

Knowing he was full of it, I frowned. With a sigh, he turned off the lights, and then walked over to me. Crawling into the bed beside me, he wrapped his arms and legs around me and whispered in my ear, "It's ten times better than having something happen to you because I lost control. Although ... even in control I still let something happen to you."

He sighed again and I twisted my body to face him. His eyes shone in the darkness, same as mine, and his face was lit in an almost ethereal glow. "I'm a vampire, and an Adams, and I'm fully capable of taking care of myself. I don't need you to be my savior and my protector. I just ... need you."

His eyes searched my face for long seconds, then he whispered, "I need you too. So much ..." His mouth lowered to mine and our lips softly searched the other's. The gentle, tender kisses didn't last long though and before I knew it, Hunter was leaning over me, and our fangs were down and our kisses were frantic. A fire started burning within me, flaming hotter over the realization that I might have died tonight. I might have died, and all this time we'd been denying ourselves ... and why? Because of my age? Because of my parents? In light of a near-death, it all seemed so arbitrary. We loved each other. We should be together. And with the bond gone, this wasn't some passion-fueled frenzy. This was us: bare, real, raw.

It was perfect, we were perfect, and I was wrong before ... this *was* the time.

As Hunter's mouth moved to my neck, I murmured, "I want you ..."

He froze above me, then shifted his head to look at me, his breath heavier. "Nika ..." I was positive he was going to start telling me all the reasons we couldn't be together, all the reasons we had to deny what we both wanted. "I thought I'd lost you tonight. I can't ... I don't want to ..." He paused to swallow a hard lump, then said, "I want you too."

His tone of voice gave me shivers, while the passion in his eyes burned straight through me. "You're not going to fight me? Tell me we can't? That it would be wrong? That it would be disrespectful? That we should keep waiting?"

His hand ran up my shirt as he shook his head. "No. I'm done waiting. And if you think this is wrong, if you think we should stop ... then you better stop me ... because I can't anymore." His hand settled between my breasts, right where the bullet had pierced me. I understood all too well why he wasn't holding back anymore; it was the same reason I wasn't holding back anymore.

"I don't want you to stop." My voice was so faint, even I could barely hear me.

Hunter's hand shifted, and began traveling toward my jeans. As his mouth lowered to mine, he muttered, "Good."

He began undressing me, and for a second, my mind spun. My dad was going to kill me if he ever found out about what we were doing right under his nose. But as more clothes were removed, I cared less and less about what Dad thought. It didn't matter. He couldn't kill me, I was already dead. And firmly in the love-of-my-life's arms. There was nowhere else I'd rather be.

Hunter's hands moved up and down my body, exploring me, caressing me. Knowing no one could hear me, I reveled in his touch, letting him know exactly how good it felt. My hands moved over the planes and angles of his body, feeling the rigidness of his muscles, the softness of his skin. His breath in my ear ignited me, and I thought I'd never been more ready for him in all my life.

"Please," I murmured, pressing my lips to the side of his neck. Feeling the blood under the surface only escalated my desire.

A low groan escaped Hunter's lips, and then he shifted his body so he was on top of me. My breath was a fast pant when I felt him pause, right where I needed him the most. A whimper escaped me, and my fangs crashed down as I lost all control.

"I love you, Nika," Hunter whispered. I wanted to answer him, but he pushed into me at the same time and all words left me.

Moving together was just as rapturous as our first time. More so, since I was so much more sensitive now. I could feel the grooves in his skin, the stubble along his jaw, the way his body flexed and moved. I could hear the euphoria in his voice as he made soft, erotic noises that were quickly driving me to a breaking point. I wished the moment could last forever, but being so in tune with everything had me on the edge much too soon. Holding Hunter tight, I arched my back as the explosion hit me so hard my head swam. Oh God …

Hunter wasn't far behind me, and he called out my name as he released. Exhaustion overcame me as my spent body started coming down off my high. And as Hunter lovingly kissed my shoulder and slid to my side, only one thought swam through my head—thank God for vampire-soundproofing.

HUNTER AND I woke up completely bare the next evening. We'd fallen asleep immediately after exploring each other. Memories of the moment flashed through my mind, making me smile. It had been just as amazing as I'd hoped it would be. And even though we had things to do, very important things to do, I kind of wanted to skip it all and stay naked in his arms all night.

"And what are you smiling about?" Hunter's deep voice said, breaking the stillness.

"Just … reminiscing. And wishing we had time to do that again."

And just like that, our door was opened. I clutched the covers to my chest as my idiotic brother stepped into the room. "Hey, guys, we're gonna head out in—" Julian cut off what he was saying the instant he realized what he'd walked into. Spinning around, he exclaimed, "Jesus, Nika! A warning would be nice! I'm so tired of seeing crap I shouldn't see!"

Making sure the sheet was tight around me, I blurred to the door and shut it before Julian could inadvertently spill all my secrets to the entire house. Great. If Dad had any worries about last night, Julian had just confirmed them all. Guess we should have found a way to lock the door.

When the door was firmly closed, I screeched, "What the hell are you doing here?"

Julian had slapped his hand over his eyes. He peeked between them, like somehow looking through his fingers would magically protect him from seeing too much. "I came to wake your lazy ass up, so I could let you know what was going on. And you should be grateful it was me, not Dad. And trust me, he wanted to come down a couple of hours ago, but Mom convinced him you needed your rest after your ordeal." He snickered and shook his head. "Rest," he muttered.

God, it was a *really* good thing he'd waken us up and not Dad. I'd never see Hunter again if that were the case, although that might still be up in the air since Julian's greeting had most likely clued Dad into the fact that his daughter wasn't entirely innocent anymore. Damn it, of all the times for Hunter and I to oversleep.

Hunter had dressed while Julian had been explaining. Approaching him, he calmly changed the subject, "What time are we leaving?"

Julian peeked at him, saw that he was dressed, and dropped his hand. "Dad wants to get to Howard's Market before Simon does, so we're leaving soon. Can you guys handle not having sex for five seconds so we can rescue Starla and Jacen?"

Hunter's eyes narrowed, but I was the one who smacked Julian. Rubbing his arm, he muttered, "Ow! Damn it, Nika. That really freaking hurts."

"Well, stop being an idiot and I'll stop doing it." While he sulked, I blurred on my clothes from last night.

Julian sighed while I was dressed. "Sorry. I think I'm just jealous. You guys are free to …" he indicated Hunter's messy bed, then frowned, "… while Arianna and I are just barely getting back on track. We kissed again last night, but I wanted … more."

He sounded so dejected, I couldn't help but feel bad for him. Tenderly rubbing the spot I'd just bruised, I gave him a sympathetic smile. "Hey, at least she can't be made to forget again. What you're building with her now will stick, and you'll get there, I promise." I exaggerated a disgruntled exhale. "I remember how the two of you were before she was wiped."

Julian nodded, then laughed. "I'm just glad our bond is gone, because ... you know." His cheeks flushed with color.

Laughing, I heartily agreed. Things were awkward enough without Julian and I still feeling each other's emotions.

I cracked open Hunter's door, hoping beyond hope that somehow everyone had missed the sound of Julian walking in on us. The hallway was empty and everyone that I could feel through the family bond was upstairs in the kitchen. Good. This level and all the rooms on it were soundproof, so as long as no one had opened the main doors right when Julian had said that, chances were good nobody had heard his exclamation. Crossing my fingers that they all had bigger fish to fry than what my boyfriend and I might or might not have been doing, and also feeling a little guilty for betraying my father's trust, I headed upstairs with Julian and Hunter in tow.

As we walked through the entrance into the living room, I noticed that the sky outside was completely dark; we'd slept all the way through sunset. Typically, we were awake an hour or two beforehand, waiting in our downstairs rooms for the rays to fade away or taking a few minutes to enjoy the view through Gabriel's miraculous vampire-strength windows.

When the three of us stepped into the kitchen, Halina gave Hunter and me a sly smile. "Nice of you to join us. Feel better after your ... long rest?" By the look on her face, it was clear to her what we'd been doing. By the stern look on Dad's face, it was clear to him too.

Clearing his throat, Dad spoke before I could say much more than, Umm ... "Yes, well, now that you're here, let's go over the plan." He pointed down to a crude drawing of the market on the table. There were little plastic army men, who I was guessing were supposed to represent us, next to the map. While Julian walked over to his girlfriend, who was standing next to my mom, beaming at him, Dad arranged the pieces on the map.

After he finished, Trey leaned over to me and stated, "I made that. Pretty smart, huh?"

Dad lifted his eyes to Trey. "Yes, it was. Good job, Trey."

He seemed to glow under Dad's praise. I had the opposite reaction when Dad's eyes swung my way. An icy shiver washed through me at the disappointment I saw in his expression. I clenched Hunter's hand harder.

Dad needed to stop seeing me as a child. I wasn't one anymore and honestly, I hadn't been one in a very long time.

Looking back down at the map, Dad started pointing out pieces. "Ben and I will stake out the back here with Rory and Cleo. Julian, Hunter and Nika will keep an eye on the parking lot, while Jake, Gabriel and Great Gran will keep an eye on the front." Looking up, Dad scanned the room. "The odds are good that Simon knows we're coming, since we busted up his party last night and took out a bunch of his guards. Odds are even better that he'll bring everything he has at us tonight, including Henry. No matter what happens, Henry cannot be hurt, or allowed to escape. We need him if we're ever going to find Starla and Jacen. Any questions?"

Olivia, standing by Tracey, who still looked furious, raised her hand. "Yeah, I've got one. You didn't say my name. Where am I supposed to be?"

Tracey immediately wrapped her arms around her daughter. "With me. I'm never letting you out of my sight again."

Olivia scoffed as she looked back at her mother. Shaking her head, she sought out my dad again. "No seriously, where should I be?"

Ben cleared his throat, his gaze alternating between Olivia and Tracey. "You should stay with your mother. She's right."

Olivia gave him a hard stare. "No, she isn't. She's scared. But I'm not, and I should go. I'm a vampire now, and you're going to need my strength."

Trey crossed his arms over his chest. "You're going to need mine too."

"And mine," Arianna said, lifting her chin.

While I was extremely proud of my friends, I felt bad for my dad. He looked like he was about to go off the deep end. "I know you all want to help, but I can't risk all of you coming." Olivia started to object again and Dad raised a finger to her. "You can be with Ben and me." Olivia smiled and Trey reached over to bump fists with her. Dad immediately shifted his gaze to him. "You get to stay here. You too, Arianna."

"What!" Trey exclaimed, instantly agitated. "No way, I'm totally going!" Dad dropped his teeth and growled at him, and he lifted his palms into the air. "Okay ... I'll stay. Relax, dude."

Dad ran a hand through his hair and sighed. "I want to get there long before Simon and his crew. We leave in thirty minutes." As people started dispersing, I turned away from Dad. His finger pointing directly at me, stopped me. "Wait right there. We need to talk, young lady."

Tracey stepped between Dad and me. "No, we need to talk, Teren. What the hell are you thinking, sending my daughter off to battle?"

Dad sighed again. "It's not a ... She'll be fine, Tracey. Ben and I won't let anything happen to her."

Tracey crossed her arms over her chest. "I've heard that before ... and now look at her."

I took the opportunity to quietly sneak away while Dad was preoccupied. I didn't disappear quickly enough though. When we were back in the living room, I clearly heard my father's voice ringing through the din of everyone talking. "We're sitting down and having a conversation about last night once this is all over with, Nika. You know that right?"

Hunter and I looked at each other at the same time. Even though Dad couldn't see me, I nodded. "Yeah ... I know."

CHAPTER TWENTY-THREE

Julian

I WAS FILLED with pride and relief. Dad had seemingly forgiven my previous blunder, and was trusting me with a huge responsibility. I wasn't going to let him down this time. I wanted to be worthy of the trust he was showing me, and knowing how much I'd screwed up last time made the desire to be better even stronger. This time, I wasn't letting anybody down.

It was a warm August night, but Arianna still rubbed her arms like she was freezing as she watched everyone who was going to the market pile into three separate vehicles. Nika and I were taking the wagon, while Ben and Dad drove their cars. Halina felt like running; she would probably beat us all there.

Nika and Hunter were getting into the front of the wagon when I stepped up to Arianna. Wrapping my arms around her, I tried to warm her up and calm her down all at the same time. "It will be fine," I told her. "Once Simon sees that Jake is okay, he'll stop all this craziness and everything will go back to normal."

"And what about this Henry person?" she asked, looking up at me with bright, luminous eyes.

Right. That guy.

Smiling, I repeated the only encouragement I had to offer. "Everything will be fine."

Arianna gave me a half-hearted smile as she rested her hands on my chest. "Just hurry back. I can't stand the thought of you being in danger." My heart starting thudding in my chest. Hearing stuff like that made me feel so good, so ... loved.

"Time to go, Julian," my father suddenly stated. He still looked upset about Nika and Hunter. I sympathized. I'd give anything to have the image of my sister and her boyfriend barely covered by a sheet scrubbed from my mind.

After giving Dad a quick nod, I turned my attention back to Arianna. "Sorry, duty calls."

Her smile turned brilliant, then she reached up and placed her lips to mine. At just that brief touch, I felt like someone had run a sparkler up and down my skin. Everything burned, in the best possible way. "Bring Simon back safe and sound," she murmured when she pulled away. "I know he's made some bad choices lately, but he's a decent guy once you get to know him."

I wanted to lean back in for her mouth, but I knew there wasn't time. I also didn't want our last words to be about Simon, but that couldn't be helped either. "I'll do my best," I told her.

When I let Arianna go and finally settled into the back seat, a figure moved at supersonic speed to sit beside me. I blinked in surprise at the image of Olivia seemingly appearing out of thin air. She had a monstrously huge smile on her face as she stared at me like I held the answer to all of life's little mysteries. "Shouldn't you ride with your dad?" I asked her.

"Nope. He said I could ride with you. So, tell me about you and this Arianna chick. You guys serious? Or are you breaking up soon? Because I think you should. You should save yourself for me. Dad says I can date when I'm sixteen. And I'm like you now, you know, so we're sort of the perfect couple."

Nika snorted, and Hunter did his best to hide his smile, but he failed miserably. While Nika started the car, I let out a long sigh. Maybe I should run there like Halina? Staring out the window at my girlfriend, I told the newly turned vampire, "Sorry, Olivia, but Arianna is the one for me. And we're never breaking up again." God willing.

Olivia immediately started in on a speech about why she thought that wasn't true. The ride to Howard's had never taken so long in all my life.

As predicted, Halina was waiting in the nearby parking lot that Dad had picked as a meeting spot. It was a little-used lot directly behind the market, and surrounded on three sides by a park populated by tall, bushy trees. It wasn't entirely out of sight, but it was as secluded as we could get in the city. Her long black hair billowing in the night breeze, Halina surveyed the area while Nika pulled into a parking space beside her. Surprisingly, Nika had beat both Dad and Ben here. Or maybe that wasn't too surprising. As Olivia's babbling had picked up pace, so had Nika's driving. I could feel Dad though, and he wasn't too far behind us. Fifteen minutes tops.

Nika and Hunter stepped out of the car at the same time, with Olivia and I a heartbeat behind them. Halina looked our way and said, "It's completely quiet. No one is around except for locals buying overpriced coffee and pork rinds." She grimaced. "Pork rinds. And humans think what I eat is disgusting."

Hunter smiled, then nodded. "Good, we beat them here. That will give us time to set up a perimeter and—"

Before Hunter could finish his statement, an arrow lodged into his shoulder. We were all so dumbstruck, we stared at it for a good five seconds before anyone moved. Olivia broke the spell by screaming. Then Hunter ripped the shaft from his body, grabbed Nika and pushed her back inside the car. As more arrows whizzed through the air striking the station wagon, I shoved Olivia into the open car door. Ben and Tracey would never forgive me if I let anything happen to her. Once we were both inside, I slammed the car door shut and hunkered down as close to the floorboards as I could get. Olivia, Nika, and Hunter all did the same, while Halina blurred away into the night. Before she vanished, I saw at least two arrows slam into her.

Muffled gunshots started ringing through the night, adding to the chaos around us. I still couldn't see anyone, and couldn't tell what direction the attack was coming from. It seemed to be one gigantic circle, with our station wagon as the bull's eye. I could hear the metal being punctured, could feel the car vibrate with each hit. What the hell was going on?

"Nika!" I yelled. "Get us out of here!"

She immediately moved to turn the ignition, and Hunter's hand shot out to stop her. "No, don't. I smell gas, I think they hit the tank."

Olivia had been holding it together pretty well, but she completely lost it at hearing Hunter's news. "What? No, no, no, I don't want to burn alive! I don't to be burned alive, Julian!"

I grabbed her shoulders as well as I could in my awkward, huddled position. "No one is going to be burned alive, okay? We're going to be fine, just fine."

Olivia calmed down some, just as Hunter hissed, "I have to go out there."

Now my sister started panicking. "What? No, that's crazy!"

"I have to help Halina clear a path so the rest of you can escape."

Just then, I started seeing people emerging from the shadows, closing in on their target—my car, my family. Our attackers—at least a dozen burly men and fresh-faced teenagers—fired continuously, like they knew if they stopped for a second, we would escape our temporary solace and rip them to shreds. As I watched my impending doom coming ever closer, I was instantly grateful Arianna was safe at the ranch. She didn't need to see me die, and I couldn't even contemplate the reverse.

Hunter was getting antsy as the shooters got closer. "I'm sorry, Nika. I can't let this happen. I love you." He gave her a quick kiss, then blurred from the car. Nika screamed his name as he left. I watched him get hit a half-dozen times in the arms, legs and gut, then I stopped watching. I heard fighting though—growls, men yelling, people shouting. He was making a difference. I had to help him.

"Nika, tell Arianna ..." Tell her what? That I was sorry? That I loved her? Yes, all that and so much more. Not able to say it, I shook my head and prepared myself to leave the small safety the car afforded us.

"Julian," my sister snapped. "Whatever you think you're about to do, don't. You're still alive, and I intend to keep you that way. Both of you!" she said, indicating Olivia.

I was just about to begin my pointless argument, when a body landed on the hood of the car. All of us looked up to see Halina snarling and streaked with blood; she looked like a wild animal. She pointed at us and hissed, "All of you, stay there!"

I immediately nodded. Halina was not someone to argue with, especially now. Nika struggled to obey, though, since the love of her life was out there, fighting alongside our grandmother. Just when it seemed she was about to disregard Halina's direct order, someone ripped off the door beside her. Nika started scrambling away, until she recognized who it was. "Simon?"

His fangs were down, and he sure looked a lot different than the last time I'd seen him. Olivia sat up when she realized who it was. "Simon! Your men are trying to kill me. Help us!"

Simon glanced her way. He seemed confused and surprised to see her. "Olivia? I thought they killed you. Like the others."

Nika moved, minutely, and Simon snapped his eyes to her. "We wouldn't kill her," my sister said. "We wouldn't kill anyone if we had a choice. And we haven't hurt your father. Jake is fine. He's coming to get you."

Simon leaned in close, invading Nika's personal space. I noticed that ever since Simon had approached the car, the vehicle had taken a lot less hits. Actually, there was a lot less gunfire everywhere now, as Hunter and Halina took out hostiles. I could slip out, run around the car, and catch Simon off guard. If I was quick enough. "Where is he?" Simon growled. "Where's my father?"

Nika opened her mouth at the same time I opened my door. I had almost blurred away, but Olivia, terrified and overwhelmed, threw her arms around me. "Don't leave me!" she screeched.

Simon looked my way and hissed. Then he raised his gun to my face, in one sickeningly blurred motion. Just as his finger compressed to squeeze the trigger, Nika slammed into him. He stepped back a few feet, and thudded onto the hood of a car that was screeching to a stop—my dad's car and immediately behind it, Ben's car. A relieved breath escaped me as our backup finally arrived.

Jake immediately opened the rear door of Dad's car and stepped out. "Simon!" He ran to his son, engulfing him in a hug.

Simon was so stunned, he looked like he'd been hit over the head with a two-by-four. "Dad? You're … okay? You're really okay?"

"Yes, I'm fine," Jake murmured, holding him tight. Relaxing his hold, he looked at the chaos around us. Aside from me and Olivia, everyone was out of their cars, fighting now. Nika had run off to help Hunter, and Dad and the rest were out securing the area. Stray bullets and arrows were still whizzing through the air while bodies tumbled, collided and fell, never to get up again. It was madness.

Jake held his son's shoulders. "Simon, call this off. It's all a big misunderstanding. I'm fine. I was always fine. You didn't need to ..." His voice trailed off as he examined his son's elongated teeth. "I can't believe you let Henry ..."

While they hugged it out again, I noticed someone behind them. A man with long, scraggly gray hair and beard, wearing an unkempt Hawaiian shirt, with an unhinged look in his steely gray eyes. I instantly recognized him from a photo at the junkyard. Henry, the reason this "misunderstanding" had downgraded into insanity. Spotting my eyes on him, Henry's expression darkened, then he turned and started running. *No.* He couldn't get away.

Looking down at Olivia still clinging to every part of me that she could touch, I gently said, "Liv, your dad is here now, and you're going to be just fine, okay?" As I began peeling her from my body, she started nodding. Once I was free of her grasp, I blurred away and left her there.

I didn't have my family's super sense of smell and extremely accurate vision, but I was slightly more advanced than a regular human, and I had little trouble chasing after Henry through the park. Now, what I was going to do with him once I caught up to him was another story. One I would worry about when I got there.

Trees breezed past me as I zipped along at supersonic speed, and an odd feeling began penetrating my concentration. I felt like my brain was trying to poke me, or wave a bunch of red flags in my face. My heart started thudding as I tried to understand what my body was trying to tell me. Something was wrong, but what? I didn't figure it out until I burst through the park and reached the sidewalk on the other side. I was alone, completely alone; there wasn't a sign of Henry anywhere.

My eyes widened as I understood. "He did the procedure, too. He's a vampire ..." That was what my body was screaming at me. I hadn't been able to catch him, and I hadn't shot past him. He'd eluded and escaped me, because he was just as fast as I was. Probably faster. "Shit," I murmured, before I turned around and dashed back to the parking lot. Even if I could find Henry, taking on a crazed, mixed vampire by myself was not something I wanted to do.

When I got back to where everyone else was, I felt completely dejected. I'd almost had him ... and he'd gotten away. There was a strange sense of stillness in the air when I got back to my car. Looking around, I could see the fight was over. A few bodies were strewn over the cement, but none of the victims were my family, thank God.

People began cleaning up as I slowly walked to my father. Nika was asking Hunter if any bullets were still inside him. With a cringe, he told her no, most of them were nicks; the one in his gut was a through and through. Dad sighed and looked my way when he felt me approaching. "Henry got away," I told him. "I tried to catch him ... but I couldn't. He was too fast." Dad raised his eyebrows in surprise and I nodded. "Yeah. I didn't see him do it, but he must be able to run like we can. He must be a vampire. Or, a partial one, at least."

Dad swung his head around to where Jake and Simon were standing close together. Simon looked very uneasy being around the monsters he'd been trying to eradicate all his life. "Is that true, Simon? Did Henry go through the procedure?"

Simon firmed his lips and crossed his arms over his chest. Even though he wasn't being restrained in any way, it was clear that he saw himself as a prisoner. Jake gently put a hand on his shoulder. "It's okay, you can trust these guys. They're not who we thought they were."

Simon flung a hand at the body Halina and Gabriel were putting into Ben's car. "You sure about that, Dad? They killed a quarter of my men."

My father's expression hardened as he turned to completely face Simon. "We wouldn't have had to kill anyone if you hadn't descended on my children with loaded weapons. You started this bloodbath, not us." Jake held a hand up to Dad and Dad sighed again. "None of that matters right now though. All that matters is that Henry got away ... and he still has Starla and Jacen."

I studied the ground, embarrassed that I hadn't been able to catch him. Dad put a comforting arm over my shoulders. "It's not your fault, Julian. None of us would have done any better. You did what you could."

Looking up at him, I nodded, and I actually did feel a little better. And besides, not all hope was lost. We now had someone who knew exactly where Henry was hiding out. Lifting my chin, I strode forward to face Simon. "If you tell me where your grandfather is hiding, I just might forgive you for pointing a gun in my face."

Simon's lips curved into a cocky half-smile. "Go to hell, vampire."

An amused scoff escaped me. "Vampire? You're still hung up on that, even though you're *one of us?*"

Eyes darkening, Simon immediately shook his head. "I'm nothing like you. I'm still mostly human."

"So am I, nimrod. We're both alive ... for now. Until our hearts give out and we become undead, just like them." I pointed to Dad, then Hunter and Nika. If Simon thought being alive lasted forever, he was in for a very rude awakening.

"What are you talking about? Why would my heart give out?" Simon spat, looking around at all of us like every word we said was some sort of trap.

Hands raised like Simon was a wounded animal, Olivia stepped forward. "You had Jacen's blood, right? Well, remember how he was different? Didn't have a heartbeat and all that. I think that's what he means. Starla took that shot to keep her ... alive. Without it, we turn into ... regular vampires." That wasn't quite it, but it was close enough.

Simon shook his head. "No ... that's not what happens. We stay alive, why wouldn't we? We're alive right now?"

I shook my head at his ignorance. "You have no idea what you've done, what you're about to become. And I don't have time to explain it all to you. Let's just boil it down to—your human body can't handle what you've done to it. You're gonna die, possibly soon ..." A thought struck me, and I suddenly wished Gabriel was here to confirm what I now suspected. Voice soft, I told him, "Oh, man ... you're too young ... you won't complete the conversion. If your heart gives out now ... you'll just die. As in, dead forever die." That was my problem too. If I died now, I wouldn't convert. I'd just ... be gone.

Jake's eyes widened. "What are you talking about, Julian?"

Wishing Gabriel wasn't busy with dead bodies, I let out a weary exhale. "It's not just Starla's blood that's a problem. It's age too. Mixed vampires ... need to be older to convert ... naturally. Nika and I were always told it would happen sometime before our twenty-sixth birthday. Simon doesn't have that kind of time. His heart won't make it."

Eyes wide, Simon looked over at Jake. Clearly, he was the only one Simon trusted. "Is that true? Am I going to ... die?"

Jake didn't know, so my dad stepped forward. "Yes, unfortunately it's true. When I turned my wife, her human body couldn't take the new blood for long. It was going to wear out her heart before our children could be born. The only thing that saved her, and Julian, and Nika, was Gabriel's medicine." Dad smiled as he looked over at Gabriel, then he shook his head and returned his eyes to Simon. "It's complicated, Simon, but ultimately, we can save you ... you just have to trust us."

Simon scrubbed his face with his hands. "Just have to trust ..." Looking up, he gave Dad a quizzical expression. "My dad and I have fought your kind for as long as I can remember, and you want me to ... trust you?"

Jake let out a long, resigned exhale. "I know it's hard to trust a vampire, son. It goes against everything we've ever believed ... but we really don't have much of a choice. Henry must be stopped, and if they can save you ..."

Simon's face hardened as he locked eyes with Jake. He turned to me with great reluctance. "Fine. I'll take you to his place. But we better go now, because he's probably already prepping to leave."

Feeling a sense of urgency, I twisted to my father. "We should run there, Dad, with everyone who can."

Expression solemn, Dad nodded. "Agreed."

Dad motioned for me to follow him, and we hurried over to Ben's car. With Halina and Gabriel's help, it had only taken a couple minutes to clean up all the evidence of the fight; even the bullet casings were gone. Ben closed the back of his SUV just as Dad approached. "We need to get the bodies out of here before someone comes by. Take Rory, Cleo, Jake, and Olivia back to the ranch. The rest of us are heading out for Starla and Jacen on foot."

Ben frowned at hearing Dad's plan. "I don't like this, Teren."

Dad smiled. "I know. But we need to get there fast, and unless you want Great Gran to finally convert you ..."

At hearing that, Halina shifted her gaze our way. "He wishes I'd put my mouth on him."

She winked at Ben after she said it and Ben rolled his eyes. "Just bring them home, Teren. And yourselves."

"That's the plan," Dad said with a smile.

"No, it's not," Jake said, coming up behind Dad. With a sigh, Dad turned to face him. "I just got Simon back," he stated, "and I'm not going anywhere without him."

"And I'm going too," Olivia added, crossing her arms over her chest.

Curling his hands into fists, Dad calmly looked at each of them. Pointing at Jake, he said, "You can't keep up, and time is of the essence. You're going to the ranch." Shifting his finger to Olivia, he said, "You're too young ... and your mother will kill me if anything happens to you. And she'll probably try to kill me anyway once she hears about what happened here. You're going to the ranch too. End of discussion." Turning his eyes to Simon, he stated, "Lead the way."

Looking as insolent as Olivia, Simon shook his head. "I'm not going anywhere without my dad. Especially with you guys."

Dad opened his mouth, but Gabriel beat him to it. Stepping forward, he coolly told him, "Starla is my child. If you refuse to help us help her ... well then, I see no reason to share my medicine with you. And trust me when I say, child, you *will* die without it. Permanently."

Simon's lips pressed into a firm line, but he didn't object any further. Jake looked like he wanted to attack Gabriel again, but he also seemed to understand where Gabriel was coming from, so he only nodded in response to his ultimatum. Olivia didn't seem as satisfied as the other two. She started to tell Dad exactly what she thought of his plan, but Ben slapped his hand over her mouth and all we heard was an annoyed series of muffled noises.

Seeing that everyone was finally finished voicing their opinion, Dad settled his eyes on Simon, like he was waiting for him to make the first move. Simon finally pointed the way I'd gone when I'd chased after Henry earlier. "That way. Follow me. If you can." He gave Dad a half-smile, then blurred away.

Dad rolled his eyes, then we took off after him. We sped toward Henry, keeping as much to the shadows as we could. With our speed, we wouldn't be much more than a trick of the eye to any human who might be looking, but the last thing we needed right now was for one of us to be exposed. Luckily, even Simon seemed to understand that, and he kept out of sight as much as the rest of us.

It was nerve-wracking, using powers openly in a city teeming with humans, and I let out a relieved sigh when the buildings and streets gave away to sloping hills and low brush. Simon stopped every few miles to make sure we were still following. When he saw that we were, he would blur off into the night again, leaving only the sound of the evening wildlife behind.

Halina and Gabriel stayed so close to Simon that they were probably stepping on his shoes, while Dad remained by my side since I was just a bit slower. Hunter and Nika stayed somewhere in the middle of the two packs. Just as my stamina was beginning to fade and I was positive we would never get to Henry's hideout, Dad and I spotted Simon and the others standing around a clump of trees. As we slowed to a stop, I looked around. There was nothing out here. Nothing but shrubs, trees and rocks. Was Henry living underground or something?

When Simon saw that we were all there, he pointed to the wall of trees behind him. "Grandfather is down in that valley, in an abandoned cabin. We made good time, so he should still be there. Your friends are in no condition to run, so he'll have to use the van to get them out of there."

Gabriel's expression darkened, and I knew why. Starla and Jacen were in no condition to run because they were being drained and starved on a daily basis. I didn't even want to think about what these last few weeks had been like for them. "Let's not waste any more time then."

Gabriel's tone was cold, emotionless, and somehow that made it even more chilling. A shiver ran through me, and Dad noticed. "You can stay here, Julian. It's all right."

I gave him a brief shake of my head. "No, I can't. This is all my fault … I need to make it right."

Dad opened his mouth, like he was going to argue, but instead, he shut it and nodded. "Let's hit him hard and fast, before he has a chance to get organized."

Simon led the way to a small trail through the trees. It led down a steep hill to a broad valley, where I could just make out a cabin in the moonlight, resting beside a wide river. I had to pay close attention to where I stepped on the rocky slope, but even still, I saw lights on in the cabin and cars parked outside. People were still there. We weren't too late.

Once we were all on the valley floor, we spread out. Halina and Gabriel stuck close to Simon, like they were worried he might start fighting on Henry's side. And I supposed that was a possibility, given his prejudice against our species—his own species now. But Simon wanted to live, and he wanted to be reunited with his father. I had to believe that would be enough to keep him on our side.

Dad gave Hunter a signal to travel around the back with Nika. We went around the other direction, while Halina and Gabriel went right through the front door. Thirty seconds later, the relative quiet of the night was transformed into a raging battle with gunshots, shouting and the unmistakable sound of fighting.

"Stay close to me," Dad hissed, as we approached the backyard. Three hunters, who had clearly gone through the procedure, blurred out of the back door of the house. They started heading our way, but Hunter and Nika ambushed them, giving us an opening. "Now!" Dad yelled at me, and we made a mad dash for the open door.

Inside was surprisingly cozy for a madman's secret base. There were deer antlers attached to the living room wall, oversized wooden furniture that actually looked very comfortable, and fishing poles in nearly every corner. Lingering over everything was the woodsy scent of pine and cedar. But for the sounds of violent scuffles coming from outside, I could easily imagine this place belonging to my family.

Dad motioned to a set of stairs leading down to a basement. Halina and Gabriel were preoccupied in the front part of the house, while Nika and Hunter were stuck out back, so it was just Dad and me heading downstairs. I wasn't sure we were going the right way until the smell of blood hit me. Dad gave me a worried look before stepping onto the basement level.

The short hallway from the stairs opened into a large room. Twin cages were set up on either side of the space, one holding Starla, one holding Jacen. Neither vampire moved, so we had no idea if they knew what was going on or not. Or if they were even still alive. In between the two cages, was that damned machine that Henry used for the transfusions, plus numerous cabinets, workbenches, and refrigerators with glass doors showing several containers of blood.

The scent of stale blood in the air was so strong, it was almost nauseating. With one hand behind himself, keeping me back, Dad stepped into the room. "Starla? Are you okay?"

Before Starla could respond—if she even could—Dad was tackled from the side. He was swept away from me like a flashflood, and I heard him and his assailant crashing into the far wall. "Dad!"

I zipped forward to help him, and saw that Dad was in a snarling, tangled fight with Henry. The older man looked deranged as he fought, with wild eyes and spittle flying from his mouth, a mouth that was punctuated with inch long fangs. "You and your diseased kind have finally met your match, creature! I will hunt down every last one of your undead cousins. With your blood fueling my army!" Henry started laughing, a maniacal sound laced with insanity.

Dad shoved him away, but like a dog defending a bone he would rather die than give up, Henry instantly leapt on him again. Henry used every part of his body to attack Dad, from his teeth to his feet. It was all Dad could do to keep him at bay. "That makes no sense!" Dad said between strained breaths. "You're the same as us now! If we're monsters ... you are too!"

Wanting to help, I looked around for a weapon. A small voice in the corner of the room said my name. "Julian? What's going on?" I looked over to see Starla slowly sitting up. Her hair was a disheveled mess, her face pale as chalk, and her skin sunken and hollow. She looked more like a zombie than a vampire, and nothing like the pampered princess who routinely played the part of my mother.

Even as I thanked the fates she was still alive, I snapped out, "I need something sharp!" With shaking fingers, she pointed to a cabinet. Blurring over to it, I yanked the doors open ... and saw all sorts of tools I wished I could erase from my memory. Saws, drills, knives, corkscrews and more deadly implements, all faintly coated with blood, like they'd been hastily wiped down before being shoved back into the darkness. Wishing I could move things without having to touch them, I grabbed something that looked like an ice pick, and then turned toward the two men rolling over the ground, each one desperately fighting for the upper hand.

"Dad! Catch!"

We made eye contact and I tossed him the ice pick. He snaked a hand free just in time to grab it, then pushed Henry onto his back and drove it into his chest. I closed my eyes then immediately reopened them. This was an unfortunate part of my world. One I couldn't pretend didn't exist. I didn't ever want to kill, but I had to accept the fact that I might have to one day. To protect those I loved.

Deep, dark red stained Henry's shirt, and he stopped moving, stopped fighting. Dad immediately stood up and backed away from him. His expression was grim, sad. Dad didn't like killing either, but Henry hadn't given him much of a choice. He'd seemed unhinged, like a drugged human who'd gone off the deep end. He'd transformed himself to give himself an advantage ... but I don't think he'd handled the outcome well. To fight the vampires, he'd become too much like one, and it had driven him mad.

I couldn't stop staring at Henry's body. At the blood, at the life draining from his eyes. A part of me was still tense, thinking he was going to spring to his feet and attack us again ... but Dad's aim had been true. Henry wasn't going to recover. Alive or undead, he would never take another breath.

Dad's hand on my shoulder finally pulled my gaze away from the dead man at our feet. "Best to turn away, Julian. He made his choice, there was nothing we could do." As Dad turned me around, I nodded. True. Hard to accept, but true.

Now that the immediate threat was taken care of, Dad turned his attention to the cages. Starla was still sitting up on her bed, holding onto the bars closest to her for support. She looked dazed, like she was struggling to focus. She was smiling though. "Hey, vamp boy. Is it over? Did we win?"

Dad strode over to her cage and ripped the door down. Tossing it to the other side of the room, he stepped into Starla's prison and scooped her into his arms. She was so limp, she looked like a ragdoll. "Yeah, it's over, Starla. Completely over. You're safe now."

Starla sagged in relief, and let out a breathy sigh that sounded like two rocks being rubbed together. She had to be so thirsty. And hungry. And tired. Those assholes.

Starla's eyes were closed when Dad brought her into the main part of the room. She almost looked asleep, or close to it. But just as Dad motioned for me to take her, her eyes popped open and she twisted her neck to look over at Jacen's cage. "Jacen? Check on him. They drained more blood from him than me, since they didn't need to worry about keeping his heart beating. He stopped talking a while ago ... stopped moving a couple days ago. I have no idea if he's ..." Her eyes turned glassy, and her face contorted in pain. I wasn't sure if that was because of her own pain ... or Jacen's.

Dad carefully shifted Starla into my arms. I braced myself for the weight, but she was so light, it was almost like the only thing left inside her was air. I followed Dad to Jacen's cage, and watched as he ripped the door off his prison. Jacen didn't move, didn't flinch, didn't make any adjustments whatsoever. He wasn't breathing, his heart was silent … it was impossible to know if he was alive or not. I supposed, only forcing him to ingest fresh blood would tell us how he was. But not here. We had to get him back to the ranch.

As Dad emerged from Jacen's cell with his limp body in his arms, Starla tried to push herself up so she could see. "Jacen? Sweetheart? Are you okay?"

I could tell from the look in her eyes that she would cry if she could. She had no tears left though. Jacen didn't respond to her, and Starla's strength gave out. She collapsed back into my arms with a whimper. "Dad," I said. "We need to get them out of here."

Dad nodded. "We'll leave the same way we entered. It sounds like most of the fighting is over with anyway." Dad looked up, to where we could feel Halina. "Great Gran, I'm going back to the ranch with Starla and Jacen. When you're done here … burn this place to the ground."

Halina responded with a low menacing growl, and something in Russian that was too low for me to make out. I was positive it had something to do with bathing in blood. Dad twisted to where we could feel Nika. I could tell he wanted to order her to leave with us, but surprisingly, he didn't. He just told her to be careful and meet us at the ranch when she could.

We headed upstairs. The living room was clear, the backdoor still open, so we took off at supersonic speed into the night. It felt weird to be leaving a chunk of my family behind, especially when some of them were still engaged in fighting, but Starla and Jacen were in desperate need of help, desperate need of blood. And I supposed, a part of growing up was knowing when to let others handle situations on their own.

Family members who had waited at the ranch were standing outside when Dad and I arrived. Jake, Ben, Olivia, and the others were with them, having returned from Howard's Market already. I was a little shocked to see them here, since it felt like we'd only spent a few seconds at Henry's hiding place.

Imogen and Alanna took one look at the bundles in our arms, and blurred into the kitchen. I could already smell the warming blood when Dad and I entered the house a moment later. Surprisingly, Trey and Arianna were still there. As Dad motioned for me to follow him upstairs to where the bedrooms were, Trey's mouth dropped wide open. "Dude, are they dead?"

Firming my jaw, I quickly told him, "No," and hurried after my dad.

We went to a guest room with a bed large enough for both vampires. After I laid Starla down beside Jacen, she immediately grabbed the comatose man's hand. Once mine were free, Arianna clutched my fingers. "Thank God, you're okay. I was so worried."

"Why are you still here?" I asked, looking down at her.

She pursed her lips, like I'd just asked her the most ridiculous question in creation. "Like I could go anywhere not knowing if you were okay or not." Glancing back at the bed, her expression softened. "What happened to them?"

Stepping away from the bed, so the adults could examine Starla and Jacen, I shook my head. "I don't know. That Henry guy drained them, starved them ... basically tortured them." Arianna gasped, and she looked so pale, I thought she might need to lie down too. "They'll be okay. They're tough ... they'll be okay ..." As I repeated it, I wasn't sure if I was comforting her or myself.

Imogen came up with a steaming thermos in each hand. Malachi was a step behind her, thermoses in his hands as well. He stopped the second he laid eyes on Starla and Jacen, and I had to wonder if he was seeing his past in their present. When we'd found him, he'd been in almost as bad of shape. Imogen gave him an encouraging smile as she indicated Starla. Malachi gathered himself, shook off his inner demons, and walked over to the woman who could barely keep her eyes open.

Starla couldn't hold the thermos, so Malachi tenderly tilted it against her lips. Closing her eyes, she took small sips at first, then larger gulps. Seconds later, she was clasping the container in both hands and drinking it down as quickly as her throat would let her. I smiled at seeing the small semblance of life returning. Arianna clenched my hand, but she was smiling when I looked at her.

Imogen tried to feed Jacen, lifting his head and tilting the cup to his lips, but he still wasn't responding. The blood she poured into his mouth, ran right out of his mouth, staining his shirt and the sheets. As I shifted my attention to him, my concern grew. If he didn't drink—if he *couldn't* drink—his body would desecrate. A fate worse than death. It would be kinder of us to stake him, then to let him degrade like that.

After another failed attempt, Imogen sighed and looked back at Dad. "If he can't drink on his own, we'll have to feed him with a tube."

Starla had finished her second thermos at this point, and seemed a lot more like herself, although still very weak. She held her hand out for Jacen's thermos. "May I?" she asked my grandmother.

Imogen smiled and handed it to her. Starla unscrewed the lid and dipped her pointer finger into the blood. Then she brought her finger to Jacen's mouth and worked her way between his lips. Nothing happened at first, but then his mouth moved, just a slight amount, like he was licking her finger. Starla did it a few more times, murmuring encouragement with each dip.

Around the fourth or fifth time, it was obvious Jacen was beginning to come around, as he eagerly sucked on her finger now. Starla gently brought the thermos to his lips, giving him a larger flow. A low growl rumbled from Jacen's chest, and Starla's face erupted into a wide smile. "That's it, baby. Drink up."

Jacen's eyes fluttered as his throat bobbed with each swallow. He stirred in the bed trying to sit up, and Imogen helped him. She propped him up so he was sitting straighter, so he could take deeper swallows. When the thermos was empty, Starla removed it from his lips. Jacen's eyes sprang open. He snarled at Starla, like she was denying him something he desperately wanted. His bloody fangs were menacing, but Starla didn't look the least bit afraid of him.

A bright smile on her face, she reached out to Malachi for the second thermos. He immediately handed it to her, and she gave it to Jacen. He used both hands to grab it, and started drinking it down like he was feverish. Tears in her eyes, Starla told him he was doing great, and she was so proud of him.

Imogen looked delighted as she met eyes with my father. "I better help Alanna make some more. Maybe we'll even butcher a cow. These two need fresh blood."

Dad nodded, also looking relieved, and from behind me I heard Arianna make a strangled noise. "You okay?" I asked, turning to look at her. Even if she had an iron stomach, this was a lot to take.

Her paleness hadn't left her, except now she also looked a little green. She forced a smile to her face though. "Yep, I'm fine. Totally cool."

Studying her, I asked, "Want to get out of here?"

"Yes," she breathed, closing her eyes. Then she reopened them and stuttered, "If you want to, I mean."

It made me smile how brave she was trying to be. I indicated the door. "Come on, let's go get some air."

Some of the bedrooms along the back of the house had balconies on them. I took her to one and led her outside, so she could clear her head and I could pretend we were alone. Leaning on the railing, Arianna inhaled and exhaled a few deep breaths. After a long moment of careful breathing while she looked out over the acres of pastures glowing in the moonlit, she gave me a sideways glance. "You must think I'm the biggest wuss."

Her words sent a spark of shock through me. "No, not at all. You're one of the bravest people I know."

She twisted her lips in an expression of *Don't lie to me, I'm not an idiot*. "I've met most of the people you know ... and compared to them, I'm not brave at all."

Her voice was almost eaten away by the breeze it was so small. Grabbing both of her hands, I squatted down until we were looking at each other straight in the eye. "I know you, and I know things you've done, things that you've forgotten ... and I've seen you be very brave." Cupping her cheek, I let myself get lost in her beautiful blue-green eyes. "So incredibly brave. And sweet, and funny, and beautiful ..."

Leaning in, I kissed her. Her lips were warm and receptive against mine, and so incredibly soft. I got so lost in the way they felt against my skin that I accidentally forgot to hold my teeth in, and they crashed down into place during a brief break in our touch. Arianna pulled away from me when she felt something different. Feeling my skin heat, I murmured, "Sorry ... you distracted me. I ... lost control."

Her smile grew playful, like she was intrigued with the idea of me losing control. My skin felt on fire. With tentative fingers, she reached out to touch a sensitive tooth. I felt the vibration of the contact all the way down my spine. "You have to hold them in all the time?" I nodded and she frowned. "Isn't that exhausting?"

Shrugging, I told her, "I've been doing it my entire life. I'm used to it."

Dropping her hand, Arianna lifted her chin. "Well, you don't have to with me. You're free to be whoever you are. And besides ... they're sexy," she added with a giggle. Then she leaned over and carefully ran her tongue along my fang.

The ache was so sudden and severe, I had to clench the railing to keep standing. A low growl escaped my chest, completely unbidden, and I felt winded when she pulled away. Holy ... God, that felt good. Arianna's eyes were wide as she studied my expression. By the way I felt, she must have been seeing pure lust and desire.

"You liked that?" she murmured, her voice low and sensual.

"You have no idea," I muttered, wishing we were someplace soundproof.

Arianna's seductive smile turned sweet and charming, innocent even, and damn if it didn't turn me on even more. "I'll have to remember that trick." That made me smile. Thanks to Trey, she *would* remember.

I was still burning with need, wanting more, but I knew Arianna wasn't there yet. Not really. "It's getting late. We should get you home."

Her lip came out in an adorable pout. "I don't want to go yet. And besides, my mom thinks I'm spending the night at a friend's house. I have nowhere to be until tomorrow ..."

My body raged with life at hearing her words. *All night.* No more rescue missions. No more danger. No more threats. Simon was safe with Jake, Starla and Jacen were recovering, and Henry was ... finished. Arianna was free from her parents for an evening, and I was free to be with her. "I don't want you to go either."

I leaned down to kiss her again, and she hungrily met my lips.

CHAPTER TWENTY-FOUR

Nika

I WATCHED THE cabin burning in the distance with mixed feelings. While I was glad that crazed man and his research had been firmly ground to a halt, the carnage and chaos left in his wake was staggering. Compulsion-proof humans, tortured vampires, disillusioned teens who thought undergoing a risky underground medical procedure was a good idea, and a madman hell-bent on wiping out my entire race. Lives forever altered. And for what? Jealousy, hatred, fear? It was exhausting, and I just wanted to go home.

"Are you all right?" Hunter asked, stepping up beside me.

Looking up into his glowing eyes full of love and concern, I forced a smile to my face. "Of course, just tired."

Hunter nodded; he looked just as worn out as I felt. "It's been quite a night … quite a summer." He sighed. "Quite a year."

Wrapping my arms around his waist, I pulled him close. "It's almost over."

He placed his arms over mine, holding me tight, comforting me with his body, if not the bond. "Thank God," he murmured into my hair. "Let's go home."

Pulling back, I looked over at Halina and Gabriel. They were studying the cabin as well; Halina's eyes were victorious, Gabriel's were speculative. Dad and Julian had left some time ago with Starla and Jacen, and were surely back at the ranch by now.

Turning my focus to the other side of Hunter and me, I looked over at Simon. It surprised me some that he'd stayed. Stayed and fought. I'd kind of assumed that he'd hightail it the minute he'd shown us where the cabin was. But he hadn't. He'd duked it out with the supercharged hunters, covered our backs, warned us of danger ... acted like one of the nest. And by the bewildered expression on his face, he wasn't sure why he'd done it.

Hoping he'd finally calmed down enough to see that we weren't all bad, I softly said his name. "Simon? Want to go see your dad now?"

He startled, like I'd woken him from a dream, then he nodded.

Halina and Gabriel led the way back to the ranch. Hunter, Simon and I followed as closely as we could without leaving Simon too far behind. He just didn't have as much stamina as the rest of us. Both Starla and Jacen were in line with my dad, abilities-wise, so Simon was at that level too. Simon would need to take Gabriel's shot from now on; if he didn't, he'd convert too soon and die. And if he wanted to stay as human as possible, he'd have to take the shot indefinitely. He was dependent on vampires now—a future he'd probably never imagined.

Simon still seemed contemplative when we arrived at the ranch. Jake, Alanna, and Grandpa Jack were outside to greet us when we got there. Alanna must have told the boys we were coming. Simon's face finally erupted into a smile when he saw his dad. He flew into Jake's arms, almost knocking him over. "Whoa, easy there, buddy. You're about a thousand times stronger than I am now."

Laughing, Simon stepped away from him, then his expression hardened. Turning to Alanna, he visibly lifted his chest and his chin, like he was gathering courage. "I'd like to see the two ... the two vampires who were used in the experiment. I'd like to ... apologize ... to them. What I did, what I allowed to happen ... it was wrong. Utterly and completely wrong."

Simon looked back at Jake with sorrow in his eyes. "I knew it too. When I saw them, saw their suffering, I knew I should do something ... put them out of their misery at least, but I needed them to save you. I needed their blood, so I let Grandfather continue ..." Closing his eyes, he let out a long, broken exhale. "I overlooked an injustice for what I thought was the greater good ... and I'll never forgive myself for it." Opening his eyes, he shook his head. "Even if they are monsters ... they didn't deserve what was done to them."

"They're not monsters," I whispered into the night. Hoping Starla and Jacen were all right, I added, "None of us are monsters."

The confusion returning to his face, Simon turned to look at me. "I think ... I'm starting to see that. Which only makes everything worse."

Eyes full of compassion, Jake put a hand on Simon's shoulder. "Come on, I'll take you to their room."

When I stepped into the house, I instantly noticed something ... weird was going on. The sounds of panting and kissing were coming from somewhere upstairs. I instantly understood. My brother was deepening his connection with Arianna, and apparently he didn't care if the entire house knew it.

Dad looked like he was just about to run upstairs and physically pull Julian and Arianna apart. Recalling that I owed Julian a little payback, I put a hand on his shoulder. "Let me handle this, Dad. I know just what to do." I blurred away before Dad could respond.

Halina was giggling when I got to the bedroom that Julian was using as his love nest. Biting my lip to hold in my smile, I burst through the door and rounded on the bed. Two figures instantly shot upright on the rumpled mattress. Breathless, Julian grabbed his shirt off the floor and covered Arianna with it. His hair was tussled, his cheeks were bright red, his eyes were wide, and his heart was pounding like it was about to explode. Arianna was no less affected as she held Julian's shirt tight to her chest—her bare chest. At least they both had their pants on, although Julian's were unbuttoned.

"Nika? Jesus, you scared the crap out of me!"

My smile was exhilarant. Payback was so much fun. "You realize that the entire house can hear you panting, right?" From the look on Arianna's face, it was clear that she hadn't remembered. Julian should have, but by the way his cheeks lost all their color, the fact that our relatives had super-acute hearing had clearly slipped his mind.

"Before Dad comes up here and gives you a three-hour-long speech on the birds and the bees, you should probably say goodnight to Arianna." With a wave to my brother and my friend, I backed out of the room.

Back downstairs, I practically skipped my way to Hunter. I suddenly didn't feel tired at all. Hunter's expression was amused when I met up with him in the living room. "You enjoyed that. A lot," he stated. I couldn't deny it, so I only shrugged. Yes, yes I had.

Dad nodded at me in approval, then turned his eyes to Gabriel. Gabriel was clearly wanting to go check on his nestmates, but he was giving Jake and Simon a moment to talk to Starla and Jacen alone. Even though I was trying not to eavesdrop, I could hear Simon stuttering on his words—all of them were awkward and uncomfortable. It wasn't every day you had to say you were sorry for doing nothing while someone was being tortured.

Clearing his throat, Dad said to Gabriel, "You told me once, that when a mixed vampire tried to turn someone, it almost always failed. Henry clearly found a way around that ... but what about the heart giving out? How much time does Olivia and Simon have?"

And Starla. Dad didn't say it, but her name hung heavy in the air. Henry had transfused her with Jacen's blood in an attempt to keep her alive, but would it work? Or would her heart give out, her conversion kick in, and the old mutation in her blood rear its ugly head?

By the look on Gabriel's face, this was something he'd been stewing on nonstop since Olivia had dropped the "Henry's making mixed vampires" bomb on us. And from what I could tell by his irritated expression, Gabriel hadn't come up with any answers yet.

"Honestly, Teren, without running a series of tests ... I just don't know. If we work under the assumption that what he did to them is similar to a successful mixed turning, then they have the same amount of time as any freshly turned mixed vampire—a couple of months, at best." With a sigh, he looked up at where Starla was recuperating. "But all of this is so new and different ... I just don't know. And I hate not knowing."

Dad nodded, like he'd expected as much. "We can't take any chances. We'll get Starla, Olivia and Simon on the shot as soon as possible. Then you'll have the time you need ... to find out their fate."

Gabriel sighed. "It's a pity you had to kill Henry. The man was clearly a genius. We could have learned so much from him. Together, he and I could have done some amazing things ..."

"Whoever he was when he was human, he wasn't that person anymore. You should have seen him come after me ... like a rabid animal. Like he was out of his mind."

Gabriel gave him a thoughtful smile. "They say the most brilliant minds are just a hairline away from madness. All it takes is the right push."

Dad studied him silently for a moment, then said, "I'm sure you'll come up with a solution."

Halina squeezed Gabriel's waist, while he gave Dad a curt nod. "Yes, I'm sure I will," he confidently stated.

Dad shook his head at Gabriel, then looked over at Mom. "It's been a long day ... let's go home." Mom sagged into his side like that was the best news she'd heard in a while. Dad smiled at her then looked up at the ceiling. "Julian, we're leaving. Tell Arianna goodbye, then get your butt down here."

Julian's response was instant. "Can Arianna stay at the house? Her parents think she's out, and it would be weird for her to stay here at the ranch without me ..."

Dad started massaging his temples. "Yeah, fine. But Trey stays too. And Arianna sleeps in Nika's old bedroom. And Julian ... your mom and I are keeping our door open all night long, so don't even bother trying something." I heard Julian hastily agreeing to Dad's terms. He sounded giddy, and Dad sighed again.

Halina slowly shook her head at him. "How do you ever expect them to give us more grandbabies like that? Have I taught you nothing?"

Dad pointed a finger at her. "You be quiet. And you taught me plenty." He smirked at that and Mom giggled. Dad rolled his eyes, then swung his gaze my way. "Ready to go, Nika?"

Knowing Dad wasn't going to like this, I squeezed Hunter's hand. "Actually, I'm staying here. With Hunter."

Dad's expression immediately turned frosty. "You're not eighteen yet, Nika."

"And it doesn't matter anymore, Dad. Hunter is my sire, my best friend, my soulmate ... and my lover. And I belong with him. And you know it. Keeping us apart because of my *human* age is pointless. I'm not human anymore."

As I studied Dad's reaction, I couldn't tell if he was going to break down ... or hit something. The house was suddenly deathly quiet. Maybe I should have done this somewhere more private, but in this family, lack of privacy was just something you got used to.

The silence ticked on for long seconds, until Halina finally shrugged and said, "At least Nika can't get pregnant. One less worry ... since you're so against the reproduction of our species."

I had to slap my hand over my mouth to not laugh. Dad turned to Halina with a groan. "Oh my God, would you give it a rest already?" As Halina curled her lips into a smile, Dad turned back to me. "Fine, Nika. You can stay here with ... Hunter. But just so you know, I don't like this."

Releasing Hunter, I stepped forward and grabbed both of my father's hands. "I know you don't, Dad. But it's time to let go."

He let out a weary exhale. "I'm not good at letting go."

A smile crept over my face. "I know that too. But you'll always be my father, and I'll always love you. You never have to worry about that."

Dad wrapped his arms around me, squeezing me in a tight embrace. "Good."

From upstairs, I heard Julian quietly ask Dad, "So, hey, since you're letting Hunter and Nika shack up, does this mean Arianna and I can—?"

Before Julian even finished his question, Mom and Dad simultaneously barked, "No!"

Halina let out a beleaguered sigh as she turned to Gabriel. "They just don't understand how it works. Maybe we should teach them?"

Gabriel smiled and Dad started massaging his head again. "It's way past time to go," he muttered.

WHEN I WOKE up the next evening, I felt different. More free, more at peace, more at ease. I was exactly where I was supposed to be—by Hunter's side—and I wasn't going behind anyone's back to be there. It was allowed, accepted. Finally.

I stretched out until my legs brushed against his, and reveled in the delightful feeling of our soft skin sliding together. We'd slept naked again, and as Hunter wrapped his arms around me, I decided that was how we'd always sleep. I just needed him as close to me as inhumanly possible.

Hunter nuzzled against my neck, his stubble sharp against my sensitive skin. "Good evening, lover," he murmured before kissing me. Then he laughed. "I still can't believe you said that to your dad. For a minute there, I thought I was going to have to make a run for it."

Laughing myself, I twisted to face him. Pressing my chest to his, I giggled and said, "Anywhere you run, I'll follow."

He gave me a long, lingering kiss. "And when the bond comes back in a few hours, you'll know exactly how to find me."

I completely stiffened in his arms. I hadn't realized what all of this being over with meant for us. *The bond.* That exquisite connection we shared that had been so harshly severed for the last several weeks. There was no reason to keep denying it any longer. Especially now that we were living together, and the insane pull we felt when we were apart wouldn't be triggered. As much. We might purposely trigger it on occasion, just to feel the passionate rush that came along with reuniting.

"That's right ..." I muttered. "You don't have to take the shot anymore."

Hunter's hand came up to cup my cheek. "We're free, Nika. In so many ways, we're finally free."

His lips returned to mine, and the desire always simmering between us began to resurface. Free. That was all I'd wanted for so long that it was a shock to the system that we finally had it. We were finally able to do ... everything we wanted to do. Rolling Hunter over to his back, I climbed onto his hips and stared down at him. With no windows to speak of, and a light-proof seal around the door, Hunter's room was very dark, and his tranquil eyes were softly glowing at me. Mine were washing him in a pale light as well, highlighting the lines and angles of his perfect bone structure. His lips were a beacon, one I couldn't resist.

Even though we'd made love the last two nights, I wanted him again. I had a feeling I'd always want him. Maybe that was a residual side effect of the bond, still in place even though it wasn't currently active. Or maybe it was just because I was head-over-heels in love with him. Probably both.

Our hands and mouths slid over each other's bodies, driving the intensity to a point where pleasurable desire was replaced with white-hot need. When Hunter rolled me to my back and moved inside me, we both exhaled in relief. He was everything I wanted, and so much more. We moved together slowly at first, prolonging the sensation as much as possible. It didn't take long for the moment to become unbearable though, and before I knew it, our movements were fast and frantic.

As I reached the edge of pure bliss, I placed my lips along Hunter's neck. The word, "Yes," escaped him and I instantly bit down. His cool refreshing blood poured into me, right as I hit the wall. I moaned as the ecstasy coursed through me, washed down me, made every nerve in my body feel like it was on fire.

Hunter's mouth searched for my skin as he continued to move over me. Releasing my own bite, I angled my neck away from him, so he'd have plenty of skin to choose from. He clamped down hard, near the base of my shoulder, and his entire body shuddered as my blood poured into him. His own climax was quick to follow, and he whimpered as he came and drank. I cradled his head to my skin, encouraging him to take more. He couldn't hurt me—not really—and the more he took from me, the longer his euphoria would last. And I wanted him to feel amazing forever.

When he finally pulled away, he laid his forehead against my shoulder and panted against my skin. "God … I never knew … I never even imagined it could be like that. That drinking and sex … could feel like that …"

A residual shudder rippled through his body. With a laugh, I kissed his hair. "Now you wish you'd always been a vampire, don't you?"

Hunter looked up at me with a smirk on his lips. Then his expression softened. "Maybe I always was … and I just never knew it."

Touched by the acceptance I saw on his face, I leaned in for one last kiss. If we waited too long to make an appearance, someone would come searching for us. Again. We might have more freedom than before, but we weren't exactly on our own yet.

With great reluctance, we both got up to get ready for the night. When we were clean and dressed, we tentatively opened Hunter's door. I still expected to see my father's angry face whenever I emerged from Hunter's room, but I think he was finally okay with Hunter and I living together. Or at least … he wasn't violently opposed to it anymore.

Seeing that the coast was clear, I stepped into the hallway with a bright smile on my face. Grabbing my hand, Hunter joined me. "I know it's early, but we should go find Gabriel, see if he made any progress on Starla's blood."

A bit of my good mood faltered as I nodded. We'd checked on Starla and Jacen this morning, before heading to our room for the day. They'd been tired, clearly still worn, but in good enough spirits considering. I had to imagine that what had happened to them would remain with them for a long time. Like how Julian had suffered from claustrophobia for years after his abduction, they would both have scars from this, I was sure.

Instead of turning to take the hallway that led upstairs, we headed across the way to Gabriel's lab. I could feel that Halina was in there, so odds were good Gabriel was too. When we entered Gabriel's carefully constructed clean room, we saw that he was indeed there, along with Halina, Jake, and a very nervous looking Simon. I gave him a friendly wave to try and make him feel better, but with the harsh way he swallowed, it was clear my presence wasn't comforting.

Halina gave us both a warm hug. Gabriel peeked up from his microscope, a small smile on his lips, while Jake gave us each a brief, almost cordial nod. Hunter pointed at whatever Gabriel had been studying. "Find anything in Starla's blood? Some kind of clue that might help Olivia?"

Gabriel's smile brightened. "I think I have. Henry was truly a genius beyond his years. His attempt to cure her by transfusing her blood with Jacen's, might have done just that. I'll need more time to be sure, but I have a very good feeling about this." With a wistful sigh, he shook his head and looked over at Halina. "A transfusion never occurred to me. All this time, and the answer to Starla's problem was practically under my nose." He lifted his arm and patted the vein running through his inner elbow.

Halina smiled as she wrapped her arms around his waist. "You're too hard on yourself, love. You can't see every angle, all the time." She frowned. "And there's been a lot of distractions lately."

"What does that mean for Olivia?" I asked.

Gabriel frowned. "Until I know for sure, and until she's of age, of course, she'll need to continue taking the shot ... just like young Simon here." Gabriel glanced down at Simon; he rubbed his arm where Gabriel must have injected him. A smile cracked Gabriel's lips as he looked back at me. "But if my theory about Starla is correct, then Olivia will merely need a transfusion of her own before she can safely convert. And with all I have learned from Henry's research at the cabin and the test subject's blood, I am confident I can safely duplicate the transfusion process. Once it has been completed, Olivia's blood will take on the characteristics of the donor vampire, almost as if it were a brand-new turning. I'm assuming that is only the case on living vampires. After the final conversion has been completed and the human part of the body dies, well, then the vampire will be stuck with those traits ... which is, of course, why we must remove Starla's blood from her."

Jake pointed at Simon. "And what about my son?"

Gabriel shrugged. "There is no flaw that I know of in Jacen's blood, he should be fine. Once he comes of age, of course. However ... if he would like to be as human as possible, then a transfusion of his own could be arranged."

Jake and Simon shared a look before Simon said, "What do you mean? Aren't I as human as possible already?"

Gabriel shook his head. "No. Being of a later generation, Julian's blood is slightly more human than Jacen's, and with this new, marvelous, *precise* procedure, I believe I can safely give you blood from a fourth generation vampire. Possibly even a fifth or six generation vampire, if we knew of one ..." Shaking his head, like he was refocusing, he said, "Unfortunately, we do not. The most human vampire in our midst, Ben, is too human. I could not get the procedure to work with his blood. But I can with Julian, and since he has the least amount of side effects of all of us, he is the best choice for you. His eyes don't even glow."

My eyes widened in surprise at Gabriel's suggestion, but ... it made sense. Besides Ben, who only had a trace amount of vampire in him, Julian was the most human. And if that was what Simon wanted—to be as human as he could be—then Julian was the logical choice. But still ... what would that do to my brother? "Will that hurt him, Gabriel? Julian ... I mean ... will that hurt Julian?"

Gabriel shrugged. "No more than a poke. We would take his blood slowly, over time." His expression darkened. "It would be nothing like what was done to Starla and Jacen." His expression evening, he looked back at Simon and Jake. "Of course, that is assuming Julian wants to help you."

While Jake and Simon contemplated Simon's future, a thought suddenly struck me. "You can safely duplicate the process ... Does that mean you can create *new* mixed vampires?"

Looking confused, Gabriel blinked at me. "I need more time to be absolutely sure, but ... yes, I'm confident I could if I wanted to." From his tone of voice, it was clear he couldn't see a reason why he would ever want to. I had a reason. I knew a few people who might be interested in becoming a mixed vampire, if it was truly possible now.

Giving Hunter an excited squeeze of his arm, I zipped upstairs. Mom and Dad were in the kitchen with Alanna and Imogen. Julian and Arianna were setting the table together, making dopey love-filled eyes at each other, and I had to wonder if all of Dad's precautions had done any good.

"Good evening, Nika," Dad said, kissing my hair. "I trust you slept well ... away from the house." He cringed after he said it, like he was making himself be civil about all of this. I was too excited to appreciate the sentiment.

"Gabriel thinks he can recreate Henry's work. He's positive he can safely make mixed vampires."

Every sound in the house stopped. Well, every sound but Trey playing basketball outside with Ben and Olivia. I could still hear Trey screeching that vampire power-jumping was illegal and unfair. Caution in his eyes, Dad slowly asked, "And why would Gabriel want to carry on Henry's work?"

Stunned that they couldn't see what I saw, I pointed at Alanna. "Because we can save the rest of our family. The ones who are still human. The ones who are going to die." Passionate tears pricked my eyes. I'd always accepted the fact that eventually some members of my family would leave me—Grandpa Jack, Ben, Tracey, Ashley, Christian, Grandma Linda ... But now we had a viable solution to save them. They only had to take it.

Alanna's face shifted to an expression of shock and disbelief. She opened and closed her mouth several times, like she wasn't sure what to say or how to feel. Julian jumped to his feet, his eyes wide as he stared at Arianna. Like we were still connected, I knew exactly what my brother was thinking—he could save her too.

Dad stared at the ground while a multitude of emotions swept over his face. He started shaking his head, and Mom gently placed a hand on his shoulder. "Teren? Maybe ..."

Dad looked up, pain in his eyes. "He doesn't want to be a vampire. He's never wanted our life. He's content to die. Right, Mom?" His gaze shifted to Alanna. They were talking about Grandpa Jack ... the one who was probably closest to his natural end.

Tears were streaming down Alanna's face now, and Imogen blurred to her side. Hunter had joined us at this point. Having heard the conversation while approaching, he remained silent. Alanna shook her head as she locked eyes with Dad. "This ... has never been an option before. I don't ... I don't know if he would want this or not."

My hands clenched into fists. I knew Adams men were stubborn, but choosing death, choosing to permanently leave the family just because of a few side effects ... in my young eyes, not taking the solution to the problem was stupid.

"We have a way to conquer one of life's biggest mysteries. We have a way to cheat death. We don't have to lose our loved ones anymore. Grandma ... you don't have to lose Grandpa. You don't have to spend an eternity alone, once he passes. And Grandpa doesn't need to worry, he won't really be a vampire. If he takes Dad's blood, then he'll be like him. He'll have fangs, yes ... enhanced speed and hearing, sure ... but daylight will be fine for him. He could live a mostly normal life, forever, with you. And isn't sacrificing steak for blood worth that?"

I looked between Alanna and my father, but before either one of them could answer me, Grandpa Jack walked around the corner and stepped into the kitchen, a thoughtful expression on his face. Everyone stared at him, waiting to see if he'd heard what we were talking about. Grandpa smiled at me, patted my shoulder, then walked over to his wife. Grabbing both of her hands, he stared deep into her misleadingly youthful eyes. "Giving up an eternity with you, with our family, for something as silly and frivolous as food and a heartbeat, would be the biggest mistake I could ever make. If you want me to do this procedure, to become a 'little bit' vampire, just like you, just like my son ... then I will. Happily."

Alanna's face contorted, then she threw her arms around Grandpa. "Yes, yes I want that. I want to spend the rest of my life with you. Literally." She sobbed as Grandpa rubbed her back. Tears ran down my cheeks too.

"Okay, dear. If it's safe, and Gabriel thinks he can make it so that I'll end up like you or Teren ... then yes, I'll go through it. For you," he whispered, kissing her head. He looked over at Dad, and I was surprised to see tears on his cheeks. Actually, there wasn't a dry eye in the room. "For both of you," Grandpa added.

Dad smiled, then hugged his parents. It quickly turned into a group hug, with everyone in the room joining in, and I inhaled and exhaled in relief. My family wasn't changing. We weren't going to lose people to the ravages of time. My family was eternal, and would always be that way. And I found a tremendous amount of strength in that.

A few hours later, when I felt a tingling sensation deep in my bones, another strength returned to me. The bond. It was reactivating, reestablishing the mental and physical connection that forever bound Hunter and me together. While severing the bond had been instant and painful, the restoration process was slow and satisfying. It filled me with a blissfulness that was only rivaled by our intimate times together. I could tell Hunter felt it too. Peace was etched into every line of his face. Joy practically radiated in the air between us. And even though I knew Halina was feeling happiness and contentment over her own reconnection with Hunter, she gave us space to revel in the moment.

Everything was as it should be, everything was right in the world. And even though my heart was still and every breath I took was unnecessary, I wouldn't have changed anything about my life. I couldn't. I was forever linked to my best friend, my lover, and my one-day husband. My life was truly everything I wished it to be.

CHAPTER TWENTY-FIVE

Julian

AS THE IMPROMPTU group hug in my grandparents' kitchen ended, disbelief and excitement rippled through me in ever-increasing waves. Gabriel, that genius of a vampire, could continue Henry's work; he could safely make mixed vampires. A few weeks ago, I'd only been hoping to save my girlfriend's mind, but now ... the possibilities were limitless. I could transform her, then we could take Gabriel's shot until we were the age we wanted to be for the rest of our lives. We could have an eternity together. If she wanted it. And given enough time to fully consider the option, I was sure she'd want it. Time. It had felt so scarce before, but now we had endless amounts of it. But instead of hoarding it or wasting it, I was going to cherish every second of it. I'd been too close to losing everything to do anything else.

While I was still lost in a sea of wondrous futures, Jake and Simon entered the happy room. With a detached sense of curiosity, I noticed them craning their necks, searching the room. Then, oddly enough, their gazes settled on me. I looked around myself in confusion, but it was definitely me they were interested in. Why?

As they approached, trepidation began filling me. I pushed the feeling aside and met them with my chest proud and my chin high. I had faced much worse than an ex-vampire hunter and his mixed vampire son. Much worse. Besides, I was pretty sure they weren't going to hurt me after everything we'd been through together. Well, Jake wouldn't hurt me at any rate. Simon would probably still try, if he thought he had a snowball's chance.

Arianna was standing beside me. She held my hand tighter when Jake stepped directly in front of us. Simon was clearly uncertain as he stood beside Jake; both of them seemed apprehensive, almost nervous. I had no idea why.

"Julian ... I don't know how to ask you this ..." Simon's gaze shifted to his feet. He looked thrown and humbled, all at the same time.

Flicking my eyes between Simon and Jake, I slowly said, "What's going on?"

Even as dread started icing my veins, Simon softly said, "I'd like your blood ... please."

I laughed. I couldn't help the reaction. Simon wanting anything from me was ridiculous. Simon wanting my blood was absolutely absurd. "What in the world do you want my blood for?" I asked.

Both Mom and Dad turned away from my grandparents to look our way. Dad tilted his head as he considered Jake and Simon, then he walked over to join our group; Mom followed a step behind him. "Jake ... Simon," Dad said with a cordial nod. "I'm sorry to interrupt, but what do you want my son's blood for? I was under the assumption Simon would complete the conversion process just fine with Jacen's blood."

Dad's words got everyone's attention in the room. With everyone silently watching and waiting, Simon seemed even more uncertain ... and nervous. "You're right, technically ... I don't need Julian's blood. But I ... I acted rashly when I thought I needed to save my father. I see now that he was never in any actual danger ..." Simon sighed and shook his head. "I did the procedure without really thinking about the consequences, and now ... I'm stuck like this. I don't want to be a vampire, but it's permanent, and there's nothing I can do. Nothing but keep taking Gabriel's shot for the rest of my life. At least I'll be able to live and die as I was meant to that way."

His eyes watered as emotion filled him, and I was shocked to see how affected he was by this. "If I have to," he said, "I can come to terms with being like this for the rest of my life. But ... if there's a way to be just a little more ... human." He swallowed a rough knot in his throat while Jake put a hand on his shoulder. Simon smiled at Jake before continuing. "Gabriel said that doing another transfusion was an option ... if the donor was willing. He said he could make it work with your blood, and that your blood has even fewer side effects than Jacen's. I know you have a million reasons to say no, but ... if you're willing to spare some of your blood for me ... I'd be forever in your debt."

Clarity immediately flooded me. Right. I was the most human mixed vampire in the family. Simon might have temporarily wanted the benefits of vampirism to save his father, but he had no desire to be one of us. He wanted a normal life. As normal as possible, anyway. I could understand that. And since what had happened to Simon was in large part my fault, and I was the one who actually owed *him* a debt ... my answer was an obvious one.

Dad looked like he was about to object on my behalf, but before he could, I told Simon, "Okay, I'll do it."

Simon, Jake, and Dad stared at me, shock clear on their faces. "Why would you do that for me?" Simon whispered, astounded.

Flicking a quick glance at Arianna, I told him, "If I'd handled things differently at the party ... been less jealous of your relationship with Arianna ... not blown up in front of everyone ... or not even had the stupid party to begin with ... then you wouldn't have found out what we were. You wouldn't have run away from us to go save your father. Maybe if I'd just talked to you at the party, I would have realized who you were, and we could have reunited you and Jake a lot more easily. Then you wouldn't be ... the way you are now. A little blood seems like a small price to pay, to try and repair the damage I caused."

Jake smiled, Simon gave me a small nod, and Mom and Dad were practically bursting with pride. But then Dad frowned. "It's not a little blood, son. It's a lot. And it will have to be taken out a little at a time, so your body can recover." He glanced up then, at where Starla and Jacen were resting in the bedrooms above us. Drained almost to the brink, they hadn't been given that same consideration. Returning his eyes back to me, he added, "And when the transfusion does happen, you'll be forever bonded to Simon."

Damn. I'd almost forgotten about that side effect. Even still, it was the right thing to do. And besides, it wouldn't be like my bond with Nika had been. Simon and I wouldn't be sharing emotions ... just locations.

Feeling the weight of responsibility resting heavily on my shoulders—bearable, for once—I nodded. "I know what it entails, Dad, and I'm ready."

"All right, Julian," he replied, pride returning to his voice.

And so began the process of me heading out to the ranch to have some blood drawn every few days. I felt a little lightheaded afterward, but it wasn't bad. And it was for a good cause. Arianna thought I was a hero for doing it, but I wasn't the only hero in the family. Dad was sitting through treatments with me, getting his blood drawn for Olivia. Dad didn't want me to have to go through two transfusions, so he'd volunteered. And unlike Simon, Olivia didn't have a problem with having a few more vampire side effects. She was loving her enhanced life.

"Thank you again, Teren," Ben said as he watched the ruby-red liquid filling up the blood bag one afternoon. "I wish I had enough vampire juice inside me to do this for her, but Gabriel says I don't. He said she wouldn't survive a transfusion from me …" He glanced at Gabriel, who nodded in confirmation. Ben sighed, then returned his eyes to Dad. "You stepping up and doing this for my family … you have no idea how much it means to me."

Dad clapped his shoulder with a warm smile on his face. "You've helped me with my family more times than I can count. I know exactly what this means to you. And besides, now we're finally even for that whole trying to wipe your mind thing."

Ben looked like he was about to protest, but then he closed his mouth and nodded. "Yeah. We finally are."

While I watched my own bag being filled up with blood, Ben turned to Gabriel. "When should we do Olivia's transfusion?" Being undead, Dad had been donating a lot more blood on each visit, so Olivia almost had enough to begin the process.

Removing Dad's full bag, Gabriel placed another in its spot. "We could do the procedure anytime, although …" Pausing, he gave Ben a serious expression. "We should wait to see how Starla's conversion goes. There might be … unexpected side effects. Or it might not work at all, and if it doesn't, there is no point in even doing the procedure. Olivia could simply continue to take the shot."

"I know," Ben sighed. "And I know she has to take the shot for the next several years anyway, until she's old enough to decide if she wants to

... kind of die ... but I'd like to give my daughter a chance to survive what's been done to her. The sooner the better."

Gabriel nodded. "Starla's conversion could happen any time now, and once it does, we'll know so much more."

Hearing that Starla had refused to take Gabriel's miracle shot that had been keeping her alive all these long years had shocked the hell out of me. I knew she wasn't thrilled that she was still aging while her boyfriend stayed forever young, but if it didn't work, she was going to die. Seemed a really big gamble to me.

"You're all set, Julian," Gabriel said, disconnecting me from the machine. "You may lie down here if you feel queasy, or you may go upstairs. I believe Imogen made cookies."

My stomach rumbled and I smiled. "I feel okay. I'm going to go eat." Dad nodded at me and Ben waved as I left the room. Honestly, I did feel a little shaky on my feet, but I wanted to go upstairs and call Arianna. My girlfriend. After that one restless evening at my house where Dad had paced the hallway all night, making sure I didn't sneak into Nika's old bedroom where Arianna had been sleeping, she was never allowed to spend the night again. She was, however, openly called my girlfriend now—by her family, by my family, and by all of our friends. It was amazing to have that back, to have *her* back. And even though it had only been a few hours since I'd left her to come out to the ranch, I couldn't wait to talk to her again.

Pulling open the large bookcase that hid the entrance to the secret underground levels, I stepped into the living room. The smell of fresh chocolate chip cookies was heavy in the air. The warm, sugary treats were waiting in the kitchen for me, but before I could get to them, I was bombarded by a faster-than-light eleven-year-old.

Long blonde hair pulled back in pigtails, Olivia had a solemn look on her face as she stepped in front of me. She put both of her hands up like stop signs, and I stumbled back a step to avoid running into her. "I forgive you," she stated, her voice completely serious.

Looking around myself like maybe Simon was behind me or something, I asked, "Are you talking to me?"

Olivia sighed, then shook her head, like she thought boys were idiots. Or maybe just me. "Yes, I'm talking to you. I just wanted to let you know that I forgive you. For dating that ... human girl. I get it. She's your age.

So no hard feelings, you know?" Her gray eyes suddenly sparkled with a devilish glow. "And anyway, I just found out that Simon is two months younger than you. That makes him closer to my age, and that makes him fair game."

She squealed and zipped away as quickly as she'd come. Wow. She was obsessed with Simon now? Oh boy. Even if she weren't a mixed vampire, I had a feeling Ben and Tracey would have had their hands full with her. I wished them luck.

The sound of light laughter turned my head toward the wall of windows along the side of the living room. Starla and Jacen were there lounging in the sunlight, and watching me with amused expressions. They both looked better now, more like their old selves. You'd never know something horrible had happened to them, except for the way they held hands a little tighter, joked a little less. There was a tightness in their jaws that wasn't there before, a rigidness in the posture, and a hardness in their eyes. Some of their carefree spark was gone, some of their brightness dulled. Yes, they were still the same, but also completely different.

"Guess no love lasts forever," Starla mused, her eyes shifting to where Olivia had streaked off. After she said it, her lips tilted into a frown. Now that I was studying her more closely, I could see that her hairstyle was softer than before, her makeup was lighter ... everything about her seemed muted.

Jacen patted her hand. "That's not true. Sometimes it does."

Starla looked up at him and her small smile returned. I thought about leaving them alone since I didn't know what to say to either of them, but instead of running away, I walked over to join them on the couch. "Hey, Mom," I said with a smile.

Normally Starla would have groaned and asked me not to call her that when we weren't pretending for the humans, but she only smiled at me, and then patted the cushion next to her. Wishing I could magically heal her scars, I sat down by her side. "Think the two lovebirds will make an appearance tonight?" she asked, her grin growing.

A scoff escaped me. She meant Nika and Hunter. They'd become almost unbearable to be around ever since Dad had grudgingly agreed to let them live together. And as Halina loved to tell us, when Mom and Dad weren't at the ranch, Nika and Hunter's bedroom door rarely opened. "If they don't come out, Dad will drag them out." He might tolerate the two of them, but only when he wasn't around to see it.

Starla laughed once, then her humor died. Jacen squeezed her hand. Feeling a mixture of guilt and unease, I unintentionally fidgeted with restlessness. Starla noticed. "You can go, Julian. It's okay." Her eyes were soft. And sad.

Wanting to comfort her, I laid my hand over the free one in her lap. "I want to sit here with you." She nodded, and we all three sat in silence for a moment. When the stillness got to be too much for me, I finally blurted out what had been going through my mind earlier. "Why did you choose to not take Gabriel's shot anymore?"

Starla met eyes with Jacen before answering me. My cheeks flushed as I waited. I shouldn't have asked her that. It was none of my business. With a soft sigh, she finally said, "I'm tired of waiting, tired of not knowing, and frankly, tired of aging. I've lived so much longer than I ever thought I would ... I feel like I've already been blessed. But after everything Jacen and I went through ..." Her voice trailed off and her eyes grew distant. Jacen kissed her head, returning her to the present. Glancing at him, she murmured, "I just want to know if I get an eternity or not. If *we* get an eternity or not. I'm sick of not knowing what my fate will be, and if it's my time, then it's my time. And besides, Gabriel thinks it will work. I trust him."

Jacen's eyes grew misty as he watched Starla. I was sure he'd tried to talk her into taking the shot for as long as possible, but when Starla made her mind up about something, she usually kept it. Kissing her head, he told her everything was going to be okay. And that was when everything suddenly wasn't okay.

Starla grimaced, like she had indigestion, and then she rubbed her chest. Jacen instantly noticed her discomfort. "Babe? You all right?"

She opened her mouth to answer him, but no words came out. Clutching at the spot over her heart, her fingers started digging into her skin like talons. She grit her teeth tight, like she was trying with all her might to stop from crying out in pain; seconds later, she started shaking.

Jacen was on his feet in an instant. Hovering over her, he grabbed her shoulders. "Starla?" Still convulsing, she curled into a ball. Her mouth finally opened, and a tortured wail left her lips; it made my skin pebble and a shiver zip down my spine.

Jacen's gaze snapped to the floor, to the levels beneath us. "Gabriel! It's happening! Now!"

Knowing Gabriel couldn't hear anything in his soundproof lab, I jumped up. "I'll go get him."

I wasn't sure if Jacen even heard me, he was so focused on Starla. She was crying now, sputtering his name in between outbursts of pain. Jesus. Were all conversions this bad? Had Mom and Dad's been like this? Would mine be ... ? Not wanting to think about it, I blurred downstairs and threw open the door to Gabriel's sanctuary. Dad and Ben were still with him, still digging for information Gabriel didn't have. None of us really knew if Starla was cured or not. But we would soon. We'd know before the night was out.

"It's Starla," I exclaimed, breathless. "Her conversion is starting."

Dad and Gabriel instantly looked up. I'd left all the doors open in my hurry, and painful sobs were echoing in my ears. If I could hear Starla, then they definitely could. Just when I couldn't stand the sound of her torment any longer, everything went silent. Gabriel closed his eyes. "Only time will tell now," he murmured, before blurring away upstairs.

Dad's face was solemn, then he looked at me in concern. "You need to leave. You and everyone else still alive. If she wakes up ... no ... *when* she wakes up, she'll be hungry. Very hungry." I could only woodenly nod as Dad and Ben urged me out the door. God, I hoped she woke up.

An hour later, I was back at home with everyone who had a heartbeat. We waited for an eternity, or what felt like an eternity. Then Ben's phone rang. "How is she?" he immediately asked.

I could hear my dad's answer on the other side, and a long, heavy breath escaped me. Grandpa Jack's gaze swung my way. "What did he say?"

Ben glanced at me and I smiled. "She made it," I told him. "She converted just fine."

Tension seemed to instantly evaporate from the room. "Thank God," Grandpa muttered. "Thank God ..."

THINGS FINALLY STARTED calming down over the next few months. Jake and Simon agreed to stay on and help with the Vampire League, although they refused to call it that. They also refused to let Hunter, Nika, and Halina continue to trance hunters to get them to see our side of things. Too much of a gray area.

The two of them took up residence in Hunter's old house, where the league used to lure vampire hunters and convert them. Jake still had the occasional visiting hunter meet him there, so he could sit down and have a civil conversation with them about willingly changing every single one of their beliefs. To my knowledge, he had yet to convert anyone to our cause, but he insisted that it would work given enough time, that people would come around on their own. Halina thought he was an optimistic fool. I kind of agreed with her, but I was optimistic too, so I didn't say anything directly to Jake. I really didn't have time to anyway. Senior year had started, and it was kicking my ass. I was now positive that all my prior years of schooling had just been a rehearsal for this one. And if I wasn't physically at school having my head crammed with copious amounts of information, I was at home studying with Arianna.

We spent most evenings together when I wasn't out at the ranch, and the more time we spent together, the closer we got. I'd thought I'd loved Arianna before, but now that we were getting really close, I realized that I'd just barely scratched the surface of my feelings for her. There was a layer of intimacy and comfort between us now that only deepened with every day we spent together. She was my future, my life, my happily ever after. I had no doubt. And now, more than ever before, I was thinking about an eternity with her. And wondering whether she would want that or not.

"So ..." My words trailed off, as my vague idea on how to bring it up to her completely failed me.

"So ... what?" she playfully asked. We were stretched out on the living room floor at my parents' place.

Scratching my head, I pondered how to ask Arianna if she wanted to be a vampire one day. "So ... how is Simon doing?"

I wanted to slap my forehead after asking her that. I knew how Simon was doing, same as she did. He was fine. He'd taken the transfusion a while ago, swapping out Jacen's blood for mine. The sire-bond had blazed to life not long afterwards. Being psychically connected to him was ... odd. But thankfully, it was nothing like Hunter and Nika's bond. Really, all that had changed was the fact that I was aware of where Simon was. And I had this annoying desire to help him out. I found myself texting him or going over to his house, just to see if he needed any help with his homework. It was embarrassing and frustrating.

As far as I could tell though, Simon wasn't suffering from any negative side effects from the procedure. He was still taking Gabriel's shot, of course, but everyone anticipated that he'd be fine whenever he chose to convert. Grandpa Jack was. He'd taken a transfusion of Dad's blood and had joined the ranks of the undead last week. He was happier than he'd ever been.

Arianna bit her lip, and I was so distracted by the movement that I completely forgot the stupid question I'd just asked her. "He's ... good, I guess. I don't know, you see him more than I do. But he seems to be adjusting just fine. He's *very* happy that you agreed to make him as human as possible, but ... he also admitted that blood wasn't so bad. I think being a vampire is growing on him." She giggled and I sighed. God, she was so beautiful.

"That's good," I said dreamily. When Arianna's brows drew together in concern, I shook my head. Right. Not an appropriate response for a conversation about Simon. Clearing my throat, I gently eased the conversation to where I wanted it to go. "So ... how do you feel about the whole vampire thing? I mean ... would you ever want to be ... ?" I cringed and felt like smacking myself again. This was not going well.

Arianna pursed her lips as she thought about my question. "Would I want to be like Simon? Would I want to be like *you*?" Her face softened with adoration.

Not wanting to appear too eager, I limited my reaction to a brief nod. "Yeah ... would you?"

She ran a soft hand down my cheek, igniting me with every centimeter she touched. Then she swallowed, and suddenly looked very nervous. "Julian ... I ... I'm ..."

"You're what?" I whispered, feeling mesmerized by the sparkle in her eyes.

She swallowed another nervous lump. "I'm in love with you." She said it so quietly, I wouldn't have heard her without my super hearing.

My heart started thudding, and my palms felt slick. Hearing her say those words was like Christmas and my birthday all wrapped up in one. It was everything I'd ever wanted. Wrapping my fingers around her shoulders, I pulled her closer. "Oh, Arianna, I love you too. I've been waiting so long to hear you say—"

Arianna gently placed her fingertips against my lips, silencing me. "I love you, and I want to be a part of your world. In *every* way," she pointedly stated. "And that means ... yes, I want to be like you. Just like you. But not right now. Not until I'm older. Much, much older," she quickly added.

I felt like I was going to start hyperventilating. She wanted to be like me. She wanted to live forever. I never thought I'd get that future. Aside from happening upon one of my kind, falling in love with a full vampire, or having a horrible fate fall upon my significant other like Hunter and Nika, immortal life with the person I loved just wasn't a possibility. Until now. "You want ... you want vampirism? You want to spend eternity with me?"

I was so stunned that she wanted what I wanted, that I could hardly think straight. Arianna cupped my cheeks. "Yes, of course I do. Someday."

I opened my mouth to ask when, but she pressed her lips to mine before I could. After that, I didn't care. She could be sixty before she went through the process and that would be just fine with me. So long as she was mine. Forever mine.

Our lips moved together in an increasingly steady pace. As fire ripped through my veins, I pushed Arianne back until her shoulders were pressed into the floor. I moved my body over hers, and baser parts of me began waking up. I wanted her. I wanted to move past all the levels we'd been stuck at for so long now and finally show her just how much I adored her, how much I worshipped her.

Her mouth was soft, her breath hot and her body inviting. My own was responding in a nearly painful way, and the world outside of the two of us slipped away. Nothing mattered but her and me. Nothing at all.

"Um, Julian, I think it's about time Arianna went home."

I snapped my gaze up to see my father leaning against the arch that led to the kitchen. Right. Not only was I not alone here, but I was in the living room, in full view and full hearing of my parents. As soon as Arianna realized that, she pushed me off of her and scrambled to her feet. "Sorry, Julian's Dad," she murmured, her cheeks bright red.

Dad gave her a warm smile. "Call me Teren, Arianna. You'll be less likely to mess up in public if you get used to it now. And from the sound of it, you're going to be around a while." He winked at her after he said it, and Arianna's blush deepened. Her skin tone was glorious—like a tropical sunset.

I wanted to be embarrassed with her, but I was too delirious with happiness. "She loves me, Dad."

Arianna playfully smacked me on the shoulder while Dad laughed. "I heard, buddy. I'm happy for you. Both of you." He pointed a stern finger at me. "That doesn't mean you're allowed to have sex under my roof though. Say your goodbyes, kids."

He walked away and Arianna buried her face in her hands. "Oh my God ..." she squeaked.

Even though I shared her sentiment, I had to laugh at her reaction. "Yeah, tell me about it."

CHAPTER TWENTY-SIX

Julian

THERE WAS AN unmistakable buzz in the air—an almost palpable energy that permeated the student body, making every student walking past me in the hall seem to shimmer, like they were radiating from the inside out. It was the last day of school, the last day of my senior year, the last day of captivity. I couldn't wait for it to be over with, and yet at the same time, I didn't want it to end. I wondered if everyone felt this conflicted about change, or if it was just me. Nika and I had fought hard to leave the ranch and be a part of normal society. It hadn't always been easy, and Nika had unfortunately been unable to complete the journey with me, but I wouldn't trade any of it. These stale halls and cracked walls had taught me so much about life—about *real* life. About who I wanted to be and who I didn't want to be. I was sad to see it go especially since, when I left, all trace of me would also be taken. No photos, no mementos, no memories left intact. Well, at least no memories that we could still influence would be left intact. Thanks to Henry's compulsion-proof vaccine, some students would always remember me until age took their minds, of course. But it was a small percentage, one my family could live with. They didn't have a choice but to be fine with it.

"Dude, why are you all sullen? It's the last day. We're almost free!" I looked over to see Trey beaming at me. His eyes were bright and clear; they had been all year. Ever since he'd found out about my family, his herbal pastime had taken a backseat. I supposed his new girlfriend helped with that too.

"Yeah, Julian, we're on to bigger and better things. All four of us." Raquel squeezed Trey's arm, and looked up at him like he made all her dreams come true. And I supposed he did. Even though it had been weird at first to see them together like that, Trey was a much better partner for Raquel than Russell, and she was good for Trey too. Life had a strange way of working out sometimes, but I had to admit, life knew what it was doing.

"I'm fine," I said. "It's just strange leaving all this behind. I'm excited for tonight though. My house, right?" My eyes shifted from Trey and Raquel to Arianna. She was smiling up at me so brightly, I felt the heat of it against my skin.

Leaning up, she gave me a kiss on the cheek. "Yep, we wouldn't miss it. Will Nika be there?" Nika and Arianna had completely rekindled their relationship. They were just as close as they used to be. And they talked about boys just as much as they used to, although, the boys in question now were always Hunter and me.

I nodded at her question. "Yeah, she'll be there. Hunter too." As if that needed to be said. Hunter and Nika were attached at the hip.

Arianna squealed then hugged my arm. "Good, this is going to be so much fun!" Twisting to Raquel, she exclaimed, "Let's get to class. We can figure out what we're going to wear tonight!"

With a flurry of giggles, they were off. I shook my head as I watched Arianna walking away from me. "They sure are excited about this graduation party."

Trey smacked my arm. "Well, duh. Your parents are letting down their guard and letting a bunch of teenagers ransack their house. It's going to be epic."

I smiled at the truth in that statement. It certainly wasn't going to be as big and chaotic as my birthday party last summer, but Mom and Dad were allowing a bunch of kids from school to come over to the house later. It was a far cry from how reluctant they'd been to just let Trey come over a few years ago. Guess they were loosening up, now that my time here was almost over.

As I went through a mental checklist of all the prep work that needed to be done before anyone arrived—the minor changes that were needed to convince the world Starla was my mom—Trey skewed his face in disbelief. His expression jostled my thoughts, and even though I knew I would regret it, I couldn't help but ask, "What?"

"I was just wondering ... how is it that Raquel and me beat you and Arianna to the sack? How is it possible that it's your last day of senior year and you're still a virgin?"

I sighed while I looked around to see if anyone had heard him. Luckily, it didn't appear that anyone had. "We're waiting for the right moment, okay? And it's a little difficult with my family watching over everything I do." And unfortunately, Arianna and I wouldn't get a break from their prying eyes this summer. Mom and Dad had already quit their jobs, so they could help with the process of moving everyone to the new ranch, and to properly say goodbye to the city. Or so they said. Personally, I think they just wanted to keep me a virgin forever. They'd only loosened up so much, after all. But even if they *were* still working, it wouldn't have mattered much. Arianna's parents had made her get a summer job to help pay for college. I'd asked Nika to compel them to change their minds, but she'd refused. Morals, or some crap like that.

Trey rubbed his jaw, like he was contemplating all of life's mysteries. "Yeah, that is a problem. Maybe Simon and I could create a distraction for you? Something to lure your Mom and Dad away for a while."

Just as I was about to tell Trey that my parents would never fall for any plan that the two of them came up with, Trey grinned and held his hand up in greeting. I didn't need to turn around to see who he was waving to, the sire-bond had already alerted me to the fact that Simon was approaching. Luckily, I no longer felt the desire to jump to my feet and ask him if he needed anything. That ... had been a truly embarrassing few months.

"Hey guys," Simon said as he joined us. He nodded hello to me, then shifted his gaze to Trey. He had an odd, devilish look in his eyes as he smiled at my best friend. "So we need to come up with a plan to get Emma and Teren out of the house, huh?" The fact that he'd heard all of that made me roll my eyes in annoyance; I couldn't get privacy anywhere. Simon's next comment though made me reconsider if that was a bad thing or not. "Maybe it could be something as simple as a league thing? A mandatory meeting. Or a hearing? We did just break up an attack, and both sides need a good talking to. I'm sure your parents would be down for that," he stated, focusing on me.

That wasn't a bad idea. Jake and Simon were all gung-ho with the league now, it was pretty much all they ever talked about, and Dad would gladly help them out if they needed advice or just an extra set of ears. Dad would also probably talk Mom into going with him if the situation were serious enough, leaving me a few hours of peace. "Yeah ... actually, that might work. Thanks, man," I said, surprised at his suggestion.

Simon shrugged. "It's the least I can do, considering what you did for me. And ... I'm happy. I love being a part of the league, it's given me ... purpose. What we're doing, stopping both sides from overreacting, it's important. Crucial even."

A small laugh escaped me. "Overreacting ... that's funny coming from you."

Simon's eyes started hardening, but then they immediately softened. "Yeah, I suppose it is. I guess I just know firsthand the crazy stuff fear can make you do. I want to help others avoid that ... if I can."

With a smile, I nodded. I understood all too well what he meant, and even though we'd had our issues in the past, I respected what Simon was doing with the league. It was painful to admit, but I was slowly growing to like him. It might be the bond that was finally changing my feelings, but maybe not. He wasn't so bad now that he wasn't an obstacle between my girlfriend and me. Yeah, regardless of how it had happened, I didn't hate Simon anymore, and I certainly wasn't jealous of him. My life was good. No, my life was great.

The rest of school alternated between flying by and dragging so slowly I was positive I was stuck in some sort of time loop. When it was over, I postponed going to my car. I wanted to walk through the buildings and commit to memory everything I'd probably never see again. The bleachers in the gym where I'd lusted over Raquel. The boy's locker room where I'd bared my teeth at Russell. The hallway where Hunter had fired a gun on my family. The supply closet where Arianna and I used to make out. The classroom where I'd futility tried to get Arianna to notice me after my grandmother had wiped her memory. The spot on campus where we met up every day after school—a huge maple tree that would sprinkle us with helicopter seeds in the fall and shade us with big leafy branches in the spring. It was where Arianna was waiting for me now so I could give her a ride home, just across the high school on the other side of a cemetery.

"Hey, that took you a while. Everything okay?" she asked. Her caramel hair was tucked up into a ponytail. I wanted to pull it free, and run my fingers through the long strands, but I knew how long it had taken her to get it that perfect; I didn't want to mess it up.

"Yeah," I answered her. "Just ... soaking it all in."

I sighed and Arianna gave me a light kiss on the cheek. "It will be okay. Whatever happens, from here on out, we're in this together."

The look on her face, the warmth in her voice, it made every nerve-ending tingle with life, made every hair stand on end. Yes. Together. "Even if together means going to college in Montana?" I asked with a playful smirk.

Her eyes brightened in response. "Especially if it means Montana! I've always wanted to visit."

I had to lift an eyebrow at that. Montana was famous for emptiness and space. *No one* wanted to visit there, and only a select few chose to live there. I was pretty certain only Alaska was less populated, but since Montana was a heck of a lot warmer, I'd heartily chosen to apply for colleges there. Truly, the isolation made it the perfect place for a bunch of vampires who wanted to lay low, relax, and keep to themselves. That was the major reason why I'd picked the state when I'd started searching out higher education. My grandmothers had given me a half-dozen locations to choose from, but right from the start that one had struck a chord with me. After everything my family had done for me over the years, I wanted to do them a favor, wanted to move near an isolated ranch that would give them peace of mind ... for a decade or so.

Arianna giggled at my expression, then grabbed my hand and started leading me to my car. The drive to her house was short and sweet. She gave me a kiss that ignited my blood and left me with an aching want that only made the separation more meaningful. When I saw her again, the missing part of me would be filled. And luckily for me, that was happening soon. The parental-approved party was starting in just three short hours. So much to do, so little time.

Once Arianna and I parted ways, I sped home to do what I hated most: clean. Mom and Dad tried to help, but I was determined to do it on my own. I even did all of the set dressing, swapping out our real family pictures for photos of Nika and me with Starla. The student body who still remembered Nika thought she had been homeschooled for the last year and a half. Nika was excited to say goodbye to all her old schoolmates. I think that was finally what made my parents give their okay to this party. Nika had never really been given a chance for closure.

When the house was as sparkling as I could get it, Mom gave me a smile of approval. Forty minutes later, the guest started arriving. An hour after that, my home was packed with kids who were either excited to be done for the year, or excited to be done with school completely. Everywhere I looked, people were having a good time. The music was loud, the food was plenty. It was certainly a night to remember, and I made sure to commit every person who walked through my door to memory.

At the end of the night, only my family and closest friends were left in the house. Trey and Raquel were hidden away in Nika's old bedroom, heavily making out from the sounds of it. From the look on Dad's face as he periodically glanced upstairs, they wouldn't be tucked away for long. Hunter and Nika were sitting together on the couch, holding hands while they discussed their future plans. Like the rest of us, they were going to Montana. Hunter didn't want to stay at the ranch though. He was trying to convince Nika to go to night school with him. "It's a chance at a normal life," he kept telling her. Personally, I thought it was a great idea. I wanted my sister to have the college experience, even if it wasn't a typical one.

Starla and Jacen were laughing together in the kitchen. They were both slowly recovering from what had been done to them. Every day, a little more light shone in their eyes. Jake and Simon chatted with my parents about the league while Arianna and I watched a movie after cleaning up the copious amounts of plastic cups left behind by the partygoers. It was all so … normal, and I loved every second of it. My life simply couldn't get any better.

It was only a few weeks later, a few nights after my birthday, that I realized how wrong I was. My life could indeed get better. I was hanging out with Trey one afternoon when I got the text that changed everything. Of course, I didn't realize it at the time.

"That was weird," I said, putting my phone back in my pocket.

"What was weird?" Trey replied, busy on his own phone. With Raquel, most likely. The two of them could barely go five minutes without talking to each other. I'd never seen Trey so hung up on a girl before. It was weird, but cool. Actually, the most shocking thing about Trey and Raquel's relationship was the fact that Trey was keeping his word about our family secret; he hadn't told Raquel a damn thing about what we really were.

Smiling at my loyal, lovesick friend, I relayed the message I'd just received. "Simon just texted me. He says everything with my parents is all set." My smile shifted to a frown. "And I have no idea what that means."

Trey's face lit up like I'd just told him I'd won the lottery. "Oh man, don't you remember?" When it was obvious I didn't, Trey shot to his feet and started bouncing on his toes. "Sex, man! That's what it means!"

A tinge of horror crept up my spine. "Simon is helping my parents have sex? Because they have a soundproof door ... I don't think they need his help. And God, I really wish I hadn't just had that thought." The image was so strong, I had to close my eyes and shake my head to get rid of it.

Trey thumping me on the shoulder caused my eyes to flash open. "No, Dude. He's helping *you* have sex. You and Arianna. Remember? He said he'd get your parents out of the house for you, and it looks like he has!" Trey brought his hands to his chest, over his heart, then swiped an imaginary tear from his eye. "I am so proud of what you're about to do, dude."

My heart started thudding so hard in my chest, I was sure my parents could hear it, even though they were at home and Trey and I were at the park. "Oh ... uh ... I see. Cool."

Trey looked irritated by my lack of enthusiasm. "Why are you not stoked right now? You should be calling Arianna and telling her the plan."

With as casual a smile as I could muster, I said, "I am stoked ... I'm just not sure if now is a good time for us. I'm not sure if we're ready."

"You two couldn't possibly get any readyier, dude." Trey's bemused expression turned understanding as he tucked his phone into his pocket. "I get it, you're scared, but it's not a big deal. Your body totally takes over. It's like eating or sleeping, you just know how to do it. And besides, we're leaving at the end of summer. This could be your last chance, Julian. You have to do it!"

I raised an eyebrow at his absurd remark. "She's coming with us to Montana, remember? And we're going to be together a lot in the dorms, with my parents far, far away ... so Arianna and I will have lots of time to ... catch up on things."

Trey frowned as he crossed his arms over his chest. "Yeah, but this could be your last chance to do it *here*. And you already missed sex on your birthday. Missing this too would just be ... sacrilege." He cringed like he was genuinely pained by the thought.

I laughed at him, then pulled my phone out of my pocket again. God ... were we ready? I'd always been so positive that we were, and seriously annoyed that my parents had never allowed us the opportunity to take it that far, but now that a genuine opportunity had been neatly placed in my lap ... I wasn't so sure. Maybe I'd only felt positive that we were ready because deep down I'd known it couldn't happen. And then again, maybe Trey was right, and I was just overthinking this. It *was* Arianna after all, and I loved her. So much.

Smiling, I texted Simon back and asked him what night my parents were going to be "occupied". After he told me to make plans for Friday, I texted my girlfriend. *'My parents are going to be gone Friday night. Want to come over? We'll be completely alone.'*

I hoped that didn't sound too forward. Or pushy. I wanted Arianna to be ready for this too, and if she wasn't, that was totally fine. We'd wait. I'd wait as long as necessary for her. Holding my breath, I waited for her response. When she gave it, I let out a long, stuttered exhale.

'Good! I've been wanting to be completely alone with you for a long time now. I love you. I can't wait to be yours.'

I turned to Trey with a dopey smile plastered on my face. Trey started laughing, and I knew I looked completely moronic. "Ha ha!" he exclaimed. "A-man is about to get laid!"

FRIDAY NIGHT TOOK forever to get here, and the entire time I was waiting, I was positive my parents were going to take one look at me and know something was up. I half expected them to cancel on Simon and stay home. Or get me a babysitter. But both options were ridiculous, and I hoped they realized that. I was eighteen. An adult. And they could leave me alone in the house so I could have sex with my girlfriend. Not that I was going to tell them about that part.

I didn't relax until Mom and Dad said goodnight and shut the door, and even then, I didn't really calm down. I was too nervous. Arianna and I had waited so long that I'd sort of built up the moment in my head. If I didn't mellow out, I was *definitely* going to disappoint Arianna. Hopefully, she wasn't expecting too much.

When I was certain my parents were gone for the night, I texted Arianna and let her know the coast was clear. She responded that she was on her way and my heart started racing. Oh God ... this was it. Moment of truth.

Twenty minutes later, Arianna was lightly knocking on my door. All of my nerves evaporated when I opened the door and saw her standing there with the most incredible smile on her face—happiness, peace, contentment, and excitement, all rolled up in one glorious grin. She had her hair loose and easy, and was wearing a simple black dress that hugged every curve—curves I couldn't wait to touch. Would she be all right if I pulled her into my arms and began stripping her right there in the entryway? Because, God, I really wanted to.

"Can I come in?" she softly asked, an amused smile on her face.

It was only then that I realized I'd been staring at her, speechless, for quite some time. Could she tell by the look on my face what I was thinking? And was she thinking the same thing? Man, sometimes I would give anything to be able to read minds.

"Yeah, of course," I said, pulling the door open wider, so she could step inside.

Almost paralyzing nerves suddenly took me over as I closed my front door. The house seemed larger, and I seemed smaller. I'd never been so completely alone with Arianna—something or someone had always been there, putting a damper on the moment. But now ... there was nothing and no one in the way. Just me and my anxiety.

Arianna's smile was confident and relaxed, and once again I felt the fear melt away. With how my mood was flip-flopping, brave one minute, terrified the next, I was sure my internal organs would never be the same after tonight. Nothing might be the same after tonight. Jesus.

"You want to ... go to my room?" I carefully asked. I hated how blunt it sounded, and instantly wished I was smoother. Hunter probably wasn't so awkward with my sister ... and why the hell was I thinking about my sister right now?

With an adorable nod, Arianna held her hand out for me. "I'd love to."

I led the way up the stairs, my heart racing so fast, I felt like I was in a gunfight again. When we got to my bedroom door, I slowly pushed it open and indicated inside. "After you."

Arianna giggled at my mediocre attempt at chivalry, and I again felt calmness returning. If only I could keep a firm hold on it. Running a hand through my hair, I shut my bedroom door. "So I don't know what you—"

I didn't get to finish my question. Arianna threw herself into my arms. Before I knew it, her lips were on mine, her fingers were tangled in my hair and her entire body was pressed against the length of me. And just like that, my worry evaporated and pure instinct took over. I wanted her. So much.

As our mouths melded in fast, frantic kisses, I walked Arianna backward until her legs bumped into my bed. Like they were acting of their own accord, my fingers ran up her spine, then grabbed the long zipper of her dress. As I pulled the metal teeth apart, Arianna let out a low groan. "Yes, Julian," she whispered into the stillness of the room. It emblazoned me. I slipped the material off her shoulders, then quickly brought my mouth to that tender flesh. She was so soft under my touch. So perfect.

Not thinking about what I was doing, I pulled her bra strap off her shoulder, then moved the cup aside. It was dark in my room, but I could still make out every curve of her breast. I sucked it into my mouth and was instantly rewarded with another erotic noise from her lips.

After that, things got even more hectic. The rest of her clothes were torn off along with all of mine, and then somehow we were lying on my bed, completely bare. Every place she touched sent bolts of lightning through my body. It was almost too much—so wonderful it was painful. I needed more, I needed it to end.

"Now, Julian ... please."

Her whimpering cry shot right through me, and as I moved over the top of her, only one thought was pounding through my skull. *God, I love this woman.* As I carefully slid into her, I let her know just how much she meant to me. "I love you, Arianna. God, I love you."

She clenched me tight as a spasm of pain ripped through her. Afraid to hurt her even more, I held completely still. I felt her muscles tighten, then start to relax. "I love you too," she whispered. "Please ... make love to me."

I found her mouth as I began to gently rock against her. It was hard to go slow, hard to stay in control, but I did it for her. I wanted Arianna to set the pace, wanted to let her decide what this was going to be like—hard, fast, rough or slow. I thought the restraint might kill me, but luckily she only kept it gentle and tender for a little while. Much to my relief, she was soon thrashing underneath me, clawing at my back and begging for more. It was erotic overload, and I could barely keep it together. Hoping I could hold out, I drove into her with abandon. Moments later, we both cried out in unison as a burst of euphoria unlike anything I'd ever felt before rushed through me.

Was this what I'd been missing all this time? *Holy hell* … I wanted to make love to her every. Single. Night. We couldn't leave for college soon enough.

The next day, I worried that my parents would notice something was different about me, but they never did. Or maybe they just didn't want to ask. Maybe they were finally letting me go, finally accepting that I wasn't that scared, lost little boy anymore. I was an adult, I was a man, and I was ready for everything those words implied.

The first thing I did after I opened my eyes in the morning was text Arianna. I just had to let her know how much I loved her, and that I couldn't wait to do that again with her. She told me she felt the same, and a sizzle went through me at just the thought of having her in my arms again. I texted Simon next, and thanked him for occupying my parents for me. Even though it was annoying to know where he was every second of every day, I supposed I could have been bonded to someone much worse. Guess Simon wasn't so bad after all.

Feeling like I owed my family for all they'd done for me, I helped out as much as I could with the move. Even though we were leaving a lot of our furniture and belongings behind, there was a lot to do with the ranch, and a lot to do with the league. Jake and Simon were completely taking it over after we all left, with Rory, Cleo, and some of the other compelled hunters staying behind to help them. They would keep us in the loop of course, but it was their baby now. I think my dad was relieved to let that responsibility go. Honestly, I think everyone in my family was grateful to have some distance from it. After what had happened with Jake, it was just more of a risk than we'd originally believed.

Olivia was the only person who wasn't happy to be leaving. Ben and Tracey were taking her to Montana with us. That fact would have thrilled her a couple of years ago, but now that she was "in love" with Simon, she was pissed. She didn't want to be that far away from her "honey boo" as she called him. I think Ben was just as eager to leave Utah as I was.

It felt like it had taken an eternity to get everything ready. Right up until the day when everything actually *was* ready. Then it felt like the entire summer had only taken a few seconds. As I gazed at the quiet, empty ranch where I'd spent the majority of my childhood, I was struck with melancholy. I didn't want to leave, but I knew I needed to. We all needed to. It was time to move on.

Nika put a hand on my shoulder, and as I twisted to look at her, I saw a familiar blend of comfort and concern on her face; no matter how old we got, Nika would always mother me. It was engrained in her DNA. "You okay, Julie?"

Smiling at her loving nickname for me, I nodded. "Yeah. Just ... saying goodbye. A lot happened here, you know?"

Nika let out an amused snort, then wrapped her arm around my shoulder. "Yeah ... I know." She inhaled a deep breath that she didn't need, and slowly let it out. As I studied her dark eyes, her smooth skin, I thought about just how *much* had changed for us here. Both of us. We'd loved, lost, and loved again. We'd watched our family struggle and triumph. We'd fought for independence, and finally won it. We'd grown, and yet at the same time we'd come to understand that there was so much we didn't know—might not *ever* know. Becoming an adult, whether you were human, vampire or some odd mixture of the two, was no easy task.

After giving my shoulder a quick squeeze, Nika said, "So, Arianna is meeting you there?"

The sigh that left my lungs was both wistful and elated. "Yeah, her parents are flying her there, to help her set up her dorm room." A room I planned on being in at every possible moment.

The sound of someone crashing into something swung our attention behind us. Trey was trying to right a bunch of boxes that he'd inadvertently knocked over. Halina hissed at him, and told him to wait in the car while she and Imogen finished packing the moving van. Nika frowned as she watched Trey sulk his way to my station wagon. "I wish Trey's parents had flown him. Why is he riding with us again?"

I looked back at her with a smile on my face. "Because he's my best friend and his parents are no-shows. He doesn't have anyone but us, Nick, so we have to be there for him. Just like we're there for Hunter." I raised my hand to indicate where Hunter was lightning-quick helping Grandma with the boxes, before disappearing into the house, probably to double-check that everything we needed was packed.

Nika's frown instantly shifted into a satisfied smile. It only lasted for a moment though. "But Hunter is helpful. Trey is just … Trey."

Closing her eyes, she shook her head. I laughed, then thought over everything Trey had done for me over the years—the stuff he remembered, and the stuff he didn't. "Maybe, but when Trey pulls through, he pulls through big. I probably never would have gotten to keep my girlfriend if it wasn't for him." And I could never repay him for that.

Nika's expression softened as she opened her eyes. She started to say something, but was interrupted by a shrill voice yelling at the top of her little lungs. "I. Don't. Want. To. Go!"

I looked over to see Olivia walking through the front doors of the house, a step behind Ben. Ben had his eyes closed, and was rubbing his temple like he had a headache. "Noted, Olivia, but for the millionth time, you're going anyway. Mom and I have decided, and once we put our foot down, there is no changing our answer."

Olivia started in on a whining diatribe of how unfair her life was, but Ben's response to her made me smile. It wasn't all that long ago that Mom and Dad used to whisper the possibility of Ben and Tracey divorcing. But now that Tracey was in the loop, and fully a part of Ben's decisions, their marriage had solidified. Another reason I was glad Arianna knew all my secrets. Hiding them from the ones you loved, never ended well. That was a cold, hard fact.

Hunter and Malachi came out of the house a few steps behind Ben and Olivia. Malachi was telling Hunter all about his time in Montana; he'd lived there as a boy, and was eager to go back. Malachi was currently telling Hunter that the woods were ripe with bears, wolves, and cougars—a veritable feast for hungry vampires looking for a little variety. Hunter was smiling like he was looking forward to a little action, and Malachi shifted into telling him about deer and turkey.

Much to everyone's surprise, Malachi and Imogen had started … well, I guess what they were doing was dating. It was weird to think of it that way. Imogen had always been single, and I was used to her being alone. Watching her wrap her arms around Malachi and give him a kiss on the cheek was just ... weird. But the smile that lit up her face after she did was pretty awesome to see. She'd been without somebody for far too long.

Mom approached while Nika and I were watching our extended family. She hugged Nika, then rubbed my shoulder. "You guys ready? Did you get everything that you want to take to college with you? God ... I can't believe you're off to college already. I swear, just yesterday you were in diapers."

Mom's comment made me groan. She'd been dwelling on our childhood a lot lately, it was kind of driving me crazy. What was a drop in the bucket for her was forever for me. I'd been waiting for this moment for far too long. As always, Nika stepped in and prevented me from sticking my foot in my mouth. "Yep! We're all packed. I can't wait to see Ashley and Grandma Linda at the new ranch."

Instead of seeing us off at the old ranch, Grandma Linda, Ashley, and Christian were greeting us at the new place. Grandma Linda was going to stay for good, while Ash would leave with her husband after a few weeks. I think Mom planned on pushing the vampire-transfusion remedy on Grandma Linda as soon as she could. I hoped she did, and I hoped Grandma said yes. Now that permanently dying was avoidable, I wanted everyone in my family to do it. Even if I had to be the blood bank for them. I'd have a pint drained from me every day if it meant my family could live forever.

Before I could remind Mom that I wasn't a baby anymore, Dad came up to our group. "We're all set. You guys have your phones on you? Mom and I will be right behind you, but better safe than sorry."

Patting my pocket, I nodded. "Yeah, we're all set, Dad." Maybe I'd have to tell both parents I was no longer an infant.

Wrapping his arms around Mom, Dad nodded. "Good. We should head out then. Get as much road behind us as we can before the purebloods need to stop." He cringed, then looked down at Mom. "Great-Gran is not excited about sleeping in the ground, but there's not much we can do about it on the road. Kind of hard to make a place light-proof on short notice. Even for Gabriel. And he's been researching it for weeks."

Dad smiled and Mom laughed. Now that things had settled down, Halina and Gabriel were just like they used to be. No tension, no drama, just a lot of awkward sexual innuendo that was completely inappropriate for family members to hear. They kind of reminded me of Starla and Jacen, although ... Starla and Jacen weren't quite the same as they used to be. They were more ... subdued now. Deeper. More appreciative of life, and everything they'd been blessed with. After spending a few minutes with those two, I loved my life so much more, and it wasn't because they were broken or anything. Quite the opposite. They were more ... alive. They had a zest for love and life that was infectious and inspiring. It was a little difficult to imagine Starla as the ungrateful, annoying spoiled brat that she used to be.

They were in the backyard now, taking in the splendor of the ranch one last time. I kind of felt like joining them, but I knew it was time to leave. Looking over at Nika, I tilted my head toward the car. "Ready, sis?"

She smiled at Hunter, and I turned to watch Hunter nod in response to her unasked question. Looping her arm through mine, she nodded. "Ready. Let's go start our new life."

We shared a laugh as we started moving toward the car. Trey was already in the back of the wagon, thumping the seats to a drum solo only he could hear. Mom and Dad had walked over to the moving truck, to say goodbye to Jake, Simon, Rory, and Cleo. I waved at Simon as we walked by. My internal radar would always let me know where he was, so this wasn't really goodbye for us, but it felt permanent as I got behind the wheel. Who knew when we'd be back here?

Nika slipped into the passenger's seat while Hunter opened the back door to sit by Trey; Hunter immediately pulled Trey out of the car and motioned for Nika to join him in the back. She giggled as she zipped into the seat with him, and I rolled my eyes. This was going to be the longest road trip ever.

As I started the car, Starla and Jacen zipped into view. Jacen opened the door of the moving van for Starla, and she gave him a brief curtsy before she got inside. Halina hopped into Gabriel's car with Imogen and Malachi. Grandpa Jack blurred to his truck—a sight that was still odd to see—and opened the door for Alanna. Ben and his family piled into Ben's SUV, and once everyone was in a vehicle, the caravan began to move.

Dad honked a goodbye to the group of humans watching the nest of vampires leaving their home. As we passed through the massive gate bearing the Adams name, I lifted my eyes to the rearview mirror, so I could watch the outline of the roof against the dark sky. I watched the steeples and chimneys, statues and shrubs that I loved so much recede into nothingness, then I forcefully shifted my eyes back to the road, and the new possibilities it presented.

On the last stoplight that would lead us out of this town and into our new life, I pulled out my phone and texted Arianna. *'On my way, babe. See you soon.'*

Her response, as always, was instant. *'I. Can't. Wait!'*

My smile was huge as the light illuminating the way turned an appealing shade of green. I couldn't wait either.

THE END

ABOUT THE AUTHOR

S.C. Stephens is a #1 *New York Times* bestselling author who spends her every free moment creating stories that are packed with emotion and heavy on romance. In addition to writing, she enjoys spending lazy afternoons in the sun reading, listening to music, watching movies, and spending time with her friends and family. She and her two children reside in the Pacific Northwest.

You can learn more at:

AuthorSCStephens.com
Twitter: https://twitter.com/SC_Stephens_
Facebook.com/SCStephensAuthor

Also by S.C. Stephens

Dangerous Rush
Furious Rush
Untamed
Thoughtful
Reckless
Effortless
Thoughtless
It's All Relative
Collision Course
The Beast Within
The Next Generation
'Til Death
Bloodlines
Conversion